D0044244

THE MYTH OF SURRENDER

THE MYTH OF SURRENDER

a novel

Kelly O'Connor McNees

PEGASUS BOOKS
NEW YORK LONDON

THE MYTH OF SURRENDER

Pegasus Books, Ltd.
148 West 37th Street, 13th Floor
New York, NY 10018

First Pegasus Books edition March 2022

Interior design by Maria Fernandez

Excerpt from "Diving into the Wreck,"
from *Diving into the Wreck: Poems 1971–1972* (W. W. Norton, 1973)

Library of Congress Cataloging-in-Publication Data is available.

ISBN: 978-1-64313-930-2

10 9 8 7 6 5 4 3 2 1

Printed in the United States of America
Distributed by Simon & Schuster
www.pegasusbooks.com

For my mom and dad,

Mary O'Connor and Stephen O'Connor

We are, I am, you are
by cowardice or courage
the one who find our way
back to this scene
carrying a knife, a camera
a book of myths
in which
our names do not appear

—"Diving into the Wreck"
by Adrienne Rich

PART I
Conception

Summer and Fall, 1960

1

Doreen

Mosel sent Doreen letters through the mail. That was what made him different; that was how it all began. She made sure to get home in time to intercept them from the mailbox in the entryway of her family's two-flat before her mother's nursing shift ended, not that Carla would have noticed or thought much about the plain white envelopes with the initials *MP* neatly written in the upper left-hand corner. MP could have been one of Doreen's friends from high school, now scattered to the winds of beauty college, typing pools, and the self-satisfied early days of marriage. If Carla had found a letter and paid very close attention, the address on South Cottage Grove might have given her pause. But she was distracted. A widow now, she had the building to manage on her own, tenants to hound about the rent, and don't think she didn't. What did Carla care if Doreen had a little pen pal?

Doreen first met Mosel when she was hanging around with a fast girl named Wanda, who was a year older and had a Brigitte Bardot beehive and perfect cat's eyes drawn in with kohl. Wanda's parents had money and believed every lie she told them; she did whatever the hell she wanted, which made her a mercurial but thrilling friend. One night, Wanda convinced Doreen to sneak out—"sneak" because although Doreen was eighteen now, Carla continued to impose Vincenzo's curfew, even though he was dead. Doreen could have made a stink, but she had other battles to wage with her downtrodden mother. So she claimed she was going to bed early and then climbed out the second-story window, scuttling across the overhang above the back door in her slip with her dress tied around her neck to keep it clean. In the alley, she slid it on, clipped on earrings, and applied her Revlon Cherries in the Snow by feel. Wanda was waiting on the corner, and they hailed a taxi to the Regal Theater on South Parkway. Only six miles away, but it might as well have been on the moon.

There were maybe five white girls in the sea of the audience, and Doreen had a brief cardiac episode when she thought about what would happen if her brother, Danny, found out she'd come here: his face would turn red, his greased hair would spark, his whole head would explode like a Roman candle. But Wanda had suggested the Regal for a reason. She knew that Doreen's own personal version of heaven was four girls onstage in matching red shift dresses and black, elbow-length gloves and eyelashes as long as feathers, singing a song about dancing with a boy. When the curtain parted for the opening act, a small-time local group called the Sweet Dreams began to coo, and Danny and all his prejudiced crap ceased to exist. Doreen was transfixed.

All the hottest acts came to the Regal—the Coasters, Ray Charles, Bo Diddley—but it had only been in the past few months that these girl groups, like the Bobbettes and the Chantels, had started coming through Chicago. Their posters, taped to the windows at Sound Town Records, got Doreen's attention, and the store's owner, Lew—a nice guy with maybe a bit of a crush on her—told Doreen to give them a listen. Those records opened a door. All her life, she'd had a hunch she would be famous someday, and now she knew how she would do it: she would get discovered by an A&R man, and he would put her in one of these groups. Doreen was only a middling singer, but she was convinced she could write hit songs, and Lew encouraged her, looking over her lyrics, letting her play the piano in the store. Doreen didn't have her heart set on being the lead. It wasn't about that. As likely the tallest one, she'd probably have to stand in back anyway. She just wanted to be there among them while they all sang a melody she had written, owning the stage without a man in sight. And getting her songs on the radio.

Wanda and Doreen found themselves seated next to two young men about their age, and the one next to Wanda struck up a conversation with her about how there wasn't a bad seat in this house because of the way it had been designed back in the twenties, by some architect with a German name he said was a genius. Doreen was annoyed by their talking over the music, but when she glanced over to nod along politely, she noticed the guy's friend. He had narrow shoulders and wore an olive-colored jacket that was too big for him, an orange pocket square, glasses with black frames. He noticed Doreen back, smiled, and revealed the small gap between his two front teeth that made her a little dizzy.

The talkative companion was his brother, it turned out, and the brother was making enough headway with Wanda to have convinced her to step out of the theater to get some air. As the two of them shimmied into the aisle, the guy in the glasses stretched his hand across the two empty chairs.

"Mosel Palmer," he said, his fingers sliding against hers.

"Doreen," she whispered. A new number was starting onstage, so they did not talk. The Sweet Dreams' choreography was a little obvious, Doreen thought, but you couldn't argue with that four-part harmony. It made her toes curl. When the intermission came, Wanda and the brother were still nowhere to be found, and Mosel just sat quietly, now and then adjusting his glasses with his left hand. He was shy, she saw at once—almost painfully so. Doreen felt for him. Just to fill the space, she started talking about her favorite topic, the Shirelles.

"Shirley Owens got them together at a high school talent show in New Jersey—can you believe that? I read about it in a magazine."

Mosel shook his head—he couldn't believe it. He had his left leg crossed over his right, his long fingers folded elegantly in his lap.

Doreen remembered how carelessly she had applied her lipstick in the alley and hoped it looked okay now that the houselights were up. Her hair was shellacked in place with Aqua Net, and there was no need to smooth it. Still, she smoothed it. "Well, it's true," she said. "Do you know they started out with a different name?"

"I didn't know that, no."

"You'll never guess what it was."

Mosel was patient, his attention squarely in this moment and nowhere else. "You're probably right about that."

"The Honeytunes. Isn't that a scream? I just love it. Do you know their song 'Tonight's the Night'?"

"Sure," Mosel said, nodding.

"A lot of people don't know Shirley Owens wrote that one. Well, she co-wrote it. Most of these girl groups sing songs other people write for them, but she's writing for the group herself."

"That's great," Mosel said uncertainly.

"You're not one of those guys who think women can't write songs, are you?"

"I honestly haven't—"

"Because when I'm up there someday, you won't see me singing anything I haven't written myself. What would be the point of singing a song that doesn't come from your own life?"

"I'm not," Mosel said.

"Not what?"

"Not one of those guys." He looked amused, maybe a little intimidated. "Who think girls can't write songs."

"Oh," Doreen said. "Well, good." She flushed. Carla always told her she got too excited about things, bulldozed the conversation. Doreen realized she hadn't asked Mosel anything about himself and was trying to think of something when the lights went down for the headliner's show.

At the end of the night, Mosel asked not for her phone number (they both knew why that was not a good idea) but her address. When he could see Doreen imagining Danny opening the door to find Mosel standing on the stoop, he clarified his intention: "I've got something to send you."

The first letter came a week later.

Dear Doreen,

It was a pleasure talking with you at the concert last week. I appreciated that you were willing to share your knowledge about the music industry. Hope you are having an enjoyable summer.

Your friend,

Mosel Palmer

Doreen read it through twice, flipped it over to see whether anything else was written on the back of the ivory sheet of stationery, but it was blank. She laughed. It could have been a card from an old woman to a member of her quilting circle. Doreen tried to decide whether to write back. A thank-you note for his thank-you note? But before she could make up her mind, another letter came.

Dear Doreen,

I have been thinking that maybe I could tell you a little more about myself this way, since you could probably tell that I am reserved and find it hard to do so in person. I am nineteen. In the fall I will start the mathematics program at Ohio State University. I hope you won't think it is conceited of me to share that I received a full scholarship after winning a contest to solve a number theory problem regarding integers. (If you are interested, the problem was to find all integers n *such that there is more than one three-digit integer* N *that is divisible by* n, *and* N/n *is equal to the sum of the squares of the digits of* N. *The answer is 6, 7, 11 and 14.) I guess I am good at solving problems. Anyway, I am grateful for that chance as my father is an elevator operator in the Loop, and though he works long hours he could not have seen to the tuition himself. I have a new problem now, though. I can't stop thinking about this girl named Doreen.*

God, what a thrill it was to see her own name written in his handwriting. She remembered how he had adjusted his glasses with his left hand—did he write with his left hand too? Why did wondering about that take the breath from her lungs? Now she knew she was supposed to write him back. Maybe it was the privacy of this mode of communication, the way it seemed to unfold in a world of its own, but Doreen felt bold.

I can't stop thinking about you either, she wrote. *And what it would be like to kiss you.*

She couldn't believe herself, but she mailed it, and a response came flying back. Soon, Mosel and Doreen were off and running, and the narration progressed from the finer qualities of each other's eyes to earlobes, collarbones, and points south. Mosel was always respectful, Doreen a little more daring, and the temperature of the letters increased across the month of July and into August right alongside the popping thermometer. The final letter from Doreen to Mosel was rousing enough to send a plume of smoke from his mailbox, she predicted with glee. She asked him to meet her on Wooded Island in Jackson Park on Saturday evening, in the dune grass off one of the trails. You didn't have to be a future math major at Ohio State to figure out what that meant.

The way Doreen saw it, if she was going to go on the road with her singing group, if she was going to live the life of a star, recording these songs about love and affection, she needed some experience. The world being what it was, she knew Mosel could not take her out on a real date. But Doreen didn't really care—she'd been on dates with boys from the neighborhood, and they seemed like tiresome children in her memory now that she compared them with Mosel. Mosel was a man. He was serious and smart, and the way he described her own lips to her made her want to scream.

Saturdays, Doreen worked the day shift at Art's Grill, six blocks from home on Taylor and Aberdeen. Business had been slow, but everyone said Art just had to hold on until they finished the new university campus. Then students would come flooding in for burgers and scrambled eggs, and it would be just like the good old days, when there were still lots of Italians and the Eisenhower expressway had not yet taken an axe to the neighborhood.

Doreen did not really have the temperament to be a waitress on any day—she was impatient and incapable of fawning—but today, knowing what the evening might hold, she was worse than usual. She fumed and stared daggers at the lingerers, who took one bite of tuna sandwich for every two columns they read in the *Sun-Times*. She watched the clock as if it were a sacred oracle.

Art—Doreen and the other waitresses called him Mr. Messina—took note of her fidgeting with the stainless steel creamer pitchers lined up behind the counter, turning all their handles just so.

"You all right, bella?" Mr. Messina asked as he cleared two plates from the lunch counter left behind by a mother and her picky son. The kid's grilled cheese was almost untouched.

"Oh, fine," Doreen said and pulled her pencil from her hair as a new customer jangled through the door. She smiled at her boss. Mr. Messina was only thirty or so. He had taken over the diner from his father, who was also named Arturo. They hadn't even needed to change the sign. Arturo the younger had married an elegant woman from St. Louis, and Carla had heard through the grapevine that she was barren. Doreen felt sad for them. *Such a shame, not to be able to have a family*, she thought, and then immediately she recognized this as something Carla would say.

The afternoon crawled on.

Finally Doreen found herself sitting on the park bench nearest the meeting place they'd agreed on. It had been a gray day, with rain falling off and on, and so the park never got very crowded. Now, with the sun already behind the skyline, only a few people passed on the walking path. Some carried fishing gear for the lagoon; one man had a new Canonet hanging around his neck and headed toward what was left of the Japanese Garden after vandals had destroyed it and the city refused to pay for its repair. Beyond the lagoon was the golf course green and, farther south, the beach. Doreen had not even thought about suggesting they go there, and not just because the activities she had in mind would require the privacy of tall grass and trees. Just last week a girl named Velma Murphy had led a group of Negro kids in an effort to integrate Rainbow Beach about ten blocks south, while white boys threw rocks at them and one split Velma's head open. Little Rock by the Shore was no place for Doreen and Mosel to go together.

Just as she was starting to worry that he might not show (and who could blame him?), Mosel came strolling up the path carrying a blanket and a picnic basket. She wondered whether this was something he had seen in a movie, because she couldn't imagine any boy she knew thinking to pack a picnic. He wore a straw hat and sunglasses, and Doreen waved when she saw him.

"Hi," she said. When she tried to say more, her mouth got tangled up and she bit her tongue. It only made things worse when she remembered that this was the very same mouth he had described so beautifully to her in his letters; suddenly it wasn't working. Her courage was failing her.

For his part, Mosel seemed calm, but shy people had more practice hiding their nerves, Doreen thought. "Hi," he said.

They sat together on the bench, the basket at their feet, and Mosel pulled out two bottles of orange soda and the sandwiches he had made for them. They were slapdash, with too-thick slices of ham he had sawed off the bone, but Doreen was charmed that he had gone to so much trouble. As they ate in silence, Doreen wondered if Mosel was also replaying the bold words from their letters, the things they had declared and asked for. An old man walked by with his schnauzer, and it occurred to Doreen that he might give them—Mosel, that is—a hard time, but the man only said good evening to them and kept on going.

The dark branches of the trees stood out against the slate-colored sky. Mosel had his hand on one side of the basket's handle, and Doreen put her hand on the other side and swung it back and forth. He grinned and looked over at her.

"I thought you said you were going to kiss me," she said. "You even told me how." And then, because she could see he was going to wait for her—he had to be sure he didn't suggest anything she wasn't okay with doing—she stood up and looped the basket's handle over her elbow and motioned for him to follow her into the thigh-high grass and tall trees between the path and the lagoon.

They weren't completely hidden. If either of them had been thinking straight, they would have realized that one person seeing them in there together could set off a chain of events that would end with Mosel in jail, or worse. But it was impossible to feel afraid with so much thrill coursing through their veins. Their own words called them into the grass like a siren's song. Doreen had written to Mosel that thinking about his shoulders made her weak in the knees. (They really were very nice shoulders, if a little skinny now that she was seeing them again in real life.) Mosel had written to Doreen that he wanted to start his fingertips at her chin and send them trailing down. Had they been bluffing, protected by the safety of the paper and pen? Now here they were, daring themselves to follow through.

Lying in the grass, they kissed and kissed and let their hungry tongues slide together, half the blanket under them and the other half pulled overtop of them like a sleeping bag. Doreen wanted to leap all the way inside Mosel's mouth, and she felt she might die if she couldn't get her bare skin up against his. Every muscle in Mosel's body seemed to be flexed, but he exercised complete control and waited for Doreen to initiate each move. She grabbed the back of his hand and moved his fingertips to the hem of her sundress, urging him to slide it up, up, up; when he touched the edge of her underpants, she felt his hot groan into her hair as she fumbled with his buckle. Panting, he stopped her hand.

"Are you sure?" he asked.

Doreen nodded, but still he held her hand. A dragonfly landed on his shoulder, and she watched its gossamer wings pulse, glint in the fading light. It flew off.

"I'd really feel better if you said the words," Mosel said, the exquisite patience in his voice at odds with his hungry eyes. "I just want to make sure it's what you really want."

"Yes, please, Mosel," Doreen said. "Please don't make me wait any longer."

He pressed his mouth against hers again and then reached into his pocket for a little packet.

"It's a Trojan. I got it from my cousin."

Doreen had heard about these from Wanda, but she had no idea where a person could go to buy one. Again she felt impressed by Mosel's foresight and conscientiousness. He tried to rip open the packet, but it slipped from his hand into the folds of the blanket. When he reached down to get it, he kissed her bare stomach and they smiled at each other in the dim light as she slid her underpants off one leg and left them hooked around the ankle of the other. His second attempt to tear the foil was more successful, and he lifted up onto his knees, though not too high, still careful to keep his head down below the line of the grass, and got himself ready. Doreen could barely breathe as she watched him.

She pulled him down and slid her fingertips up the back of his shirt. The sky above them was violet and suddenly filled with dozens of dragonflies, vibrating and darting in their strange patterns. She watched them as she felt for the first time the shock of what it was to be entered, as she fell into the pure enjoyment of his body and hers, so sleek and lovely in the evening light. Now a pair of the dragonflies landed on Mosel's shoulder, locked in their own strange embrace, and Doreen felt certain that a kind of magic was all around Mosel and her, a spell of protection on the dune grass.

When it was over, he kissed her and kissed her, salty sweat on his upper lip, and told her she was so pretty it hurt to look at her, and she thought that this was everything she had hoped for, more than that; she counted in her mind that there were enough days left before Mosel moved to Ohio to do it thirteen more times.

2

Margie

Margie kept her secret for as long as she could.

In the beginning, this involved merely a tidy compartmentalization, the alarming fact sealed away alongside other alarming facts in her brain's deep storage. Like the time she saw her grandfather's penis when his robe splayed as he was getting out of bed. The terrier in the middle of Northwest Highway, flattened but still breathing, that she did not even try to help. There was a safe place for shame, and it was under lock and key.

But "the truth will out," as Father Keene liked to say, menacingly, and in Margie's case it was making its debut along the waistband of her flannel school uniform skirt. When it would no longer zip, she considered using some of the money she'd made over the summer as a nanny for the Grebe family to buy a new uniform. Mr. Grebe owned Grebe Jewelers, the nicest store in Sycamore Ridge, and the family had paid Margie well for taking Susan and Richard to the country club pool every day. But the skirt would have to be ordered from the school store, and she didn't think she could do it without her mother, Verna, finding out. Instead, Margie bridged the gap first with a small gold safety pin and next with an old diaper pin she found among the clothespins on a shelf above the washing machine. When she was forced to make one last pathetic attempt with a kilt pin, the bottom two buttons on her blouse straining like faulty bolts in a dam, she realized she was going to have to tell Verna the truth.

The next day was Saturday, a gray October morning. Verna was in the yard of their redbrick bungalow wrapping burlap around her rose bushes. Margie stood quietly behind her, her hands clenched in fists inside the pockets of her wool coat, as Verna's expert fingers tied the twine on the final bush. When she stepped back to admire her work, she fished a cigarette from the pocket of the cable-knit cardigan she wore over her apron.

"Lord, Margie!" she said as she nearly stepped on her youngest child. "Don't sneak up on people."

"I'm sorry, Mother." Margie realized she was just going to have to say it. There was no way to bring the conversation around naturally to the topic of mortal sin.

"Did you salt the roast like I asked you?"

Margie winced.

Verna shook her head and took a slow drag on the Chesterfield. She had long arms and fingers and a narrow face pinched with exhaustion. She had raised four other children and seemed determined to get this one launched into the world so she could lie down and die. Had she always been this way? Margie sometimes wondered whether Verna had a glamorous past, back in the years before the war. She might have styled her coppery hair in big, soft curls and worn a fitted green dress. She might have danced to big band music in a dance hall. But Margie didn't dare ask Verna about those days, if they'd ever existed. With Verna, the only hope of temporary alliance involved anticipating what she might complain about next and impressing her by doing it first. In this case, however, Verna's scorn would only be directed at Margie herself.

"What is the matter with you?" Verna asked.

Margie took a breath. "I've got something to tell you. I—"

But Verna saved her from having to say the words. Verna was no dummy. With the cigarette still in her fingers, she wrenched open Margie's coat and pressed her palm to the low part of her belly. Touch was rare in the Ahern family, so it was a strangely intimate experience.

It might have been a comfort—someone was finally acknowledging Margie's miraculous bulge with a warm, soft hand!—if the reprimand weren't so swift.

"You little idiot," Verna said. She struck Margie hard across the face with her open palm. Then she put her head in her hands and shook it, ash cascading down the backs of her fingers. "I knew you looked heavy." When she opened her eyes, she glanced over the fence into the Cunninghams' yard, then in the other direction to the Jensons'.

Overhead, a plane passed on its way to Midway. Its belly, too, looked round and full. Margie wished it would fall out of the sky and plow her into the ground.

Verna yanked Margie's coat closed. "Get inside."

They stood in the kitchen in silence. Margie felt a strange mix of dread and wonder—of course things were only going to get worse from here, but she was genuinely surprised that her mother had believed her right away. Before today, Verna had reacted with skepticism to every last thing Margie had ever told her. When Margie had an obvious fever, Verna would swipe a hand across her daughter's forehead and pronounce her fine. When Verna had discovered Margie crying on the floor of her bedroom closet in her homecoming dress—afraid to go to the gym because what if nobody wanted to dance with her?—Verna stared at her, hard, and said, "Stop making up problems just so you can deliver a tearful monologue." After four other children, nothing that happened to Margie would ever be impressive or delightful or tragic. The only reaction she would ever get from Verna would be irritation.

"We're going to have to get your father to come home from work," Verna said. Frank Ahern was an insurance salesman in a dreary office just a few blocks away from home. Verna lit another cigarette and called him from the wall-mounted phone next to the pantry. Because Margie couldn't bear to listen to that conversation, she wandered out of the kitchen, through the dining room, and into the pale-peach front room. She pressed her stockinged feet into the rug. There were two elegant sofas facing each other, a brick fireplace with gleaming brass tools her parents never actually used. A bookshelf full of old *Reader's Digest* issues and an oversized copy of *Lives of the Saints*. Its gory pictures had scared Margie to death when she was little.

Off to the side was a framed portrait of Jesus, light cascading over his rolled-back eyes. Margie turned her head. She wasn't going to think of him right now.

Instead she thought of all the girls she had met in books, hoping for a kindred spirit. But Jo March hated boys—she sold her hair without a thought! Mary Lennox and Sarah Crewe were brats; Nancy Drew had Ned, but Margie had strangely always imagined him like a nice priest or one of Susan Grebe's boy dolls, neutered by his unbudging plastic underwear. Nancy was made of tougher stuff than her, Margie thought. Nancy never would have allowed herself to get in trouble. All the plucky heroines were loved for being unconventional, but they were only unconventional in safe, charming ways. What Margie wouldn't give for an alternate *Anne of Green Gables* that began with a missed period.

She heard the receiver click back into place, and her mother's twitchy energy began to propel her from one task to the next. Cupboard door to sink to stove to refrigerator, *thud*, *clink*, *swish*, *whoosh*, like a choreographed dance. There was probably a track in the linoleum floor that marked out her steps.

Margie came back into the kitchen to see that Verna was salting the roast. It was a little disappointing to learn that even this, the end of the world, could not disrupt her mother's plan for dinner.

"I'm going upstairs to change my dress," Verna said. She dried her hands on her apron and hung it on a hook inside the pantry door. "Your father is going to meet us at church."

Margie felt a rush of blood to her brain. Somehow it hadn't occurred to her that this would be her mother's first move, though now it seemed obvious. A few moments later, Verna flew back down the stairs, her part newly slicked so that the fine hairs coaxed out by the October wind wouldn't be seen in the house of the Lord. She threaded her handbag over her wrist and snapped the frame shut. "Well, come on."

The more worked up her mother got, the more still Margie felt—not calm but wary. She was a bird on her nest, merely turning her head from one direction to the other to monitor threats. A question had not yet occurred to her mother, but it would come, eventually—someone had to ask it, didn't they?—and Margie had to think how to answer.

St. Paul of the Cross was eight blocks away, and Verna and Margie dutifully tied on their plastic rain bonnets for the walk through a stinging drizzle. Verna wasn't going to let that roast languish unprepared in the refrigerator, and she wasn't going to let their hairdos get ruined either. Margie remembered Verna teaching her how to wrap her hair on hot rollers when she was about ten years old, the smell of singed hair, the pads of her fingers waxy by the end from handling the blistering ceramic. Then there was the waiting—her head wobbling like an overblown sunflower on its stem—for the rollers to cool. Together they unwound them from her hair, and Verna warned her not to yank, not to grow impatient—she'd heard of a girl who got the rollers so tangled they had to be cut out, and that imbecile walked around looking like a scarecrow for a year. On some level, Margie understood that all these warnings were for her own good: peril was all around, and Verna wanted to protect her from it. Verna was as hard on herself as she was on Margie.

But despite Margie's extreme caution with her hair, even now, as the rain rustled against the plastic printed with yellow daisies; despite never allowing her nose to grow shiny; despite clean white gloves, buffed shoes, very fine table manners, an A in French class, a perfect track record of smiling appropriately and answering "I'm just fine; how are you?" enthusiastically to every single person who asked since she was in kindergarten,

Margie had somehow still done the thing that all those fine qualities were cultivated to prevent.

Verna said nothing. Margie kept waiting for the question to occur to her. But maybe it already had and she couldn't bear to hear the answer. Maybe she already *knew* the answer, Margie realized. But how could she know?

Her dad's Plymouth Belvedere was parked on the street in front of the church, which had an ornate set of double doors in front, with one additional entrance on each side. Margie had always thought of the doors as the Father, Son, and Holy Spirit—three ways in, pick your poison. "She liked the Holy Spirit best because it could be whatever you needed it to be. A bird, the wind, tongues of fire. But in order to get to the priest's office, the Aherns had to enter through the Son, the blood and guts guy. The words *Lord have mercy on me, a sinner* echoed through Margie's mind.

It was a sin, even though she hadn't chosen it. So how to account for the orange glow spreading within her like a swallowed sunrise? How to explain the peace she felt, the trill of awe?

Frank Ahern stood in the dark vestibule, waiting for them with his hands folded across his belly, and Margie felt her usual pity for him. He looked physically uncomfortable all the time, in clothes that were too tight, and he was often sweaty and startled looking. Verna was mean to everyone but meanest of all to her husband. She made no secret of the fact that marrying him, at the ancient age of twenty-nine, out of desperation born of the fear that she would live with her parents forever, had been the biggest mistake of her life. Over the years he had been a decent father to his five children. He worked diligently with very little success to build his business (he was a lamentable salesman), but he made enough to keep them all fed and clothed and to send Verna to the beauty parlor each week.

None of it mattered. She persisted in hating him.

When Frank saw his daughter, he threw up his hands. "I feel as though I don't even know you, Margaret." Gone was his affectionate nickname for her, Mars Bar. She couldn't remember him ever calling her Margaret.

He kneaded the back of his neck. His eyes darted to Verna, but he seemed afraid to look at her straight on. With them in the vestibule, as they waited for the priest to open his door, was Mary, her blue ceramic mantle fixed and yet flowing over the edge of her niche in the wall. If Mary was doling out any mercy today, Margie had yet to experience it. She watched her father's face; she could see that the question hadn't occurred to him either. Was anyone going to ask it?

Father Keene's office was a cramped space with molded plastic chairs and heavy drapes that obscured the dim light. He stood behind his desk when they entered.

"Hello, Father," Verna said.

He reached across the desk and put his hand on her shoulder, and she broke down, shaking with sobs. Frank, ever hopeful, put his arm around his wife in an attempt to comfort her, but she shrugged it off, irritated, and began rifling through her handbag for a handkerchief.

"There, there, Mrs. Ahern. It's an awful thing, that's for sure. No one should have to go through this."

Margie watched her crying and receiving the priest's comfort as if she were watching a play. No one spoke to her as she sat down in a chair by the door. Frank and Verna took the two chairs directly across from the priest's desk.

"My heart breaks for the two of you," Father Keene said.

Verna pressed the handkerchief to her lips.

"You are so well regarded in our community. I hate to think of the gossip and cruelty a family like yours might face."

Verna looked at Frank, a new horror occurring to her. "This could destroy your business. You can barely keep it alive as it is, and now you could lose it. We will be *destitute*," she spat over her shoulder in Margie's direction, the first acknowledgment that Margie was even in the room.

Frank put his head in his hands. "We went wrong somewhere along the way, Father. I just don't understand. My other girls were so good." His voice broke.

"Now, now," Father Keene said. He had thick black hair he almost certainly dyed and thick fingers he wove together under his chin. "The main thing to do here is keep our heads. Let's talk about the facts of this situation and leave the emotions for our prayers. Whatever you've done wrong, God will forgive. They are sins of omission, after all. How could you have known?"

Frank nodded, relieved to be taken in hand.

"As I said," Father Keene said, "the social consequences of this business could be quite severe for the both of you, and for your other children. But my concern is something even more dire—the theological consequences. An illegitimate baby born of mortal sin cannot be baptized into the Church."

Verna whimpered.

"That means the child will spend its life separated from God and spend eternity in Limbo, beyond the reach of God's grace and peace."

This idea had not occurred to Margie, though it should have, as she had been hearing stories about Limbo all her life. She pictured someplace like the waiting room at her pediatrician's office, but bright white and endless, with babies crawling all over the floor with no mothers to care for them.

Father Keene shifted in his chair, relieved to have delivered the worst of the news. "But there is another way, something that might save this child and protect your own family. A way to give Margie a fresh start."

Verna sat forward and blew her nose.

"First, am I right to assume that the young man has not stepped forward?" Father Keene asked.

Verna and Frank turned in their chairs and looked at Margie, who froze now that the question was finally, finally upon her. Her parents looked chastened—until this moment they had been so horrified by her, it must have seemed her condition arose spontaneously. Margie held her breath.

If she told the truth, they would not believe her. She tried to stop the memory of that day from flooding in, but so far it had proved more powerful than any prayer she could think of to stop it. Mr. Grebe's turquoise

Eldorado Brougham pulling into the driveway in the middle of the day for no good reason. The creaking stairs to the basement, painted blue over an old coat of red that shone through in shards. Passing by the laundry room, the smell of Tide and mildew, her eyes fixed on the swirl in the back of Mr. Grebe's hair. In his workshop behind the boiler was a long workbench, his gemology tools arranged on a shelf hanging above it. There was a safe with an oversized handle, and Mr. Grebe spun it this way and that, and then the door clicked open. He'd said he wanted to show her what a raw diamond looked like. He spilled the little nuggets from the velvet bag into his palm and handled them so delicately, just moments before he pinned Margie's shoulders to the floor.

Father Keene didn't bother to hold her gaze for long. "Well," he said, "there are many good Catholic families who desperately want to have a baby but cannot conceive. A baby adopted by one of those couples could be given a legitimate life and therefore be baptized and raised into full membership in the Church. The stain on Margaret would not follow him or her into childhood, adulthood. The child would never have to know."

The stain on Margaret. The room felt very hot just then. A few white pinpricks danced in her field of vision.

Verna looked at Frank and gave him a curt nod. "Adoption, yes. Whatever it costs, we will find a way."

"Actually," the priest said, "the Church will pay for her care—room and board in the home until her time comes, medical care at that point, and costs associated with placing the baby. When it's over, Margaret can return home, resume her education, and one day, God willing, marry, begin her life."

Father Keene opened the calendar on his desk. "Do we have a sense of the timeline?"

Verna sighed. "I don't know. We haven't been to the doctor. But I've carried enough babies to know she's four months gone, give or take."

"Four months!" Frank cried. "Four months she's been living in my house and lying to me."

"Longer than that, for all we know," Verna said.

The priest counted. "That would put the date in April. I will put in a call to Sister Simon today to make the arrangements. It may take some time for a bed to become available. Unfortunately, these days, the homes are very full. Sometimes we can find placements in the homes of generous parishioners in other cities during the waiting period. She can't stay in Sycamore Ridge, of course. There will be talk."

"But . . ." Frank said, initiating the first bit of hesitation shown by any of them, "what about her studies? Can't she at least finish out the semester?"

Verna looked at him like he was an even bigger idiot than she'd imagined. "She can't stay in school now that she's showing. They will expel her."

No more school. The walls of Father Keene's office began to tip toward Margie. No more French class. No more furtive hours in the library enthralled with Shelley (*Weary wind, who wanderest / Like the world's rejected guest / Hast thou still some secret nest / On the tree or billow?*). No more yearbook committee, gossiping afterward by the lockers with her best friend, Pamela, when the halls were empty except for the custodian sliding his enormous amoeba-shaped broom across the floor.

Pamela. Thinking of her finally made the tears come. So many moments these past weeks, Margie had wanted to confide in her, but she didn't have the courage. How many times had they whispered, with a mix of awe and disdain, the names of girls rumored to have gone all the way? How many times had they vowed to save themselves for boys they really loved? Margie couldn't bear to imagine what Pamela would think of her now. If Father Keene was offering her a way to keep the secret for the rest of her life, Margie would do it.

3

We

No one told us how our bodies worked.

When we started bleeding at twelve, thirteen, fourteen, we thought it meant we were dying but kept it to ourselves because we didn't want to be any trouble. If a girl wore white pants to school, it put everyone on edge, and now and then we'd see that girl crying in the bathroom and wringing them out in the sink.

We saw boys see us and at the same time stop seeing us. Some of them hounded us until we swatted at them, until we found another way to get to school, another door to use, an empty classroom in which to eat our lunch. Some of them loved us, truly, and we loved them back. We knew it was our job to draw them in and keep them away, both at once, just like in the movies. And so we said no but then yes or yes but then no or maybe later, maybe now, and saw up close the seams of sofa cushions, the humid crush of shirt collars, our own wrists twisting to break free of their grip.

When we understood we had started something that couldn't be stopped, we still tried to stop it. We asked for help from everyone and no one; we kept it completely to ourselves. Using an address we found at the library, we wrote the president of the United States requesting aid. We drank castor oil by the quart. We sprayed Lysol between our legs.

We stood at the top of the stairs and let ourselves tip. Down two flights, breaking a shoulder, chipping our teeth. But still we could not dislodge it.

The boys said they would marry us when they graduated and got the money together. Or they'd like to, but their parents wouldn't let them. Or they were sorry, but they had plans. They were going to college, to welding school, to the army. They had people counting on them—other people. Didn't we know how big the world was, how much of life was ahead of them? We knew.

The boys said nothing and inched out of the frame over the following weeks, hoping no one would notice.

The boys said they'd never laid a finger on us and then got every player on the football team to say we'd made the rounds, that it was impossible to pin the baby on just one boy.

After all, who could trust girls like us?

PART II
Gestation

Winter to Spring, 1961

4

Doreen

Since the Coniglios did not own a car, Doreen got Danny to borrow his friend Benny's Oldsmobile 88 for the drive to the Holy Family Home for the Wayward near the downstate town of Prairie Creek. Aka Hicksville. Did they even have radio stations there? Did the girls dress like Laura and Mary Ingalls? Doreen had never been out of Chicago, and the idea of empty fields and hawks and wolves—hadn't there been a wolf in one of those books?—scared the hell out of her.

Initially, Doreen had assumed it would be just her and Danny making the trip. A pipe dream, of course, thinking she could sidestep Carla. When she'd sat her mother down and told her she was pregnant but not to worry because she planned to give the baby up, Carla had stared at Doreen. First, she shouted. *What are you talking about; that baby belongs with us; this is not what Sicilians do!* Doreen had to stop herself from rolling her eyes at this. Since when had Carla made a big deal about their heritage? She couldn't stand the old-school nonnas, always shaking their fingers at someone and refusing to speak English. When they had fled the neighborhood for the safer suburbs ("No Negroes," they said), Carla had cheered. Good riddance. *Doreen* wasn't even an Italian name. It was Irish, for a childhood friend of Carla's who had died of the measles. But apparently now she was a proud and dramatic Sicilian mother. First up, she announced that she was taking to her bed. Danny and Doreen didn't see her for two days, save her trips to the refrigerator and the decanter of Chianti.

Doreen knew exactly what Carla was doing during those two days, and it wasn't rending her garments. She was thinking. Family was the most important thing in the world—that was a given. And this baby, despite the shameful event that had led to its creation, was family. The idea of giving away a member of your family when, for generations, the Coniglios and her side, the Consumanos, had fought so hard to stay together—across the ocean, through poverty, through burying the old ones who'd arrived in this country to be spit on in the grocery store, through all the sleepless nights over their children—was outrageous. What kind of person just gives their family away?

And yet. And yet. Carla was a widow. (This was what she wailed every time she could not open a pickle jar, every time a lightbulb burned out—"I'm a *widow*!") Vincenzo had been a good man, most of the time, but his death was sudden and his affairs so out of order that it took months to learn he'd left them with nothing. Carla was still reeling from the knowledge that they were broke. Another thing she knew: her son was an idiot, but her daughter was not. Doreen had a spark—Carla told her this all the time. Doreen had a spark, and a baby would douse it forever, and in her thinking Carla came to an alarming conclusion: she loved Doreen more than she loved that anonymous baby.

But what kind of Sicilian mother would she be to voice such an unholy thought? Carla would have to make a big show of her grief. She would have to walk around in black and clutch her rosary and insist on coming along in the car to try to change Doreen's mind. But Carla was really there, Doreen was pretty sure, to make certain she went through with it.

So now the three of them bobbed south along Route 66 in the green-and-white 88, long past the far suburbs. Danny gripped the bottom of the steering wheel with his upturned right hand, his other elbow propped on the window ledge. He was always carefully posed like this, in case some girl popped out from nowhere and he needed to impress her. Doreen looked out at the fallow fields that lined the highway and noticed a scarecrow whose stuffing hung out of the bottom of his shirt, not unlike a pregnant belly. *Is everyone knocked up?* she thought. The world felt unreal, like a painting she could poke her finger through. But she was working like hell not to give in to those kind of thoughts.

Carla's head rested against the passenger window, and Doreen watched her mother's springy black curls quiver in time with her sobs. Danny reached over and patted her arm. Then he turned up the radio so he could hear "It's Now or Never" over her whimpering.

"Ma," Doreen said, knowing she had her own role in Carla's little play. "It's all right. Well . . . it will be all right. You'll see."

"You're trying to break my heart," Carla said. "You're trying to kill me. Thank God your father is dead."

"I'm in trouble" was what Doreen had said to the nun who answered the phone the first time she called Holy Family. Doreen had walked past the leaflet on the corkboard at the Roosevelt branch of the library many times, noticing it but dismissing it with relief because it did not apply to her. How things could change in a day. She called the number from the pay phone across from the circulation desk. Sister Simon wasn't warm, exactly, but she also wasn't scandalized.

"When is the baby due?" she asked, and Doreen could hear the swish of paper.

She hesitated. "The spring?"

"Have you not been to see the doctor?"

Doreen clutched the cord. Her sense of smell was in overdrive, and the inside of the phone booth smelled like cigarettes and BO. She tried not to breathe through her nose. "Not yet. I mean, I'm going to. I mean, I think I am."

Sister Simon sighed. "We have a very good doctor who sees our girls. We also provide food, lodging in our dormitory, and spiritual preparation as you await the baby's birth. I think you should come as soon as possible. We have an opening. The world is not kind to girls in your situation. Holy Family is a safe haven."

Doreen's morning sickness was mostly behind her by now, but her stomach buckled at the thought of a dormitory, grim iron beds in a line in one big room, a bunch of sad girls in nightgowns like the ones Carla wore, with the bows cinched up to their necks.

"How much does it cost?" Doreen asked. Part of her hoped Sister Simon would name an impossible number so that she wouldn't have to face this place. But if she couldn't get in there, what was she going to do? Doreen was eighteen and broke, halfway an orphan. The only thing she knew how to do to make money was waitress and sing, but she couldn't do either of those things with a kid on her hip. Not to mention this baby would be born with hair too curly even for a Sicilian.

They had used a Trojan only that first time. Mosel had waved to her from the window of his Greyhound bus bound for Columbus months ago—a final goodbye, they both knew—and he was blissfully ignorant of the pregnancy because Doreen didn't have the heart to tell him and derail his plans. He could be the next Einstein, and a Black one to boot, for all she understood about what he scrawled in the little notebook he kept in the breast pocket of his shirt. The only time she ever saw him lose his temper was when a particularly robust thrust of her hips had sent the notebook flying from his pocket into the damp grass behind her head and he'd gone scrambling after it with his bare butt still hanging out over the top of his pants. Mosel said he loved her, but she knew he loved his equations even more.

"The Church will cover all your expenses," Sister Simon said, "provided you go through with surrendering the baby so that it can be placed with a good Catholic family."

"It might take me a while to get there, but sign me up," Doreen said, and spelled out her last name very slowly.

❧

"Please don't do this, Doreen," Carla said now in the car with her handkerchief pressed to her forehead.

"I know what I'm doing," Doreen said with confidence.

Carla broke character briefly to snort at this. Then she wailed. "There has to be another solution."

"Ma," Danny said a little too sharply. "Enough of this. You should be grateful that Doreen wants to do this. Now you don't have to explain to the neighbors how your daughter got knocked up by a mystery man."

Doreen reached across the seat and punched Danny hard in the shoulder.

"Ow," he said, flinching, the car wrenching to the right and then back into the lane. He made eye contact with Doreen in the rearview mirror. "No, I'm serious. She says she's never going to tell us who did it. Never."

"That's right," Doreen said, and she meant it.

"Was it Sam?"

"Ew," Doreen said. "Are you kidding me?"

Danny looked at her. "Not Benny. Not in this car!"

"God, no. Come on."

"Stop," Carla wailed. "You are going to kill me. It's like you want to!"

Danny was such a chucklehead, he wouldn't give up. "Anthony? So help me, if it is Anthony, I am going to beat his ass—sorry, Ma—into next year."

"None of the above," Doreen said. She leaned back against the green upholstery and crossed her arms. "I told you, it was an immaculate conception."

Carla whirled around in shock. "You get the Holy Mother's name out of that filthy mouth of yours. Both of you." She pointed in Danny's face and then threw up her hands. "God is punishing me with two terrible children. What did I ever do to deserve this?"

Danny wasn't joking about hunting Anthony down and giving him a beating, Doreen knew. If that was what he would do to a kid he knew, a friend, there was no telling how far it would go if he found out about Mosel. She couldn't stand to think about the things Danny and his friends got up to after dark, armed with baseball bats and worse, when they went out looking for boys they thought didn't belong in the neighborhood. Danny wasn't the mastermind behind this posse, but he followed willingly, and she knew they all thought of themselves as protectors—heroes—for holding the color line.

Thinking about this almost made Doreen say yes, it was Anthony, just to stop the Spanish Inquisition and make sure Danny would never find out about Mosel. But once, in third grade, Doreen had fallen off her bike on the way to school, and it was Anthony who had stopped to help her. He walked her bike the rest of the way so she could hold his handkerchief on her bleeding elbow. Anthony was a nice boy. She couldn't tell a lie like that about him. Anyway, when the baby was born, everyone would know it wasn't Anthony or anyone else from their parish. She thought of Mosel's kind brown eyes, shielded by his glasses with a chip out of the right lens just at the bottom. She thought of the feel of his smooth bare chest against hers. Doreen knew she would love him forever and that she could never see him again. That was why Holy Family was the only way.

An hour later, Danny slowed and turned into a long driveway flanked by two redbrick pillars. Even though it was a late March day, the sun had come out and it seemed almost warm. Bits of gravel plinked against the car as they passed through the trees. On the other side, a large brick building came into view. Three stories high, it looked like a school—or maybe a prison. The main entrance was at the top of a set of grand stone stairs. On each side, Doreen counted five windows. Curtains hung in a few of them, but the rest were bare. There wasn't even a sign.

"Well, this is goodbye," she said to Carla and Danny. "I'm going in alone."

"Wait," Carla said, whipping around. This time, the fear in her eyes was real. "What . . ." She sputtered for a moment. "What do we even know about the doctors? Are you sure it's really safe here?"

"Ma, I'm sure. It'll be all right. I just want to get it over with."

"Let me at least get your suitcase," Danny said.

Doreen got out of the car and stood next to him at the trunk. "Just carry it up to the top of the stairs for me, okay? But then you have to go before I ring the bell."

"All right," Danny said.

Carla got out to say goodbye, and in the sunlight she looked awful, nearly green. She was obviously thinking about all the ways this could go wrong. Women still died in childbirth. That wasn't just a thing in old books.

"Ma," she said, "I'll be back in a few months. And no one's going to know. You can tell all the nurses at the hospital what we talked about, that I got a job at a dinner theater in Detroit, okay?"

"You can change your mind, if you want to. You can always come back home."

Doreen shook her head. "Practice saying it, okay?"

She cleared her throat. "My daughter, Doreen, is going to be away until May," Carla said in a strangled voice. "She got a job singing at a dinner theater in Detroit."

Despite everything—how strange Doreen's body felt, how terrified she was of giving birth, how lonely she felt now that the fun was truly over, probably forever—hearing this lie gave Doreen a little ping of hope. When all of this was over, maybe she could make that lie into the truth. Maybe she *could* get a job singing in Detroit, maybe even all the way in New York. Girls got discovered that way, and there was still time for it to happen to her. Maybe.

"That's right, Ma. You say it just like that. Pretty soon, I'll be back home. And it will be like this never happened."

Carla hugged her daughter and got back in the car. Doreen started up the stone steps. Halfway up, she began to feel the burning in her thighs and a taste of rust in her mouth. Danny followed behind her with the suitcase, and when they finally reached the top, he was panting too.

"Too many cigarettes," Doreen needled him. "You can't handle a little exercise."

Danny ignored her and smoothed his hair.

"Well, you can just leave it here. I'm not going in until you go."

"Dorie, what if it's locked?"

"It's not locked," Doreen said, not at all sure that was true. "Come on—go."

Danny took her by the shoulders and looked at her. "I gotta be serious for a second."

"No, you don't," Doreen said. She would have paid any price for him to taunt her some more like he had been doing back in the car. Anything to feel normal.

"You're doing a good thing," Danny said. "I know it's going to be hard. I'm proud of you."

And then he—*Good lord!* Doreen thought—he *kissed* her on the forehead like some kind of chump and took the stairs two at a time back down to the car. She heard the clunk of his dropping it into gear, and then it crawled away. Over the engine and the sound of the tires she could hear Carla wailing all over again.

Doreen took a long breath, held it, let it out.

The bell beside the front door was black, encircled with a brass collar. When she pressed it, she felt the vibration it made down the length of her finger.

Nothing happened for a long moment, but then the door opened halfway to reveal an older woman in a black habit with dark eyebrows and a chin that looked set in concrete.

"Excuse me. What are you doing?"

"Are you Sister Simon? I think we spoke on the phone. My name is Doreen Coniglio—"

"You may not use this door."

"Oh, I—"

"This door is for adoptive parents only," she said. "You girls have to come in the back, around to the left." Sister Simon closed the door, and

Doreen heard a bolt slide into place. She stood there staring at the carved oak, the panes of frosted glass. If Mosel were here, she knew, he would carry her suitcase. But he wasn't. She really had to stop thinking of him.

With the handrail supporting her right elbow, she heaved it down the stairs, sweat springing out at her hairline and down her sternum. At the bottom, she stopped to take a few breaths and lifted it once more, the back corner dragging intermittently on the gravel path she followed around the left side of the building. There were more windows but no faces looking out of them. Not even one was open so much as a crack. Off to the left was a sprawling lawn framed with trees and a double garage with its doors open, revealing an old black Chevy truck.

For the past few weeks, Doreen had felt the strange urge to take a pinch of dirt from the ground and put it on her tongue. She hadn't done it, obviously, but she couldn't stop thinking about how it would taste, like salt and iron. The warm day had brought the smell of the soil up to her nose, and her mouth began to water. Out of breath, Doreen dropped the suitcase too hard, and it tipped over onto its side. One of the buckles snapped open. She sighed. With the side of her boot, she kicked the case through the dirt the rest of the way to the back door. She felt like an elephant.

Again, a black doorbell with a bronze collar. By now she had her doubts, but it was too late to turn back.

5

Margie

Margie sat in the second row of chairs, with two empty seats between her and Ingrid, the youngest and, paradoxically, most self-assured girl at Holy Family. Why was it that the less you knew, she wondered, the more confident you were? Morning meeting, Margie had learned, was typically a boring hour of housekeeping details—girls needed to be reminded to wipe their hair out of the drain and not leave curling irons sitting on the laminate counters in the bathroom. You wouldn't think anyone would need a curling iron at a home for unwed mothers, but you would be wrong.

Occasionally, however, something interesting happened during the gathering. They might find out that one of the girls had gone into labor in the night or received a care package from home or lost town privileges for a rule violation, like using the phone to call her boyfriend. One time, Sister Joan, the youngest nun, who was an object of fascination for being both witty and pretty, read the girls a poem.

This poem was by a woman poet—a *poetess*, Sister Joan called her—who was young, not even ten years older than the Holy Family girls were now. "Think about that," she had said solemnly to them. "In ten years, you could be a published poet." It was a strange poem, nothing at all like Shelley's flowery, old-fashioned language that Margie had loved memorizing in school. This poem was both plain and yet somehow more cryptic. Margie understood exactly what it was about, but she couldn't explain how she knew.

The girl in the poem was standing in a field, watching a bunch of horses in the evening light, when suddenly a splinter flew into her eye and made it water and burn. She could still see the horses, but now they were warped and strange, like beasts out in the desert that you suspect might be a mirage. For a week, the girl could not get the splinter out of her eye, and even when she finally did, nothing was the same. All she had was the memory of the way the horses had looked before. She never saw them the same way again.

"Cheer us up, why don't you," Yvonne had shouted from her chair by the window when Sister Joan got to the last line. Margie honestly couldn't blame her. It was a strange poem to read to a bunch of girls whose lives were forever changed. Or maybe, because of that, it was just the poem they needed to hear.

Now Sister Simon swished into the cafeteria, and someone Margie hadn't seen before followed her in. The girl was as tall and interesting looking as Margie was short and plain, with dark brown hair held back by a pink headband, a mohair sweater stretched over her belly, and gold hoop earrings.

"Girls," Sister Simon said, clapping unnecessarily to get their attention. "We have a new young lady joining us. Please say hello to Donna."

Everyone murmured their hellos as Donna took her seat, and Margie wondered what Donna's real name was. At Holy Family, you weren't allowed to use your own name (Margie had been renamed Minnie) or say where you were from or keep in touch with anyone after you left. Sister Simon said this was to protect everyone's privacy. It was the kind of rule Verna would approve of, no doubt.

"Now. I want to tell you a story. Two stories, actually. I guess you could call this 'The Tale of Two Girls.'" Sister Simon folded her hands in front of her so that the sleeves of her habit came together and made them disappear. Behind her was a long table and the serving window that connected the dining area to the kitchen and its panoply of smells. Breakfast's scrambled eggs had faded into bleach, but the smell of lunch was there too, last night's meatloaf reheating in the warmer. Margie swallowed down her nausea.

"The first girl—we will call her Jane—despite being brought up in a good Catholic home, with parents who sacrificed in order to provide for her, got herself into trouble with a boy from school."

The chairs around Margie creaked as all the girls shifted forward more or less at the same moment. This was far more interesting than another discussion of the chore chart.

"Jane believed they were in love and that this boy would do the right thing: marry her and make the baby legitimate. Maybe no one would ever have to know, Jane thought, that her baby was conceived in sin.

"Things seemed to be going along well. The boy even gave her a ring. But after a month or so, he got to thinking about what kind of future he really wanted. What kind of woman he really wanted to have for his wife. Was Jane that kind, given that she had allowed herself to get into this predicament? No, not really. The boy decided he would like to grow up a little more, have some adventures out in the world, as boys must do, and then, when he was a little older and wiser, he could choose the kind of wife who would make his family proud. He asked Jane to return the ring."

Margie knew where this story was going, but still she found herself picturing Jane, hoping against hope.

"Now Jane, humiliated, was left expecting a child who would not have a father. Though she had no means to provide for the baby, her family having cast her out, she had grown attached to the romantic idea of becoming a mother. Jane thought she would find a way to care for the baby so that she could keep him. Because of this selfish wish, Jane got further and further away from God. She gave birth all alone.

"She had to do anything and everything to earn money to provide for the child." The sister closed her eyes and shook her head. "Things I won't even mention here in polite company. Meanwhile, her little boy was called a 'bastard' on the playground and mocked and pitied by the other children. His mother's life was lonely—after all, who would marry a young woman in such a situation? Not to mention she didn't stay young for long.

"More importantly, the boy's life was lonely too. He was deprived of all the things a child needs to thrive. A father, a happy and comfortable home, a mother who spends her days caring for him instead of out in the world trying to earn a dollar. Girls, the story of the first girl is a tragedy.

"But now we come to the second girl's story. This girl's story starts out the same way as the first. Many of you will recognize it: an illegitimate child created in sin, destined to a life of shame. But instead of focusing selfishly on her own desires, the second girl thought about her baby. She knew he deserved better, and she did not want to make her parents and her community suffer through embarrassment. She knew she was not the rightful mother of this child, considering the poor decisions that had led to his creation. Instead, she realized that God had chosen her to *carry* this baby for another woman, a married woman who had tried and failed to conceive. There are so many women like this out in the world today. Their greatest wish is to have a child, and this girl had the chance to make that wish come true. Yes, she was frightened. She knew it would not be an easy path, but this girl decided to go away to a place like Holy Family.

"The baby was born and placed with a grateful couple—he, a successful doctor; she, a beautiful, refined wife. With this couple as his parents, the boy will grow up going to the best schools, traveling, maybe even to Europe. He will be dressed well and excel at sports and his studies. And of course he will be raised a faithful Catholic. Surely he himself will go on to become a doctor, perhaps a surgeon."

Margie stole a glance at the other end of the row of chairs, where the new girl, Donna, now sat. She had a look of amusement on her face, almost as if she didn't believe the story was true.

"I'm sure you're wondering what happened to the second girl. After her time at the home, she returned to her family. They recognized that she had made a noble choice to make up for the sinful one, and they welcomed her with open arms." The sister unearthed her hands from her sleeves to drive the next point home, speaking slowly and chopping the edge of her hand onto her palm with each word. "Life. Went. Back. To. Normal. The girl was able to finish school and earn a spot in a well-respected secretarial college. Her first assignment was as an assistant to an up-and-coming attorney in a large firm. He was a bachelor, but he would not stay that way for long."

Every girl in the room was now leaning so far forward they risked falling out of their chairs.

"They had a lovely wedding. A photographer from the newspaper even came. A honeymoon to Niagara Falls. And this young woman went on to become a mother three times over, this time the right way, and the only reason all this was possible for her was that she had made the right decision when she got into trouble as a girl."

Margie absorbed the lesson like the good student she had always been: The sister was offering them a way out. They could wipe the slate clean, and nothing would have to change. Maybe their lives would turn out even *better* than they otherwise would have because they were doing such a selfless thing. God rewarded girls who were good.

After the story ended, Sister Simon moved on to regular meeting business, and Sister Joan appeared at Margie's side. "Come out in the hallway with Donna and me," she whispered.

"Minnie," Sister Joan said, "Donna is going to be staying with us until her time comes. The two of you have due dates very close together, and I think you might be a good fit as roommates." The sister hurried back into the meeting, leaving them alone in the hall.

"Hey, Minnie," Donna said, and rolled her eyes a little at their names.

Up close, Donna was even more intriguing—and intimidating—than she had first appeared. How could Sister Joan think they would be a good fit? Donna had rich, dark eyes and red lipstick, expertly applied. It was March, but her olive skin still held a tan. And, Margie noted with bitterness, Donna's face didn't show her pregnancy in the flesh around her jawline. Margie, on the other hand, had gone soft everywhere. Even her fingers looked pregnant.

"Want to see our room?" Margie asked.

Donna nodded, and Margie led her down to the far end of the hall and to a room that contained two single beds and two dressers on either side of the small window that looked out over an empty field.

"I think Sister Joan will bring up some sheets," Margie said. "The beds aren't so bad. I promise I don't snore or anything."

Donna gave her a faint grin and sank onto her bare mattress. "I really can't believe I'm here."

"I know what you mean," Margie said. "You feel like the whole world is out there going on without us."

Donna leaned back on her elbows. "That's because it is. How about that story Sister Simon told? What a crock."

"Totally," Margie said, her heart sinking. She knew she had been naïve to hope it was true. "Definitely a huge crock."

No doubt Donna was missing out on a lot more excitement than Margie was. That makeup. Her outfit. She couldn't help but hear Verna's voice in her head, calling Donna *trashy*.

"God, I'm starving," Donna said.

Margie checked her watch, which she now had to buckle on the last hole. "Lunch is not for half an hour. Do you want a snack?"

"You have snacks?"

Margie lowered her voice. "We're not supposed to, but my dad sends them. I think he feels sorry for me." She pulled a large cardboard box from under the bed—Frank had even written "Schoolbooks" on the side so as not to raise suspicion—and opened its flaps to reveal about a dozen chocolate bars, cans of shoestring potatoes, little cream-filled cakes wrapped in plastic.

Donna took one of the cakes, oatmeal with maple cream, unwrapped it, and took an enormous bite. "Oh god," she said, chewing with her eyes closed. "You are a godsend. This tastes so good."

Margie thrilled at the praise. "I wish I could say the food downstairs does too, but . . . well, you'll see. Has anyone shown you around?"

"Not yet."

Donna finished her cake, and Margie secreted the wrapper back in the box and shoved it under the bed. "The girls are two to a room on this and the other side of the ground floor," Margie explained when they were back in the hallway. "We're grouped by due date—the ones on the other side have longer to go, and we don't see them much except at meals." They took the stairs next to their room up to the foyer on the main floor. It was quite pretty, with an intricately tiled floor of tiny white and brown squares in the shape of an enormous fleur-de-lis. A chandelier hung above a round table with a vase of silk flowers in the center.

Donna whistled. "This is *nice*. Like a hotel."

"Those doors over there lead to the common room. That's where we can play games or read or whatever. And we have classes, either there or in the dining hall. Sewing, bridge, sketching, religion."

"Bridge?" Donna said. "Do they think we're forty years old?"

Margie laughed. "I know. But you'd be surprised what you're willing to do to pass the time. The days are long. I'm taking a history class so I can graduate on time."

"What kind of history?"

"European. World War I." Margie had been reading about the hours soldiers spent digging trenches. She would think of them standing in the drizzle, leaning on their shovels. Young, handsome, trying to light their cigarettes in the damp. A sudden explosion might blow off their limbs or miss them entirely.

"Is there a piano?" Donna asked, looking for the first time, Margie noticed, just a little desperate.

"No."

"And no radio either?"

Margie shook her head, taking a little pleasure in seeing Donna look so deflated. So far she had seemed impervious, cool as a cucumber. "And that's the chapel," Margie said, pointing at the door to the right of the common room.

"Oh," Donna said. "I hadn't thought about that. Do we have to go?"

"Every morning," Margie said. All the other girls complained about chapel, but Margie didn't mind it. She felt drawn to the dark space, the quiet. It was the only time in the day when what was happening inside her head—dark, eerie shadows moving across a wall of fear—matched what was happening outside it.

"And then the nuns' offices and quarters are on this side," Margie said. "But you can only get to them through the parlor."

Margie walked Donna to the carved double doors and opened them just wide enough to reveal a lavish room with a fireplace, two brocade sofas, and a fine Persian rug. "We're not supposed to go in here. It's for the visitors, when they come to put in an application."

"The adoptive parents, you mean?" Donna said.

For a quiet moment they stared at the furnishings, so different from the plain beds and cheap dressers in their room.

Donna gave Margie a slightly naughty look. "You said no radio, but there's a hi-fi in here."

"So?"

"So we could listen to music."

Margie shook her head. "No way."

Back in the dining room, the rest of the girls had already started on lunch. The windows overlooked a tawny prairie that Margie thought was very beautiful. Its tall thatches of grass were peppered with meadowlarks and the occasional tree, and Margie had already spent a good amount of time in a chair by the window, noticing how the birds clustered in denser segments of grass to get out of the wind. She found it restful to watch them in the same way she found Shelley's poetry restful, and the soldiers getting their arms blown off in France. Anything that kept her from thinking about Mr. Grebe, about what was happening to her, was a welcome distraction.

"God, this really is the middle of nowhere," Donna said, gawking at the field. "There isn't even a billboard to be seen."

"You don't think it's pretty?"

Donna shrugged.

They each took a tray from the stack and joined the line of girls moving past the kitchen window. The scent of onions and ketchup made Margie's mouth water, despite the fact that she had been disappointed by this same meatloaf last week. This kind of hunger was new to her. As the youngest of five children, she was used to getting the dregs at the supper table. These last few weeks, her focus on food had been an intense, galvanizing thing that woke her out of a sound sleep at night. There was a kind of violence lurking behind the urge. If there were only one hamburger left in the world and she saw another girl reaching for it first, Margie thought she might casually throttle her to death.

Donna pursed her lips and turned her head to the side when the nun working in the kitchen, smiling in the shadow of her hairnet, slopped the slice of meatloaf onto a plate and handed it to her through the kitchen window. "Oh my god," she said, loudly enough that Margie's eyes went wide. "I can't eat this."

"Didn't you say you were starving?" Margie asked, taking her own plate and an extra roll from the basket as they moved down the line.

"Yes, but this smells like dog food."

They carried their trays to a large, round table, joining three other girls drinking milk and dipping bread into the meatloaf's watery sauce. Though Margie would have liked to be the one to introduce Donna to the others, to impress Donna with how well she knew her way around, Margie had mostly been keeping to herself since she had arrived a few weeks ago and did not actually know the other girls' names.

But again Donna surprised her, handling so easily a situation that Margie would have agonized over. "Hiya, girls," she said. "I'll start. Donna, from Chicago. And you know Minnie."

Margie gave them a shy grin, fairly certain they *didn't* know.

"I'm Yvonne," said the girl to her right, who wore dark-rimmed glasses and had enormous front teeth. "From Peoria. I love your hair," she said to Donna. "I think you look just like Mrs. Kennedy."

Next was a tall, frail-looking girl with a ballerina's bun on top of her head. She was thin all over—even her midsection was narrow, but it jutted out so far she could barely reach the table. Her plate, which contained just a roll with butter, sat untouched. Margie had the thought that the baby was draining the life out of her face, it looked so hollow, nearly gray. "Laurel. Lake Forest."

"I'm from Ellisville," the next one, plump and freckled, said, and when everyone stared at her blankly, she blushed. "It's a farm town just down the way."

"No," Laurel whispered. "Your name."

Margie did know her—the youngest one.

"Oh!" She giggled and wiped her mouth with her napkin. "Ingrid."

Laurel waved her graceful hand toward the empty chair at Ingrid's side. "And that," she said, "is where Patsy would be sitting, but she went over the day before yesterday."

Donna looked at Margie. "Went over?"

"Over to the hospital," Margie said, "to have her baby."

Donna whistled. "So that's it, then? You won't see her again?"

"Sometimes they don't come back," Laurel said, "and we never really know why. But maybe it is just too hard to see us again, you know?"

"Or maybe she died," Yvonne chimed in, and plastered a smug look on her face when she saw the reaction to her words. "I just mean, how would we even know? No one tells us anything."

"Well," Laurel said, shaking her head in irritation, "*Patsy* didn't die. She's coming back in a couple days, actually, to get her things. Her father is driving up from Springfield."

"Do you know what she had?" Margie surprised herself by asking. She pictured Patsy in a hospital bed beneath a white blanket, holding a bundle in her arms that looked like a football.

"A little boy," Laurel said in a whisper, and the air around the table grew suddenly heavy, the way it does just before a storm. All at once the girls exhaled, quietly, and Laurel kept her eyes on Patsy's chair.

Margie wondered about how all the girls had come to be here, even though she knew she would never get the answer. Unlike Laurel, who talked often of Bill, the wealthy boyfriend who claimed he would marry her just as soon as he finished up at Princeton, and Yvonne, whose puppy love had matured rather suddenly in the back of a station wagon, Patsy had never said how she came to find herself in the family way. And Margie couldn't help but speculate. Maybe Patsy's story was about love. Maybe, like Margie's, it was not. And now, of course, there was Donna to wonder about.

Despite being the new girl, Donna wasn't at all shy about piping up. "But isn't it good news? She made it through. Now she can get back to her life."

Ingrid stuck her chin in the air. "That's right," she said. "It's like Sister Simon always says: God chose us to give these babies to couples who can't have children. It's an important job." She scooped a bite of meatloaf into her mouth.

"Or we just got knocked up by accident and none of us have the money to take care of it like the rich girls on the North Shore do," Donna said. "No offense, Laurel."

Laurel looked at her in shock. "I can't believe you would even *say* that."

Donna shrugged. "Why not? It's the truth."

Ingrid's eyes were wide, and her hand went to the little gold cross she wore at her throat as she chewed and swallowed. The room had filled up with the rest of the girls, and the chatter was getting dangerously loud. Sister Simon did not like chatter at meals.

"Be careful talking about back-alley doctors and that," Yvonne said, smacking the gum that was forever in her mouth, even, mysteriously, as she ate. "Ingrid's a tattletale." She winked at Donna.

"I am not!" Ingrid said.

"Then how did Sister Simon find Laurel's letters to Bill?" Yvonne spat back.

"It's not my fault if someone chooses to break the rules," Ingrid said.

Laurel scoffed and pushed her chair back from the table.

"Well, it's not," Ingrid said. "She's not supposed to have contact with him. It's for her own good."

Laurel snatched up her plate. "Nice to meet you, Donna. I've got dish duty." She stalked off toward the kitchen. The chill in her voice made Margie wither.

Donna, however, seemed unperturbed. "So, Yvonne," she said, "what's the first thing you're going to do when you get back home?"

Yvonne rubbed her belly. "I know I should say something *other* than food, but all I can think about right now is a cheeseburger and a chocolate milkshake."

"Ingrid?"

"I have a horse," Ingrid said, "and I really miss her. Her name's Clover."

"Of course it is," Yvonne said, rolling her eyes.

Margie gave her a look. Ingrid was only fourteen, a child. It gave her a shiver to imagine how she had ended up here. "Come on, Yvonne."

After a beat, she looked at Ingrid. "I'm sorry. He sounds nice."

"He's the kind of horse who doesn't like just anyone," Ingrid said pointedly. "But he likes me."

"What about you?" Donna asked, looking at Margie.

Margie chewed on the last bite of bread, still hungry, and contemplated this. She wanted to regain her parents' trust, of course. She wanted them to see her as they had before: the child who never made too much trouble, the child they more or less forgot about most of the time. She thought of her parents' cramped house in Sycamore Ridge with its front room furniture arranged for an interrogation, the sofa and chairs set too close together; she thought, too, of the nook in the kitchen where they ate their silent meals. Margie's own room, which she had shared as a baby with her older sister Alice until Alice had left for college, or so Margie had been told—she was still small then, watching the line of dolls on a shelf that would stare at her all through the night. Margie knew she should want things to go back to normal, but the idea of returning to the Ahern house made her want to scream.

To Donna she smiled and said blithely, "There's no place like home. I can't wait to get back."

Donna studied her for a moment, and Margie had the strangest feeling that Donna knew she was lying, that she could see right through her words to the truth.

6

Doreen

The following Wednesday, Doreen once again passed the dumpsters that marked the only door the birth mothers were allowed to use at Holy Family, her breath making clouds in the cold morning air. Her pink saddlebag purse thumped against her thigh. Inside was the last of the tip money she had earned before leaving town, a compact, and her tube of lipstick. Doreen hadn't known what to bring along when Sister Simon told her it was time to go see the doctor, but she figured that the main thing was already with her, always with her, straining at the waistband of her skirt.

In the circle drive out front, Hugo, Holy Family's only man and mysterious caretaker who lived in an apartment above the garage, sat waiting in the black Chevy truck she had noticed the first time she trudged up this path with her suitcase. She had seen Hugo inside the building once or twice wearing his oil-stained tool belt.

"Careful there, miss," Hugo said as he opened the door for her. She hoisted herself into the cab, but he didn't look her in the eye. How many girls had he driven to the doctor's over the years? Did he always act so embarrassed for them? When he came around to his side of the truck, he adjusted his cap and ground his cigarette out with his heel before he got in.

The past twenty-four hours had been so strange. Doreen wasn't used to being around all these milk-fed country Protestants. Even the Catholics seemed like Protestants. And to make matters worse, most of them were younger than her. They hadn't graduated from high school. They'd never had jobs or their own money. Some of them didn't even have pierced ears. About once an hour she had to talk herself out of leaving. Yet, miserable as this place was going to be, it beat the alternative.

Didn't it? Ever since Minnie had given her the tour and showed her that fancy parlor with the fireplace, Doreen couldn't stop thinking about the kind of people who came to sit in it. People with money. White people. Who wanted a white baby. What would happen if her baby couldn't pass for Italian?

"How far is it?" she asked, eager to fill the silence with something, anything.

"Just ten miles up this road to town," Hugo said.

They passed a farm where cows nosed a fence, a little brick church with a white bell tower. Next came an L-shaped, single-story building with a few trucks parked in front of its many red doors. It had green shingles and shutters and a painted sign that read THE STARLITE MOTEL. Then it was a few more miles of open fields and what seemed like ten thousand birds picking through the empty acres for something to eat.

"It's my first time going there." Doreen's nerves made her chatty and fidgety, and she took out her compact to reapply her lipstick. Carla always told her the shade was too bright, but Doreen liked the way it brought out her eyes, the nice contrast it made with her dark hair.

Hugo nodded. "Well, they've got the best doctors in the county over there, so you don't have anything to worry about."

"Best in *this* county?" Doreen said. "Wowee."

Hugo didn't even crack a smile. Maybe he had been told not to talk to the girls or ask them questions about their lives. He had to wonder about their stories, didn't he? It was so human to want to know everything you weren't supposed to know.

The hospital was a newer building, a gray concrete box with small square windows. Saplings with woodchips mounded up around their trunks lined the parking lot. Hugo pulled up to the entrance and took the truck out of gear. Concrete benches that matched the building's concrete walls stretched along the edge of the drive. Three nurses in white uniforms with hats that looked like crushed paper airplanes clustered near one, smoking with their elbows propped in their hands.

Hugo came around to her side and opened the door to help her out.

"It's okay for you to leave the truck here?" Doreen asked as her shoe, which she could no longer see, made contact with the ground.

"Ah." Hugo shook his head. "I can't come in with you. But they are expecting you. I'll be back to pick you up at eleven thirty."

Doreen looked at the slender watch Carla had given her on her last birthday. It was only nine. She took a breath and put on a cheerful face, as if what Hugo did or didn't do mattered little to her. The truth was, she was terrified. She had never been to this kind of doctor before. "Okay, see you then."

Doreen slung her purse strap over her shoulder and marched into the lobby of the hospital.

"Good morning," said the receptionist, an older woman wearing large glasses attached to a chain draped around her neck. "May I help you?"

"Yes, I have an appointment to see the doctor," Doreen said.

The receptionist smiled. "All right. What is the doctor's name, dear?"

Doreen gave a slow shrug and turned up her palms.

"Obstetrics, is it?" the receptionist asked with a nod to Doreen's belly.

"Yes."

"Why don't you give me *your* name."

Doreen's heart began to sink like an elevator. Was she supposed to give her real name, or the fake name the home had assigned her? The receptionist stared at her, likely wondering what kind of person struggles to answer a question about her own name. Despite the cold April weather, Doreen felt a trickle of sweat trail down her lower back.

The receptionist looked at Doreen's left hand, the bare ring finger. "Oh. Are you here from Holy Family?"

Doreen exhaled. "Yes."

Suddenly the woman's eyebrows moved into Bette Davis arches, and she didn't seem so nice anymore. "Go through those doors and down the hall," she said in a flat voice, pointing over her shoulder. "There's another desk where you can check in."

"Thank you," Doreen said, but the way the receptionist continued to stare at her made her think she hadn't yet been dismissed. "Should I go . . . now?"

"You know, someone should tell you that you shouldn't be making a spectacle of yourself in your condition."

"I'm sorry?"

"That lipstick. *Really*. Now, go on."

Doreen stalked off with her head held high, but her cheeks burned. What, exactly, did the receptionist think was an appropriate way for her to exist during these nine months? Should she walk around in rags with her hair uncombed as penance? Fade to invisibility like a ghost that could pass through walls?

The woman at the next desk was nicer. She took Doreen's name down—Doreen gave her the real one—on a slip of paper and asked her to wait. The place didn't seem all that busy. Most of the chairs in the waiting area were empty. Two heavily pregnant women sat in the row behind her, one at either end, and their two husbands stood by the window, smoking near a tall brass ashtray. *Oh, to be a husband.* They seemed to have it made.

A nurse appeared and escorted Doreen to a room at the end of the hall. Inside was a stool and a table with two long metal arms extending from its end.

"Hang up your coat," the nurse said, pointing to a hook, "and your purse." She weighed Doreen, whose eyes nearly popped out at the number on the scale, and then made some notes on a piece of paper. "You're here to determine due date, is that correct?"

Doreen nodded. "Yes, and just to . . . make sure everything is all right." She was surprised to hear herself say that part. These last months she had been doing her best *not* to think of the bump as anything other than a bump.

The nurse opened the door to go out. "I'll be back in a minute with the doctor. You take everything off and lie down on the table."

"Everything?"

"Yes," the nurse said and went to the door.

"Do I get a gown or something?"

"We don't do those extra things for you girls."

Doreen took a deep breath and exhaled. The room was very bright. She unbuttoned her dress and hung it on the same hook as her coat, unhooked her bra and slid it off. Unfastening her garter, she rolled down the stockings, folding them neatly inside the cup of her bra, then slid down her panties and folded them up too. She shoved the little packet of unmentionables inside the sleeve of her cardigan so that the doctor wouldn't see them.

It was cold in the exam room, and as Doreen lay back on the paper it crackled, making her think of the sound of ice under her boots. On Taylor Street on a snowy day, the owners of the shops—what was left of them these days, now that the new highway had split the neighborhood in two and every third building was abandoned—were out at the crack of dawn without fail, shoveling the sidewalk and casting big handfuls of salt in front of their doors. Suddenly Doreen felt a pang of homesickness. She could nearly hear the scrape of the metal shovels on concrete, the easy banter of the men in their wool caps, old-timers arguing in Italian as they debated how many more inches were coming, counting down the days until baseball season.

It won't be much longer now, she told herself. Soon, the pregnancy would be over and she could put everything behind her. She could get back to her piano, her notebooks full of songs. She thought about getting thin again, fitting back into the dress she had worn on Mosel's last night in

Chicago. When he'd seen her walking toward him, he'd clutched his chest, miming a heart attack.

The door opened, startling her. In her reverie Doreen had almost forgotten she was lying uncovered on the table. She draped her arms across herself, though it was no use trying to cover the white dome of her belly, the skin stretched taut, her veins visible under the fluorescent lights.

The nurse came back in, followed by the doctor. The first thing Doreen saw of him was the horseshoe-shaped bald spot on the crown of his head, because he did not look at her. He appeared to be about her father's age, or the age her father would be if he hadn't dropped dead. He had deep creases in his forehead and a trim beard. "Miss Coniglio?" he asked.

"Yes."

"I'm Dr. Samuels."

"Pity we had to meet like this," Doreen said. The joke failed to cover the tremor in her voice.

He didn't laugh. He put the tips of his stethoscope in his ears and slid the cold disk over her stomach. "Strong heartbeat," he said to the nurse, who wrote something down. "Scooch down," he said.

The nurse unfolded the metal arms at the foot of the table and showed Doreen how to fit her bare heels into the stirrups as the doctor stretched gloves over his hands. Doreen inched a little closer to the edge, but the muscles of her backside and thighs clenched involuntarily and she could not move down farther. As Dr. Samuels sat down on the stool and slid it toward her, she imagined his view and felt her cheeks burn.

"I said scooch down," he barked. With his right hand, the doctor grabbed her hip, yanked her toward him, and forced her thighs apart. The nurse came around to the head of the table and put her hands on Doreen's shoulders to keep her from creeping back up the table.

Doreen let out a whimper. *Goddamnit, don't cry*, she told herself. The nurse patted her shoulder. Nothing happened for a moment, and then Doreen took a soundless breath when she felt the shock of the doctor's thick fingers. He spread her apart with one hand and jammed the fingers of his other hand inside her.

"That *hurts*," Doreen said, twisting her torso and looking up at the nurse for help, but she only pressed her lips into a line and looked at something just beyond Doreen's face.

Dr. Samuels only grunted in reply. Next came the sound of metal sliding on metal and then the thing was inside her, cold and hard and stretching her open. "What is that?" she moaned. "What are you doing?"

Dr. Samuels leaned to the side so he could see around her leg and gave her an exasperated look. "Listen, you got yourself into this. If you would have kept your legs together, we wouldn't have to be doing this now."

He disappeared again, and Doreen felt the relief of the metal device coming out of her and landing with a thunk in a metal bowl.

"You said your last monthly was in early August, so some lucky couple will become parents to this baby in early May."

Doreen stared at the stippled ceiling tiles. Hearing the word *baby* still startled her. "Is it . . . all right? Nothing to be concerned about?"

Dr. Samuels didn't answer the question. "It's very late in the pregnancy for you to be seeing a physician for the first time." In his voice was the particularly male form of contempt telegraphed by high school vice principals and landlords and supervisors at crap jobs. Exasperation that she had not done as she was supposed to do curdling what would otherwise be mere pity for her stupidity. "Do you feel the baby moving often?"

Though Doreen usually tried to ignore the sensation, of course she felt it, especially when she was lying in bed at night. Each time it happened, it took her breath away.

Dr. Samuels nodded. "Well, you're fortunate that nothing has gone wrong."

"And you're one lucky girl to be able to see Dr. Samuels in particular," the nurse chimed in, her fingers still curled around Doreen's clavicles as if even at this late moment she might try to escape. "He donates his time every Monday to provide obstetrics care to you Holy Family girls. The rest of the time he practices up at the University of Chicago, the kind of doctor with a waitlist a mile long."

All through this chitchat, Doreen continued to lie on her back, stark naked. Her nipples ached with the room's chill. "Can I get a blanket or something?" she asked.

The nurse took Doreen's cardigan off the hook and draped it over her chest. The carefully assembled pile of her underclothes slid down the sleeve toward the floor, her panties fluttering like a pink butterfly to the tile. If she hadn't been wishing so completely to be delivered by death, she would have laughed. How innocent she had been back then, some ten minutes ago, when she had worried about the doctor seeing her bra.

7

Margie

On Friday afternoons while dinner was cooking, the sister who worked in the kitchen set out platters of food that was about to go bad to make space for the grocery delivery that arrived Saturday mornings. This motley feast typically involved textures ranging from slimy to grainy to chalky dry. But today there was carrot cake left over from Sister Simon's birthday party. The girls had not been invited to the celebration, which had taken place in the nuns' private sitting area, but judging by how much was left over, it seemed that the brides of Christ were not so keen on carrot cake. Maybe it was the raisins. Some people hated them, Margie knew, but she could not agree. Raisins were perfectly fine.

She cut herself a slice the size of a paperback novel and took her plate and fork and a cup of tea with cream and sugar back to her room. She had a feeling they were not supposed to take food to their rooms, but lately Margie was struggling to keep track of all the rules. It could be that they weren't supposed to take food out of the dining hall, but it was equally possible that they were *supposed* to eat this weekly snack somewhere else so that the kitchen staff could do some kind of chore she had forgotten. It was the same for the laundry procedures. Was she supposed to leave her dirty clothes in the hallway, or carry them down to the basement herself? At some point she had been told—this she was sure of—but she couldn't remember who had told her or what they had said.

Some of the girls called this forgetfulness "baby brain," but Margie thought the term was incomplete in that it was not just her brain but her entire body that seemed to be forgetting things. Her hands couldn't quite remember how to twist the elastic band over her ponytail so that it stayed in place, or how to fold hospital corners at the foot of her mattress, though Verna had trained her to do it by the time she was nine years old. The worst part was, Margie didn't even mind that she seemed to be in a boat drifting away from all the things she knew. She couldn't muster the energy to grab the oars and fight back against the current. She just wanted to eat her cake and take a nap.

But sleep was no escape. Almost every night since she had arrived, she'd dreamed of a place that appeared to be just like Holy Family but was off somehow: the hallways were zigzag instead of long and straight; the square mosaic tile that adorned the floor ran all the way up the walls and across the ceiling. Instead of electric lights, gas lanterns illuminated the hall.

Margie always wore the same thing: coarse, heavy cloth that draped her shoulders and dragged on the floor behind her as she moved through the oily yellow darkness. The other thing that was always the same was the baby. It moved alongside her. To say it hovered or flew was wrong, and yet it remained in her field of vision even as she went from one room to the next in the byzantine layout of the dream. Margie didn't know if it was a boy or a girl because it was wrapped in oatmeal-colored muslin and its face was covered by a cloud.

What changed each night was the particular form of torture. First there was Margie like Saint Agatha, when the men came and ripped down her drape to saw off her breasts. Slowly, the way she had seen her father carve the turkey at the head of the Thanksgiving table, sweat breaking out on his brow as he fretted over whether he was supposed to go with or against the grain. The next night she hovered above the flames like Joan; then came the cascade of stones battering her face, breaking her teeth, hammering her knees until they sluiced like jelly inside her skin. Another night she felt the crush of an eight-hundred-pound weight bearing down on her torso. That was the way Saint Margaret Clitherow died, pressed to death. In the dream, Margie saw her own eyeballs pop out of her head. The baby, faceless and therefore eyeless, was nonetheless watching, hovering like a precious dust bunny.

Margie reached the room to find Donna lying on top of her pink-and-green quilt with her shoes still on and her eyes closed. She set the tea and cake on her dresser.

"How was it?" Margie asked.

Donna turned her head to the side and looked at Margie out of the tops of her eyes. "So much worse than I possibly could have imagined."

Margie sank down onto her own bed. "I know. I'm sorry."

"So you've had the pleasure of Dr. Samuels's company too?" Donna asked.

Margie nodded. "Yes, it was awful. Did he confirm your due date?"

"Early May," Donna said.

"I'm April 21," Margie said.

Donna propped herself up on her elbow and looked at Margie. "Wow, Minnie. You only have three more weeks."

Despite all the things Margie's brain and body had forgotten, all the routines and instincts that had been dulled by hormones and sleepiness, April 21 remained a destination marked in red on the map of her mind. Sometimes as she walked the halls of Holy Family she would chant it like an incantation. She had learned from the other girls that the due date was just a guess, but she felt sure April 21 would be her baby's birthday. If anyone had asked during the day, Margie would have said that April 21 felt like a holy day, the day on which she, right along with her baby, would be born into some new existence. But of course no one asked. Her baby wasn't hers; she had no right to be changed by the fact of its passing through her body.

At night it was a different story: at night she was flayed like a salmon steak while the baby watched. Instead of explaining this alarming fact to her roommate, though, Margie said, "We're probably right next to each other on the chore chart. Has anyone shown it to you?"

"No, but if it involves getting up off this bed, I'm not interested," Donna said.

"Come on, it'll just take a second."

Donna groaned but pushed herself off the bed and followed Margie to the double doors outside the dining hall, where a single piece of paper was pinned to a corkboard. A typed column listing chores ran down the left side; next to each one, a girl's name was penciled in along with a date.

"Most of us will only be here for about six weeks," Margie explained, "so there are six chores, and when you first get here your name goes at the bottom, with the easiest one." She pointed at the row that said *wipe tables*. "Then when the girl at the top of the list goes over, everybody moves up."

Donna's eyes moved up the list. "I'm not scrubbing anybody's toilet."

Margie shrugged. "It's not that bad. It's only for a week."

Donna stared at the list. "Hasn't anyone ever just said no?"

Margie laughed. Never in a million years would that have occurred to her. Despite Donna's traumatic morning with Dr. Samuels, she seemed unfazed and impatient, as if being at Holy Family was merely a tedious interruption of her otherwise absorbing life.

When Margie tried to express her admiration for this, what came out was embarrassing: "I like the way you are."

Donna looked at her with a deep furrow between her brows. "What?"

"I like how you just say whatever you're thinking."

Donna snorted. "Ask my mother how that's working out for me."

"I think you could be famous someday," Margie said. She hadn't known that was what she thought of Donna until she said it aloud, but now it felt wholly true. Donna had a kind of spark, but it wasn't just beauty—it was a quality Margie typically associated with men, a kind of hearty energy that swept other people up in its path. You just wanted to watch her to see what she would say next.

Donna positively beamed at hearing this. "Well, good, because that's the plan," she said.

"It is?" Margie asked.

Just then, Donna put her hand to her head like a mad scientist. "Oh my god, I feel like if I don't hear the radio soon I'm going to die."

"I know what you mean," Margie said. "I've never seen a place with so many teenage girls that's so quiet."

"Isn't this what dictators do?" Donna asked. "Ban dancing and burn all the music?"

Margie glanced into the dining room to make sure it was empty. "Sister Simon says we are here to contemplate what we did. That if we're allowed any distractions, we're just delaying facing up to everything."

Donna rolled her eyes. "And what do you think about that?"

"I think . . ." Margie considered whether to say what she knew she was supposed to, or what she really thought. "I think she's never been pregnant before."

Donna bugged out her eyes. "Obviously."

"I mean, I think she can't know how we think about it all the time, that there's no distraction big enough to really take it out of your mind, even for a minute, you know?"

Donna stared at her. "I do." Then her eyes went wide. "I have an idea."

"What?"

"Hugo."

"Hugo?"

"Come on." Suddenly full of energy, Donna raced to the other end of the hallway and pushed open the door to the stairs. Margie followed close behind.

"Where are we going?"

"For a walk."

"It's almost time for dinner," Margie said, thinking of her uneaten carrot cake drying out on the foot of her bed. "And we don't even have our jackets."

Donna stopped and, turning to touch Margie's hairline with her finger, laughed. Both of them had broken into a sweat after just two flights of stairs. Margie's legs felt like they had dumbbells attached to the ankles, and her pelvis ached. Maybe that was why she had become so forgetful—it took every bit of concentration and energy just to move from place to place. And not pee her pants.

Downstairs, Donna opened the heavy outer door. The cold blast of air felt like heaven, Margie had to admit. Sister Simon did allow them to take walks around the grounds, as long as they went with someone, but they were supposed to check out at the front desk and be back within fifteen minutes. Margie half expected the open door to trip an alarm, but all she heard was the sound of birds and, in the distance, the trucks on the road.

"If he's there, we'll just stop to chat," Donna said. She did not seem plagued by the same heaviness Margie felt. You could still see the bones in Donna's wrists, and she could still button her little boots all the way up to her ankles. From behind, Margie noticed as she struggled to keep up, you couldn't even tell Donna was expecting.

"What are you talking about?"

Donna broke into a trot, and Margie followed as best she could. At the garage, Hugo was nowhere to be found, but the door was open and the truck was inside.

Margie froze when Donna went around to the driver's side and opened the door. "What are you doing?"

She squealed with delight. "God bless these country people. The keys are in the ignition." She heaved herself up into the seat, slid over, and cranked down the passenger window. Then she opened the door for Margie.

"Donna. This is crazy. We can't steal his truck."

"Why not?" Donna's expression was full of mischief.

"Because! We'll get in trouble!"

"Hon, I've got some news for you—we're already in trouble." Then she laughed. "Minnie, don't be a drip. I don't want to steal his truck. I just want to listen to the raaaaadio."

She stretched the last word out longingly. Margie wondered if she herself had ever needed anything as much as Donna seemed to need to hear some music. There was danger in wanting something so much, but Margie got in the truck.

Donna turned the knob and waded through the static until she found a station playing Billboard hits. She instantly relaxed.

"Yvonne told me that when Hugo was young, he was in prison. He held up a gas station."

"And you believe her?" Donna asked.

"I guess so. She said the nuns took him in and gave him a job when no one else would. Why would she make that up?"

Donna shrugged. "For the hell of it? You shouldn't be so gullible, Minnie. Someone will take advantage of you."

"Will You Love Me Tomorrow" came on next. When it ended—because talking while it played seemed akin to interrupting the Lord's Prayer—Donna asked, "Do you ever listen to WLS at home? You can get it out in the burbs, right?"

Margie scoffed. "Of course. Sycamore Ridge is not *that* far—just past Glen Park. It might as well be the city."

"Sure," Donna said, laughing. "Sure it is." From the pocket of her dress she pulled out a little bottle of red nail polish and began touching up her chipped nails.

Margie felt she needed to insist on this point. "I'm just saying—we have the radio. We have dances."

"Ooh, dances. Is *that* how you got yourself into this mess?"

Margie felt her throat tighten. She pointed at the bottle. "You should be careful with that. If it spills, we are going to get it."

Donna peered at her. "Such a Goody Two-shoes. Minnie, is this your first time?"

Margie reddened. "What are you *talking* about?"

Donna put her hand on Margie's arm, her wet nails glistening in the fading light. "No, hon, I just mean, is this the first time you've ever gotten into trouble? Ever disappointed your parents? You seem like a *good* girl."

"And you're not?" Margie said. She had meant it to sound like a reproach, but it landed as a sincere question. Back in Sycamore Ridge,

Margie didn't really know anyone who wasn't a good girl. Pamela's biggest rebellion was insisting on playing the hand bells at St. Paul of the Cross when her mother wanted her to sing in the choir. It was only in the last year that Margie would meet her after rehearsal to get sodas at the counter in the Ben Franklin and speculate about what it would be like to kiss a boy. Pamela, like everyone she knew in Sycamore Ridge, thought Margie was visiting her dying aunt in Dubuque. If she found out the truth, she would never speak to Margie again.

Donna considered Margie's question. "I think it's a little different where I'm from."

Margie blinked, clueless. "What do you mean?"

"Because I don't have money, dummy."

"Oh . . ."

"It's fine. Nothing will happen if you say it out loud, I promise. The sky won't crack open. You just don't see a lot of twin sets and pearls on Taylor Street is what I'm saying. My dad died three years ago, and he didn't leave my mother a dime. My brother is a meathead, and he still lives with us. He says it's because he's the man of the house now and has to take care of us. But he's a complete drain. He can barely hold down a job."

Margie shifted quickly from the shock of hearing so many personal details so easily shared to elation at what the sharing might mean—did Donna actually want to be her friend? "Does he have a temper?" Margie asked, scrambling to keep the conversation going. "How did he take the news?"

"Put it this way—I called home from a pay phone to tell him so I wouldn't have to be there when he started breaking stuff." Margie must have looked horrified because then Donna said, "It's all right. He has a good heart. I mean, he's an idiot, but that will end eventually. Maybe. Carla—that's my mother—says we have to be patient with men. It takes them longer to grow up."

"That's funny," Margie said. "I call my mother by her first name too. I mean, when I'm not with her. I never thought about why I do that."

"What's her name?"

"Verna."

Donna smirked. "As in, 'Verna's being a real bitch today'?"

Margie's hand flew to her mouth to cover a snicker. "I guess so."

"Don't worry, Minnie. She can't hear us." Roy Orbison came on, and Donna tipped her head back against the seat. They listened to Ike and Tina and Elvis and the Lettermen and Bobby Vee. Donna knew the words to every single song. After a while, she turned on her side so that she could face Margie.

"So, what was it? Your first love?"

Before she could think of a clever deflection, Margie said, "I don't want to talk about it."

"Heartbreak, then?" Donna pressed.

"No. Nothing like that." She could feel the memory pounding on the door to get in, but she wasn't going to let it.

"I don't mind telling you about mine," Donna offered. She inspected her nails, waved them aimlessly to dry. "If you want to know."

Margie blinked, attempting to recapture the conversation's thread. *Love.* "Was he *your* first love?"

Donna looked to the truck's ceiling in contemplation. "Well, I had a few false starts before him. But he was definitely . . . different."

"What does he look like?" Margie asked and then cringed because she knew her dreamy voice made her sound childish.

"Big brown eyes," Donna said. "And he always dressed so nice, you know? He was one of those guys who took a lot of pride in his appearance. His skin was soft. He smelled good."

Margie whispered. "Did he . . . die?"

"No! *What?* Why would you ask that?"

"Oh, you're just talking about him in the past tense. It made it sound like maybe he had passed away."

Donna shook her head. "But he might as well have. He went away to college. And our families . . . well, they wouldn't have gotten along."

"What did he say when you told him?"

Donna made a face like she was mugging for the camera, but just before the grin slid into place, Margie noticed her eyes pucker just a bit. The word *sorrow* flashed through her mind. "Now, why would I do that?" Donna said.

Margie thought maybe she shouldn't ask any more questions. For a long while they sat in the cab of the truck and listened to the music as dusk fell across the meadow. She felt the spooky sensation of an elbow or a heel sweep from her ribs to her hip and tried, and failed, to picture the baby in her mind. He was only a shape now, a direction, an idea. Uselessly, she grasped and grasped at it.

Donna's eyes were closed, and her hands rested on the globe of her stomach. She seemed completely unperturbed, and Margie envied her. Why couldn't she ever just be in the moment like that? Why couldn't she listen to a song without wondering what the song meant or how long it would last or what would come on next and whether she would like it? Even now, it was happening. She didn't let herself look at it, not yet, but she felt the face of her watch with her fingers, and time itself goaded her. With every second, they were getting closer to the cataclysm. And no one was talking about what was going to happen. How could she just sit, listening to the radio in the face of that knowledge?

When "Everybody's Somebody's Fool" ended, Margie said, "Donna, I think we should go in."

"Eh, I'm sick of *Donna*. Let's cut the shit—what's your real name?"

Margie felt the same pang she had earlier, when they were standing in front of the chore chart. *I like the way you are*, she'd said to Donna, or whatever her real name was. She liked the way the world looked through her eyes.

"You don't have to say your last name."

"Margaret," she said. "But most everybody calls me Margie."

"Oh, that's a relief. Minnie is . . ."

"Ridiculous?"

Donna laughed. "Yes." She switched off the radio, and they got out of the truck. The temperature had dropped, and the grass crunched under their boots as they headed back toward the building.

"So," Margie asked, almost afraid it was too personal, that Donna would make up some other fake identity rather than reveal anything more, "what's *your* real name?"

Donna paused her steps and stooped down to the ground for a moment. Margie couldn't be sure in the dim light, but it looked like she scraped up some dirt with her fingers. When she stood, she put it in the pocket of her skirt. Finally, she said, "Doreen."

Doreen. It was the perfect name for this girl, and Margie knew it really *was* her name, that Doreen was telling the truth. She was glad they were walking side by side so that Doreen would not see the elation in her face. This was Doreen and she was Margie, and whatever else happened they were going to be friends. Why Doreen walked around with dirt in her pocket was just something that would be revealed in the fullness of time.

The exterior light beside the stairwell door was on, and so it took a moment for Doreen and Margie to see Sister Simon's dark shape in the window, waiting for them.

8

Doreen

"Well, you're off to a great start, I see," Sister Simon said to Doreen. "Both of you, come with me to my office." They followed the sister down the first-floor hall to the last door on the right. "Close the door and sit down," Sister Simon said.

"Sister, I will admit that we lost track of time, but all we did was go for a walk," Doreen said. She looked to Margie for support, but she was looking down at her hands in her lap, her lips curled in and pressed between her teeth.

"Just a walk?"

"Just a walk," Doreen said.

"Are you sure that's not a lie?"

"I'm so sorry, Sister," Margie suddenly wailed. Her ponytail shivered as she heaved into her hands. "I tried to stop her, but Donna made me go with her. She *made* me get into the truck."

Doreen whipped her head to the side to glare at Margie.

"*Into* the truck is your story now?" Sister Simon said, and it was clear she already knew this. Hugo must have seen them from his apartment over the garage.

"She wanted to listen to the radio," Margie said. "I knew it was wrong."

The sister sat forward and looked at Doreen. "Well?"

It took every ounce of self-control for Doreen not to remind both of them that she was eighteen goddamn years old, that she could drive a car, vote in an election, walk into a bar and order a whiskey. And since she had not been convicted of a crime, she was not in jail and could listen to the radio whenever the hell she wanted. Instead she said, "Marg—Minnie—is right. It was my idea. I would have gone and done it on my own if she wasn't there."

"So you broke into a vehicle."

"We didn't *break into* anything. It was unlocked!"

"Why are you here?" Sister Simon asked.

Doreen sighed. "I think we all know."

"Humor me."

"Because we are expecting."

Sister Simon sat back in her chair and folded her hands across her chest. She shrugged. "There are many women in Illinois who are expecting the birth of a baby, but they are not spending their pregnancies in a place like this. Why are you?"

Eventually, Margie couldn't take the tension. "Because we aren't married."

"That's right," Sister Simon said. "And for girls in your situation, Holy Family is the only place that can make it possible for you to have a future. You both have just about a month to go. You're so close to putting this behind you. It's disappointing to see your lack of self-control."

Margie sniffled, and Doreen glanced at her sideways to see that she was crying. Just a few moments ago in the truck, Doreen had been feeling almost sisterly toward Margie—the girl was so clueless it was sweet, not to mention impossible to imagine that she'd actually gone all the way with a boy, despite the proof sitting right on her lap—but now Doreen wanted to smack her. Crying was exactly what Sister Simon wanted them to do. She'd like them to crawl on their knees across the gravel parking lot.

Doreen's secret weapon was that she did not care whether Sister Simon thought she was a common slut. But poor Margie cared, and she was going to punish herself a thousand times worse than the nun ever could, probably for the rest of her life.

And yet the sister was right about one thing. This was the only place that could get Doreen out of this mess and make it possible for her to live the life she wanted. This chapter of her life had to end, and quickly, if she had any hope of getting back to singing the songs that rang in her ears all night long. Because of that, she couldn't be stupid. She couldn't get herself kicked out.

Sister Simon sighed. "You may go get sandwiches from the kitchen. Then you will go up to bed. Tomorrow we will begin again. And you will show the proper gratitude for the gift Holy Family is giving you."

"Thank you, Sister," Margie said. In the hallway, she tried to catch up to Doreen. "Doreen, I'm sorry."

"Sorry about what?"

"I shouldn't have done that. I shouldn't have blamed you. I panicked."

Doreen couldn't stand girls who did this, playing to whatever crowd happened to be in front of them at the moment. Back in the office, Margie would have informed on every girl in the place if it had raised her status in the sister's eyes. Now she would be glad to cast off her confession, her contrition, if it would get her back in Doreen's good graces. Everything was up for negotiation with a girl like Margie. She was merely a reflection of whoever happened to be standing across from her. "Give me a break. You knew exactly what you were doing."

"I *said* I'm sorry." Margie sounded surprised. Her apology hadn't worked the way it was supposed to.

Doreen stopped and looked at her. "And I don't care." She raked her hands through her dark curls. The hallway was lined with bright-pink and green wallpaper, cabbage roses over a striped background, and just looking at it made her dizzy. Whoever had picked out the pattern was deranged.

That night Doreen waited until she was sure Margie was asleep, and then she slipped quietly out of bed to where her skirt hung on a hook and tipped the contents of its pocket into her hand. It was about a tablespoon of sandy dirt, and she craved it like she craved a piece of chocolate cake.

She held her palm up to her mouth and dipped her tongue into the little mound. The grains that stuck to it made her salivate and tasted just the way she had expected they would: salty and metallic. Disgusting, but she wanted it anyway. The taste made her remember putting a penny in her mouth once as a very young child, and Carla squeezing her jaw until she spat it out with a bubble of drool. “No,” she'd said sternly, her eyes locked on Doreen's to make her point. “You don't put coins in your mouth—you could choke.” Doreen guessed that was how she had learned the meaning of that new word: *choke*. It was staggering to think that she had learned the name of everything a body could do—sit, stand, walk, hop, breathe, laugh, cry, choke—from Carla. How in the world had her mother even seen her slip the penny between her lips? She must have been watching Doreen's every move, even as Danny ran circles around them in his beloved cowboy outfit with the real leather fringe. How did mothers do the work, day in and day out, of keeping humans alive, much less teaching them anything? Would the woman who adopted her baby be as good a mother as Carla had been? Even to a brown baby that didn't look like her? She didn't want to think about the answer.

She took one more lick of the dirt and then, disgusted with herself, brushed her hands off over the wastebasket next to her dresser. Wouldn't Sister Simon be pleased to see her literally eating dirt.

Doreen lay back on the pillow, wide awake. Now she needed to wash the grit out of her teeth.

Up from the bed once more, she slipped her robe over her nightgown and borrowed Margie's slippers—Doreen didn't have any of her own, and that little snitch owed her—and moved quickly into the hall so the light wouldn't flood the room.

The double doors at the end of the hallway led right into the dining hall, and she was surprised to find a light on in there. It had to be after midnight by now. Sitting at the table closest to the kitchen window was a woman in a flannel nightgown with her red hair in a long braid down her back. She was young but not that young, too old to be one of the residents.

She looked up when the door clicked back into the frame. "Oh, Donna," she said. "Have I woken up the house?"

"Oh, no. I haven't been able to sleep. I just wanted to get a drink of water." She smiled so that she could study the woman's face a little longer and realized it was the young nun who had stood behind Sister Simon during morning meeting on her first day. Doreen hadn't recognized her without her habit. On the table in front of her was a stack of books.

"Care to join me?" she asked when Doreen walked back through with her cup of water. "I'm Sister Joan. I'm sure it's hard to keep us straight."

Doreen grinned. "Well, it's easier when you're wearing your own clothes. Now you look like . . ."

"Like a person?"

"Oh, I didn't mean—"

"No, it's true."

Sister Joan had eyebrows with a high natural arch and full lips that broke easily into a smile, the kind of features the most popular girls in school had seemed magically to have. Doreen could picture the sister wearing a letterman's jacket to a pep rally, giggling with a trio of girls in evening gowns and giant corsages. Had she done those things before she ended up here?

Sister Joan rose from the table. "I'll be right back."

Doreen waited at the table while she went into the kitchen. She skimmed the titles of the sister's textbooks. *Introduction to Physiology. Basic Pharmacology.* Each one three inches thick.

A moment later, Sister Joan came back carrying two mugs of cocoa with tiny freeze-dried marshmallows floating in the foam.

"Oh," Doreen said in surprise. "Thank you." It was the first kind thing she had seen one of the sisters do since she arrived.

"I was planning to get one anyway. Told myself I would if I made it to the end of the chapter."

"You're still in school?" Doreen asked.

"I'm taking a few courses at the community college. If I do well in those, I can enroll in nursing school."

"They let you out to go to class?"

Sister Joan laughed. "Donna, I'm not in prison. And this isn't a cloistered order either; otherwise, you girls wouldn't be here. Our charism involves working with unwed mothers, and some of us get training to help us do it better." She took a sip of her hot chocolate. "How have you been feeling?"

Doreen sighed, remembering that just five minutes ago she'd been lapping dirt out of the palm of her hand. "A little strange," she said.

"Well, strange makes sense, considering you're growing a whole new person," Sister Joan said. "And you've never done that before."

"No, I haven't. I'm having all kinds of weird symptoms."

Sister Joan raised her movie star eyebrows. "Like what?"

"My skin is so itchy. Especially the bottoms of my feet."

Sister Joan nodded. "That happens to a lot of girls. Hormones are slowing your liver down, and it's not moving bile as well as it usually does. It will go away when the baby is born. What else?"

Doreen pursed her lips and looked away, trying not to laugh. "You're going to think I'm crazy."

"Pregnancy makes girls crazy. It's not your fault."

"I want to—I mean, I think about—*crave*, I guess—dirt. I want to eat it."

Sister Joan grinned. "That *is* a weird one. Pretty uncommon, but I've seen it. It even has a name: pica."

"No way."

Sister Joan nodded. "Sure. That's normal too. Although you probably shouldn't eat the dirt around here—who knows what kind of farm chemicals are in it. It means you need minerals, probably iron. Take an extra helping of beef if you can stand it."

Doreen gave her a dubious look. "How do you know so much if you haven't even started nursing school yet?"

"My mother was a midwife. I was helping deliver babies by the time I was ten years old."

"No kidding."

Sister Joan nodded. "My people are from a tiny town in the Ozarks, on the Missouri side. It's just trees and a handful of people, and my mother was the one you called when you went into labor. The closest hospital is a couple hours' drive."

"Is that why you became a nun? Seeing how awful childbirth is, you just wanted to avoid the whole thing?" Doreen asked this with a little trepidation, fully aware that she didn't yet know how bad it actually would be.

Sister Joan shook her head. "I didn't even know what a nun was back then. We weren't Catholic. I'd never met a Catholic. In Sunday school we learned they worshipped Mary like a false god, that they thought they could get drunk every weekend and raise all kinds of hell, as long as they went to confession on Sunday."

Doreen thought about Danny and his friends. The Protestants maybe had that second part about right, though all her conditioning could never allow her to admit it.

The sister pushed the textbooks to the side and wrapped both palms around her mug. "Then one year we had rains like you wouldn't believe, and terrible flooding. The governor sent in the Army Corps of Engineers, and volunteers came to help people who were stranded. And some Franciscan nuns came down from St. Louis and set up a clinic in our schoolhouse. Everyone in Shook—that's the name of the town—thought they were strange and even dangerous, but I could not take my eyes off them. They wore brown habits and white veils, and from a distance they all looked exactly the same."

"*That's* what you loved about them?"

"I loved that they were all women. They ran their own programs without any men telling them what to do. They went out into the world, wherever they were needed. I thought they were like superheroes. I knew right then I wanted to be a part of it."

"What did your parents think about that?" Doreen asked.

"Oh, they hated it. I found out there was a boarding school run by another order in St. Louis, and I made it my goal to go. When I converted later on, my parents took it as proof that all they did there was brainwash you."

"Well, did they?" Doreen knew she was pushing the line asking such a direct question, but Sister Joan didn't seem to mind.

"If they did, I guess I'd be the last one who could tell you, wouldn't I?" She laughed. "Brainwashed into loving the Lord. It's not so bad, I've got to say. Jesus is the best boyfriend I ever had."

"He never got you knocked up," Doreen said. "That's a point in his favor."

The sister gave Doreen a complicated look, amusement softened with sympathy. "You know, you're only going to be here for a very short time, and then it will be over. You *will* move on from this."

Under the table, Doreen dug with her index finger into the cuticle on her thumb. This promise disappointed her somehow. Why was that? "There's a Catholic in the White House now," Doreen said with a shrug. "Anything is possible."

Sister Joan laughed, then gave her a decisive nod. "You will. Now, off to bed with you and let me get back to work. And no sneaking outside for a handful of dirt. If Sister Simon caught you at that, you'd never hear the end of it."

Doreen couldn't help but smile. "Good night. Don't work too hard." She waved over her shoulder as she made her way back to her room, but the moment of ease was quickly surpassed by the itching in her palms. She rubbed them on the coarse sleeves of her terrycloth robe. The rhythm of the *scritch scritch scritch* sounded familiar. She was going nuts, clearly, but she also knew she had heard it somewhere. It was a mark of how starved she was for music that it came to her just as she was lying back down in bed. *Long, short-short. Long, short-short.* The pattern from the opening line of "I'm Sorry" by Brenda Lee.

9

Margie

Saturday arrived again, another week gone by. Seven days of ferrying their dishes to and from the kitchen, of chapel and chores. Seven days of reading about Verdun and, when she could safely get away with it, reading instead from the contraband copy of *Peyton Place* someone had snuck in.

After breakfast, the girls scattered to do their chores, and eventually Margie drifted into the community room, an old parlor at the front of the building that now contained two large tables, a handful of red folding chairs, and stacks of beat-up board games. Three of the black checkers were missing and someone had fashioned replacements out of bottle caps. Dice from one game had migrated into a box for another game that didn't even involve dice. And the jigsaw puzzle of the Chicago skyline was a disaster. Even if you could complete it, and that seemed impossible, the missing pieces would leave holes in the architectural marvels, as if someone had thrown bricks through their windows.

All her life, Margie had played with toys whose best days were behind them. She hadn't quite known what to say when Doreen had so baldly proclaimed in the truck that Margie's family had money, because while it might have been true on paper, the reality was more complicated. Yes, Margie got new clothes whenever she needed them, especially when it came to dances and holidays. Verna never made her wear her next oldest sister Catherine's hand-me-down dresses. Of course, that was partly because Catherine was a size four, like Verna, and Margie had been a size ten since she was fourteen. But as the youngest of five children, she knew well what it meant to bring up the rear of the parade long after most of the spectators had exhausted their handfuls of candy and gone home. No matter how she tried to distinguish herself from her siblings, Margie had never caught her parents by surprise with a precocious insight or clever talent. It was impossible to delight them after the four sagas that had come before and were now complete. Kenneth in seminary, Alice married, living in a Lincolnwood bungalow now, Bud in the air force, and Catherine away at college in Minnesota. Margie wasn't that much younger than them, but she had grown up with the constant fear of being forgotten that stemmed from having been left out of all the things that happened before she came into existence. And the proof of the fun they'd had without her was board games just like these, the corners of the boxes, surely ripped by accident in the unimaginable revelry, taped back together.

Just when Margie was about to rifle through the shelf for a deck of cards to begin setting up solitaire's bleak rows, Ingrid came into the room with two of the dining hall's brown melamine cups of lemonade.

"Want to play something, Minnie?" she asked.

Margie took the cup and smiled. "Sure, if you want to. Thanks for this."

"I love lemonade," Ingrid said. Every day she wore her hair in two long braids pinned up in the back. Maybe it was the hair combined with the wide, freckled face, but she looked like she had just come from milking the cows.

Margie drank the contents of the cup down in two big gulps. "I'm just so thirsty all the time," she said. "You'd think I was walking through the desert."

"Well, it's just all going to the babies," Ingrid said. "Don't you just love thinking about how happy we're going to make these parents?" She gave herself a little hug. "I bet they never knew someone could be as nice as us."

Margie nodded and searched for a neutral reply. "I never thought about it that way."

This week Ingrid was assigned to the laundry, two spots behind Margie's job dusting and washing windows. That put Ingrid's due date around the end of May, Margie calculated, though Ingrid had been here a good deal longer than Margie had. Margie grinned distantly at her so as not to be rude, but the truth was she hadn't let herself think at all about anything that might take the edge off her guilt, even though she was only a couple weeks away from the main event. Maybe *because* she was only a couple weeks away. It seemed indulgent to convert this disaster into something noble in her imagination, patting herself on the back for *doing it for the adoptive parents*, as if from the moment of conception she had known it was her destiny to perform this act of generosity. Sister Simon didn't want them walking around feeling good about themselves, but it would also be counterproductive to the Holy Family enterprise to have girls throwing themselves off the roof in despair before the coveted babies were delivered. Anyway, Margie didn't think she was despairing. Low self-regard came naturally after a lifetime of practice, like slipping into a comfortable, if ugly, old coat. She hadn't known what would happen to her when she followed Mr. Grebe down the basement steps, but she should have known. She'd been as naïve as Ingrid seemed to be still, somehow. That was no excuse.

"What should we play?" Margie asked in the hopes of changing the subject.

"Oh, I have a better idea," Ingrid said and opened one of the drawers in the built-in beneath the shelves to find paper and pencils. "Let's make a list of names!"

Margie tipped the cup to her mouth again, but only a single drop of lemonade remained. She felt something near panic. "I don't think that's such a good idea."

"Why not?" Ingrid asked.

"Well, it seems a little . . . wrong," Margie said gently. "I mean, *we* won't be naming them. That job will be left to the parents."

Ingrid's face fell. "I hadn't thought of that. You're probably right. I just thought it sounded sort of fun to imagine. Maybe Charlene? Or Tracy? Then again, it could be a boy."

"But we might not know," Margie said. Again, this notion had the feel of a bird she'd expended a lot of energy keeping stuffed in its cage, but flinging now from her mouth, it felt true.

"We won't know what they name them?" Ingrid asked.

Margie wondered if she disliked Ingrid so much because she was afraid people saw her the way she saw Ingrid: Dull. Naïve. Those wide-open eyes like a fish's that keeps stupidly swimming into the glass.

Margie sighed. "No, I mean we won't know anything. That's what adoption is. After the baby is born, it will have a whole different life that has nothing to do with us. But do you see why that's probably for the best?"

Ingrid put down her pencil. "I guess so," she said. "But it's just . . ."

"What?" Margie felt her muscles pull her shoulders even higher. She could swear she was ready to strike. Why did she feel like a cornered animal?

"Minnie, you keep calling it *the* baby. Not *my* baby. But aren't they ours, a little? At least for now?"

"No," Margie said, fast. If she admitted what she really felt there was no telling what might happen. "We're borrowing them. Like library books. You don't get to keep them."

"We don't use the library," Ingrid said in a superior tone. "Mother says the books are covered in germs."

Just then the front door chimed, and they heard footsteps coming from the nuns' offices in the opposite hall. Margie and Ingrid bolted up and ran to the window. Parked in the curved front drive was a green-and-white Oldsmobile. Whoever had driven it was now standing too close to the front entrance to be seen from this vantage, but they heard the heavy door open and close, felt the burst of cool air that seeped under the community room door. Sister Simon's voice, plus a young man's, rose up as they passed into the visitors' parlor. Moving as one eager entity, Ingrid and Margie slipped to the community room door to open it a crack and see what they could see. Sister Simon had left him alone for a moment, and he sat in the parlor with his back to the hallway. All they could see was dark hair slicked down with pomade, the bottom of his shoe resting on his knee.

A few minutes later, Sister Simon reemerged, followed by Doreen, whose hair looked very nice, Margie thought with a burst of affection. She wore a black-and-yellow plaid dress and a black handbag looped over her arm. The dress's belt rested just below her breasts, and the heavily pleated skirt cascaded over her belly like a waterfall.

"Is that her boyfriend?" Ingrid hissed.

The guy punched her on the shoulder lightly and put his arm around her. This had to be the brother—Danny.

"How should I know?" she whispered back to Ingrid, trying on Doreen's snappy tone.

Danny asked something, and at first Sister Simon shook her head firmly. But when he broke into a smile, Margie could see her body language change even through her shapeless habit. Danny finally got her to nod. She went to a cabinet on the far side of the room, took something out, and put it in Doreen's hand before disappearing back into the parlor. Then Doreen turned to the common room door, and Margie and Ingrid scrambled to their seats. Ingrid tossed half the deck of cards in her direction.

The heels of Doreen's boots clicked into the room. "Margie," she said, ignoring Ingrid completely, to Margie's glee, "do you want to come to the movies with us?"

"Really?"

"Who's Margie?" Ingrid asked, still holding the hasty hand of playing cards. They were facing the wrong way.

"Sister Simon said I could?" Margie said.

"She didn't want to, but Danny wore her down. He's good at that."

"Let me get my purse," Margie said, and it took all the self-control she had not to break into a run.

10

Doreen

When Margie appeared at the end of the hall, forcing herself to walk slowly, trying hard not to appear eager, Doreen had to suppress a grin. Whether she was eager or trying not to be, Doreen thought, the result was the same: the trying. Margie tried so hard at everything. Her whole life—her words, her deeds, even her private thoughts—seemed calculated for the sake of the judges she imagined sat on a dais she dragged with her everywhere she went. But the score never came in. The reward for all that trying was simply getting to do it all over again the next day. Doreen wasn't even mad at her anymore for the business with Hugo's truck. She knew Margie simply couldn't help it.

"Margie," Doreen said more gently than she would have expected, "this is my brother, Danny."

"Good to meet you, Margie," Danny said, doing an impression of a functioning adult. The three of them tromped single file down the path that ran along the side of the building to the front drive. When they got there, Danny swept his arm toward the Oldsmobile. "Your chariot awaits, ladies."

Doreen started to give him a look, but Carla's voice cut through her mind: *Would it kill you to be nice?*

Maybe, she would have said back, had her mother been there.

Danny opened the passenger-side door, but before they got in Doreen fished two rings from her pocket. She put one on her left hand and gave the other one to Margie.

"What's this?"

"It was the only way Sister Simon would allow us to go out. We have to wear them."

Margie slipped the plain gold band on her left hand and looked at it, her fingers splayed out. "Do you think anyone would really believe *we're* married?"

No way in hell, Doreen thought, when it came to Margie. But she herself? Maybe.

"And . . . is the idea that you're both married to me?" Danny asked. It was a valid question. Sister Simon hadn't thought the plan all the way through.

"It's stupid," Doreen said, "but I think people will believe whatever you put in front of them. Anyway, who cares what they think?"

Without having to say a word, Margie's whole being screamed *I do.* And now it was clear she was indulging in a little fantasy of what her imaginary wedding had been like. Pink bridesmaids' dresses, no doubt, miniature roses tied with pink ribbons. A reception at "the club," that mysterious place suburbanites were always talking about on TV. And then, for a brief, painful second, the mental equivalent of a hard pinch, Doreen thought about what it might have been like to marry Mosel. Just the two of them, for practical reasons but also because it was what they really would have wanted. City Hall, Doreen in the exact same dress Sophia Loren had worn in *The Black Orchid*. Mosel's warm cheek against her own as he whispered, "My wife."

Doreen helped Margie into the back seat and then got into the front herself. Danny circled around the front of the car to the driver's side and made the engine roar to life. Doreen glanced back at the building, and there was Sister Simon in the visitors' parlor window, staring out at them. She noticed other faces too—Ingrid's childish pout in the common room window, Sister Joan looking out from the second floor.

"I can't believe they're letting us out," Margie said in a voice hushed with wonder.

"Jesus, I think I got here just in the nick of time," Danny said, his eyes bobbing to Margie in the rearview mirror. "You're talking like a couple parolees." He turned to Doreen, his leather jacket squeaking against the seat. "You know, that Sister Joan ain't half bad, if you imagine her without the getup."

"Danny, you are an idiot," Doreen said and switched on the radio, the vibration of the tires beneath her feet sending her into a kind of euphoria. "Take Good Care of My Baby" came on. Over her shoulder she locked eyes with Margie as the opening line led into the chorus. It was so ridiculous—you couldn't have scripted it better. But then everything about their lives now was ridiculous. They howled with laughter.

The town of Prairie Creek looked like a set for a TV show instead of a real place where people actually lived. Doreen spotted no overflowing garbage bins, no cheap aluminum fencing, no shrines to Our Lady filled with last fall's mucky leaves. There was a lunch counter with a sparkling sign that read DELUXE DINER, a five and dime, a ladies' boutique with a display of gloves in the window. The awnings of all the shops matched, green and white stripes, and all the pickup trucks parked parallel out front were new and sparkling clean. In the muddy month of April. She didn't trust any of it.

"Where in the hell are we?" Doreen asked.

"Not in the community room," Margie said pointedly, and Doreen had to give her that. The movie theater was in the middle of the block, and Danny strutted to the window to request three tickets for *Come September*. Doreen had brought her purse and Margie had her own money, but he wouldn't let them pay.

"It's on me," he said casually, though Doreen could spot his secret pride from a mile away. He said it loudly enough for the girl in the ticket booth to hear too, of course. Carla must have given him money, Doreen thought, trying to keep hold of her hard edge, but she couldn't help feeling elated at going out to do something normal for a few hours. In the lobby, Danny bought them three huge tubs of popcorn with extra butter, and boxes of Sno-Caps and bottles of Pepsi, and they found seats in the exact center of the theater, Doreen sitting between Danny and Margie.

Come September was a movie about Rock Hudson's character trying to rendezvous with his mistress at his Italian villa, only to discover that his business partner had rented the villa out to a bunch of teenage girls. From his moral high horse as a man who has just broken up his mistress's engagement, he lectures the teenage girls about how important it is for them to stay pure. Bobby Darin was in it, too, and behaved like a cad.

When the plot dragged, Danny lobbed a piece of popcorn at Doreen without looking her way and then pretended it had come from the guys next to them. Doreen threw one back; Danny's return shot hit Margie, who surprised them both by deftly casting an entire handful square in Danny's face. A few pieces went down the front of his shirt, and he had to stand to knock them out. The couple behind them began sighing in annoyance and signaled the usher, whose flashlight came bobbing over. He told them to pipe down. They said they would try.

When the movie ended and the girls stood, Doreen heard the snitching woman behind them gasp as the annoying teenage girls' silhouettes came into view.

"You should be *ashamed*," she said, the credits on the screen rolling across her thick glasses.

"Of what?" Doreen shot back. She wanted to make the woman say it out loud.

"Come on," Danny said and pulled her arm toward the aisle. But Doreen stood firm. Beside her she could feel Margie winding up to apologize. Doreen was ready to smack Margie if that was what it took to stop her.

"You . . . you were very disruptive during the film," the woman said.

"Oh, *that's* it, then. We should be ashamed of laughing at the movies?"

"In your condition, you shouldn't even *be* at the movies."

Doreen had her half-full Pepsi in her left hand and was ready to dump it in the woman's lap, but Danny knew her too well and was one step ahead. He gently grasped the bottle and coaxed the girls into the aisle.

"We're so sorry," Margie began saying over and over. Doreen glared at her.

"You should be," the woman said.

"Hey, lady," Danny said. "Why don't you drop dead."

They hightailed it to the diner and got a table in back, hoping the local couple wasn't planning to eat lunch there, though the town didn't appear to have any other restaurants. Margie excused herself to the bathroom. Doreen had to go too, but she was newly starving and wanted to get a look at the menu first. The smell of the fryer was making her homesick for Taylor Street and her job at Art's. It was strange to think she might be back there again in a month or two, regaling the other waitresses with stories of her adventures at the fictitious Detroit dinner theater. She'd have to come up with a good name for the place, maybe a few stock stories, to make it believable to Wanda and her other friends. Meanwhile, this little baby would be in its crib, in its new home. Assuming Sister Simon could find parents willing to take it. And what if she couldn't? What did they do with a baby if no one wanted it?

"So," Danny said.

"So."

"How's it going over there in lockup? Margie seems nice. She's your roommate?"

Doreen nodded. The waitress came, and Doreen took the liberty of ordering burgers and fries all around. Margie had been talking about getting a burger when they were in the car. "She's fine. She dresses like a Sunday school teacher." Doreen rubbed a finger over her lip, trying to smudge away the line she knew was all that remained of her lipstick. "But it's not like I'm looking my best these days either. I know the nuns think my clothes are trashy. They talk about how we're all going to go on to get married, so we have to learn how to dress and do our hair the right way to attract the right kind of man. I'm just trying to keep a low profile until I can get out of there."

"You will," Danny said. "Get married, I mean."

Doreen shrugged. "How's Ma? She sent you to check on me, I know."

"I wanted to come."

"Sure."

"No, really. I wanted to talk to you about something."

It seemed like Margie had been gone a long time. Doreen glanced over her shoulder at the bathroom door, wondering if she should go check on her.

"I think I understand now why you won't tell us who the father is, Dorie," Danny said.

Doreen whipped her head around to face him. "You do?"

"And it's really okay. I can see why you didn't want to tell me, but give me a *little* credit."

Doreen waited. If Danny revealed himself to be a little less racist than she had always believed, maybe she could tell him the truth, which meant maybe she could tell Mosel the truth. In which case, maybe there *was* a way she could keep . . . but no. She had made her choice. She had so much she wanted to do in this world, and it had nothing to do with baby food and diapers. The kid would be better off with real parents, ones who knew what the hell they were doing. Wasn't that for the best?

Danny took a breath and laid bare his revelation. "He's a mick, isn't he? Maybe even a rich one. A married one. It makes me sick, I won't lie, but at least we're still talking about a Catholic here."

Doreen stared at him for a long moment, mystified. "What?"

"The father—he's Irish, right?"

Doreen stared at her brother. Here was a representative of the half of the population that ran the entire world. The stronger, smarter sex. She tipped her head down and started to laugh.

"What?" Danny asked, sounding truly wounded. After all, he had been so magnanimous to offer her a way back in after she had betrayed the Coniglio family name with a redhead named Sully. And here she was laughing at him.

"I'm gonna go check on Margie," Doreen said.

At the end of the diner's back hall, she knocked gently on the locked bathroom door. "Margie, it's Doreen. You okay in there?" With her forehead tipped against the door's peach paint, she could hear movement, a shuffling of feet, then nothing. "Margie?"

A moment later, the door opened a crack. Doreen went inside and closed it behind her. Margie was sitting on the bisque-colored linoleum with her legs straight out in front of her, her belly like a watermelon resting on her lap.

"What's going on?" Doreen asked. "Are you okay?"

Margie looked up at her, eyes glassy, face pale. "I think so."

"Did something happen?" The obvious question dawned on her. "Do you think you're in labor?"

Margie shook her head. Her breath was a low pant, but she seemed to be coming back to herself. "This happens sometimes. I have these . . . dreams. But I'm awake, or at least I think I am. In the dreams, bad things happen to me. Punishments."

Doreen sat down beside her. "Punishments?"

"Stuff like what the saints went through. Torture." Margie put her hand on her stomach with great trepidation, as if she were touching a throbbing hornet's nest. "And the baby is always there in the dreams. Watching. But I can never see its face. It's just flat and white, but there are no eyes or nose or mouth. It's . . . hard to explain."

"That sounds horrible," Doreen said. Though she was a couple years older and about a thousand times wiser to the world than Margie, Doreen realized she had come to think of Margie as the one leading the way through these last weeks of the pregnancies. She was further along, closer to the cliff, and surely had access to shrouded wisdom about what Doreen herself would soon be going through. She had experienced no dreams of martyrs and pain. Was that what awaited her?

"Doreen, do you believe in hell?"

She gave Margie a startled look and scanned her friend's forehead, looking for a mark. Had she fallen and hit her head? Experienced some kind of seizure? "I don't know. Hell? Maybe for murderers and stuff. I guess I don't really think about it."

Above them, the exhaust fan whirred like the blade of a blender. Margie was looking at her palms, which she held clutched together in her lap. "What about for us?"

Doreen grabbed her arm. "Margie, no. Come on. It's like the nuns say—we stumbled. We got brainwashed by movies and magazines about romance. We met a couple of guys we couldn't resist, and it went too far. Think of all the girls going all the way—well, we're just the ones who got stuck with the evidence."

"That's not what it was like for me." Margie's voice was flat.

"What do you mean?" Doreen asked.

"Romance. A nice guy."

Suddenly it made sense. Margie was nearly as naïve as Ingrid, but she never pined for her boyfriend or asked any of the other girls for details about theirs. Margie was only sixteen, but the way she carried herself through the world made her seem about a thousand years older, as old as the saints in her dreams. Margie hadn't conspired with her steady to make him her first. Someone had *done* this to her.

With a little coaxing, Doreen got Margie to tell her the story. Mr. Grebe, the father of the children she nannied for over the summer, had been so nice to her at first, paying her special attention, complimenting her—a new barrette, the pearl earrings she had gotten for her confirmation, the shade of her nail polish. When he closed the jewelry store for the lunch hour, he would come home and linger even when his plate was empty, asking her questions about her plans with the children for the afternoon. So when he told her he had something he wanted to show her in his basement workshop, the creep, Margie didn't think much of it. The door had a lock on it, she told Doreen, and by the time she heard that bar slide closed, it was too late to stop him.

"Oh, Margie," Doreen said.

"I really didn't want it. I didn't even know what . . . you know . . . what *intercourse* was. I didn't know what went where. No one ever told me. You have to believe me."

"Of course I believe you."

"I didn't try very hard to stop him, though. My whole body just went stiff. I could barely blink my eyes."

"You must have been terrified."

"I should have tried, though. Why didn't I try? I can't stop thinking that I'm going to burn for it."

Doreen softened her face, her hands, her voice. "Margie, we're young. We didn't do anything wrong—especially you. People like us don't go to hell. I promise."

"It's just . . ." Margie said. "I've seen it, in these dreams. In the beginning, it's almost a relief because you know you deserve it. But then it gets really bad, and it goes on and on and on and on . . ."

"Hon, you're scaring me. I think we should take you to the hospital."

"No," Margie said. She blinked a few times and then took a deep breath and stood. "I'm really fine. I just got lost there for a minute."

Doreen peered at her. "Are you sure?"

"Danny's going to think we both fell in," Margie said and giggled in a way that made Doreen feel slightly more assured. Side by side, they washed their hands in the little sink. Doreen watched Margie in the mirror and felt a new tenderness for the awful mustard-colored sweater she was wearing. She plucked some paper towels from the dispenser and handed them to Margie, who patted the clamminess from her cheeks and forehead.

Doreen wanted to ask Margie what had happened when she came out of that basement. Did her father know? Had they called the police? But she knew she couldn't ask. Instead she said, "I hope it's okay—I ordered you a burger. Our food's probably at the table by now."

"I'm starving," Margie said. "I'm going to order a milkshake too. Why not, right? I'm already a rhinoceros."

"Let's both get one," Doreen said.

PART III
Labor

April 1961

11

Margie

From where she lay in her gurney at the end of the hall past the elevator, Margie could hear at least three separate call buttons going off in proper hospital rooms and the squeaking footsteps of the nurses who rushed to answer them. Margie, of course, had only the steel cord of the window shade to pull on, shoved as she was up against the wall. No call button. No IV. Thankfully she still wore her watch and could time the spates of lucidity between the pain, which wrapped her from ribs to knees and pressed like Saint Margaret Clitherow's eight-hundred-pound weight, but she would make that analogy only in retrospect, when sense had returned to her. For now there was just the sweat and the whimper and the iron taste of blood on her bottom lip.

After a while—maybe an hour, maybe six—the nurse who'd rattled her into this dim corner reappeared, flustered and irritated. Her hair was a halo of gray, Margie saw through her squint. Cotton candy without the color. "Oh, you're still here," she said. As if Margie would have gotten up and wandered off, her white pettipants still sticky with amniotic fluid. "Why are you still wearing your clothes?"

"Could I have some water?" Margie said.

The nurse ignored her. "You'll need a gown."

"How do I get one?" Margie asked. When she imagined lifting her arms over her head to pull off her sweater, she thought it would be easier to combust and drift in particles up the air vent. It was simply impossible to imagine.

The nurse stalked off. Back at Holy Family, when it had been clear to Sister Simon that Margie's time had come, she sent someone to find Hugo and he pulled the truck up to the kitchen door. Running through the beams of the headlights, with rain pummeling his black hair, he helped Margie up and into the cab. All the way to the hospital she made a strange panting sound through her nose, and when he pulled into the circle drive, she opened her own door before he even had the truck in park, out of pure desperation to move from that cramped position. There in the rain, her water broke. She'd heard the girls talk about this part, and Yvonne had said—Yvonne was always authoritative—that the drama of it was overblown. The waters didn't break so much as trickle, she explained, and sometimes they didn't even do that. *Well, shit, Yvonne*, Margie thought, almost laughing in the midst of her misery because her water broke like a balloon. Even above the noise of the rain it made a small splash.

It was not hospital policy, the nurse had told her, to give Holy Family girls a room. After all, how would it make the married women feel to see an unwed mother have access to the same kind of treatment? Who on the happy day she had earned wants to be reminded of a blight on the world? That last part was Margie's addition, as she thought about the shame and then, when the contraction came, transitioned from *thinking* about the shame to embodying it—or feeling it embody her, as if it were the shell and she its sticky yolk.

Gripping the steel chain, Margie raised the blind. She would have sworn the moon was moving across the glass in front of her eyes. When it was close to the center of the pane, the nurse returned. This time she had a gown and a blanket and a little bag.

"Let's get you undressed," she said and sat Margie up.

At the moment, she was between contractions, able to speak, though she didn't. The nurse helped her raise her arms, and she did not explode but merely groaned like a bear.

"Enough of that," the nurse said. "You're lucky that Dr. Samuels is here tonight and will be delivering you. But you should know he doesn't like noise."

Somewhere in the recesses of Margie's mind a pinball made a mirror spin: a doctor was coming to help her. This was a true surprise. She clamped her mouth shut, and a moment later her damp clothes were balled up inside the bag and she wore the soft cotton gown and felt cool air on the bottoms of her feet. She now loved this nurse more than she loved life itself.

Now the gurney was moving. The contractions were almost continuous, and the nurse looked down at her, alarmed. "Why didn't you tell anyone your water had broken?"

Later, Margie would figure out that eight hours had passed. But now she only said, "How do they hide it?" The words sounded jumbled to her ears, not what she had meant to say.

"What?" the nurse said, distracted. Now they were in a new place, and she drew a peach curtain along its track to shield them from the hallway. From the drawer of a metal cart, she took a men's shaving razor and a tube of cream, then a squat tube with a long hose attached. "I've got to prep you."

But Margie insisted. "The scar from where they get the baby out. I've seen . . ." Margie took a breath. "I've seen women at the club pool in bikinis, and I know they've had babies." Another breath. "But you can't see where they came out."

The nurse looked at Margie for a long moment, maybe a month. She pressed her hand to her own cheek. "Do you not know how babies are born? How is that possible?"

"They don't come out of your stomach?"

"They come out," the nurse said, her voice nearly a wail, "the way they went in."

The nurse went out again. Margie felt a visceral longing to be comforted by a mother, but she knew her particular mother wasn't the comforting type. The voice of a long-ago catechism teacher rose to her mind's surface: *Turn to Mary.* But shouldn't Mary, if she was really there to offer the kind of succor the teacher promised, be the one to turn to her? Surely this was an hour of need like no other, and yet Margie had never felt more alone. She tried to imagine soft hands pressing a cloth to her brow, the sweep of that blue mantle.

A while later, Dr. Samuels came in and left the peach curtain open to the hallway behind him. He had no memory of having met her before. "Margaret Ahern?" he asked, looking at the chart that sat at the end of her bed.

Margie nodded, breathing through her nose. She shifted on the gurney. There was so much sweat under her lower back it felt as if she had wet the bed. Maybe she had.

"I'll need to check your progress," Dr. Samuels said. He lifted the sheet from the foot of the bed and draped it over her knees, leaving her bottom half completely exposed to the hallway, and pulled a glove from his pocket. A janitor passed, rolling a mop bucket in front of him. Margie closed her eyes and tipped her chin to the ceiling and tears leaked down her temples.

"All right, prima donna," Dr. Samuels said, clucking his tongue. "Trust me—no one's looking at you." He thrust his fingers inside her without warning, and Margie bellowed from deep in her chest. The pain of it sent white flashes across her eyes.

"You're getting there," he said, pulling his hand out, and snapped off the glove.

"How much longer?" Margie asked through her bottom teeth, the words a hiss of air.

Dr. Samuels grinned, and Margie felt a dangerous thing she knew was forbidden: murderous fury. "That's for me to know and for you to find out," he said, all of this a little game for him. He pulled the sheet back down to her feet. "We're going to get you some medicine."

For the rest of her life she would look back at this moment as the last chance she had to stop it. Everything in front of Margie's eyes came into sharp relief—the silver of the stethoscope's disc that hung over his chest pocket, every whisker on the doctor's face.

"Don't put me under," she said.

Her hand was on her stomach. The baby was so close to her fingers. Just this thin layer of skin and blood and muscle was keeping her from getting it in her hands. Every cell in her body was lining up for this fight. She would not be here if Mr. Grebe had not forced himself on her. But this was her baby, however it had come to be. And she wanted it. They were not going to take it from her.

Dr. Samuels ignored her and marked something in her chart. He went out again as the nameless nurse came back in. She towed an IV cart inside the curtain.

"No," Margie said, intending the word to carry power, but it landed like a marshmallow, nearly soundless. The nurse prepped Margie's listless arm, impervious to Margie's attempts to bat her hands away.

"Now stop," the nurse said. "You've lost your senses."

"Don't put me under," Margie begged. Her lips now felt like two pieces of sandpaper, her tongue a parched mound of sand. She moaned through its grit.

The needle went in, and through the tube came a liquid that flooded Margie's whole body with cool relief. She became aware of the softness of the inside of her eyelids. She swallowed, and the sound of it in her ears was like something heavy dropping into the ocean. The nurse hovered over her, backlit by the overhead light, and her cotton candy hair got whiter and whiter until it filled the room.

Margie sank through liquid blackness to the bottom of a vat of melted licorice. It was a warm and sticky bath, and then all of it rushed away, sucked down by a vacuum, and there was a door. Margie turned its silver knob. As she passed through, she realized she was hopping. With her left hand, which looked nothing at all like her left hand, she smoothed the coarse fur on her right shoulder and arm. Her whole body felt bigger, sturdier, especially her wide hips and her short legs and her long brown feet, covered in the same fur. Margie hopped. Margie understood that she was no longer a girl. Margie was a kangaroo.

Just below her ribs was a warm slit, and with the pads of her paws she felt the fine hair and impossible softness of her baby's head. A human baby, not a joey. And then the baby took her breath away by shifting back and lifting its eyes to Margie's eyes. In all her dreams of torture, the baby had always been with her, but its face never had come out from behind the cloud. Now, the blue-black eyes looked up into Margie's own.

Knowing that the baby was safe inside the pouch filled her with the peace that passeth all understanding. She hopped on through the sand, her weariness gone, a wiry energy in her back legs. She thought casually of the power of those legs to leap, to rip to shreds any other animal that might come near.

On the other side of the hill, a crowd of people were gathered, and with surprise she saw herself, Margie, in the center, sitting on a molded plastic chair like the one in Father Keene's office. The people began to holler at her, and the stones they held began to fly through the air. Saint Stephen, the first martyr, had been stoned to death; now it was Margie's turn. Again she saw the stones as she had felt them in the other dreams; they broke her body apart. But this time she was not inside *that* body. This time she could turn away. She put her paw on the baby's head once more and hopped farther down the path.

Margie hopped and hopped and hopped until she arrived at the place she knew she'd find. The rocket was on the launchpad. The door hung open, and inside was a red seat with straps just the right size for a kangaroo. Flipping her tail up behind her, she slipped each steel buckle into its socket and closed the door. As the engines rumbled beneath her legs, they ignited into a fire like the one that had consumed Joan of Arc. But this fire was going to save Margie, and it was going to save her baby. She began to lift the baby out of her pouch to hold him—*him*, *him*, she knew in her heart—in her arms, to let him see through the tiny window the holy tongues of fire that would deliver them, and that sensation of his sliding out of the pouch, her arms lifting and lifting and lifting, went on as the rocket soared into the endless blackness. The baby—his name was Timothy—was moving up but also down and out, and she could not get him into her arms.

When Margie opened her eyes, she was alone inside a new curtain, this one mint green. Her fur was gone, her belly sunken. With her mouth wide open, she took the deepest breath of her life, all the air around her rushing into her lungs, and let out an animal's growl.

"My baby my baby where is my baby" was how it began, but soon the limits of language failed to convey what roared within her, and the words collapsed into pure sound, a scream that came from the fire in her throat.

A nurse came running in, a new one she had never seen. At first, she pressed Margie's shoulders down into the bed, but Margie thrashed her way out of the nurse's grasp. "Where is my baby where is my baby give me my baby."

"Now, hush," she said. "You've lost your mind. You don't know what you're—"

Margie lifted her right arm, and though it wobbled like a strand of spaghetti, she managed to backhand the nurse across the face. "Goddamn you," she slurred. "Give me my baby."

The nurse stepped back, stunned, and her hands flew to her face. Margie threw her leg over the bedrail, heaved her whole body over like a corpse coming out of her grave. She fell with a slap to the linoleum. Blood from between her legs gushed in a wave onto her feet, and she found that her brain could not command her legs to stand. For a long moment, she was a howling pile of sticky wrath there on the floor, until the nurse came to her senses, loaded a syringe, and brought the night sky across Margie's eyes once more.

She felt herself surface for a moment and sink again maybe ten more times, maybe twenty, so she knew that at least a couple of days had passed when she woke all the way up and opened her eyes. The skin around her fingers and ankles felt tight. Even her face felt puffed out along her jawline. The IV bag dangled above her, the steady flow of fluid the reason she wasn't hungry, the reason she would have made a *pop-splat* sound if anyone stuck her with a pin.

There was a woman sitting beside her bed. At first Margie thought it was Verna, but as the room came into focus, Margie saw this couldn't be the case because this woman had smiling eyes, high pink cheeks, and curly hair. "There you are, dear," she said, like someone's British grandmother.

Margie closed one eye and squinted at her. Did she actually have a British accent, or was that in Margie's imagination?

"Well now, you have caused more of a stir around here than we've seen in quite some time. I wouldn't have guessed it to look at you."

Timothy. Margie's hand went to her stomach, and her heart clenched as she recalled that he was out and gone. She recalled the rocket ship and something strange about fur. She recalled the soldiers in the trenches and their severed arms. She recalled that she had been screaming and she knew why, but for some reason she did not scream now. It was as if the part of her brain that could observe was up and running, but the corresponding part—the part that could react to the information—was still under anesthesia.

"It's all behind you now, dear," the woman said and patted Margie's hand. "You'll be glad to know you're getting out of the hospital today. Back to Holy Family to collect your things. Your parents will be waiting for you there to take you home."

When she took a breath to speak, she felt a constriction around her ribs. With her fingers, she touched the ridge of something under her gown. A bandage wrapped tightly around her breasts. "Who are you?"

"I'm Mrs. Yeardly, your social worker."

Another memory: his impossibly fragile scalp. The bones against the pads of her fingers. "I have a social worker?"

"Of course, dear." Mrs. Yeardly opened the folder resting on her lap. From her pocket she took a black ink pen with a gold nib. "Now," she said, and the sound of the metal cap sliding off the pen set Margie's teeth on edge. "You've already gotten through the hardest part. It's all behind you now—you're nearly home! There's just the formality of signing the papers."

Margie held very still. Somewhere along the way she had been told about this part, though she hadn't thought much of it at the time. The bandage was growing wet. Her breasts were leaking.

Mrs. Yeardly cleared her throat, which was the closest to impatience Margie had seen from her yet. When her entire brain turned back on again, she would cringe over everything she had put the nurses through: the inconvenience, the extra work. She had made so much *noise*. But in her present state of mind, these facts scrolled past and she could make no judgment of them.

"Did you hear me, Margaret? It's time to sign the papers now."

"I have to read them first," Margie said. "And I'm too tired right now."

"Margaret." Mrs. Yeardly scooched to the front of her chair, folded her hands atop the paper. She smiled brightly. "I know you are not at your best right now and that once you've gotten some rest and can see things more clearly, you'll realize that several people have gone to a great deal of trouble—in good faith—to solve this problem for you, to clear a path so that you can move forward with your life."

When Margie still said nothing, Mrs. Yeardly's voice turned a little colder. "A great deal of trouble and a great deal of *expense*, Margaret. And I know you wouldn't dream of putting your parents in a difficult situation. If you don't sign, they will have to come up with the money to pay Holy Family back for your care. You're a good girl. You wouldn't do that to them."

The other part of her brain was waking back up now. Margie's thoughts still had to travel a great distance to reach it, but it was there. When she closed her eyes, she saw Verna and Frank, Father Keene, Sister Simon. She saw how many Catholic school uniform blouses Verna had ironed in her two-plus decades of motherhood. She saw Sister Simon, a vessel of the Holy Spirit, devoting her life and her labor to the care of girls like herself, the wayward, the lost, the ones who had strayed. What had happened to girls before there were places like Holy Family?

So many people had gone to a great deal of trouble.

But then she thought of Timothy. Had she really seen him, touched him, reaching down between her legs in the moment of his crowning? Had she run the pads of her fingers over the slick skin, only to have her hands swatted away? Or had she only dreamed of him in her twilight sleep? Did it mean anything? Margie had believed in eternity before—how it had been impressed upon her from her earliest days!—and this was no time to abandon its horrors, nor its gifts. Her baby had come to her—and through her and out of her and back into her again—because they were tethered, wheeling through the empty space but bound to one another the same way her arm was bound to her body at the shoulder.

"Margaret," Mrs. Yeardly was saying, shaking Margie's hand. "Margaret."

"I think I'd like to take a walk to think about it," Margie said, though she could barely raise her arm from the bed.

"A walk!" Mrs. Yeardly said, as if it were the most bizarre suggestion in the world. "Now that's enough. Let's not stall any longer."

Her baby. No one would ever understand what she felt, how she could love the result of the awful thing Mr. Grebe had put her through. How was that possible? And yet she could no more give up her baby than she could pluck her own eyeballs out of her head and place them in Mrs. Yeardly's waiting palm. But so many people had gone to a great deal of trouble. A great deal. Verna and Frank had succeeded in raising a good girl, and good girls didn't make a fuss or impose on their hosts. They kept themselves small and tidy and under control so that no one ever had to be uncomfortable. Good girls—the best girls—trained themselves not to want anything at all.

Margie picked up the pen. She watched her fist move across the paper.

12

We

The official term was *relinquishment*, but it is hard to relinquish what you don't understand to be yours.

The people at the home said, "Don't you understand? You don't have any money for food, for rent, the layette, the christening gown. You will never be able to buy him a bicycle."

They told us the new father was a doctor. The new mother was from a rich family. The baby would go to private school, ride around in brand-new cars, maybe even with a driver. He would ski. He would go to the ocean. He would live in a skyscraper penthouse or a country mansion. He would want for nothing.

They said he would be free of us, and because of that he would have the chance to be happy. In wanting to keep him, we were thinking only of ourselves, they said, which proved we were not real mothers.

We signed, because if we signed they would let us go back to sleep. We were barely out of twilight when they came to us. We signed with the wrong hand because we couldn't remember which hand we wrote with. We vomited into the wastebasket, we wailed, we begged. *It will be all right*, they told us. *You will see your baby again in heaven.*

We understood that no man would ever want us if he knew what we had done. Good men, the kind we should want, would think, *What kind of girl lets herself get into trouble like that?* Though later on we couldn't shake another question, a question we would use to chase love from our door: *What kind of girl gives her baby away?*

By then we knew we had put our parents through so much we were willing to do anything to regain their acceptance. We were wretched, like prisoners who had given up trying to escape. We didn't speak to lawyers. We didn't know there were laws, that we had rights. Sometimes, we didn't even get a copy of the document, and so all we had was the memory of the black lines of type. We never saw a birth certificate.

They said, "You would have to be crazy to think you could do this on your own."

Well, we felt crazy. Overcome by exhaustion, grief, anesthesia, we believed we could melt the locks on the doors with our eyes and fly to our babies and kill anyone who tried to stop us. We wanted to hurt people. We wanted to hurt ourselves. We did.

We were sent to asylums. We were sent back home as if nothing had changed. But every cell in our bodies was different.

"Now things can go back to normal," our mothers said after we signed. "*Now* we can forgive you."

13

Doreen

Doreen could not get the taillights of Hugo's truck out of her mind. Margie doubled over in the front seat, the driving rain, the long drive ahead of them. What had happened when they arrived at the hospital? The rumor mill had been surprisingly quiet, and she couldn't get information out of anyone.

"Sometimes they just don't come back," Yvonne said at breakfast between bites of scrambled eggs. "Holy Family will box up her things and ship them back to her parents' place. You know"—she shrugged—"maybe it's better, in a way?"

The idea of this being the end, that she might not ever see Margie again, filled Doreen with alarm. But Yvonne didn't need to know that. "It's only been four days," Doreen said. "She must still be at the hospital."

"Sure," Yvonne said, "but I'm just saying her parents might go straight there. We might not find out anything more."

"But what about the baby? Where does it go?"

"Depends," Yvonne said. "Most of the time the adoptive parents come here, to the parlor. And that's where they pick up the kid. But sometimes it happens at the hospital."

"Why at the hospital?" Yvonne's intel was frustratingly spotty.

She shrugged. "I don't know. Maybe they don't want to wait? All I know is we've seen it both ways. Sometimes we hear the baby crying up on the third floor. Sometimes we don't. But one way or the other, both the girl and the baby go away."

Doreen sat back hard against her chair, folded her arms. "Why am I even asking you? You've only been here two weeks longer than I have. How do I know anything you're saying is even right?"

"Well, excuse me for living." But Yvonne smiled like she always did, good-natured, with those big front teeth, her orange Pippi Longstocking bangs hanging in her eyes. She was what Carla called a shit-stirrer, and Doreen was falling for it.

Doreen left Yvonne at the table to torment someone else and carried her tray to the kitchen. It was so odd, the way she felt about Margie. She didn't really even like her. Well, that wasn't quite right. Margie was very irritating. Her clothes were a disaster. She didn't know anything about music. She tried too hard to please the nuns and her parents and almost certainly her teachers too. She was squeaky clean in a way that Doreen never had been, never could be. Didn't *want* to be, Doreen reminded herself. But then Margie had told her about those dreams, and it was like the mask came down for a moment and Doreen could see that behind it was something else entirely, a deep well of sadness and maybe wisdom too. It was unsettling to realize that Margie understood some things that Doreen might never have thought about. And now Doreen needed to know what they were. She had the uneasy suspicion that Margie understood what was happening to both of them far better than she could.

Sister Joan was dusting in the chapel when Doreen found her. The room was dark, with small stained-glass windows on just one side, and the light they cast on the dark wood altar was pink and yellow.

"Hi, Donna," she said, and draped her rag over the back of a chair in the second row. "How are you feeling today?"

"I'm all right," she said, running her hand over her stomach. "I was really having a hard time breathing this week—it's just so crowded in there—but today I feel like my lungs have opened up a little."

Sister Joan's eyes jumped to Doreen's. "Really? When are you due again?"

"Early May was the best he could say," said Doreen.

Sister Joan's forehead creased. "Huh," she said.

"What?"

She paused but then shook her head. "Oh, it's probably nothing. Is there something on your mind?"

"I've been thinking about Minnie, wondering how she's doing."

Sister Joan nodded. "She has been on my mind too." This she said somewhat automatically but then seemed to take notice of Doreen's tense posture. "You know, when I worry about you girls, it helps me to remember that your bodies were made to do this work. Giving birth is completely natural, and it doesn't have to be scary."

"Easy for you to say."

Sister Joan laughed. "That's true."

Doreen couldn't help but press. "Have you heard anything about how she's doing? She must have had the baby by now, right?"

"Oh, yes. She—" Sister Joan stopped herself. "Now, Donna, you know how important it is to the mission of the home that every girl's privacy be protected. You know I can't tell you anything about Minnie's case."

So whatever Margie had imagined and dreamed about and dreaded had already happened, Doreen thought. The baby was out of her body now, separate from her.

"But can you at least tell me"—Doreen's eyes felt hot, her voice clenched in her throat—"whether she will be coming back here?"

Sister Joan tipped her head in sympathy. "I can tell you honestly that I don't know the answer to that. Sister Simon handles all those arrangements."

Doreen nodded. She sniffed noisily, the way Danny often did, and the harsh unfeminine sound of it was just enough to keep her tears from spilling over.

"Have you done your chores yet today?" Now Sister Joan's voice was cheerful. "Work can help to take your mind off things."

"Not yet," Doreen said. "But I guess I'm headed there now. Bathroom duty."

Sister Joan sighed. "I wish you girls could rest a little more in these last weeks."

Inspiration struck when Doreen was on her knees in front of the third toilet, yellow rubber gloves up to her elbows, scrubbing Comet into the porcelain. She sat back on her heels and peeled the gloves off, one by one, draping them over the green can. Her initial moan was quiet. No one heard it, of course. This was just for practice.

"Uhhhhh," Doreen said, louder this time, and placed her palms on the newly cleaned tile to push herself to standing. "Is anybody there?"

In the hallway she was harassed once more by the horrid cabbage rose wallpaper and let it inspire a desperate sound. "Ohhhhhhhh."

Finally Ingrid's blond head poked out of her door. "Doreen. Are you all right?"

Doreen kept her hand on her belly and shook her head. "I don't know. I think these might be contractions. Uhhhh."

Ingrid leapt into the hall and took Doreen's elbow, and together they walked down to the room she shared with Margie. Doreen hobbled a little, but she didn't want to oversell it. She didn't know much about what labor was actually like, but she did know that it was supposed to progress, so she should save some material for a few hours from now in case it took a while to convince Sister Simon.

Ingrid settled Doreen on her bed. "Do you want a glass of water?"

She shook her head with what she hoped came across as stalwart courage. "I'll be all right. But I think you'd better go get Sister Simon."

Ingrid's eyes widened. "Is this . . . oh my goodness! Is it time? I can't believe it's time and that *I* get to be the one to tell!"

"That's right." Doreen nodded. "It's your big moment, Ingrid. Now go."

Ingrid scurried into the hallway, leaving Doreen to her faux contractions. She closed her eyes and touched the skin all around her belly, stretched taut like a beach ball, and she imagined what it would feel like when the pains really did start to come.

Lying down was dangerous—she could drift off to sleep at any moment, but that would foil her plans. She kept awake by wondering what Mosel was up to right at this moment, a spring day of his freshman year of college. Maybe he was finally seeing the sun after the snowbound months in the library and the stale air of his dorm room. Mosel's face came into her mind, the quirky smile with the gap in his front teeth, and she smiled back at him in the empty room. "I'm having your baby, Mosel," she whispered, almost playful. "I'm having your baby, but I'm going to give it away." It could have been a song.

Doreen heard footsteps and felt the rush of tension that came into any room the moment before Sister Simon entered it. "Uhhhh," she moaned, loud enough for them to hear her in the hallway.

When Doreen opened her eyes, Sister Simon was beside the bed. She peered over her glasses. "When did this start?"

Don't overplay it. "I've been feeling strange since last night. But about an hour ago I started having pains."

"Hm." The sister clearly possessed a professional-grade bullshit detector, and Doreen suddenly realized that trying to fool her might be a bad idea. "What kinds of pains?"

"Here," Doreen said, sweeping her hand over her stomach in a vague pattern. "I feel another one coming."

Sister Simon lifted her black sleeve to look at her watch. "High or low in the abdomen?"

"High?"

The sister made a little satisfied sound in her nose. "Then it's probably false labor. You're at least a couple weeks out from your due date."

Doreen pictured Margie checking out of the hospital, the plastic bracelet still on her wrist, her dad helping her into the back seat of his car. It was unacceptable that Margie could just disappear forever. "There's something else," she said in an attempt to buy more time.

"Any bleeding?"

"Yes," Doreen said, probably a little too emphatically. Over the sister's shoulder Doreen could see two heads in the doorway, Ingrid and Yvonne. Yvonne was chewing her gum at a faster-than-normal rate. "Definitely. Definitely some bleeding."

Sister Simon sighed. "Well, I'll tell Hugo to bring the truck around. I have to send you over, just to be on the safe side, but I'll tell you that I lose a lot of time and energy to girls who can't tell the difference between a little discomfort and actual labor." She stuck her finger in Doreen's face. "Believe me—there is a difference."

How the hell would you know? Doreen wanted to say. She hoped when her time actually came it would be Sister Joan who found her and helped her through. "Thank you, Sister," Doreen said in her best imitation of quiet bravery. "You know my only thought is for the baby."

"As it should be." Sister Simon turned on her heel, and the gawkers scattered back into the hallway. They returned only when they were sure she was gone. "We'll help you pack a bag," Ingrid said, tiptoeing back into the room. She opened the top drawer of the dresser and took out a sweater. Yvonne lifted the side of her blouse and pulled the latest issue of *Seventeen* out of the waistband of her skirt. "You can borrow this," she said. "There's a real good tutorial on eyeliner in here."

"Thanks, hon," Doreen said. "You girls are the best."

At the hospital, it didn't take long for the nurses to realize Doreen wasn't actually in labor—it turned out they had some pretty foolproof ways of determining that, no doubt putting to use some of the facts about anatomy that Sister Joan was studying in the wee hours. But by the time they cleared Doreen to return to Holy Family to wait for the real show to begin, Hugo had already left and wouldn't learn that he was supposed to come back to get her for at least another half hour. The nurse told Doreen to get dressed and wait in the lobby.

Instead Doreen stepped into her too-tight underpants, fastened the brassiere that had become a joke—a rubber band restraining a pair of cantaloupes—zipped her dress over her bulges, and walked the hallway of the maternity ward looking for Margie. The patients' names were posted on white cards thumbtacked to each closed door, and she looked for *Ahern* but didn't find it. Through the window of one door she saw a cluster of balloons and a crowd of people, but the hallway was mostly quiet, the nurses occupied at the desk. This section of the hospital was not where the actual laboring was done, Doreen realized. She shuddered to think that happened elsewhere, in some soundproof, windowless place. A few of the doors were unmarked and ajar, and at those Doreen poked her head inside, but she saw only a bare mattress on a metal frame, just like the beds at Holy Family. The scent of rubbing alcohol was everywhere, the signature not of cleanliness so much as of messes discovered and disappeared, the shock of them still lingering.

Doreen came to the double doors at the end of the hall and passed through them, imagining she would find yet more rooms, yet more new mothers resting comfortably. Instead she encountered a long room on the interior side of the hallway with windows that extended from the waist-high wall to the ceiling. The space was brightly lit and contained some medical equipment, a small bathtub and a pile of linens, and a rocking chair. In front of the windows was a row of eight white bassinets.

Doreen's palms began to itch, and she rubbed them on the sides of her dress as she stepped toward the glass. There were no nurses in the room at the moment. Only four of the bassinets were occupied, and each baby was wrapped in the same white blanket with a pale blue stripe. Three wore pink caps and one wore blue, and the three girls fidgeted: one with an arm loose and cold, one hollering, her face a crimson raisin, one whose cap had slipped, revealing the tiniest ear in human history. And then there was the boy. He slept, his face the color of an apricot, puffy crescents beneath his eyes. She might have thought he was a little statue except that his chest lifted by about a quarter inch every few seconds. Lifted and fell, lifted and fell. A whole, real person, packed tightly inside the white-and-blue blanket. Doreen tried to wrap her mind around what she was seeing. This was what it all led to. This was what was inside her too, inside all the girls. She felt a wave of dread like she had never experienced. Was she making a mistake to think she could walk away?

Her eyes went to the foot of the bassinet, where a white card read *Ahern*.

Had Margie seen him? Would she? Should she? Her eyes still locked on the baby's face, Doreen was startled to see two hands enter the frame the bassinet made around him and pluck him up. She took a little step back and watched a nurse take him to a table on the other side of the room, change his diaper, and wrap the blanket around him once more. Then she took him out a door that led to the hallway where Doreen was standing and began walking away.

Doreen kept her eyes on the tip of his blue hat, visible above the cradle of the nurse's elbow, and followed the pair of them. She relaxed when she realized her timing had been perfect. The nurse would lead her right to Margie's room.

She tried to hang back and be patient as they walked down the long hallway, past six closed doors and then another nurses' station.

"Excuse me," said a nurse with short blond hair that curled around her chin. "I think you're going the wrong way." The nurse carrying Margie's baby turned left at the end of the hall.

"No, I know where I'm going," Doreen said, glancing after them, touching her belly. "I'm not here for me, actually—at least not yet." She kept walking, waved to the nurse, and hoped she'd sit back down to her paperwork. "Just visiting a friend."

Doreen took the corner in time to see the nurse stop in front of a waiting room.

"Well," she said cheerfully to the baby, "are you ready for your big moment?"

Coming closer, but not too close, Doreen watched as the nurse took the baby into a room full of red chairs. On the wall was a row of framed prints of leaves in all seasons, from vibrant green to red to desiccated brown. Doreen scanned the room. Margie was not there. Instead, the nurse was carrying the baby to a waiting couple.

Maybe it was surprise that stopped her from taking in what was happening, but Doreen noticed the woman first because she looked Italian. Her brows were very well sculpted, and it was the kind of thing Doreen noticed because she aspired to live up to that standard herself. The woman's hair was up, and she wore a stylish hat and a plaid cape, and though Doreen did not think she had ever met her before, she seemed familiar. The nurse stooped down and put the baby in the woman's arms, and the woman let out a sound that was between a sigh and a moan, a sound of pain and of relief all at once. The woman looked at her husband, so Doreen finally did too.

She took a breath. It was Art Messina, the owner of the diner where she had worked for years. Her eyes darted back to his wife, and she made the connection, the woman who was barren, the woman Carla had told her about. *Such a shame, not to be able to have a family.* This baby was going to live in her neighborhood.

Doreen took a few steps back from the doorway, though the Messinas were so engrossed in the moment they wouldn't have noticed a freight train passing through the hall. She couldn't understand what was happening. It was startling to see that Art was weeping, his mouth stretched down, as he touched the baby's head. Doreen put her palm to her chest. He always had been such a kind man.

He wiped both his eyes with one hand. "Now, don't you agree with me? It should be Nicholas. It's a good fit," he said to his wife, and she nodded and helped guide his arm beneath the bundle so that he could hold the baby. Art held him up so that he could look him in the eye. All the jostling had gotten him crying too, and Art's wife began to cry, so all three of them were crying, all three of them wailing in the same key. It was the first time they were hearing the voice of their son. "You've made us very happy, Nicholas Francisco Messina," Art said. "It's nice to meet you."

Holy Family had worked hard to build a wall between the babies' origins and their futures, and almost all the people on either side of that wall had the good sense never to hoist themselves up to peer over it. *Have you ever met a rule you haven't tried to break?* Carla liked to say to Doreen, and this moment was no exception. Doreen had seen something she shouldn't see. And because of that, she knew something she shouldn't know.

Doreen retraced her steps past the nursery, back through the maternity ward, with her coat unbuttoned, hanging off her shoulders. She walked and walked, her heart pounding. What was she supposed to do now? She couldn't tell Margie. Wasn't it better to let her stay on their side of that wall?

In the lobby there were benches, a large window that looked out over the circle drive, and she was surprised to see the streetlights on. Hours had passed, and it was evening now. Doreen did not yet see Hugo's truck, but there on the bench closest to the window, a little leather overnight bag at her feet, was Margie.

14

Margie

The scent of Aqua Net reached Margie in her stupor. Doreen. Doreen was in the hospital. Doreen was sitting beside her on the bench.

"What are you doing here?"

Doreen's belly was still there, and it was clear she hadn't given birth, but her face was ashen.

"Are you all right?"

Doreen winced in a way Margie had never seen before, her poise gone. She seemed flustered, struggling to find words. Finally, she said, "Margie, are *you* all right?"

Margie didn't reply. Beneath her skirt she wore a pad as big as a diaper, and every time she shifted on the bench she could feel a new wave of blood spill into it. The nurse who discharged her had explained she would need to keep binding her breasts for a few more days and watch for mastitis. Right now they were only rock hard and painful, but not infected.

Doreen looked around the empty lobby. "Are your parents here?"

"No. I'm waiting for Hugo to take me back to get my things. My parents are coming to Holy Family." She thought back to instructions that had come to her somehow from Sister Simon, maybe over the phone. "I don't think we're supposed to talk to each other."

"Margie." Doreen turned until her knee touched Margie's knee, and she tried to take Margie's limp hands. "I came to see *you*. I faked contractions so I could get to the hospital. I was afraid you would just leave and I'd never see you again."

Margie couldn't really control her gaze. She watched Doreen's mouth and heard the words, but then her eyes drifted out to the circle drive, where a few brown sparrows were prodding an abandoned donut, then darting away as if it might fight back, then returning, pecking around the chocolate frosting with their beaks. It was starting to snow. Snow in April.

"Hon," Doreen said. "Do they have you on something?"

Margie could tell Doreen was scared, but she couldn't muster the effort required to reassure her. "Normally they wouldn't let a girl who's gone over ride with someone still expecting," Margie explained. "Sister Simon said that it's important for me not to talk about the last few days with you. Because it's confidential." Margie felt like a parrot, repeating that word: *confidential*, *confidential*.

"I understand," Doreen said. She looked almost a little relieved, Margie thought. Maybe it really was better that she not know. After all, there was nothing Doreen could do to escape this fate now, unless she did what Margie could not do and changed her mind.

"Thank you," Margie said. "For coming to see me. That was really nice."

"Oh, Margie," Doreen said, her eyes filling with tears. "You look like you've been through a war."

Margie tried to straighten up. Verna always complained about her posture. It just didn't reflect well on her, she knew. It made her seem weak, like she was courting sympathy. "I'm fine," Margie said to Doreen. "Really. And look." She pointed out the window. "Here's Hugo."

The wind had picked up, and the snow was falling harder now. It coated Doreen's hair in the time it took them to get to the truck. Doreen offered to sit in the middle so Margie could lean against the door if she wanted to rest. Margie did want that, more than anything. With her cheek pressed against the cold glass, she remembered sitting in this same truck while Doreen painted her nails red. Margie had hoped Doreen would want to be her friend. Maybe now Doreen finally found her interesting enough.

"Hugo," Margie said. "Could we listen to the radio?"

"Of course, girls. Of course," he said. She knew it would make Doreen happy, and she needed not to have to talk.

Hugo let them choose the station, and Doreen found "Please Stay" by the Drifters. She listened with her eyes closed, her head tipped back against the seat, and Margie wondered whether she was picturing that boyfriend, the baby's father, off at college. It seemed so strange to Margie that her own life was over and Doreen's was still going, at least for now. And all that separated them was this one event, this one day.

Margie's mind returned again and again to Timothy: Where was he now? And now? What about now? Would the nurses care for him until the people came to adopt him? Would he go to some kind of foster home first? No one had told her anything about what was going to happen next. She hadn't even known what to ask. The questions were only coming to her now, as the fog in her brain receded.

Hugo crawled along the country road. In the time it took for the wipers to make a full pass across the windshield, the glass clouded over with snow again. The trip took nearly an hour.

When they finally arrived back at the home, Sister Simon was waiting just inside the back door and ushered them in, waving to Hugo, who turned to take the truck back to the garage. "Well, look," she said to Doreen when she pushed the heavy door shut. "It's the girl who cried wolf. Good luck to you when your time really does come. We'll see if anyone helps you then."

Doreen stared at Sister Simon hard. They faced off for what felt like an eternity, and Margie held her breath, curious to see which one would look away first.

"Why are you such a hateful woman?" Doreen asked. "Miserable, hateful, cruel. And you enjoy it."

The sister scoffed. "We've gone to an awful lot of trouble to help you, young lady," she said. "The least you could do is show a little gratitude."

An awful lot of trouble. The words rang in Margie's ears. The same ones she'd heard from Mrs. Yeardly. It was as if all of them were reading from the same script.

"Get out of my sight," Sister Simon said dispassionately. "Go to Vespers, and then to the common room. Someone will bring you a blanket and pillow. You'll be sleeping there tonight."

"What?"

Sister Simon ignored Doreen and turned to Margie. "I'm sorry, Minnie, but your parents had to turn back because of the weather. They will come tomorrow. So you will be with us one last night, and I want you to have your room to yourself. It's important for you to rest, and the last thing you need is Donna and her theatrics."

"It's *Doreen*," Doreen yelled. Margie, startled by the sudden noise, took a step back and felt the strands of the mop hanging on the wall press wetly against her neck. "Margie knows my name is Doreen, and I know her name is Margie." Doreen was crying now—why was she crying? She wiped her nose on the sleeve of her coat, defiant. "We *know* each other's names. We know lots of things about each other. She's my friend."

"That's enough," said Sister Simon. "Minnie did a brave thing today. She doesn't deserve to have you upsetting her."

"I know she did." Doreen sniffed. "I know."

"Don't talk about me like I'm not here," Margie said softly.

"I'm sorry, Margie," Doreen said.

Margie nodded. "It's okay."

Sister Simon pointed to the stairs. "Go," she said to Doreen.

"This is a loony bin," Doreen said before she walked away. "You can't treat people like this. It should be against the law."

Sister Simon led Margie to her room and helped her take the clothes from her dresser drawers and fold them carefully into her suitcase, all except her nightgown and the clothes she would put on in the morning. The sister draped a white blouse and a brick-red skirt with box pleats over the chair in the corner. In Holy Family's sewing class, Margie had learned how to alter the waistband with elastic on either side so that she could keep wearing it until she lost the weight. "There. Now we have everything ready," she said. "I'm sure your parents will be here first thing."

Margie nodded. She imagined Verna and Frank, staring straight ahead at the road. She imagined herself in the back seat, staring out too. Would they speak? It seemed unthinkable that she could let herself be put into a car and driven away from the place where Timothy slept. But she had already done it once today. She would do it again.

Sister Simon was watching her, performing the kind of risk assessment a job like hers required. Was Margie going to turn out to be a troublemaker, a girl who changed her mind? Was she going to make a scene and become hysterical? "I think you're doing very well, Margie," she said. "I know it doesn't seem like it now, but you will get past this. You will move on with your life."

"I want to go to bed," Margie said. It was only early evening, and she couldn't remember the last time she had eaten, but she didn't care. She began, as if the sister were not standing there and she was in the room alone, to take off her clothes. She unzipped her skirt and let it fall to the floor. She pulled her sweater over her head. Still wearing her slip and the clay-colored bandage stretched tight across her breasts with metal clips, she pulled back the quilt and got into bed.

"You don't want your nightgown?" Sister Simon held it out to her. It was red flannel with a white lace collar. She had worn it for the Christmas morning photo Frank always insisted on taking when all his kids were back home under one roof. Margie had crowded in with her siblings as if they were a bunch of strangers on a train, apologizing that her hips were too wide, that her shoulder was in someone's way. Her whole life she had received the message that she took up too much space in the world. She wanted to be smaller—not just thinner but less like a solid and more like a vapor. She wanted her molecules to move farther apart.

Margie turned to face the wall. "I was in hell."

"What?"

"I was in hell, and my baby was there," Margie said. "He stayed with me the whole time."

This shut Sister Simon up for a moment. She seemed to choose her next words carefully, as it was becoming clear that she was dealing with a mentally fragile person. "You've been through a lot these last few days. But try to remember, Margie, that God chose you to give a baby to a couple who longed for one. They can have a family now, because of you."

"God wasn't there," Margie said thickly. Sleep was already claiming her, making it hard to speak. "You don't understand what I'm trying to tell you. I was in hell, actual hell. God was not there. But my baby was. And he has a name—Timothy. He stayed with me the whole time. He never left me."

The soaked bandage woke her at four in the morning, and she got up and took some gauze and a new Kotex pad from the bag of supplies the nurse had given her and shuffled down the hall to the bathroom to change her various dressings. The smell of her milk surprised her. It was sweet and smelled, well, of milk. She wasn't sure why she hadn't expected that. She hoped Timothy was getting good milk. She wondered if he had noticed that she was gone. As long as someone, somewhere, was holding him, it was better than nothing. But she still felt crazy. She was not sure whether she was awake or dreaming. Margie shivered at the sink, shocked to see the bare skin of her deflated stomach hanging down like a rope beneath her belly button.

Back in her room she stepped into her slippers and pulled the nightgown over her head. The flannel was good quality and soft, and for a moment Margie appreciated the comfort of a single familiar thing. The last echoes of the drugs they had given her at the hospital had finally worn off. She was in pain but also awake. On top of the dresser was the pink headband Doreen had been wearing the day she arrived. Seeing it, this thing connected to Doreen's life outside this place, snapped Margie into action.

She took the front stairs two at a time, silent in her slippers, slow but moving. She crossed the fancy foyer to the common room's open door. Doreen lay on the blue couch with her feet propped on one arm, a blanket covering her body up to her chin. Margie had planned to shake her awake, but Doreen's eyes were open, searching the ceiling, and she jerked up when she saw Margie enter the room.

"What's going on?"

"Doreen, I have to talk to you."

Doreen scooted over to make room for Margie. "Are you all right?"

Margie shook her head. "You have to get out of here."

"What?"

"I know. I know I probably sound crazy."

Doreen put her hand on Margie's shoulder. "What happened to you? What was it like?"

"It's over now for me. I already signed the papers. I can't change it. But there's still time for you. You don't have to go through that."

"Margie, look at my stomach!" Doreen said in a too-loud whisper before Margie shushed her. "I definitely have to go through it."

"I don't mean the birth," Margie said, and from the look on Doreen's face, Margie could see she understood. "I mean what happens after."

Doreen rubbed her forehead with the heels of her hands. Stress radiated off her.

"Just listen to me, okay? Don't do it. Get out of here before you go into labor. Call Danny right now. We can . . . I don't know. We can hide you in the garage until he gets here."

Doreen shook her head. "But even . . . even if I am having doubts—and I am, Margie, because this baby . . . isn't going to be what Sister Simon expects. I just don't know if the kind of parents who come here to adopt could ever . . . Well, I can't even say it."

Margie gave her a confused look, and Doreen shook her head.

"Never mind. All I mean is that *if* I change my mind in the end, they can't *make* me give up the baby."

"They made me," Margie said. "They knocked me out, and when I woke up, he was gone. I don't even know for sure that he is a he, except I *know*. I know him. I named him: Timothy. He comes to me in my dreams."

Doreen looked stricken. "I believe that you know, Margie," she said. "There's no doubt in my mind that you had a baby boy."

"Doreen, even if you could change your mind, if you don't relinquish, Holy Family will make you pay for every cent they've spent on you. Every disgusting piece of meatloaf, every square of toilet paper."

Doreen's expression was moving from shock to fear. "Won't they still try to make me pay if I leave?"

"Maybe. But they would have to come after you to get it. And you'd have your baby. You have to try."

Her eyes darted to the clock. "You're saying I should just leave? Now, in the middle of a snowstorm?"

Margie went to the window. "Shit. I forgot about the snow."

Even in the midst of such a grave conversation, Doreen smiled hearing Margie swear. "I'm rubbing off on you."

"It's actually stopped," Margie said. "It looks clear out. I don't think it's very cold. Just below freezing."

"What are you saying?" Doreen stood up. She seemed charged with excitement, though Margie couldn't tell whether it was the excitement of possibility or terror.

"Your coat's right here. That's good. You won't have to go back up to our room." Margie picked it up off a chair and handed it to Doreen. Then she crossed the room to a crate they used as a lost and found. "And we can find a hat and mittens for you in here. There's a pair in there that belong to Laurel. She hasn't even noticed she lost them."

Doreen expelled a disbelieving breath. "You want me to walk? Walk *where*?"

"I just want you to get away from here, Doreen. You can have your baby in Chicago, with your family there. You have to listen to me."

"Margie, you don't seem like yourself. You seem . . ."

"Crazy? I feel crazy. But the sun will be up soon. I'll call Danny and tell him to come. If you get to town, you can wait for him in the diner. I promise I'll have all your things sent to you."

Doreen stared at her a moment, swallowed. "I already called him."

"When?"

"A few hours ago. I was lying here stewing about Sister Simon's big fat mouth and I thought, you know, I don't have to take this crap anymore."

Margie pulled Doreen into a hug so hard their collarbones bashed together. "Good." Margie let her go and picked up the coat again. "He'll be almost here. He'll pass you on the road to town."

"You really think I can't wait for him?"

Margie shook her head. "They will try to talk him out of taking you. They will remind him about the money. Anything could happen—you have to listen to me. Please, Doreen. Just trust me." Margie looked at the clock again. It was 4:50. The nuns would be getting up soon for morning prayers. "Please."

Doreen took the coat and slipped her arms into the sleeves. She didn't need any more convincing, Margie could see. It was almost as if Doreen knew more than she was letting on. It reminded Margie of the feeling she'd had in the dining hall on Doreen's first night, when Doreen had gotten the girls to go around the table and say what they missed the most about home. Margie had lied about what she missed, and Doreen had known she was lying. It was like Doreen could see right into her soul.

"Do you have money?"

Doreen nodded. "In my pocket. And my lipstick." She pulled on her boots. Fortunately they were her practical pair and not the little suede ones under the dresser upstairs. They were lined with black fake fur and came up to her shins. As she fastened just the top button on her coat—no others would connect—Margie turned her collar up in back and pushed her into the foyer. The building was completely quiet except for the distant clank of a radiator.

"If they hear the door, they're going to come," Margie said as she pulled it open and the cold air rushed in. "Go. Walk fast."

The sky had turned from black to gray ahead of the sunrise. Soon Doreen would be walking in the light. One more time, Doreen pulled her into a hug. "I'm so, so sorry, Margie."

"No," Margie said. "Sorry—why?"

Doreen looked at her, eyes sorrowful and full of tears. She shook her head, as if there was something more she wanted to say.

"Don't be sorry. Just *go*."

Doreen took off down the steps, waddling as fast as she could, which wasn't very fast, through the snow that Hugo had yet to shovel from the front path.

She stopped and turned back. "Margie?"

Margie glanced behind her into the foyer, afraid she would see Sister Simon standing there. The most important thing in the world at this moment was to get Doreen out of there, to save her friend from what she had gone through. Margie felt like a prophet singled out to deliver this one piece of wisdom to this one girl. She frantically waved her hand and mouthed the word *go*.

Doreen grinned. "Tell Sister Simon I used the front door."

15

Doreen

Crunch-crunch. Crunch-crunch.

After an endless and noisy day—the chatter of the girls in the cafeteria, the hospital's bustle, Timothy's crying, Art's crying, his wife's crying as they named Timothy Nicholas—the world had suddenly gone silent. There was just the empty road stretching out before her and the sound her boots made in the snow as she tried to outpace her dread. What in the hell had she just done?

Crunch-crunch. Crunch-crunch.

I-am. Cra-zy.

I-am. Cra-zy.

Margie had been right: it wasn't that cold. Maybe just around freezing, and the sky was concrete gray now. Doreen's nose was cold, and the tips of her fingers ached inside the cashmere gloves, but the rest of her felt like an engine running hot, the kind that came into the mechanic's shop where Danny worked, steam pouring from the car hood's seams.

It wasn't that Doreen didn't know how dangerous it was for a pregnant woman to set off walking in the dark in the middle of nowhere. She knew very well. It was just that Margie had scared the shit out of her about how dangerous it would be to stay. She didn't know what would be worse—that they would take her baby, or that they would see the baby, see its dark skin, and reject it. She had to get away, to control what was going to happen next. She was far enough along the road now that she could no longer see Holy Family behind her and had to rely on her watch and a guess at her rate of speed to figure out how much progress she had made. The only thing to do was keep walking forward.

Crunch-crunch. Crunch-crunch.

And this wasn't the only irreversible decision Doreen had made in the past day. She thought about Margie, sitting on the bench in the lobby of the hospital. The brief moment in which she could have told her what she knew: Timothy was safe, and the people who adopted him were good. But what good would it do Margie to hear that? To know where her baby was but not be able to go to him? To know that *Doreen* could see him, but she couldn't? It would be too painful. There were some things it was better not to know. By now Timothy would be in a crib in his new home, blocks from the Coniglios' two-flat. Doreen couldn't tell Margie where he was, but she could check on him. She would look after him. It was a promise, starting today.

Crunch-crunch. Crunch-crunch.

Holy Family would come after her for the bill. Doreen knew all too well that you couldn't run away from a debt, couldn't hide. Vincenzo had *died* and even that made no difference to the creditors he had left unpaid. But she could see so clearly now that no one would love and protect her baby the way she would. So it was two promises today, one to Margie and one to herself.

Crunch-crunch. Crunch-crunch.

When the first contraction came, it wrapped all the way around her torso like a vise.

"Ohhhhh," Doreen moaned to no one, making the same sound she had made while scrubbing the toilet at the beginning of this endless day, but this time she wasn't faking. "Shiiiiiiiiiiiiiiit."

Doreen tried to breathe through her nose. Every time she exhaled, she felt a little puff of hot air on her top lip. And then all at once the tension eased and the pain disappeared. Doreen started walking again. This can't be it, she told herself. I have another week or two at least. But a few minutes later, another contraction took hold and she had to stop again. Now that she knew to expect it, it really wasn't so bad. She thought that if this was as bad as it was going to get, she could probably take it, but her legs were getting tired.

The original plan had been to walk toward town, hoping Danny would find her somewhere along the way, but she had not signed up for giving birth on the road like a woman on the goddamn Oregon Trail. What was she supposed to do—go back? The situation was so absurd and impossible that, perhaps simply to survive, her brain narrowed its view down to a window of a single minute. Breathe and walk, breathe and walk, get through this minute. Then she could think about the next one.

Doreen continued to make progress this way. The sun was up now behind her, giving her the shadow of a giant. She watched the giant's head bob. All at once Doreen was overcome with a memory of her family walking to Mass at Our Lady of Pompeii when she was about four years old. She had wanted to hold both Carla's and Vincenzo's hands, but she also felt urgently that Danny should hold both of them too, and the only way to make that happen was for the four of them to arrange themselves in a circle. Carla and Vincenzo tried explaining the problem to Doreen, but she would not listen. She was inconsolable. Couldn't they see? Everyone in the family had to be connected. Vincenzo found it very amusing that they had to shimmy this way down the block, their closed unit, everyone touching each other. Doreen could remember Carla's blue hat with its bobbing sprig of cherries and the yellow morning light that made them into one continuous long shadow.

Now there would be one more person in that circle.

Crunching gravel brought her to her senses, but the sound was coming from behind her, which meant that it couldn't be Danny in the Oldsmobile. Doreen turned to see Hugo's truck approaching in the middle of the road, and her first instinct was to run. But where?

She kept walking as the truck pulled up alongside her. She didn't even turn her head. *Crunch-crunch. Crunch-crunch.* The truck stopped for a moment, and as Doreen moved past it she heard the squeak of the window cranking down.

"Doreen!"

Doreen turned her head in surprise at the sound of a woman's voice.

"Stop, please." Sister Joan's veil fluttered behind her shoulders. Some of her red hair was sticking out from the band that went across her forehead. She looked like she'd put the whole getup on in a hurry.

"You can go back," Doreen said. "It's okay. Danny's coming to meet me in town."

The sister looked so small in the truck's big cab, her slight shoulders barely rising above the wheel. "Doreen, this is crazy."

"Did Margie send you? I thought she was trying to help me."

"She was and she is. She got worried when she realized you hadn't taken any food with you. She woke me up to ask me what to do."

Doreen sighed and kept on walking.

"Get in the truck and warm up. We can talk."

"No thanks."

Just at that moment, of course, another contraction took hold. Doreen tried to keep walking without missing a step, but this one was stronger than the last and sharper too, deep in the bones of her lower back. She slowed, stooped.

"Oh, for God's sake!" Sister Joan yelled. She stopped the truck and flung herself out the driver's side door, hustling around the front to where Doreen stood. "How many of these have you had?"

Doreen felt the hot air on her upper lip, the condensation of ice melting out of the air to form droplets on her skin. She didn't try to talk.

"So, more than a few? You're in labor, honey." Sister Joan looked at her watch. "It's 6:35—remember that."

"I can't be. It's still April."

"They must have miscalculated your due date. I was thinking that this morning when you told me about getting your breath back. Your baby dropped. That usually happens the day before labor."

She opened the passenger door, and this time Doreen did not fight her.

The sister got back into the driver's seat and put the big truck into gear. "I think it's about eight more miles. Just sit tight."

"No hospital," Doreen said.

"What are you talking about? You are about to have a baby. Maybe sooner than we think."

"I'm not going in that building. If you try to make me, I will just lie down in the parking lot and have it there."

Sister Joan looked mystified. "But why?"

"I changed my mind, okay? I want to keep my baby."

The sister nodded, her eyes on the road. She was driving faster than she had been, but not too fast. "Okay, Doreen. That's your decision. Nobody's going to take your baby away."

"Don't give me that shit," Doreen said. "I know what they did to Margie. She told me all about it." She peered at the sister, feeling her irritation balloon to fill the truck's cab. "You know, I really thought you were different. I trusted you. But I can see you're just like them."

Sister Joan absorbed this slight without a shred of defensiveness. "What do you mean they took her baby? *They* who?"

"At the hospital. They put Margie under, and when she woke up, the baby was gone. They wouldn't let her see him. No one even asked her whether she planned to give him up for adoption. They just assumed. They made the decision for her. And then she was too drugged to speak up for herself. She was even drugged when she signed the papers."

Sister Joan looked stricken.

Doreen sucked her teeth. "Oh, come on. You didn't know that's what they do?"

She sighed. "I guess not. I've only been assigned to the home for a few months, and Sister Simon handles all the arrangements with the doctors and the adoptions. I guess . . . I didn't know what it was like."

"Well, now you know," Doreen said.

"I promise—I will stay with you the whole time."

"No. I'm not going in there."

"But what exactly do you propose we do instead? You are having a baby, one way or another."

"Didn't you tell me that your mother was a midwife?"

The sister's eyes went wide. "Doreen, just because I helped my mother years ago doesn't mean I am prepared to deliver a baby today!"

"Well, you're going to have to try, because I am not going to the hospital."

Sister Joan stared at Doreen for a moment. Then she looked back at the road and didn't say anything for a long time.

Another contraction seized Doreen's middle. It was a hundred times worse sitting down. She arched her back to relieve the pressure on her hips. "Goddaaaaaaaamnit."

Sister Joan looked at her watch again. "Five minutes. This is going to happen soon."

When the pain eased, Doreen tipped her head back against the seat with her eyes closed. She was grateful that the sister was not talking anymore. The sound of her voice, the talk of the hospital, was making it hard to take things one minute at a time.

The truck slowed, and without opening her eyes, Doreen could feel that they had taken a left turn and come to a stop. With great effort, she lifted an eyelid a sliver. They were in a parking lot in front of a red door.

"What is this place?"

"I can't believe I'm saying this, but I have an idea," Sister Joan said. "Stay here."

Done, thought Doreen. *You don't have to tell me twice.* For about a minute she used her thumb to trace a circle around each of her fingernails. Then she took ten breaths, each six seconds long, just for the hell of it. Just to keep her mind from going crazy. It gave her the strength to open her eyes properly and look around. A large sign on two wooden posts stood in the grass between the building and the highway. THE STARLITE MOTEL was painted in red and outlined in green with a large star in place of the dot on the *i*. The red door in front of the truck was one of several that stretched along the side of the building, and only a few other cars were parked in the lot. At the front was the office, accessed by a glass door. As if unearthing a tablet buried under a few thousand years of sediment, Doreen recalled having seen this place on the drive to and from the hospital. A lonely outpost in a lonely place.

Sister Joan emerged from the glass door carrying a huge stack of towels and a block of wood with a key dangling off the end. She climbed back into the truck and put it into gear.

"How'd you get those?" Doreen asked.

"I told him I like to take a lot of baths. Trust me, no one ever questions a nun."

She backed out of the space and drove to a different red door at the far end of the motel building's L-shape and pulled in, then turned off the engine. "I also told him to put me as far from the road as possible. I like the peace and quiet, you see."

Doreen noticed that the sister was in a funny mood, almost giddy, but she seemed to be trying to restrain herself. She turned to Doreen. "Now, I need you to listen to me. What you are asking me to do is dangerous. I know you don't believe that, but it's true. This is crazy. It's not too late to change your mind. We can drive right on to the hospital now, and I think we should."

"No."

The sister rubbed her forehead and sighed. "Well, then I have no choice. But you need to know that once we get into this, there's no going back. It could happen this morning, or it might not be until tonight. or even longer. If I think it's getting out of control, I am going to call an ambulance, end of discussion. Okay?"

Ambulance was a scary word, Doreen thought. "Okay."

"I don't know how much you know about what this is going to be like. Do you have sisters or cousins you've talked to?"

Doreen shrugged.

"It's going to hurt. A lot. And it's messy. I'm about to get pretty up close and personal with you. Can you handle that?"

Doreen recalled Dr. Samuels and his torture device. Anything had to be better than that. "I think the question is whether *you* can handle it," Doreen said, trying to lighten the mood while she had the chance. Soon, she figured, she would be screaming at the top of her lungs. "Say goodbye to your purity. I don't think this is in your job description."

"My job is to try to be the hands and feet of Christ, and today that means getting this baby born."

The room was small and shabby but fairly clean. Sister Joan ushered Doreen to a chair in the corner just as another contraction took hold. "Five minutes again," she said. "Don't sit down. Put your elbows on the back of the chair like this and hunch over." She demonstrated. "It will take the pressure off your back."

From that position, Doreen watched with her head tipped to the side as the sister set down her bag, took off her coat and hung it in the wardrobe. She closed the drapes and turned on the room's three lamps. Then she stood in the middle of the room for a long moment, maybe wondering what to do, maybe praying. After that, she went into the bathroom, and Doreen could hear the shower rings rattling. She came out with the curtain trailing behind her and pulled all the covers off the bed, then draped the shower curtain over the bare mattress and laid the flat sheet on top of it.

Next, Sister Joan set the metal trash can from the bathroom next to the foot of the bed. "They're not going to be too happy when they see the state of this room when we're done with it. But we'll cross that bridge later."

"What's that for?" Doreen asked, pointing to the trash can.

Sister Joan opened her mouth to answer but stopped when Doreen contorted her face. This contraction lasted a long time. The sister looked at her watch. "That one was over a minute long. They're coming faster now, aren't they?"

She went into the bathroom again, and Doreen could hear the water running. When she came back out, her habit and veil were off and she was wearing just a cap-sleeved undershirt and her woolen leggings. Her hair was twisted into a tight bun. "Okay, I'm as scrubbed up as I'm going to be. I want to check you out, and then I'm going to have you get clean too."

She got Doreen to lie down on the bed and let her knees fall apart so she could see where things stood. It was embarrassing, but not as bad as it had been with Dr. Samuels.

"I'm going to help you get your briefs off, okay?"

"Okay."

They came off with a wet *thwap*. "Honey, did you know your water broke?"

Doreen shook her head. She could barely feel anything below her hips. There was so much pressure pushing down. "I feel like I need to go to the bathroom." She closed her eyes. There was no dignity in any of this. "Number two."

But the sister wasn't fazed. "That's normal. Don't push yet, though. Okay? I'm going to feel with my fingers."

It hurt so much, Doreen screamed, a sharp, piercing sound. There was just so much pressure.

"I'm sorry," the sister said. "I can't believe how fast this is moving. You are almost ready to push. But we need you to wash off so everything is clean for the baby."

Sister Joan helped Doreen step into the tub and ran the water scalding hot. Doreen braced herself with her palms on the tile walls, and the sister scrubbed her hard between her legs and down to her knees with a washcloth. It actually felt good to be in the heat of the water, but the sensation of everything—the scrubbing and the pressure in her hips and back and the stinging inside her and the urge to squat down and push—was so overwhelming that the room started to go white in front of her eyes. "I have to get out," she said.

"Okay, okay." The sister helped her step out and dried her off. "Let's put your slip back on, and we'll just keep it tied up around your waist." Doreen lay back down on the bed and laughed, a brief moment between contractions. She was just naked in all her glory in front of a nun, and a real live baby, Mosel's baby, was about to come out of her body. This was, by far, the craziest goddamn thing that had ever happened to her.

"Waaaaaaaahhhaaaaaaa. I need to push I need to push I need to push."

"Okay, here we go," Sister Joan said. She was crouched on the floor with a mound of towels spread across her knees and the floor beside her.

Until then, Doreen had felt helpless, like her energy was diffused across the peaks and valleys of her labor pains and the colossal effort it took to keep her mind from devouring itself. But now she had a task, and the will of her mind and muscles merged into a kind of tornado spinning down, down, down. Doreen pushed.

"That's it," Sister Joan said, her voice coming from far away. Doreen's eyes were clamped shut, and she was propped up on her elbows. "Tuck your chin to your chest and give it all you got."

A rest, and then another push. The sister's voice again. "Put your hand down here. Touch." A slick mound. Doreen's hand fell away. "The baby's head is coming, Doreen. You're doing so well."

She pushed and pushed for who knows how long. After a while came the awful shoulders, first one, then the other as the baby turned, and a wave of fluid gushed out, probably all over the sister's lap and arms.

And then there was her voice ringing like a bell. "She's here, Doreen. Open your eyes."

Doreen opened her eyes, and up onto her stomach came a purple creature turning pink, streaked with white gunk, and crying a grinding cry. Up came a towel too, and Sister Joan helped her cover the baby and slide her up her chest. Her skin was olive, like Doreen's, and she had black curls slicked to her head with amniotic fluid. Two dark eyes.

Doreen wailed. She could not take her eyes off the baby's eyes. Her baby. A little girl. The sister said something about not moving her legs too much. Something else was happening down there, more fluid, a thunk into the empty trash can, but all of it might as well have been happening in another room, in another motel.

"Hello," Doreen said to the baby. After another long moment of adoration, she turned her head to the side and vomited suddenly, a violent spurt of yellow on the sheet.

"Oh dear," the sister said, looking up casually from her cleanup efforts. "Don't worry about that. It happens."

Doreen spit and dragged her lips across her bare shoulder to wipe them off. Sister Joan helped her sit up a bit and move the baby to her breast.

She turned back to her baby and the dark eyes, which were blue and brown and black all at once, a color that only existed in the otherworld from which she had just arrived. She thought of Mosel and the time they'd had together as if it were a dream, a summer not just in the weather but a summer of her mind, of her heart. A warm carefree space apart that could only be what it was because of its limitations. And yet here in her arms was something lasting, a whole new life they had made.

"How are you two doing?" Sister Joan asked in a gentle voice.

Doreen couldn't tell if ten minutes had passed or an hour. For the first time, she took her eyes off the baby and looked squarely at the sister. "Thank you for helping me," Doreen whispered and heard in the sound of her own voice that she was weeping. All she could think was that someone could have tried to take her baby if it hadn't been for the sister. If it hadn't been for Margie. She clutched her closer as if she were clutching her own life.

Sister Joan held her gaze and nodded, one sure bob of her head. Then she kissed Doreen's hair and laughed. "I can't believe you did this to me. But you did great. Don't panic, but I found a doctor in town willing to come out here to check the two of you—"

"Not that Dr. Samuels," Doreen said warily.

"No." Sister Joan shook her head. "One of the good ones. Now you two should rest."

That sounded nice. Doreen's eyes were heavy. A blanket appeared and enveloped the baby and her, and as she closed her eyes, honest to God, she heard the swell of an orchestra and a lyric sung by Shirley Owens's voice: *Today's the first day of my life in love with you.*

The violins were a little old-fashioned, but it had all the makings of a hit, Doreen thought as she faded to sleep. What could be more romantic than love at first sight?

PART IV
Postpartum

Five Years Later
1966

16

We

After it was over, after we truly understood that it couldn't be reversed, we went home.

We went back to our job as a bank teller, as a carhop on roller skates, as a sales girl at the department store makeup counter; we went back to trigonometry and pep rallies and graduation parties. We explained away any discrepancies in the cover stories our mothers had come up with. Nothing had changed. Everything was back to normal.

And we tried to make that true by going with our old friends to our old haunts and having fun the way we had before. We let the boys at the ice rink pour whiskey into our hot chocolate when no one was looking, and we drank it down and skated as fast as we could until our blades tangled up and we collapsed into a pile. We howled with laughter because everyone else was howling, but it felt like a performance instead of a good time, and when they called us the next Friday night we pretended to have a cold.

No one ever talked about it again. That was surprising. We had so many things we wanted to say, so many stories we wanted to tell, but even speaking the name of the home aloud, even saying "the baby," was like throwing a stick of dynamite into a room. There were so many of us in every county, in every state across the country, but we didn't know about each other, and we never would have dared to ask around.

We knew then, and it only became clearer as time passed: we would have to carry our stories alone.

17

Margie

Margie ran down the dormitory steps in her slick-bottomed flats, the spine of the Norton Anthology taking bites out of her ribs. If she wanted to be on time for class, she would have to run at full speed past the rows of bronze mailboxes in the lobby, out the door at one end of the portico and into the door at the other end, then take a sharp right down the next hall to the lecture room. But in her three years as a student at Mount Mary College, she had not once passed her mailbox without opening the tiny door to see what was inside. What if there was finally news? What if she missed it?

Shifting her books to her left hip, Margie fished out her key and turned it in the lock to find three white envelopes. She snatched them out and resumed her dash to class while glancing down at the return addresses: the library, no doubt a final warning about her overdue fines; her great-aunt, sending a belated card for Easter. She pulled the third one to the top just as she reached the classroom and was shocked to actually see the words she had been looking for all this time: the Archdiocese of Prairie County, Illinois.

Professor Butler, one of the first women who was not a nun to teach at the college, had already begun her lecture and glanced at Margie now through the glass door with a curious look. Margie slipped inside and found the nearest empty seat, in the second row. She placed the letter in her lap, opened her composition notebook to the first blank page, and wrote *Gerard Manley Hopkins* at the top. Keeping her eyes forward, she worked her fingertip under the flap of the envelope and began to tear, but the noise of the ripping paper seemed comically loud in the quiet room, and she gave up. It would have to wait until after class.

So Hopkins, then. "The Windhover." Funnily enough, maybe the only thing that could distract Margie from wanting to know what was in that letter was a lecture on this particular poem, a Catholic school classic, which she had loved when she first read it as a high school junior. But that was before she had gone away. Now it only irritated her.

Professor Butler began to read the poem. In "The Windhover," the speaker watches a kestrel fly and dive on its prey, and praises the role God plays in everything that happens. "As a skate's heel sweeps smooth on a bow-bend: the hurl and gliding / Rebuffed the big wind. My heart in hiding / stirred for a bird . . ." The sound and rhythm of the words were almost scandalously beautiful, too honest and full of emotion for the stale air of the classroom. Margie felt again the spell they had cast on her the first time she read the poem. The speaker seemed to be saying that God shows up in nature not as the bird nor the sky nor the summer air through which the bird moves, but as *flight itself*, the invisible yet undeniable force that lifts the bird. In the final stanza, the speaker describes his surprise when dead black embers fall away from a log to reveal a blazing gold-and-red inner core, still burning. According to Hopkins, even mundane firewood contains the hidden presence of God.

Here was where Margie's irritation came in, what she would write about in her upcoming term paper if she had the courage to be honest. The reader gets to watch that kestrel hover in midair, but the poem does not follow the kestrel as it dives down to the ground to tear a mouse's head from its body. Maybe flight was marvelous for the bird, and for the poet who watched it soar, but how did it feel for the mouse, who had no choice but to become the bird's prey?

For the mouse, the bird's supposedly holy flight meant only pain and suffering. Where is God *then*? What kind of terrible God loves only the strong and abandons the weak? If he isn't there for the mouse, then he isn't there at all. She grinned faintly, hearing Doreen's voice in her ears: *This poem is a big ol' crock of shit.*

Doreen. Margie remembered the mix of jealousy and relief she had felt as she watched Doreen walk away from Holy Family in the snow. Later that same day, when she was sitting in her room waiting for her parents to arrive, Margie overheard Sister Simon and Sister Joan arguing in the hallway about Doreen.

"You should have brought her back here *immediately*," Sister Simon hissed in a tense whisper. "We have a system. Hugo takes the girls to the hospital."

Sister Joan's voice was calmer but firm. "But she refused to go. She was terrified that they would put her under and take that baby away. And it sounds like she had good reason to be."

"Don't be dramatic."

"But the mission of this home is to *help* these girls. Tricking them, bullying them, the way the hospital treats them like they're nothing—how is that in line with what we are here to do?"

"You think it would help these girls to let them take their babies home and play house? Pretend they can make a life for these children?"

Sister Joan sighed. "No, of course not. But . . . this should be a safe haven. We can help them while they make the decision on their own. Don't you have any compassion for them at all?"

"I have compassion for these innocent babies. That's why I screen the adoptive parents so carefully, why I interview them and make them show their financials. Because these babies deserve better than a lifetime of shame. They deserve good homes, with good people."

Sister Joan's voice had gone quiet then for a long moment. Finally, she said, "I can't be a part of this."

A cruel laugh. "Don't worry. The diocese will terminate your placement here by the end of the day."

Margie had waited until Sister Simon stalked off and then went into the hall. "So Doreen's all right?"

Sister Joan nodded. She looked drawn, deflated. "She's fine. She had a little girl." She gave Margie a faint smile. "I'm not supposed to tell you that, but as you probably heard, breaking that little rule is the least of my problems."

"It was good what you did," Margie said. "It was the right thing."

Sister Joan touched Margie's elbow. "I wish I could have helped *you*, Margie."

Margie's eyes had filled with tears then. It was so strange to hear a person in charge acknowledge what had happened to her. "I know," she said. "I know you would have done something if you'd known."

"You should get ready. Your parents will be here soon."

"Okay," Margie had said. "But about Doreen's baby—she's going to keep her?" It hurt so much to ask, but she needed to know that her friend had been able to choose for herself.

"Yeah," Sister Joan had said, a knowing look on her face that was both relieved and regretful. "She's going to keep her."

Now in the classroom at Mount Mary, Margie glanced at the clock and willed the time to pass as her finger went to the envelope's flap once more. Two weeks after she left Holy Family, Margie had returned to her high school in a state of shock, still in so much pain from the injuries of Timothy's birth that she soaked pad after pad, could barely sit down without seeing stars. Her longing for him crowded out every other thing. Her arms ached to hold him; her mind galloped around the question of where he was, whether he was all right. The rest of that year she felt she was encased in glass, separated from the rest of the world and even herself. Her best friend, Pamela, stopped coming to Margie's locker after third period and slipped away into the crowd of kids who gossiped about the real reason for Margie's absence from school. After she failed two of her classes and missed application deadlines at colleges she had once dreamed of attending, Frank had called the admissions office at Mount Mary in Milwaukee and begged them to take her.

An all-girls college housed in the stone buildings of a former convent, Mount Mary felt like a cloister, but in the best possible way. Margie's only job was to read—now that her prerequisites were out of the way, she took only literature classes—and write papers and attend seminars. There, and in the stacks of the library at nearby Marquette University, where the girls had borrowing privileges, she could get lost in all the eras that had come before her own, never forgetting Timothy, not even for a minute, but allowing herself to forget from time to time that she had once been like the mouse Hopkins left out of the poem.

Margie didn't want to be the mouse, doomed to suffer. She needed to know whether Timothy was all right—would always need to know, *deserved* to know. And one day, a few months back—maybe it was the passage of time; maybe it was new confidence stoked by once again succeeding as a student—she decided to do something about it. Using half her laundry money, she called Holy Family long distance from a pay phone in the lobby of the library and asked to speak to Sister Simon.

"I'm sorry, she's not available right now," the woman who answered the phone said. "Is there something I could help you with?"

Margie cleared her throat to muster courage. "I would like to know the process for accessing the file of a baby born there in sixty-one."

"And you are the adoptive mother?"

Margie paused. "No, I'm the one who gave birth to him."

The woman's tone grew wary. "Oh, I misunderstood. We don't give out that information to you girls."

Girls rankled Margie. She was twenty-one now and felt like she was about fifty-five. Hadn't she earned the right at the very least to be considered a woman? "I don't intend to contact him or bother him," Margie said. "I just want to know if he is all right."

"Those records are sealed by state law. We have to respect their privacy. If you'd like, you may send a letter, and we will place it in the child's file, which is unsealed when the child comes of age. Then he or she can decide whether to make contact."

"But that's in *thirteen* years."

"It's the best I can do."

In fact, Margie had already filled one of her composition notebooks full of letters to Timothy she had written over the years, fragments extracted from the radio static that played in the background of her mind at all times. But she couldn't imagine sending one of those. Instead, she wrote to Sister Simon, who was still, no doubt, telling the story of the bad girl who kept her baby and the good girl who gave her baby up. The story, she now understood, of Doreen and Margie. Except that the rewards of being that good girl had never materialized, and that made her wonder about the consequences of being the bad one. Was Doreen living on the street, turning to prostitution to keep body and soul together? Somehow, Margie doubted that. She waited weeks for Sister Simon's reply, but it never came. Being ignored stung, but had she expected anything else? Margie's resolve hardened.

She thought about how, on the rare occasions when Verna was unhappy with the service at Field's, her mother went up the chain and demanded to speak to the department manager. Margie needed to go up the chain, she had realized, to the archdiocese that oversaw Holy Family and who knows how many other homes like it. She drafted her request in plain terms: access solely to any information that would confirm Timothy's current health and well-being, and nothing more. And here was the reply.

Margie waited through the rest of Professor Butler's lecture, imagining what she would do if the letter actually contained good news. Timothy would turn five in a week. He might be living anywhere in the country now, watching spring take hold in a city park, in the desert, on the prairie. If she could only know that the people who had him, wherever they were, made sure his coat was warm enough, made sure his shoes weren't too tight. In her reverie she saw a comb passing through sandy-blond hair, a cowlick, long slender fingers that were a miniature version of her own. Would she ever get to see his picture?

When at last the other girls filed out of the room, Margie stayed at the table and tore the rest of the envelope away.

Dear Miss Ahern,

This is a response to your inquiry of February 3 requesting information on a baby born at Prairie Creek General Hospital and surrendered for adoption to the State of Illinois. In accordance with the Illinois Revised Statutes of 1945 on the Adoption of Children, all petitions, decrees, and all other papers and records relating to the adoption have been impounded by the clerk of the court. The archdiocese has no authority to supersede the dictates of this law. Therefore, we must deny your request.

It was the only answer that made sense, of course, perfectly predictable, and yet it landed like a punch in her stomach.

"Margie?" Professor Butler paused in gathering her books and papers and turned to her in concern. "Are you all right?"

Why was it that, anytime someone asked that question, you couldn't tell the truth?

18

Doreen

"Mom."

"What?"

"Mom." The bathroom door in the Coniglios' apartment was solid oak. On the other side of it, from the hallway, Summer's voice sounded tiny.

"Is it an emergency?" Silence. "Because, unless it's an emergency, you really shouldn't bother people when they're in the bathroom."

Doreen was sitting on the closed lid of the toilet bowl with a small pad of paper on her knee. This was the only place in the apartment where she could be alone long enough to jot down the lyrics that zipped through her mind, good ones, sometimes, but always fleeting, and she could never count on remembering them after Summer finally went to bed. By then she was too tired to keep her eyes open. She had a melody in mind for this one, a chorus that sounded kind of like if "I Know a Place" and "I Hear a Symphony" had a baby, which she understood made no sense. But she still needed to write it down.

Another shuffling sound in the hallway, the shadow of two little feet. "Mom?"

Doreen sighed and tipped her forehead onto her knees. She stood up, slipped the pad of paper in the pocket of her jeans, and opened the door.

Don't be mean, she reminded herself. Summer was easily offended. "Hi, sweetie. How's my birthday girl?"

Summer was five today. Five! It hardly seemed possible. To mark the occasion, she had chosen a flowered A-line dress over a pink turtleneck and pink tights, showcasing her mom's flair for fashion, her father's endless eyelashes, and the fawn-colored skin that was all her own. She leaned to the side to look behind Doreen into the bathroom, then gave her a high school principal's skeptical stare. "Why were you in there so long? I'm hungry."

Doreen looked at the clock in the hall. It was past one. "I'm sorry, kiddo. I lost track of time. Let's get some lunch."

It was a typical Saturday in the Coniglios' two-flat. Carla was up at the emergency room working the second half of a double shift. Danny was at the garage working on a rush paint job (likely helping one of Taylor Street's most accomplished car thieves dodge arrest, but hey, it paid well). And Doreen had to finish payroll for three of her bookkeeping clients while somehow shooing Summer out of trouble until everyone came home at dinnertime. Weekends were for union workers and rich people. For all the Coniglios but the youngest one, every day was a workday.

Summer took her mother's hand and walked her into the kitchen as if she were afraid Doreen might wander off without her supervision. "Peanut butter and jelly?" Doreen asked, and Summer nodded.

As Doreen spread Peter Pan on a slice of white bread, her eye caught the box of birthday candles she had bought at the drugstore last week. "Oh, Summer—we can't forget to pick up your cake before the bakery closes. Let's go after lunch."

Summer's eyebrows went up. "Is it the kind with words on it?"

Doreen nodded. "Yep, a birthday cake."

"With *my* words on it?"

"You mean your name? Yes, it's going to say 'Happy Birthday, Summer.'"

She thought about this. "But not 'summer' like the season. Summer the name, with a *big* S."

Doreen smiled. "That's right."

"In purple?"

"In purple." She cut the sandwich into two triangles—she might as well throw it in the garbage if she cut it into rectangles by mistake—and placed it on a yellow plate, then set Summer up at the table with a glass of milk. This was the same table where, just shy of five years ago, Doreen had sat motionless in her nightgown, afraid to move for fear a creak of her chair would wake newborn Summer, finally quiet in the bassinette at Doreen's feet after hours of endless crying. A few weeks before that, Doreen had opened her eyes in the bed at the Starlite Motel to see Danny sitting beside her holding Summer, Sister Joan showing him how to cradle her head. "I'm an uncle! I can't believe it!" he had said over and over, so proud, as usual, of himself.

What no one told you about having a baby was that the misery of pregnancy was a dream compared to the shitshow of taking care of a newborn. For a while Doreen wondered if she had picked up some kind of tropical disease, she was so exhausted and full of malaise. Every part of her body ached, the arches of her feet, every muscle in her eye sockets, the tips of her pinky fingers. She was trapped in an endless cycle of rocking, swaying, setting down, picking up, filling bottles, putting them back in the fridge. All through it Summer cried until she shivered, cried until she dropped into sleep in the middle of a wail, as if someone had turned off her brain like a light switch.

But then, deep in the night, Summer's eyes would find Doreen's in the dark, and she would break into what Doreen knew could not yet be a smile but *was*, and her lips would loosen from the bottle's nipple and milk would drain down her chin. Doreen would laugh and help Summer get the bottle back in, and then she would begin to cry—Doreen, that is—thinking about how hard Summer was working to learn how to be awake and how to be asleep and how to drink and pee without creating an international incident over it. In the dark, in her exhaustion, Doreen would beam with pride. *My baby is a genius. My baby is going to be the first woman on the Supreme Court, the first woman on the moon, the first woman from this block to buy a car in her own name.* She was in awe of Summer, and now that this girl could walk and talk and read and work the television and mouth off like a convict, Doreen's admiration had only grown.

The brown phone hanging on the kitchen wall rang, and Doreen reached in from the table to answer it. Mrs. Quinn, the tenant who lived upstairs with her ailing husband, couldn't get the door of her linen cupboard unstuck. While she claimed she was not looking for help but just wanted to "make sure they knew" about the problem (which, Doreen understood, meant Mrs. Quinn was planning to deduct five dollars from the rent on account of it), Doreen told her she would be right up. She settled Summer on the carpet in front of *Gidget* and headed upstairs with Danny's Phillips head and a small crowbar. She passed through their twin front room, this one choked with doilies and the Quinns' cuckoo clock collection, the dining room, and the hall that opened onto three bedrooms. The linen closet was beside the bathroom. After quite a bit of tugging, some wrenching, and a terrible sound of wood cracking away from wood, Doreen opened the door to Mrs. Quinn's cheers.

She clucked her tongue. "I just don't understand why that keeps happening," she said.

Doreen sighed. "My brother didn't let the paint dry all the way before he put the door back on."

"Well, you've saved us, dear. As always."

Doreen smiled, reminding herself to tell Carla to keep an eye on that five dollars.

Back downstairs, she put the tools away and tiptoed past Summer, catatonic in front of the television, and into the bedroom to the ledgers and envelopes of receipts she kept under the bed. The waitresses' carbons from DiMarco's restaurant, dotted with olive oil, the receipts from the laundromat, owned by Mrs. Quinn's nephew and one of Doreen's first clients. The pristine slips from Mrs. Mallory's gauzy white-curtained hosiery and undergarment boutique were stamped with a purple butterfly, and Doreen took pains not to crease them or leave them lying around after she tallied the numbers. If Summer got access to a pen and thirty unmonitored seconds, every slip of paper in sight would be covered in drawings of cats.

About three weeks after she came home to Taylor Street, the bills from Holy Family started to arrive. The girls from the diner had cooed at Doreen to come back to work there. But she didn't think she could stand to see Timothy's picture taped up beside the register next to the plaster statue of Mary, infant in arms, to be reminded every day of the life-altering secret she had kept from Margie. Instead, she scraped together thirty dollars for a LaSalle Extension School bookkeeping course she saw advertised in the back of *Good Housekeeping*. Her customers probably wouldn't like to see that she did their books fifteen minutes at a time, spread out on her bed and balancing her adding machine on a pillow, sometimes dozing off, sometimes interrupted to deliver juice, soothe a nightmare away, plunge a toilet, throw a frozen lasagna into the oven, but Doreen knew she did good work for them. And the money that came in was enough to pay down the debt, little by little.

A while later, after she had prepared about half the paychecks to be signed, Doreen stretched her legs and walked into the kitchen. Summer was still watching TV—was that bad? What time was it? Once Doreen was standing beside the sink, she couldn't remember what she had come in for. Had she ever eaten lunch? She opened the fridge. She had just read an article about how you should never eat on your first impulse to eat, because it was probably just boredom and not actual hunger. This was very irritating to Doreen because she had no time whatsoever to be bored. But she wanted to have sex again before she died—it was one of her most cherished goals—and she would have to be able to fit into the clothes from her former life, currently shoved to the back of her closet, if she had any hope of pulling it off.

Suddenly, Summer wailed from the front room. Doreen closed the fridge and rushed in to find her sobbing, her fist clenched around her index finger. "What's the matter?"

"I got a splinter!"

"You got a *splinter* while watching TV?"

Summer wailed, nodded, and pointed at the broken-down coffee table with a leg that a long-dead family dog had gnawed into a few sharp edges.

Doreen sighed. "Come on, let's take a look." She kissed the top of Summer's head and walked her into the bathroom, where she kept her mother's kit of torture devices: tweezers, iodine, and the badge-of-honor Band-Aid you could earn if you were brave. As soon as Doreen opened the medicine cabinet, Summer began crying even harder.

"It's okay," Doreen told her. "We'll get it out in just a sec, but you have to be very still." She sat down on the lid of the toilet again, Summer standing in front of her, and pulled the pad of her index finger into the light. The sliver was small and long, a dark-brown shard with a distinct edge protruding from her skin. "Oh, look, it's already halfway out. This one will be easy."

Summer screamed before the tweezers even touched her skin. Doreen stopped and gave her a look. "Kiddo, meet me halfway here."

Inhaling through her nose and straightening her shoulders, Summer steeled herself for the pain. With deft fingers, Doreen grasped the tiny end of the splinter and pulled, then pressed the iodine-soaked cotton ball on her finger and winced through a new round of wailing before she got the Band-Aid on.

"There. All done."

Summer instantly stopped crying and opened her eyes to admire her wound of war.

"I think you're going to make it. We won't even have to amputate."

"I was brave," Summer said, her eyes challenging her mother to contradict that version of the story.

"Oh, very," Doreen said. Even as she felt the fleeting sense of accomplishment at solving this one minor problem, she had the same feeling as she'd had in the kitchen, standing next to the stove. She was forgetting something, but her brain was too fried to remember. "How about I help you set up your dolls to play school, and then I've got to get some work done." She raised her wrist to look at her watch but realized she had forgotten to put it on that morning.

"Okay, but we need all the chairs."

Doreen held up her hand. "Two. We can do two chairs. I'm not carrying in any more than that." Watching the older kids in the neighborhood go into and out of the mysterious place called school had made Summer so jealous she begged Doreen to teach her what went on there, so they had developed a game that involved arranging her eight dolls into a single row of enraptured students, their hands folded primly in their laps. Over time, Summer evolved the game into an ever more baroque sort of play, with scripted lines they both had to follow. Doreen's role, of course, was to play the principal who popped her head into the classroom every now and then to tell the students how lucky they were to have Summer as their teacher.

Class began with the Pledge of Allegiance—despite Doreen's coaching, Summer always said "one nation, under God, invisible"—and then the dolls began to learn about the letter B. She watched as Summer stood with her hands on her hips, her shoulders erect. Her pink headband was struggling to hold back her uneven curls. Summer's students stared at her, unblinking, all of them white, most of them blond. There wasn't a curl on any of their heads. But it was impossible to find a doll with brown skin and hair like Summer's. Doreen had tried every department store and toy store in Chicago.

She was doing the best she could with Summer's densely curly hair, but she had no idea how to care for it or coax it into any shape other than a halo, and only within the past year had it grown long enough to style. Most days Doreen put it in two little untidy buns, but today it was loose and wild. Doreen loved the way the wildness matched Summer's animated personality. Not everyone would it see that way, though, Doreen knew, because people treated confident mixed and Black girls differently from confident white ones. It would only get worse once school started, and the pressure to be obedient, to sit still, would turn Summer's natural exuberance into a liability.

When Doreen had first brought Summer home, Carla fell head over heels for the baby she said looked just like Doreen and Danny had at birth, the same Mediterranean skin, the same fuzzy black hair. And Danny was already in love. But Doreen knew it was only a matter of time before the truth came out and they learned about Summer's father. She had read that mixed-race babies' skin could darken as they grew, and Summer already seemed more brown than olive. Beautiful and perfect, but spilling Doreen's secret nonetheless.

Carla hadn't even noticed the letter Mosel sent while Doreen was gone, mixed in with the rest of the mail. He was back home after his freshman year at Ohio State, working at a sandwich cart in the building in the Loop where his father was an elevator operator. *There are a lot of pretty girls in Columbus, but none of them are as pretty as you, Doreen. I still think about you and Wooded Island. Do you think about me? Are you still working at the diner? I'll be here until September. Can I see you?* Doreen let herself cry for ten full seconds, then sniffed and shoved the letter between her mattress and box springs, where it remained.

One day when Summer was six months old, sitting in her high chair, Carla was cooing over her and had a sudden realization. She ran her fingers over Summer's head and said, "Her hair is getting *so* curly."

What happened next was burned in Doreen's brain forever. She tried to keep her voice cheerful. "Danny had curly hair as a baby."

"Not curly like this," Carla said. And then she turned to Doreen with wide eyes. "Doreen."

Doreen was folding Danny's laundry, and the couch was piled with work shirts, boxer shorts, gray-white socks. She straightened the hem of an undershirt, matching the edges up in a perfect line.

"Doreen, look at me."

Summer banged on the wooden high chair tray and babbled. She had so much to say even then. Doreen raised her eyes to Carla's.

"Who is Summer's father?"

"I've told you—that's private."

"And before, when your plan was different, I could respect that. When you were planning to give her up—"

"*Hey*." Doreen had dropped the undershirt, blood rushing to her head. "Don't ever talk about that in front of Summer."

Carla put her hand up and closed her eyes. "I'm sorry. It's just that now that we're all together? In this house. In this *neighborhood*. I need to know what we're up against here, Doreen." Carla sat on the edge of her chair, her back completely straight. "Is her father a . . . a . . ."

"A what?" Doreen had asked with a smirk. "A sea captain? A trapeze artist?"

After Carla looked at her for a long moment, she put her head in her hands and began to weep.

"Oh, here we go."

Carla looked up. "Did he force you?"

"What? No!" Patient, gentle Mosel, listening to her talk endlessly about songwriting and girl groups. As she looked at her baby, it was easy to say it out loud. "I loved him."

"You *loved* him." Carla blinked. "Who was he?"

"I'm not going to tell you his name. Why should I? Look at how you're acting. This is exactly what I thought you would do." Doreen's voice shook. "I'll tell you this: he's brilliant. Not like these idiots around Taylor Street. He won a math scholarship to a university. He'll probably be a professor someday."

And Carla had looked at Doreen like she was describing an encounter with a UFO. "You are asking me to believe that the father of my granddaughter is a colored mathematician who is off at college."

"I don't give a damn what you believe. It's the truth."

Summer chose that moment to fling her spoon across the room, and she watched in wonder as it ricocheted off the edge of the brass reading lamp and landed on the windowsill. "Ahhhhhooooo!" Summer trilled in glee.

"My sweet baby," Carla whispered and touched the back of Summer's hand. To her own daughter, she said only, "How could you do this to me?"

"To be honest, Ma, I wasn't really thinking about you at the time."

That was the shot across the bow. Carla crossed the room to Doreen in two steps and slapped her twice across the face, first with her palm and then with the back of her hand, Nonna Francesca's ruby ring biting into Doreen's cheek. With her cupped hands, she grabbed Doreen's jaw and shook it.

"What is the matter with you?" she shrieked. With a wild sweep of her arm, Carla shoved the stacks of folded laundry off the sofa onto the floor and kicked at the clothes with her stockinged feet until they were twisted in a heap on the carpet.

"I," Carla said, breathless, her mascara like ashes beneath her eyes, "am a *widow*."

Then she had gone into her bedroom and slammed the door. Doreen could still hear the sound of it five years later. And just as she had when Doreen announced her pregnancy and intention to give her baby up at Holy Family, Carla stayed in that bedroom for two days.

"*Mom*," Summer said in the bedroom now, clearly not for the first time, "you're not listening."

"I'm sorry, hon. What?"

"It's line-up time. For the kindergarteners?"

"Right," Doreen said. "Of course." She dutifully "walked" each student, scissoring the dolls' vinyl legs back and forth across the bedroom to the doll bed, where they sat in a heap when Summer was done playing with them. "Thank you, Mommy," Doreen prompted.

"Thank you, Mommy," Summer said, beaming with satisfaction that she had so accurately re-created the school experience. They heard keys in the door. "Nonni!"

"Where's my angel?" Carla always cried when she came home, in a big dramatic voice that Summer loved. She peeled off her soaking raincoat and hung it on a hook on the back of the door. Then she scooped Summer into her arms, which was getting harder to do now that Summer's toddler days were long behind her. Her legs dangled down Carla's thighs.

Carla had stayed in that room for two days, making an absolute stink but also, again like last time, Doreen knew, thinking. She had to decide who she was going to be, whether she believed love had its limits. When she emerged, she went to baby Summer and held her contritely for hours. She corralled Danny the next afternoon, when Doreen wasn't home, both to tell him and to threaten him that if he said a single thing about it to mother or daughter she would kill him in his bed. Life more or less resumed where it had left off, though the challenges of the neighborhood lay ahead: where Doreen could go with Summer, where it wasn't safe. And Carla never apologized to Doreen.

"Is Danny home yet?"

Doreen shook her head. Carla sank into Vincenzo's armchair and slid off her rubber-soled shoes. "What a day. We had three boys playing with a chainsaw, a motorcycle crash, a woman with a toothpick stuck in her eyelid."

"In her *eyelid*? How in the hell did that happen?"

Carla shrugged. "How do you think? She was drunk. Went down like a tree into her Reuben."

Summer pulled on Carla's arm. "Nonni, come look at my birthday shoes."

"Okay, let's go see. Then I need to change my clothes so we can start dinner. Did you pick up the cake?"

Doreen winced. "Shit." That was what she had forgotten.

"*Mom*," Summer said, scandalized.

Carla, who had remembered to put on her watch that morning, looked at it. "You've got ten minutes before they close."

Doreen was already pulling on her rain boots, had grabbed the jacket she would slip her arms into on the way out the door, when Summer said, "I want to come too."

"There isn't time, hon."

"But it's *my* birthday. It's *my* cake."

Doreen groaned. Why did every last thing have to be so hard? "All right. Hurry up!"

Summer kicked off her shoes and put on her own boots, found her yellow rain jacket, and Doreen hoisted her on her hip so they could run down Ada Street to the corner. The whole city was engulfed in the fog that sprang from a warm day suddenly chilled by a storm off the lake. The puddles were deep, and water splashed over Doreen's boots, soaking her socks. Summer was slipping down her hip.

"If I put you down, can you run really fast?"

Summer nodded, determined, and took Doreen's hand. They ran. The fog obscured the striped awning of the bakery two blocks away, the little yellow table that sat outside, but Doreen knew it was there. They just had to keep going.

19

Margie

Margie peeled the tab off a can of pineapple juice, careful not to scuff her pink nails, and took a sip as the Hiawatha Service to Milwaukee cut through the backyards of houses in a small farm town north of Chicago. The sun was low outside the windows on the opposite side of the train, and the sky to the east was the pale peach of a peaceful day ending softly. Somebody's day, though not Margie's, since she had spent the past two with Verna in Sycamore Ridge, and they had been anything but peaceful. But the visit home was done now, and she was on her way back to school. Her cheeks puckered as she sipped the juice, somehow at once too sweet and too sour.

A moment later she sensed the presence of a man in the aisle and turned to him.

"Is this seat taken?" he asked.

He wore gold-rimmed glasses and had a navy trench coat draped neatly over his arm. When he removed his hat, she saw that his face was freckled, his hair thinning.

"Please, sit down," Margie said, and moved her purse from the seat to the floor beside her feet.

"Thank you." He laid his coat on the metal rack above them and sat down, giving her a tight, close-lipped smile.

Margie preferred to sit by herself on these train rides because she had learned some men—the back-slapping salesmen who took this line to call on customers, college boys from the North Shore who roved in packs and filled up a whole train car with their noise—viewed a woman in solitude as an invitation. They would pepper her with questions about what she was reading, and why, and what she was writing in that notebook with the black marbled cover. Was it "Dear Diary"? But when this man sat down, he opened his own book, a paperback mystery, and paid her no further attention.

Still, she wasn't going to tempt fate by pulling her things out now. Margie turned her eyes back to the window. With the can of juice still clutched in her hand, she watched the trees grow farther apart, an open field and flock of sparrows that made long shadows across the still-dead grass. Up and down they moved together on the currents of air. The shifting shapes they made were hypnotic, and at some point Margie drifted off to sleep.

"Ah!" the man beside her yelped.

Margie's eyes flew open, and she blinked to see him grabbing the tumbling can of juice and swatting at his trousers. "Oh no! I am *so* sorry." Flustered, she rifled through her purse for a hanky and offered it to him.

"Oh, it's fine." The ambiguous close-lipped smile again. He dabbed at the gray wool near his hip. He wore a shirt that was too big for him, in a loud pink pattern. "Just took me by surprise. It was nearly empty."

"Still," Margie said, "I feel awful."

"I actually love the scent of pineapple. It reminds me of vacation." He folded the hanky in half and handed it back to her, this time with a real smile.

"Well, that's lucky, because you're going to be smelling it for the rest of the day. Thank you for being so understanding."

He offered his hand. "Theo Barrett."

"Margie," she said, and shook it. Now that she had spilled juice on him, she felt obligated to make conversation. "Headed home?"

"No, I live in Pottawatomi. Do you know it? Small town about an hour northwest of Chicago."

Margie nodded. She knew it only as a dot on the map. If you drove much beyond Sycamore Ridge, it was all farms.

"I work in the Loop. It's my mother-in-law who lives in Milwaukee—I'm making a quick visit up to see her, and it's easier taking the train straight from the office than going all the way home and driving. Actually, I spend a lot of time on trains these days."

Margie looked behind him for a woman who matched his appearance. Maybe plain but with interesting earrings? Maybe beautiful but heavyset? "Did your wife find a seat in another car? I could move."

Theo shook his head. "I'm on my own today." He paused. "And every day, actually. My wife passed last year."

Margie's hand went to her chest. "Oh, I'm so sorry."

"Thank you," Theo said, obviously well practiced at receiving condolences. "It has been very hard on her mother, so I try to get up to see her every month or so, just to check in."

One of the worst things about what had happened to Margie was that now her first response to kindness, even kindness that had nothing to do with her, was to be wary. Was he telling her this to con her into believing he was a good person? Then again, no wife with a breath left in her body would allow her husband out in a shirt like that. "Well. How nice." Margie didn't ask what had happened to Mrs. Barrett, and he didn't explain.

Theo slipped his book into the pocket of the seat in front of him. "Is Milwaukee home for you?"

"No. Well, yes, temporarily. I'm at Mount Mary," Margie said.

Theo brightened in surprise and seemed to look at her with new respect. "A student! How do you like it?"

Another of those questions you weren't supposed to answer honestly, she knew, but Margie considered what she would say if she could. College gave her something like freedom, though not that exactly, since Mount Mary had plenty of rules, and she took her coursework seriously enough that she never took the liberties a truly free person might—skipping class to go to the movies or out to lunch, staying in bed on a snowy morning with *Northanger Abbey*. Margie was nothing if not a dogged rule follower. Instead, what she had there, for the first time in her life, was privacy. Using her earnings from her summer job, she had paid the extra fee so she could have a single room in the dorm. That eight-by-ten cell meant the world to her because, inside with the door closed, Margie could let down the guard she kept up at all other times. She could rest.

But trying to explain that was the fastest way to make this man think she was nuts. "Mount Mary is great," Margie said. "I feel so lucky to be there."

"What are you studying?"

"Literature," Margie said. "I might get my teaching certificate. I'm still deciding."

"I loved school," Theo said, to himself as much as to her, and looked caught up in a memory. "University of Michigan."

Examining those glasses, his thinning hair, Margie wondered how long it had been since he had finished college. Could he be thirty-five? Forty? She couldn't decide if his age made him look distinguished or vulnerable, like a creature losing its protective fur. His eyes were kind, his fair skin covered in freckles the color of cinnamon. He was, actually, handsome, in a kind of funny way, despite the odd clothes. "And what do you do now?"

"I work as a statistician for the city."

Margie's face must have looked pretty blank, because he smiled.

"A number cruncher. We look at how the mayor's policies are playing out in the real world—who uses certain services and why, where a proposed budget cut might hit the hardest, things like that."

Margie tried to picture Theo approaching Mayor Daley's desk to hand him a report he would throw in the garbage. "Do they actually listen to what you tell them?"

Theo laughed, delighted. "Excellent question. No, not very often."

"I grew up in Sycamore Ridge," Margie said. "I try to come back to see my parents every few weeks. My mother doesn't like it when I stay at school through the weekend. She thinks I'm going to get into trouble. She doesn't understand how much we have to study."

Theo nodded sympathetically. "History was my subject," he said. "Kings and empires and battles. I had quite a talent for those blue-book exams, if I do say so myself. Not that they do me much good these days."

"You must have done well in math too, to be doing what you are now."

He nodded. "I thought I would use my history background more, actually, since it seemed to me that politicians might want to learn from the past. Turns out that's not the case, though. It's all about the future with those gentlemen."

Those gentlemen. He seemed not so much older than her, though of course he was, as from another time. In her years at Mount Mary, Margie had been to a few mixers at the Sigma Chi house at Marquette, and she tried to square what she had learned of those boys with what she was learning of Theo. Some of them were very handsome, yes, in particular the one who had pulled her out on the fire escape of his window and pawed her in the darkness. She had thought she wanted him to kiss her, but as soon as she felt his thumb on her nipple, her stomach dropped and her pulse began to hammer and she was back on that basement floor with Mr. Grebe holding her down. Later, after she had managed to get away from the fraternity boy and back downstairs to the party, he got so drunk that he walked around with a bra draped over his head. Not Margie's, though everyone had assumed it was. She looked now at the freckled backs of Theo's hands, his soft, almost pink scalp. She tried to imagine him doing a thing like that.

They chatted effortlessly for the rest of the journey to Milwaukee, about how the trees in Chicago were beginning to bud but Milwaukee's were still bare, about the Polish bakery on 16th Street that Theo always visited on these trips because his mother-in-law was choosy about her kolaczki, about an Italian restaurant not too far from Mount Mary that made good meatballs.

"Dante's," Theo said, snapping his fingers as he recalled the name. "Do you know it?"

Margie did. She had been there a few times when the parents of her dormmates had come to visit and rounded up as many girls as they could to give them a decent meal. She had even tried the meatballs in question, and they were every bit as good as Theo claimed. But he seemed so pleased to be able to share the recommendation; impulsively, Margie lied. "I think maybe I've heard of it?" Her voice was nearly coy as she squinted, pretending to remember. "I don't think I've ever been there."

"Ah, well," Theo said. "You'll have to try it sometime."

"I will," Margie said, feeling a little deflated that this was the end of it. They were pulling into Milwaukee's new Union Station, a vast improvement over the old crumbling one that had greeted her for her first two years. The idea that a massive stone building could be knocked down and carted away so that no trace of it remained was unsettling but thrilling too. Nothing was set in stone, not even stone itself.

With her purse on her lap, Margie pulled her overnight bag out from under the seat in front of her and balanced it on top of her penny loafers as the train entered the darkness of the tunnel. Theo stood and slipped on his coat, put the paperback in the pocket. Then he sat back down. He seemed to be trying to decide something. Margie hoped she knew what it was.

"Margie," he said, and took a business card from his wallet, "if there's ever anything you need, if you find yourself downtown or in Milwaukee, since I come so often, this is my office number. My secretary gets me my messages."

Margie took the card and slipped it into her purse. For some reason she didn't want him to see her look at it. They stood and followed the stream of passengers onto the platform and into the station. Theo offered to help her carry her bag; Margie declined.

"Is someone picking you up?"

She nodded. She would take the bus, but she thought this might sound pitiful to him.

"Well. It was a pleasure to meet you, Margie." Theo shook her hand.

Even as this encounter had taken her by pleasant surprise, she couldn't wait to escape it now. She could feel herself starting to want something, and in Margie's experience, wanting something was a bad idea. "Likewise," Margie said and headed for the door.

Back in her dorm room, she set Theo's card faceup on the back corner of her desk, where she could see it when she was working at her typewriter. THEODORE BARRETT, it said. SENIOR STATISTICIAN, CITY OF CHICAGO. Margie tried to imagine a circumstance in which she would call him, but they all seemed to start out with terrible emergencies. Getting mugged on the way to the train station. Getting lost somewhere in the city or not having enough money for the bus. She could never call him just to say hello. It would be far too forward. And anyway, what would be the point? Had he given her the card like a helpful uncle might? Or was he actually interested in her? If he was interested, he would want to get to know her better, and Margie had too many things she couldn't let anyone know. She stared at those little block letters for a week. Then she threw the card in the garbage.

20

Doreen

The previous week, the dusty register tape from A+ Hardware had not even come close to matching what the ledger said the owner had deposited in the store's account. Doreen's customers were the small business owners holding together what was left of the neighborhood she had known all her life, and she loved them. The chief way she demonstrated that love was making sure somebody wasn't screwing them out of their money. Sure enough, a late-night attempt to reconcile the numbers made it clear someone in the store was ringing up duplicate transactions, probably so he could later claim his hand had hit the button twice and pocket the extra cash. It wasn't a lot of money—$137.42—but that still didn't make it okay.

On Mondays, she delivered weekly reports to her customers, along with checks she had prepared for their vendors and employee paychecks, ready for signature. She saved A+ for last. With Summer slipping in and out of view—Doreen saw her glide down an aisle with a hundred hanging hammers on display and set them swinging with her index finger—she opened the ledger on the counter to show the owner, Glen, the discrepancies. He drew his mouth into a line and looked up at her. Summer reappeared with two paintbrushes sticking out of her hair, huge green gardening gloves on her hands.

"Go put those back!" Doreen hissed. "I'm sorry, Glen. I have to call them like I see them."

Glen nodded. Next to the key cutter was a display of light bulbs, and Doreen followed his gaze there, where Glen Jr., his younger son, stood unpacking boxes. This was the son enrolled in some kind of graduate program that was keeping him out of the army. Glen's older son, Marty, the more reliable one, who had been handling the books until last year, had been sent to Vietnam. Glen Jr. was wearing a positively gleaming pair of Beatle boots in black leather.

Glen sighed. "Thanks, sweetie. You always do such a good job. *Too* good a job."

Summer was back, with her hand in the bowl of orphaned screws and nails and hinges and bolts of various sizes that sat beside the register.

"You hear that, peanut?" Glen said to her. "Your mom is the best there is."

Summer shrugged. That everyone in the neighborhood loved her mom was old news.

They said their goodbyes, and Doreen led Summer by the hand back out onto the sidewalk. "What's on your fingers?" she said, turning over Summer's sticky palm. As she stooped to look, they kept walking, and her hip collided with a person walking the opposite way.

"I'm so sorry!" She straightened up and put her hand on the woman's slender elbow. "I should have been watching where I was going."

"No, I'm sorry," she said. "I shouldn't be in such a rush."

Doreen's eyes widened with recognition, and she felt the rush of mild panic that gripped her anytime she ran into Luisa Messina, Timothy's adoptive mother, around the neighborhood. But, of course, he wasn't Timothy. He was Nicholas, five years old now, just like Summer.

Mrs. Messina's forehead was creased with worry. Doreen had never seen her look disheveled, but she did now, the silk scarf tied over her hair slipping to reveal a crown of frizz. Of course, she still looked beautiful—natural was just another "look" she could pull off—but Doreen didn't like to see any signs of trouble around Timothy.

"Is everything okay, Luisa?"

Summer was tugging at Doreen's sleeve, looking to collect the cookie she had been promised for being good while Doreen gave Glen the bad news. Whether Summer had indeed been good was open to interpretation, and first they would have to find a place to wash the glue or caulk or whatever it was off her hands. Doreen gave her a look, and she paused her interruption.

"Well." Luisa shifted the scarf forward over her hairline. "I just got to the beauty parlor for my appointment, but there was a message waiting for me at the reception desk that Debbie—that's the babysitter; she's home with Nicholas now—has to leave because her grandmother was just taken to the hospital and—"

"Why don't I watch him for you?" Doreen said spontaneously. "Give me your key. Go back and keep your appointment, and we'll be waiting for you at home when it's over."

Luisa's eyes widened in gratitude and maybe a bit of wariness. "Are you sure? Aren't you on your way somewhere?"

Doreen shrugged and tried to seem at most indifferent to the possibility of seeing Timothy up close. The truth was that she had spent the past five years keeping an eye on him in the most inconspicuous ways she could think of—at Mass, at the playground, "bumping into" the Messinas at the market once she had aligned her shopping habits to theirs. As she had walked through the snow, away from Holy Family, she had silently promised Margie that she would watch over Timothy, and she intended to keep that promise. When they were still babies, she pushed Summer's carriage every evening past Taylor Street's open windows, homemade curtains billowing out, the shouts of kids playing baseball in the alley ringing around them and the air filled with the smell of hamburger on charcoal, to the Messinas' block on Lexington. They owned the nicest building across from the park, a two-flat with a double-wide stone porch and three containers of red geraniums on the stoop. Luisa often gardened in the little front yard after dinner while Timothy lay on a blue blanket. Doreen would walk past as slowly as she could without raising suspicion, noting that Timothy kicked his legs, that he wore a little cotton cap because he still had no hair. Sometimes Luisa waved in the casual way of neighbors who knew each other but were not particular friends. Sometimes she didn't even notice Doreen walking by.

But Doreen noticed everything, saved every detail in her mind as if she were preparing a report for Margie. In those early days, Doreen had been so consumed with Summer's care that sometimes days went by when she did not think about what she had done to Margie. Then, out of nowhere, the guilt would fill her mind like a swarm of bees, and she would be forced to recount once again the choice that she had faced in the lobby of the hospital and in those frantic hours back at Holy Family before Doreen set off walking into the snow. The truth she could not bring herself to tell Margie. Doreen knew it was her duty to watch over Timothy for the rest of her life. Margie had given her Summer. The least Doreen could do was make sure Timothy was all right.

"Well, if you're sure . . ." Luisa opened her purse and gave Doreen her house keys, on a heavy gold ring with a monogrammed charm.

"Of course. Don't miss your appointment. Getting my hair set is the best part of my week." That was a lie, since Doreen could only afford to go once a month, and even then often canceled at the last minute and put the money in the jar on the top shelf of the closet. Instead, she and Carla took turns doing each other's hair on Friday nights.

"Thanks again—you're a lifesaver!" Luisa called as she hurried back the way she had come.

Doreen turned to Summer. "I have a treat that's better than a cookie. We're going over to Nicholas's house to play."

Summer put her hand on her hip and turned her dark eyes on her mother in disapproval. "That is not better than a cookie."

Doreen pulled her along to Lytle Street. "Okay, fine. You've got two cookies coming to you if you can help me out here. Be sweet, okay?"

Summer's expression the entire walk there could only be described as sour, but when Doreen put the key into the handsome oak door, she brightened. "This place is *nice*." They had never been inside before.

"Manners," Doreen whispered.

Poor Debbie was out the door in a flash. Things did not look good for her grandmother. So, within seconds of stepping into the Messinas' front room, she was alone with the kids.

"Summer," Doreen said, compelled by a strong force to touch her daughter's shoulder at this moment, "you remember Nicholas. He is five, just like you. And his birthday is in April, just like yours." Summer raised her eyebrows, impressed. It wasn't everyone who was worthy of being born in the best month of the year. April belonged to her.

Nicholas stopped in the middle of a complicated Lincoln Logs construction project and looked at Summer. "You can help me with this if you want." He handed her one of the flat green pieces, and they entered into a relaxed, wordless collaboration. Meanwhile, Doreen sat on the edge of the sofa, feeling like the ends of her hair were on fire. This was the closest she had ever been to him.

Timothy had fine, sandy hair that was parted and combed into place just so, and dark brown eyes rimmed with the kind of lashes they put on the girl mice in Disney cartoons. Luisa had dressed him like an English country gentleman, tweed slacks and a starched white shirt with a forest-green sweater vest. Margie would have approved of this prim aesthetic: Timothy would not have been out of place at the Sycamore Ridge Country Club. *Poor kid*, Doreen thought. At least Luisa had let him roll the cuffs up to the elbows. When Doreen's gaze trailed down to his hands, her breath caught for a moment. There was something about seeing his fingers when Margie had never seen them, delicate and so capable with his familiar toys. It just made her ache.

She looked again at Timothy's hair and coloring, wondering whether he took after Margie or that son of a bitch who had attacked her. The Messinas both had very dark hair and rich complexions, with dark eyebrows that dominated Art's face and that Luisa surely spent good money sculpting into the elegant arches that framed her eyes. Timothy didn't look like them, of course, but he wasn't different enough from them, at least as a little boy, to prompt any questions from strangers.

When Luisa took him with her to Field's, no one at the beauty counter would even think to ask whether he was actually hers. What a crock of shit. Almost every day, some nosy woman took a long look at Summer and asked Doreen that, usually with a kind of dread in her voice. "She's *your* daughter?"

As if on cue, Timothy looked up from the chimney and asked, with genuine curiosity and not a hint of meanness, "Why is your hair like that?"

"Like what?" Summer said. She had found a pad of paper and a red marker on the coffee table and was drawing a blob that Doreen knew she would tell her was a cat. Summer desperately wanted a cat.

"Like cotton candy, all up in a ball."

Doreen cringed.

"It's not a ball," Summer said, irritated. But then she changed course and explained gently, as if to a simpleton, "That's how God made me. And he made you like you are too. That's why your chin is like that. Nobody can know what God is thinking. It's a secret."

Timothy's eyebrows went up at this, perhaps some new information for him to absorb. Doreen stifled a laugh. He did have a slightly weak chin, too small for his face.

"God is really old," Timothy said.

"Older than my nonni," Summer agreed.

"God made a flood. That's how we got all the animals."

Summer knew about this too. "Especially cats. They are the best kind of animal."

They played for a while longer, and then Timothy asked for a snack. Doreen went into the kitchen, trying not to die of jealousy over its gleaming tabletop range and built-in ovens, the big double sink. She pulled a bag of celery from Luisa's sparkling refrigerator and cut a few stalks, filled the boats with peanut butter and dotted them with raisins.

"Nicholas, have you ever had ants on a log?" Doreen brought the plate into the front room and set it on the coffee table.

"Ants to *eat*?" he asked, horrified.

"It's a snack," Summer said. "The celery is the log, and the raisins are the ants." She munched on a piece, her desperation for a cookie now forgotten.

Timothy examined one of the ants with his pinky finger. "What's the peanut butter?"

"Oh, that's just to get the ants to stick," Doreen said.

Summer shook her head. "Mommy, that's the mud. Logs have mud on them."

"Oh," Doreen said. "Well, that makes sense." She thought she could sit and listen to these two talk all day long. Part of her was itching to go down the long, pointless road of regret—Margie would never get to listen in on a conversation like this. She would never know that her boy bit down on the side of his bottom lip when he was concentrating, that his most treasured possession was a book about sharks that he showed them with the reverence of a monk unfurling an ancient scroll—it was impossible not to wallow in all that Margie had lost. *Because of me*, Doreen reminded herself. But she couldn't change it. She couldn't go back.

A while later, she heard the front door creak open, and there was Luisa, restored to her usual glamour. "Well," she said, hanging her purse and jacket in the front closet, "how did it go?"

Doreen stood up from the sofa, afraid Luisa would be put off to find her so comfortable. "Oh, fine," she said and picked up the empty plate. "They've been playing very nicely this whole time. I made them a snack—I hope that's okay."

"Of course." Luisa stood watching the children for a moment. "Summer always looks *so* pretty," Luisa said.

Doreen grinned faintly and felt her reliable paranoia—or was it just an ability to size things up?—wash over her. Luisa had never once mentioned Summer's race, but there were a thousand subtle ways to imply that Summer was working with a deficit, that she was a child to be pitied instead of admired or even just plain liked. Wasn't it a pleasant surprise, Luisa seemed to be saying, that a girl like Summer could look so pretty? Doreen knew she wouldn't be able to shield her daughter from these casual dismissals much longer, if she had even succeeded in doing it so far. She would have cut off her arm if it would make the world treat Summer the way she deserved.

Or maybe Luisa was just trying to be nice. She turned to Doreen suddenly and smiled. "I usually have a glass of wine in the afternoon. Would you like one?"

"Sure," Doreen said, and then felt guilty for having assumed the worst about the woman's inner monologue. They went into the kitchen and sat at the laminate bar, Doreen on the end and Luisa to her right side, with a bottle of valpolicella between them. It was quiet for a long moment. Maybe too long, or maybe they were both just tired.

"Are you still writing songs?" Luisa finally asked.

Doreen looked up in surprise. "Oh. No. Not really. Well, a little." She shrugged, trying to show it didn't mean that much to her, even though the mention of it brought a pang of sadness. "It's hard to make space for it."

"Oh, that's a shame. I remember Artie saying how talented you were, going on auditions, talking about making a record."

"Well, that's behind me now. My days are for Summer, and in the evenings, I do my bookkeeping work. Payroll waits for no man," Doreen said as lightly as she could manage. It had taken her five years, but she had nearly paid down the bill from Holy Family. And she had Summer. "Things change."

"That's for sure," Luisa said. She had already drained her first glass of wine and was pouring a second. "To tell you the truth, it's a lot harder than I thought it would be."

Doreen absorbed this surprising moment of candor.

"I mean, he's an angel. He's the answer to years of prayers."

"Of course he is," Doreen said.

"And Artie is an absolute born father. He just adores every part of it."

"Well," Doreen said gently, "I have a feeling *you* are the one in the trenches most of the time."

Luisa laughed at this. "Imagine if men had an inkling of the work—the toilet training and accidents, the tantrums in the grocery store. Getting up in the night with them endlessly."

"They'd run screaming on the first day," Doreen said.

Luisa's face changed, and she put her hand on Doreen's elbow. "I'm sorry—that was so insensitive of me. I am blessed to have Artie. It must be so hard for you . . . on your own." She was too polite to probe about why that was.

Doreen shrugged. That was how you survived a light conversation about the hardest thing that had ever happened to you. "Well, you know I live with my mother. I couldn't do it without her help, but I honestly don't know how much a man could really bring to the table. My brother, Danny, is a man—he lives with us too—and his main contribution is more dirty laundry."

Luisa laughed, and so what she said next caught Doreen off guard. "When you found out you were expecting, did you ever think about giving"—but then she held up her hand and shook her head—"actually, never mind. That's none of my business. I'm sorry. It's just . . . as hard as this is, sometimes I think about the girl who gave birth to Nicholas and wonder, how could she? How could she *give* up her own baby? I think there must be something truly wrong with a girl who would do that, you know?"

It was suddenly very hot in the kitchen. Doreen blinked hard to stop herself from telling Luisa that she didn't know what the hell she was talking about. If Margie had known where Timothy was, would she have fought harder to get him back? Margie hadn't given him up. Rather, Doreen had helped preserve the lie that he was gone forever.

Choosing her words carefully, Doreen said, "I actually do know someone who went through it. It's hard to explain, but she really did love her baby. Sometimes . . . sometimes a choice isn't really a choice." The entire process of the Holy Family adoptions was arranged so that the new parents never saw, or even thought to ask about, the experience of the girl with the womb. The man and woman who adopted the baby needed to believe not only that the girl had not suffered but that she had been indifferent, callous and selfish and damaged, because that made the act of taking the baby heroic. They had *saved* him from a bad life. They *deserved* to have him more than she did, and so they were not responsible for what happened to her. They owed her nothing.

But what would the Messinas think if they knew Margie had been intimidated and coerced by the bullies at the home and in the hospital? That it hadn't really been a choice, because how could someone with no power and no money and no freedom at all be said to have *chosen* a thing? The fact that Timothy was better off with the Messinas because they were married and had a nice house didn't erase what Margie had been through.

Luisa shook her head. "I guess so. She was probably very young. Still, it's just so hard to imagine how she could give him up."

You've got that right, Doreen wanted to say. *You cannot possibly imagine.* And then she asked a question that scared her. "Will you tell Nicholas about her?"

Luisa nodded. "We've talked about it, and yes. We don't want to lie to him. It's not 1935, you know? People are so much more open about adoption now." Her eyes were wet, and she touched the corners with her manicured ring fingers. "I don't plan to give him many details, but I want him to know he was chosen, that we wanted him so much."

"I think that's wonderful. He deserves to know about that love." Doreen swallowed the last sip of her wine, took a breath. "When you tell him . . . promise me you won't say that she gave him up. That really isn't—it's so much more complicated than that. He should know she loved him just as much as you do."

"But if that's true, then how could she—"

"Just trust me on this, okay? It doesn't have to be you against her." Doreen knew she had let too much emotion creep into her voice. She tried to shake it off. What had happened with Margie was awful, but what good would it have done, really, for Doreen to tell her she knew where Timothy was going? Margie had already been through so much—raped by that man, giving birth alone. This would be one more heartbreak.

Luisa was looking at her a little strangely, with suspicion, as if Doreen had somehow tricked her into sharing all this information, instead of the truth: that Luisa had brought it all up because she was lonely and desperately needed someone to talk to. Someone to tell her it was all right to feel that motherhood had not turned out the way she expected.

"Nicholas is a great kid," Doreen said, finding her easy smile once more. "And he is very lucky to have the both of you as parents."

Luisa rested her chin on her laced fingers. "I will always be grateful to that girl, wherever she is now. I hope she doesn't torture herself over what she did."

21

Margie

Margie stared at the paper curling out of the top of her typewriter. She had written what she thought was a perfectly serviceable introduction to the term paper she was calling "Fieldmouse Theology: Exaltations and Omissions in 'The Windhover,'" and beside her was an outline for the rest that she had written out the night before after turning down an invitation from some girls on her hall to go out for pizza. It had all made so much sense as she was sketching out her main points, but now every sentence she typed felt forced, and she knew she was taking at least one of the quotes from the poem, on which her argument rested, slightly out of context. Her thesis was weaker than she had thought.

She let her eyes roam from the paper to her twin bed, neatly made with a log cabin quilt, the small armchair, and the braided rug she had found in a thrift store. The nightstand was stacked with books, as was the floor around the nightstand and the small table beside the door, their spines more colorful than the quilt's patchwork. The books seemed to reproduce while she was sleeping. The clutter was becoming a bit of a problem—Margie knew it would drive Verna crazy. Which was maybe why she let the books spread like mushrooms on a forest floor and happily stepped around them.

A muffled sound followed by a yelp came from the window, and Margie left her typewriter to see what it was. On the quad, some Mount Mary girls, Shawna and Bette, and a few guys Margie recognized as their boyfriends, were sitting on a blanket eating sandwiches. The day had suddenly turned warm, Wisconsin's short-lived spring arriving at last, and people were flocking to the first weak patches of sunlight. The yelping was coming from two girls roller-skating down one end of the long circle drive, a steep hill to take on wheels, screaming in alternating terror and delight.

The paper could wait. Margie slipped on her loafers and a light wool jacket, knowing the wind off the lake could still cut through you into May, and grabbed her purse and notebook of letters for Timothy on her way out the door.

Margie wasn't friendless. Just last evening she had been sitting on the floor of Shawna's room while Bette sorted through records and Shawna flipped through an issue of *Cosmopolitan* on the bed behind Margie. "Have you heard about the Cucumber Diet?" she had asked Margie. "You skip breakfast every other day, and there's no fruit, no cheese, no bread. You can have chicken, but no sauce. But with cucumbers, you can have as much as you want." Shawna had leaned forward to touch Margie's shoulder for emphasis. "As *much* as you want." Margie had laughed, but she tried to imagine what it would feel like to have as much as she wanted of anything.

Margie waved and called to the girls that she would be back later. Right now she craved the relief of going from being alone in her room to being alone in public, basking in the restful company of strangers who wouldn't notice her at all. The used bookstore was the perfect place for wandering, and she could be sure anyone she encountered in its nooks and crannies was just as eager as she was to be left alone.

Most people, it seemed, had chosen to take care of errands on foot today to enjoy the fair weather, so the bus wasn't very crowded. In her seat about halfway back, Margie grasped the clips and slid the window down to let in the wonderful warm air. An older woman across the aisle nodded appreciatively. Then Margie pulled the pen and black-and-white notebook from her purse.

Though the outside was identical to her school notebooks, Margie guarded this one with her life. But anyone who found it probably wouldn't be able to make much sense of it. In the beginning, she had planned to write real letters to Timothy in here that she might someday type and send, but as with anything she tried to write these days, whether for a class or for herself, her words seemed to have a mind of their own, to land strangely on the page. She couldn't express anything straightforwardly.

Dear Timothy, she wrote now. *You are 1,833 days old today. I wonder if the people who are with you all the time have told you that springtime smells different from winter. I don't mean flowers, and we don't have those yet anyway, but the dirt itself, if you can get near enough to it to scrape away the frosty top layer with a stick. Creeping things reanimate, unlatch the hatching new, new, new made out of the dead.*

What in the hell was that?

At the next stop, a woman in a red coat stepped on, and when she turned to walk up the aisle, Margie saw that she was carrying a little girl who wore a corduroy jumper and a yellow jacket with a matching yellow hat. A pink terrycloth bunny that had seen better days drooped in the girl's hand, and she continued to clutch it as her mother took a seat nearby and settled the girl on her lap. With her chubby hand, she pulled off the hat to reveal a swirl of strawberry-blond hair like frosting on the top of her head and examined the hat in her hands, her glistening lower lip curled down in concentration.

Even though Margie turned away as fast as she could, there was no avoiding the surge of anguish. Flustered, she slapped the notebook closed and pulled the cord to request a stop, though she was still blocks short of the stop closest to the store. She would walk ten extra miles if it got her some distance just now. On the sidewalk, she took a few deep breaths and waited for her ruffled nerves to subside. It was just a baby, not a nuclear bomb. The world was full of them, more than she had ever noticed in her younger years, and it was plain silly that her body still had this reaction every time she saw one. *Walk*, she commanded her legs, and as always, moving eventually helped pull her mind out of its spin.

She found plenty to distract her in the bookstore and then crossed the street to the diner and ate a grilled cheese at the counter. It was time to get back to her paper, she knew, but instead she wandered a bit more. When she eventually circled back around the block to the nearest bus stop, she saw a sign on the door of an office she had never noticed before: GEORGE D. MICHELSON, FAMILY LAW.

The words jolted her to attention. The letter from the archdiocese said that the records were sealed according to Illinois state law. Did that mean she could explain her situation—that she didn't intend to contact Timothy or disturb his parents in any way, but that she just wanted to know if he was all right—to a judge to see if he might be able to do something? To talk to a judge, she knew, she would need a lawyer. Why hadn't she thought sooner that someone like him might be able to help?

The bell on the glass door tinkled when she stepped inside the small office. To her left were three chrome chairs with vinyl cushions, striped with sunlight from the partially closed blinds, and a coffee table with a neat fan of magazines: *Car and Driver* beside *Good Housekeeping*. Mr. Michelson was covering all the bases. Framed on the wall above the chairs was a line of awards: Top Verdict in Milwaukee County, 1962. Top Settlement in Milwaukee County, 1965. Recognition by the Wisconsin Trial Lawyers Society for "zealous advocacy of the needs of families."

The typewriter on the receptionist's desk had its cover on, and Margie was just about to conclude that the office was empty when a male voice called from behind a partially open door behind the waiting area. The door swung open to reveal a man with carefully parted and combed hair in shirtsleeves and a tie with half a turkey sandwich in his hand.

"Hi there," he said and waved her in his direction. "Carol went home sick, so the only welcoming committee you've got is me, I'm afraid." Margie followed him into his office and took the chair he offered that sat across from his desk. "Excuse the mess. And the sandwich." He folded it up in waxed paper and wiped a smear of mustard from his cheek. "How can I help you?"

Margie swallowed and felt her heart begin to race. She hadn't really thought about how it would feel to have to tell her story to a stranger. "Well . . ." She stalled.

"Listen, I don't know if it will make you feel any better, but I've heard just about every story you can think of—affairs, cross-dressing, disinterest in the bedroom, falsified life insurance, wife beating—husband beating!—I mean, you name it. So there's no need to be embarrassed, whatever it is. You are a bit younger than my typical client, but it seems like you kids are living a coupla lifetimes before you turn thirty these days."

Margie gave him a weak smile. "I'm actually here about a child. My child."

Michelson nodded, unruffled. "Okay, we're talking about a custody situation, then."

"Well, not exactly."

"Why don't you close the door?" When Margie did, he said, "Maybe you know this or maybe you don't, but anything you say to me in here, I can't tell anyone. Even if I don't become your lawyer. Okay?"

Margie nodded and threaded her fingers together in her lap. "A few years ago—five, actually—I had a baby at a maternity home downstate. I didn't want to go there, but my parents made me, and I didn't want to give up my baby, but the people there took him anyway while I was still under twilight sleep, and I never saw him again. I've been trying to access the file, but they won't tell me anything."

Mr. Michelson nodded. "Well, first I'll say that I don't do much work with adoptions. I'm mostly a divorce attorney, as you probably guessed from my list of greatest hits. But I do know that the state seals records to protect the privacy of the child and adoptive parents." His voice grew gentler as he said, "I guess the thinking there is it's best for everybody to make a clean break."

"I understand that, but they must have broken the law. You can't just take a woman's baby from her."

"Well, you weren't a woman at the time, correct?"

Margie shrugged.

"In cases like these, there are always two questions: whether the other side broke the law and then whether the injured party could actually win in court." The lawyer sat back in his chair. "They would put you through a lot, I think, because for better or worse, a judge's sympathy will be with the married couple who is raising the baby. He will want to know if you have a job or the financial support of your parents, whether the father is involved and what he might say if called to speak. The judge will say that the child is five years old now. What good would it do to tear him from his parents at this late stage, when you are a stranger—"

"Oh, I don't intend to do that. I wouldn't contact them." Margie took a breath to steady her voice and banish the thought of Mr. Grebe having any say in this at all, banish the word *stranger.* "In all my requests to the home by phone and letter, I've made that very clear. I just want to know if he is all right. Just some kind of confirmation. I don't even know for sure that someone *did* adopt him. You have no idea the possibilities that go through my mind."

Mr. Michelson opened his hands, and the gentle voice was back, to Margie's dread. "It sounds terrible. But you can see, can't you, how they really can't open the door to that at all? Even if you would respect the boundary, and I'm sure you would, some other girl out there might take advantage of the access and make life hell for the adoptive parents. They can't risk that, so the rule has to be the same for everyone."

"I just don't want to give up," she said, and a tsunami of tears were behind that sentence, but she did not let them fall.

"I wouldn't be a very good lawyer if, when there was so little chance of winning, I let a client put herself through all that."

Margie shook her head. "But that's the thing. I don't care about what happens to me at all."

Mr. Michelson sighed through his nose, and there was a finality to it. "Miss, that's such a sad thing to hear you say."

"So you won't help me?"

"How about this: Let me take down some information—your name, the name of the home, the date of birth. I will see if I can find anything out. But I don't want you to get your hopes up."

Margie wrote out everything she could think of that he might need to know. Then she stood to go. "Well, thank you for your time."

When she was at the door, he said, "You are a young woman with your whole life ahead of you. In time, maybe, it will get easier and you will be able to move on."

She smiled politely. Since no one was going to reassure her, she might at least be able to reassure him so that he could get back to his sandwich in peace. What he didn't understand, she thought as she crossed the street to the bus stop, and what she knew in her bones to be true, was that time meant nothing. She felt exactly the same about them taking Timothy away as she had felt five years ago on the day he was born, and she would feel this way when she was eighty years old, on her last day on the planet. Someone took her baby away, and she hadn't fought hard enough to stop them. That truth would never soften. Perhaps, if she had been given enough time to hold him, to come out of the anesthesia, she would have concluded that the best thing for Timothy was to be raised by someone else. She wasn't stupid, even then, as a teenager. She would have seen that she couldn't keep him, and she would have said goodbye. But what they did to her at the hospital was as bad as what Mr. Grebe had done as he gripped the back of her neck and moved over her on the cold basement floor—they decided for her what would happen to her. They knew what they wanted, and they forced her to give it to them.

22

Doreen

Saturday was cleaning day at the Coniglios, and woe unto any woman who had other plans for how to spend her day. (Danny, of course, was sleeping in.) Carla wore a scarf over her hair and the pink zip-up apron that predated D-Day, and the last thing she would do before she went to bed was wash it and hang it on the line in the scrubby yard behind their two-flat, where it would wave like a victory flag.

"Oh, these are filthy!" she said as she wiped the front room windows with newspaper dipped in vinegar. She said this about every object of her attention as she cleaned, and it was never actually true. Nothing would be so audacious as to get dirty in Carla's home.

Doreen had just finished her duties in the kitchen, and when she'd set the last pan from breakfast on the drainboard, she wiped her hands and sat down at the piano to play one of the exercises Vincenzo had taught her long ago to develop her dexterity. He would play it, and then little Doreen would follow, though her fingers inevitably would get tangled as she tried to keep up with him.

Carla twisted the cap on the bottle of vinegar and took up her feather duster. She always began with the framed pictures on the walls, then turned to the lampshades before she ran the soft feathers over every piece of wood furniture. Nearing Doreen's side of the room, she said, "That's pretty."

Doreen could hear the caution in her voice. Carla didn't want to spook her. Within the last year, Doreen had finally started playing again, but she usually just goofed around with "Old McDonald" and "Itsy Bitsy Spider" for Summer, adding some improvised harmonies and exaggerated flourishes, anything to get a laugh. Summer was fascinated by the sound that came out of that old upright and loved to sit beside her mom as she played. Maybe she could sense what a hold the instrument had over Doreen, as much when she *wasn't* playing as when she was. Doreen had loved the piano all her life; now she hated it too. It reminded her of everything she had once wanted. Still wanted, shouldn't want, couldn't want, wouldn't have.

But she wasn't thinking those dreary thoughts at the moment. Instead, she began to play "Ave Maria," and though she had her back to her mother, she could sense Carla's delight in not having had to ask for it. Doreen sang out slowly in her lusty alto. *Ave Maria, gratia plena . . .* Summer, who had been drawing with crayons on the floor in their bedroom, came running out at the sound of her singing. This, that Summer might feel a little of what she felt for music, that she was compelled to come running toward the sound of her mom's voice, gave Doreen a burst of pride. Pride was an awfully rare feeling in these days of putting one foot in front of the other.

Carla came near and moved a stack of ledgers and Doreen's adding machine off the top of the piano. She whisked her duster across the framed portrait of Vincenzo that watched over his daughter's playing. As she sang, Doreen thought again of the two of them playing together, of the nights he would play down at Pepper's Cafe to make some extra money. In the morning, while he sipped coffee at the kitchen table, he would let Doreen count it, stacking the bills and coins into neat piles.

When the song was finished, Carla said, "I know what I want for my birthday."

Doreen laughed. "Is that right? I've got to tell you—the budget is somewhat limited."

Carla was on the other side of the doorframe in the dining room now, crouched to attack the slats on the ladder-back chair. "Well, that's fine because this gift doesn't cost a thing. I want you to write me a song." When Doreen laughed again, Carla straightened up and looked at her. "I'm serious."

"Come on, Ma," Doreen said. Beside her on the bench, Summer banged on the keys.

"You don't remember how you used to write songs for all of us? There was that one about Danny's smelly socks. And then when we got the new car and you wrote a jingle for it? Like that, but serious. A serious, real song. That's what I want."

"Too bad I'm retired." Doreen gently lifted Summer's finger to help her plunk out the happy birthday song. She couldn't help but think that Carla knew exactly what she was doing. Every time Doreen touched the piano, the longing to fall in with music and writing again welled up in her. Carla had to know that too. Mothers always knew. It was so very annoying. Doreen didn't know if she could stand to let herself care about music again now that her life was so different and so much of what she had imagined for herself was impossible. "I haven't even bought a new record in years." A slight exaggeration, but not by much.

"Well, why don't you go buy one, then?" Carla said, as if it were that easy, as if a person could abandon her dearest held dream for five years and then one day pull it out of the trash and start admiring it again. She took her purse out of the front closet and handed Doreen ten dollars.

"Are you nuts? I can't spend money on records."

"Of course you can. Go see what's new. Come on," she said with a grin.

"Right now?"

"Yes. I'm sick of the sight of you."

"But we're not done cleaning."

"Summer and I can take care of it. Can't we, hon?"

Summer nodded. She was still wearing the ankle-length flannel she called her princess nightgown. "Mommy, isn't that your mommy?"

"Yep."

"Aren't you always supposed to do what your mommy says?"

Doreen narrowed her eyes in suspicion. "Why are you being so nice?"

"It's not nice," Carla said, turning back to her dusting. "I told you, I'm sick of the sight of you. You'd better go before I change my mind."

Doreen shook her head in wonder. "Well, all right."

Doreen changed into a sharp green minidress she had dug out of a bin at a rummage sale and put on eyeliner. Then she took the bus to Sound Town Records on Illinois Avenue, just north of the river off Wabash, trying to remember the last time she had been out of the neighborhood. When the bell on the door jangled, Doreen felt a pang of recognition. A few years ago—a lifetime ago—Sound Town had been her favorite place in the world. It wasn't just the sense of possibility lingering in the smell of cellophane—some new song she might discover, the first out of all her friends to hear it—it was the feeling that, someday, she was going to make a record that would be filed in these bins alongside all the others. Of course, this was preposterously unlikely, especially now, and yet for years Doreen had been dogged by the premonition. She could picture the sleeve with her name on it. *Doreen Coniglio.* Or maybe she would have to change it to a stage name. *Doreen Connie. Doreen Marie,* her middle name. Her songs would be on every radio in America. If she had tried to explain this certainty she felt to anyone, they would have thought she was expressing a wish, a pipe dream. But the knowledge was much more solid than that. It felt like something foretold.

"Am I seeing a ghost?"

Doreen turned to the counter to see Lew, the owner, who had to be in his early thirties now but was still wearing his signature black-rimmed glasses, a rumpled white shirt with the sleeves rolled up. He was one of those guys who in high school had probably seemed older than all his friends. His true age had finally caught up with him. He had a little less hair now, but the smile, the steady way he stood inside his own shoes, was still the same.

She smiled. "Boo."

"Where in the hell have you been hiding? I haven't seen you for ages."

"I was away for a while, but I guess I'm back now."

"College?"

"Something like that." Doreen had to admit it gave her a thrill to leave Summer out of this, to pretend for a moment that she was her same old unencumbered self.

"Well, take a look around," Lew said. "You've got some catching up to do."

When Doreen had come in as a teenager, Lew had always been so kind to her—and never in a creepy way. He answered all her questions and let her listen for a long time to anything she was thinking about buying. She cringed thinking about it now, but she had even played some of her songs for him on the piano in the back of the store. He had encouraged her to keep writing.

Doreen walked the aisles lined with wooden crates and the hand-lettered signs that listed price and genre. There were nicer places to go, shops that didn't smell like day-old French fries and mildew, that didn't have water spots on the tiles of the drop ceiling. You could buy top-forty records at Sears now. But Lew always seemed to have the things you couldn't get anywhere else. And anywhere else, you couldn't get Lew.

Doreen picked up Simon and Garfunkel's *Sounds of Silence* and held it under her elbow while she flipped through the nearby bins. She still loved the girl groups like the Shirelles, the Chiffons, Diana Ross and her Supremes. But lately she was starting to get into John Phillips too, and Dusty Springfield, because they wrote their own material. She couldn't get very excited about singing someone else's songs. Singing her own was a different story.

She picked up "Have I the Right" by the Honeycombs. In the picture, the men wore dark suits and skinny black ties and crowded around a girl playing the drums. A girl drummer! She had short hair teased up high and flipping out behind her ears, and she was wearing her own suit, just like the boys in the band had. Behind Doreen, the door to the office opened and a guy she had never seen before came out. He looked a little like Lew, with the same strong jawline and dark eyebrows, but without the glasses, younger, better looking.

"How's it going?" he said, turning sideways to move past her in the aisle. Her hip bone brushed his jeans. He stopped to look down at the Honeycombs record in her hand. "Oh, you don't want that. That's garbage."

Doreen raised an eyebrow. She had picked the record up somewhat randomly and hadn't really been thinking of buying it, but now she felt the need to defend it. "They might be a one-hit wonder, but I wouldn't call this garbage."

"I'm just saying. A girl drummer—it's a gimmick. You could do better." The way he stood, with his arms crossed and his overgrown hair falling in his eyes, a lopsided smile, made her wonder whether they were still talking about records. "Come on. I'll show you."

Two bins away, he plucked out a record and handed it to her. "You know about this, right? Unless you've been living under a rock." It was *Aftermath* by the Rolling Stones. "Do you like 'Paint It Black'?"

Doreen *had* been living under a rock, it turned out: a boulder in the shape of motherhood. She had bought the latest from the Beatles—Summer loved to shout the heys on "You've Got to Hide Your Love Away"—but that was all the keeping up she had been able to manage. As for the Stones, she didn't really know much about them. A couple years ago, she and Carla had watched Dean Martin mock them mercilessly on *The Hollywood Palace*, but she wasn't about to mention that for fear she would sound as old as her mother.

Next he pulled out another record by a band called Neptune Avenue. "These guys are just all right, but look." He stood close to her and flipped the record over to point at a name on the back of the sleeve, and she could smell the toasted scent of his cigarettes. "That's my buddy Jimmy. He played bass on this album."

Now he had her attention. "Really?"

"Do you play?"

"Piano. What I really like to do, though, is write songs. But, I mean, not like this." She felt suddenly flustered. Why had she said that? "It's not serious or anything. I do it just for fun."

He looked at her. "Is there any other reason to do it?" His eyes were brown, framed by dark brows. "I'd like to hear those songs. What's your name?"

Doreen thanked the Lord above that she had changed into the minidress instead of wearing the old brown flowered one she usually kept on all weekend. "Doreen. You're Lew's brother, aren't you?"

"Cal," he said, and he ran his hand down the back of his hair. Doreen wondered if he did that every time he said his name, like he was posing for a catalog ad and was contractually obligated to make the gesture. "First time in the store?" he asked.

She laughed. "Oh no. I used to come in here all the time a few years ago. But I never saw you here."

"I was probably off on my ill-fated attempt at college. I didn't read the fine print. Turns out you actually have to go to class or they won't let you stay."

He had a vertical line of consternation on his brow, and Doreen couldn't tell if it meant he was a deep thinker or just confused. And then there was that wry smile again. She could see what he was trying to do to her while at the same time acknowledging that it was working pretty well. She felt a thrill whisking through her chest, lighting up cells that had been knocked unconscious for more than five years. She tried to slow down her brain. "How did your friend get on the record?"

"What? Oh, Jimmy. Yeah, it's funny. The band was coming through Chicago, actually, for a show, and their regular bass player got the flu. Couldn't even get out of bed. They knew Lew through a friend of a friend and came in here looking for a backup. I just happened to be there that day and told them about Jimmy. He helped them out that night, and six months later when their guy quit, they called him up."

"Just like that," Doreen said.

"Just like that, the bastard. Left his own band high and dry. We're called the Suspects. Speaking of which . . ." Cal looked at his watch. "I've got to go. We're meeting downstairs in a few minutes for rehearsal. You know, Lew's got a studio down there now. He said if we can get our material together, he might help us record something."

Doreen nodded, though she hadn't known about the new studio. Cal started walking backward down the aisle.

"If you don't have somewhere to be, you should come too, check out our music. Maybe I'll see you down there?"

Doreen grinned, shrugged. Tried not to laugh. She had somewhere to be every minute for the next thirteen years at least. Carla had given her a long leash this afternoon, but her generosity would run out by the time Summer had her first tantrum of the day. Lately Summer had been melting down when it was time to leave the playground or the library, just losing it completely, speaking in tongues, throwing woodchips or books or whatever was at hand. Doreen tried to imagine explaining Summer to Cal. She was nearly in kindergarten now and smart as hell but . . . also kind of like a caged animal? A little professor who sank to the ground, as if drunk, and wailed when you dared to ask her to pick up her dolls. On the other hand, she made Doreen valentines any old time, even in May, even in October. Her plump little lips, in sleep, were a marvel of creation. Doreen felt so grateful she had lied by omission to Lew when she first arrived. Now she didn't even have to try to explain.

When Cal got halfway to the door, he turned around again. "You should come. I play better when there's a cute girl watching."

It turned out that was all it took: he had called her cute. Doreen would have followed him off a cliff now, skipping the whole way. She took her time picking out a few more singles to go with the Simon and Garfunkel: "Good Lovin'," "Monday, Monday," and "You Can't Hurry Love," though she hesitated for a moment over whether to take it. She wondered whether Cal thought the Supremes were already stale. Then she was mad at herself for caring what he thought.

She didn't want to seem too eager to get down to the basement. But ten minutes later she was in a chair and tugging at her too-short hem while she watched the Suspects tune their guitars.

"Boys, this is Doreen," Cal said to the other three: Earl, with the big front teeth, was the new bass player. Charlie was on drums with a cigarette hanging out of his mouth that dropped ash into his lap in time with the beat. Norman played keyboard and the harmonica suspended in front of his lips on a rack. They all had the same mop-top haircut, so it was hard to tell them apart. When they smiled and muttered that it was nice to meet her, Earl offered her a swig of the bottle of Jim Beam they were passing around, and she took it gratefully, hoping it might calm her nerves. Cal played electric and sang lead, of course, and she was trying not to look at him.

Later, when she broke the spell of his gaze and was able to think straight again, Doreen would realize that, objectively, the Suspects were not very good. Sexy, but not very good. They were going for something edgy like the Kinks, but Cal didn't really have the voice to carry the song they were working on, which was about a broken date and structured on power chords that built to a raspy vocal peak. Every time they got to the guitar solo, they decided to take a break to smoke or drink or piss or adjust something with their amps, so the hour-long practice session yielded about twenty minutes of actual playing time, and they never played the song all the way through.

But it almost didn't matter that they weren't very good. Doreen was enthralled, and not just by the sweat around Cal's temples or the way his forearm flexed against the body of the guitar. These guys had ballsy confidence that was infectious. They had no doubt that they could be a band, that they could play their instruments or fake it well enough. They weren't talking about it or wishing someone would notice them and invite them to try. They were just doing it. Doreen wanted to get at that certainty. She wanted to touch it with her fingertips.

When they wrapped, the rest of the guys went upstairs to look at records, and Cal walked over to Doreen with his hand in the pocket of his jeans. Most people would have asked, *So, what did you think?* but Cal didn't. Either he didn't care or he assumed he already knew. His swagger almost made Doreen giggle, but she couldn't deny its effect. Her cheeks were flushed pink; somehow she had ended up holding the bottle of whiskey for the second half of the rehearsal. She stood up, a little wobbly, and handed it to him.

"Thanks for coming," Cal said and took a swig. He wiped his mouth with the back of his hand.

"Thanks for the invitation," she said.

He moved in close, almost like he was going to kiss her, but stopped short and said, "Can I call you?"

Doreen's knees went loose like a couple of new guitar strings yet to be tightened. His cleft chin was about three inches from her mouth, and she had the urge to bite it softly with her teeth. That was how she realized she was a little drunk. "Sure," she whispered. He found a scrap of paper and a pen on the top of the piano, and she wrote down her number, even as she imagined Carla answering the phone, Danny, maybe even Summer herself: "Coniglio residence. Summer Coniglio speaking," in her tiny Minnie Mouse voice.

Doreen sighed, and the weariness of the whole world was in it. "I've got to get going," she said.

23

Margie

Margie was thinking about the moon as she moved through the crowded arrivals area of the Milwaukee train station, blue light against black trees outside a kitchen window described in the poem she had been reading, so the chatter and jostling of her fellow travelers barely registered in the cool remove of her mind. When the man bent over the drinking fountain stood up and wiped his upper lip with the back of his hand, the first thing Margie thought about him was that his arms at his side looked nothing like the gnarled limbs of a yew tree. Then she came to her senses and realized the man was Theo.

"Mr. Barrett, hello."

He smiled broadly. In his hat was a pheasant's feather, slightly theatrical for Milwaukee, she thought, and yet she liked it. "Margie, please call me Theo."

"I didn't see you on the train."

"I actually saw you when I got on, but I hated to bother you. You seemed to be so engrossed in your book."

"Oh, well, you should have." Margie tucked her hair behind her ear. "Said something, I mean." She grinned. "Not that it would have been a bother." In fact, she had been so absorbed in her reading that she felt she was still coming up from under water. On Friday she had gone back to the bookstore and stumbled on the slim volume of poetry called *Ariel*. It took her a moment to identify the snap of recognition: Sylvia Plath. This was the same poet whose work Sister Joan had read to the girls at Holy Family, the poem about the girl who got a splinter in her eye and could never see anything in the same way again. Plath, a mother of two young children, had killed herself a few years ago—Margie had read a brief article about it in *Life*. And now, seemingly from beyond the grave, came more poems. But they were nothing like poems she had seen before. Plath wrote about what it was like to give birth, to wake in the night with a crying baby, to look at the sky and long for comfort but receive only the moon's cold face in reply.

She looked at Theo, looking at her. His eyes had the soft crinkles in the corners that fair-skinned people got from squinting against the sun. There was something solid about him, as though he usually knew what was going to happen next and how he should react to it. "What's on your schedule this evening?" he asked.

It was about five o'clock. Back on campus, she had the option of Sunday supper in the cafeteria, or she could make a peanut butter sandwich in her room as she sometimes did. The semester was over now, but she had managed to get into a summer poetry seminar so she wouldn't have to move back home with Frank and Verna. Margie straightened her shoulders, felt the cap sleeves of her blue sundress stretch slightly at the backs of her arms. She was finally learning to dress for her figure. Verna always urged her to wear clothes that made no sense for a girl with hips and a soft middle and then complained about how she looked in them. Thank God she wouldn't have to go back to Sycamore Ridge for the summer. "I don't really have plans."

"How about dinner?" Theo asked.

He took her to Dante's, of course. Though she had been there before, Margie felt that going to the restaurant on a date, if that's what this was, changed it somehow. She didn't recall having seen the little red jars with candles inside that sat in the center of each table, or the dim glow from the stained-glass light fixtures in the shape of lanterns that hung from the ceiling on delicate chains. *They make it dark so that you can't see your food* was what Verna would have said, but Margie liked the low light. It relaxed her. She also liked that when Theo asked for his usual table, a stocky older man with a crisp white apron cinched around his belly led them to a booth cocooned in the corner next to the bar.

"For the lady?" their waiter asked Theo after he ordered a gin martini with a twist, but instead of answering for her, he turned to Margie and lifted a hand.

Margie, as on every other day of her life, thought not of what she wanted but what she *should* want. "Red wine?"

"Excellent choice, miss," the waiter said, and turned for the bar.

"Well." Theo folded his hands under his chin. He wore a brown plaid jacket and a yellow shirt. The pheasant feather had been just the beginning of this outfit, but he seemed entirely comfortable.

The usual worries were queuing up to spoil her nice time, like a lot of annoyed people lined up at the DMV: What did Theo think of her? What did she *want* him to think of her? How could she keep from making a fool of herself? "Well," she replied, and tried to grin.

The drinks came, and they ordered their dinner. When the waiter left a second time, the same awkwardness descended once more. But Margie knew it was bad form to be dull, so she scrambled for a conversation starter. "Did you hear that the Beatles are going to perform in Japan? I was amazed the government gave them permission."

"Yes, I think I did hear something about that," Theo said with mock uncertainty. He laughed. "I don't think there's a person alive who doesn't know about that. It's impossible to get away from those guys."

Margie felt instantly silly. "You probably don't care for them particularly."

"Are you implying that I am too old to like the Beatles?"

Her cheeks colored. "No, I—"

"I'm only kidding, Margie. I probably *am* too old to like them, but I do like them. I don't understand the haircuts, I will admit that. They look like they've got wigs on backward. But the music is good."

Mercifully, the food arrived and gave them an excuse not to talk for a while. Theo offered her a taste of his veal, and when she said yes, he politely cut her a bite and laid it on her bread plate. Somehow, this echoed his choice not to order her drink for her: he was offering something, but she got to decide when and how she would receive it. Margie wasn't used to navigating such favorable terms.

"This is delicious," she was saying about the veal, when an enormous crash silenced the dining room. Margie whipped her head toward the sound and saw that the stained-glass fixture that hung above the table beside them had fallen and smashed on the tabletop. Marinara sauce was splattered across the bust of the pale-pink dress the woman sitting alone at the table wore. Two women at the table next to her leaped out of their chairs. Others screamed and gasped. Because of the red sauce and the general confusion about how the fixture had fallen, no one seemed to notice that a three-inch shard of green glass was sticking out of the woman's shoulder, and blood, a deeper shade of red than the tomato sauce, was pouring down her arm and pooling on the tablecloth.

Theo stood, laid his napkin on the table, and went straight to the woman, crouching beside her chair to find her eyes. Margie thought she must have been in shock. She sat very still, her hands trembling, and looked from her shoulder back to Theo. A waiter rushed over with a wet rag to help with the cleanup.

"Please call an ambulance," Theo said to him. His voice was loud but completely calm. "Miss, I want you to breathe through your nose. Everything is going to be all right. Some people are coming to help."

Margie's pulse raced at the sight of all that blood. The woman nodded once and began to moan.

"You're doing just fine," Theo said. "Is your husband in the men's room?"

She nodded, and her head started to loll as if she were going to faint. Theo grasped her hands. "Let's try to stay awake now, all right? Keep taking those breaths through your nose."

The husband returned. "Fran, my God! What happened?" he cried, and his panic spread like a fire across the room. "She's bleeding. Oh my

God, look at this!" he yelled pointlessly, while Theo stayed crouched just where he was, holding the woman's hands until the paramedics arrived and took her away.

On the sidewalk ten minutes later, after Dante himself had insisted on covering their meal and begged them to come back another night, after Margie thought that it would probably be years before she could stand the sight of marinara sauce again, they stood together waiting for a taxi. She kept glancing sideways at Theo, trying to think of how to say what she was feeling.

"You were . . . really something just now," she finally said.

Theo looked at her. "What do you mean?"

"What do I mean? You stayed completely calm when all those other people were losing their minds. You knew exactly what to do and what to say to that woman. If you hadn't been there, she would have been all alone."

"Oh, I don't know about that. Someone else would have helped her."

"Not her husband. He was in a frenzy. And the rest of the people didn't even notice she was hurt. How did you stay so calm?"

Theo didn't answer right away. He seemed to be genuinely thinking about the question. Finally, he said, "I don't know. I guess I just told her what I'd want someone to tell me in that situation. That everything is going to be all right. That help is coming. It's a lie, in a way, I guess, because I didn't actually know. That glass may have pierced her artery. She might need surgery. But in another way, no matter what happens, what I told her was true."

"What do you mean?" The evening breeze fluttered the restaurant's striped awning. It was dark now, and the occasional passing car painted the pavement with its headlights.

Theo sighed. "Well, I told myself I wasn't going to talk about her, but I guess it comes from what I went through with Lorna. When things get really bad, you need someone to tell you it's going to be okay, even if you know that is impossible. When you're teetering on the edge like that, you need someone to believe it for you when you can't. It wasn't ever okay again with Lorna. But in another way that reassurance turned out to be true. There was a new kind of okay. I am still here. I am still breathing."

Margie felt transfixed by him. She knew he probably saw her as a naïve girl who couldn't possibly understand what it was like to experience that kind of loss. And yet she had. And because she had, she knew the truth of his words. Nothing was ever okay again, no matter how much someone tried to reassure you, but you went on anyway. Unless you planned on going the way of Miss Plath, you had no choice.

Theo was watching the outward signs of these thoughts cross her face, and her eyes locked on his. With his cupped palm, he made a little cradle for her elbow. A gentle, comforting gesture, but a question too. "Margie?"

"Hm?" The bizarre turn of events had shaken her self-consciousness loose, and she felt the awareness of simply standing here with him. Her mind right here in the moment, inside her head; her hands inside her pockets, her toes inside her shoes.

"May I kiss you?"

Margie nodded slowly and moved closer to him, surprised that she didn't feel nervous. Theo's kiss was like a question—his lips pressed against hers for a thrilling moment before he pulled back an inch and waited to see if her mouth would follow. It did. He kissed her again and then slid his cheek along her cheek. She smelled the Aqua Velva at his neck.

"You know, I don't talk about that much. But it's the oddest thing. I feel as if I could tell you anything."

Margie felt a muscle in her chest constrict with dread. She would have to be careful not to let his comfort with her trick her into letting down her guard.

"Are you sure I can't take you up to the door?" Theo asked when the taxi driver stopped where Margie had asked him to, at the beginning of the long driveway that led to her dormitory.

"This is fine," Margie said.

"I'd like to see you again." Theo opened the door for her. "Maybe next weekend?"

Margie took his hand and climbed out. She tried to shake off her dark thoughts. "Does it have to be so far off?" she asked in a breathy voice that sounded like a heroine in the movies. She wasn't putting it on, though. She *felt* breathy. She felt carried away.

Theo slipped his arm around her waist and touched his nose to hers for a moment. "Well," he said, "there is the problem of my job. But let me see what I can do. I might be able to come up on Wednesday. Will you get into trouble if I come to pick you up?"

Margie imagined the house mother shaking Theo's hand in the foyer as she took in his hairline and funny clothes. "They might gossip about me a little, but I don't mind."

He kissed her again. "I'll drive up in my car. Take you out to dinner."

"Anything but Italian," Margie said, and Theo laughed as he got back into the cab and it drove away.

Margie slung the heavy overnight bag over her shoulder. Clutching her coat at the collar, she walked up the hill in the darkness. At the top stood the gray stone buildings of Mount Mary with golden light shining through their windows. In so many ways it was the safest place Margie had ever been, but then she instantly doubted whether that was true. Safe places could be the most dangerous of all.

She hardly knew him. As soon as Theo was gone, she began to doubt everything she had felt in his presence. He might forget what he said about Wednesday. He might not actually come, and then she would be disappointed. She should put him out of her mind.

And yet she thought of him as she took the stairs to her room, passing the small alabaster holy water font affixed to the wall outside her door, a vestige of the dormitory's first life as a convent. She thought of him as she brushed her teeth and, later, lay in the dark in her twin bed staring at the ceiling. It was as if the woman's freak injury in the restaurant had accelerated their connection and turned this first date into a third, a tenth. Margie liked Theo's calm competence in the moment of emergency, the way he crouched beside the woman instead of talking down to her from above. She wondered if she was the first girl he had kissed since his wife. She replayed the soft kiss outside the taxi. Then her trickster mind replaced the image with his wife's lifeless lips, purple and pumped full of formaldehyde in the darkness of her grave. Never to be kissed again. Margie felt she had no choice but to linger on this image. Why was she like this? Why did she have to take every nice thing and pull it up like a rock to discover what darkness was writhing beneath it?

She let herself suppose that Theo would arrive on Wednesday as promised and that he might ask to do it again. And again. How many dates before she would have to take her clothes off? How many dates before he would want to meet her family? Would she be able to keep Timothy a secret forever? It had been a week since she spoke with the lawyer, but she hadn't yet heard from him. How might it change things if she did?

Margie switched on the lamp and opened the notebook of letters. She wrote *May 8, 1966* on the first blank page, feeling the dread already beginning to eclipse the brief joy of the evening. *Are you cold right now, wherever you are? Every time I see a mother wrap a blanket over her baby, I think of you. I think of my own feet, chilled in my socks. You are the draft in every room. You are the goosebumps on my skin.*

She wanted to tell him what this evening had meant to her, but there was no need to explain it in the letter. Timothy was always with her in a way that made going to the trouble of describing the events of her day seem absurd. He had been there with her through the drinks course and the falling glass and the kiss, just as he had been with her every day before that, back to the day of his birth. Further. Even though she knew it was impossible, Margie could shuffle through memories of his presence in her own childhood, at her *own* birth. When Margie was still in Verna's womb, the single cell that would become her son was already waiting in her tiny ovary.

Margie's mind still played these tricks on her, years after she had left Holy Family. She still slipped between what was real and what was not. And she wanted to get better. She wanted to make her life about things she could see and touch when her eyes were open. But what if that meant letting Timothy go?

24

Doreen

Seeing the confidence that fueled Cal and his band, even when it was, let's be honest, completely unwarranted, made her hungry to try—really, seriously try—to see what she could do with her own music. Those guys could be careless with their time because they were men, because they were freer than they could ever understand, but Doreen didn't have the luxury of wasting a minute of her limited time alone. Every day she tried to write at least one melody. Sometimes she put lyrics to it, sometimes she didn't. Her old notebooks from high school were full of ideas for songs and half-finished verses, none of them very good, because the rhymes went sideways or the syllables stretched to breaking to fill a measure. But at least she had something to start with. And after five years of not writing at all, mostly because her circumstances made it impossible, but sometimes, maybe, because she was deliberately denying herself the pleasure, when Doreen opened the hatch, *a lot* came out.

In addition to the more serious efforts, she worked on the tune for Carla's birthday. She experimented with the chords, looking for a progression that kept the song light and bouncy but didn't sound too bright, too much like a children's song. Every now and then when Summer was off shopping with Carla or at the park with Danny for forty-five minutes, she would stop to look around the empty front room and swim in the silence as if it were the healing waters of some sacred spring. Even when the writing wasn't going well, being engaged with doing the work the wrong way until she figured out the right way felt like heaven. It was repairing something in her that she hadn't known was broken.

Doreen leaned over the bathroom sink to sweep mascara on her upper lashes. She was careful not to add too much more than usual, or Carla might get suspicious. She could always put more on in the cab.

"Big night out?" Carla asked as she passed the bathroom on her way to change out of her uniform.

"Oh, not really," Doreen said as casually as she could. "You remember Wanda and those girls from my class? One of them is having a house-warming at her new apartment." Not a complete lie, in that the party was taking place in an apartment and it was, in theory, possible that some of her friends from high school might show up there. Chicago was big but not that big. It was a free country.

Carla crossed her arms. "Have fun—I mean it. You never see anyone anymore." Most of the time, Carla had sympathy for Doreen's plight as a single mother: always lonely, never alone; all work and no play.

"Thanks, Ma."

"Just don't forget that I'm on at seven tomorrow. Be quiet when you come in, or I'll strangle you."

The party was in a redbrick coach house in Lincoln Park, which the drummer for the Suspects rented along with his brother and another guy named August, who, when Cal introduced Doreen around, said he was a sculptor. There was something a bit off about him, she noticed: he wore an expensive-looking sweater, and his eyes were a bit glassy. Doreen maintained her smile through the introduction, waiting for the punchline, but none came.

"He really is one, you know," Cal said when they went into the kitchen to get beers from the door of the fridge. "A sculptor."

Doreen bugged out her eyes. "What does that even mean?"

Cal laughed. "He sculpts. He's an artist."

"But not for a job. He must have some other job. Who gets paid to *sculpt*?"

Cal popped the top off their beers with a church key lying on the counter. He handed one to Doreen. "I don't know how that part works. I think he's from the North Shore."

She glanced at the sink overflowing with dishes, the gashes in the linoleum floor. The place barely had any furniture. "Then why in the world does he live here?"

Cal gave her a look. "Freedom. And drugs."

She laughed, even as she felt a surge of what could only be described as hatred for the guy. To be rich, to have absolutely no responsibilities—it was like he was an alien. Probably everyone else at this party, too, could do whatever they wanted, whenever they wanted. Doreen felt the dangerous pull of bitterness dragging her into its orbit. Instead of giving in to that, she admired Cal, who was looking as scrumptious as he had last week in the record store's basement studio. Tonight he wore a chambray shirt so faded its navy blue was gray around the edges of the collar, and it fit him like a dream. His hair curled around his ears, and just now he took one step closer to her, placing his hand on the counter beside her hip. "I'm glad you came."

Just when he was about to kiss her, the kitchen door that led to the sidewalk burst open and five new guests threaded past the stove and into the living room, waving, setting bottles on the counter as they went.

"I guess we should go be social," Doreen said, though she didn't know a single person at the party.

"We won't stay much longer." Cal hadn't stopped looking at her face throughout the interruption, at her mouth, really. "Then we could go back to my place, if you want to."

The heat between them was as delicious as it was unbearable, especially now that he had planted the image of his bed in her brain. She shrugged, grinned. "Eh, I could take it or leave it."

He grinned back at her, one eyebrow up. "Well, in that case, never mind." They went back into the living room where more guests had gathered, clustered in groups of two or three. They sat on the couch and sipped in silence. "Eight Miles High" was playing at a deafening volume on the hi-fi. It was hard to talk, but hard not to talk, and the truth was that she and Cal didn't have all that much to say to each other. Next to them, August was explaining in a very loud voice, to a bored-looking redhead twisting a lock of hair around and around her finger, about how the artist Henry Moore was creating a sculpture at the University of Chicago to commemorate nuclear energy.

When August started in on the process of heating bronze, Doreen turned to Cal. "Help."

He pulled her back into the kitchen, slid his palm against her face, fingers curling into her hair, and kissed her. It had been so long, she had almost forgotten that, as good as you imagined this would feel, it felt better. *This is happening*, Doreen thought. *This is definitely happening.*

They took a cab to Cal's studio, which was a block from the record store in a run-down building with garbage bags lining the hallway, not that Doreen noticed them or the smell as they stalked toward his door, their hands intertwined. Inside, she had her fingers on the buttons of his shirt before he had even closed the door. Underneath he wore a white undershirt she had to extricate from his waistband. Undressing Doreen was much faster: Cal popped her shift dress over her head and there she stood in her heeled sandals and underwear. She hadn't been able to find a clean bra at home. "Well, that's efficient," he said.

Afterward, they lay in the tangle of sheets on the mattress on the floor. It was not the bed she had imagined back at the party, but it had gotten the job done. Cal lit two cigarettes and handed one to her, and she hesitated only a moment before taking it. Carla hated the smell of smoke, and mostly to avoid her lectures, Doreen hadn't smoked since back in her fast days running around with Wanda. But she wanted to stretch out for as long as she could these moments in which she didn't have to be herself.

Cal set his cigarette in the ashtray on the floor next to his pillow and rolled onto his elbows above her, his tan shoulders still muscled from his days on the high school baseball team, and moved one of her curls off her forehead. She took a long puff on her cigarette and put it down in the ashtray on the floor beside them.

"Sorry if that party was a drag," he said.

Doreen laughed. "It was fine. It was brief. Everybody was about to drop acid when we left."

"Probably. It was just an excuse to get you here."

She ran her fingers over his shoulder. "Well, it worked."

He peered at her like he was thinking hard. On Cal this looked like an uncomfortable activity. "You know, I really feel like I can trust you."

"With what?"

"What do you mean, with what?"

"Trust me with some kind of secret?"

Cal looked bewildered. "No. *Trust* you, trust you. Depend on you. As in, you don't seem like the kind of person who would go behind somebody's back."

Doreen laughed. "You don't even know me." Though he had meant what he said as a compliment, she would have preferred to keep him at a distance. She had grown very fond of Cal in the last half hour in particular, learning that being a mediocre guitar player did not make him mediocre at everything else, but she was not at risk of falling in love. He was no Mosel, in other words, but that was fine because she also was no longer the girl she had been when she and Mosel were together.

"Sure I know you," he said. "I know that Lew says you're a nice girl. And you are."

Doreen sat up, no longer drunk. "Do you know that I write songs?" She was getting irritated again, which depressed her. All she had wanted to do with this evening was preserve for a brief time the sense that her life *could* be different, if she wanted it to be. That she had the option.

"Yeah, you told me," Cal said. "Good for you, baby, that's great."

She remembered the condescending thing Cal had said about the female drummer for the Honeycombs—that she was a "gimmick." He probably thought about her songwriting that way too, a little hobby she kept up, jotting down lyrics in a diary she locked with a little gold key. Maybe a few unicorns drawn on the cover. Doreen didn't want to get angry, but she could feel it bubbling up. She took a long drag on her cigarette and blew the smoke in his face, pretending it was unintentional. "I gotta go soon."

"Can't you stay a little longer?" He pressed his face into her neck, the scrape of his whiskers sparking electricity. After a moment, she ran her fingers up the xylophone of his backbones. The hair on the back of his neck was damp with sweat, and she decided to channel her frustration in another way.

As they moved together, she felt it again, the liberation, paradoxically, that came from her precise control over what he knew about her, what he didn't. In this moment she was not a mother to Summer, not a daughter, not a sister, not the friend who had made a solemn promise to look after someone's son. She was only her own body and its sensations and the songs she could make, wherever they came from. She didn't have to be anything else.

When, a couple hours later, she finally told Cal she had to go, he slipped into his white boxer shorts and took her hand to "walk" her to the door, all four steps from the mattress to the studio's only entrance.

"So the guys and I have finally scraped together enough money to make the demo. We're going to record in two weeks. Saturday morning, real early. Lew's going to help us, but he's bringing in another guy to run the board, and we have to pay him." He turned her hand over and touched the inside of her palm. "Will you come? I think I play better when you're there."

"I'll try," she said, but she wasn't sure if she wanted to see them record. It was so easy for them to set up an opportunity like that, and so easy for them to take it for granted. Besides, how would she explain to Carla that she needed to be away from home so early in the morning, before the record store was even open?

Carla. Doreen looked at the clock on his nightstand. It was past three. "Shit."

"Ah, don't worry, baby," Cal said. "We've got nothing but time."

The cab took so long to come that it was nearly four when she slipped into the apartment and tiptoed through the front room. She was dying for a glass of water but decided to head straight to the bedroom. When she turned the corner into the hallway, though, she saw that the light in there was on. Carla sat on the bed next to Summer, whose cheek lay on an old towel covering her pillow. She opened her eyes. "Mommy."

"Ma, what's going on?"

Carla looked at Doreen with murderous rage. "A stomach bug, I think. She'll be fine, but it's been a long night."

Doreen's heart sank like an elevator. "I am so sorry. Go to bed, Ma. I've got it from here."

"No, you don't. One of us has to stay here, and the other one needs to start on the laundry. She has diarrhea too."

"Oh, hon." Doreen bent over Summer and kissed her forehead. Her cheek was hot and clammy. "Ma, I really am so sorry. If I had known, I would have come home right away."

Carla ignored this and gently helped Summer sit up. "I want you to take the tiniest sip of water, angel. Just one little one." Summer sipped, and Carla handed Doreen the glass to set back on the nightstand.

Carla pulled the blanket back up on Summer's shoulders. Without looking at Doreen she said, "I asked you not to stay out late. I am on in three hours."

Doreen sighed. "I messed up." She choked on the words, trying not to cry. Just a couple hours ago she had been relishing the feeling of being unencumbered, of pretending Summer and Carla didn't even exist. Was she a bad person for thinking she deserved just a single night off? Life was so relentless, every damn day. She knew she should just absorb the drubbing she had earned, but her weaker self tried to deflect it. "Danny does shit like this all the time," she muttered.

Carla gave her a long look, her jaw moving slightly as if, for Summer's sake, she were grinding the sharp edges off the words she really wanted to say. "Danny is not the mother of a five-year-old child."

25

Margie

By the time she walked into the perfumed air of Marshall Field's on Theo's arm, past the clerks dressed in spring florals who held up mirrors to women trying on shades of coral, pink, and poppy, past a tower of straw handbags displayed on a red gingham picnic blanket, Margie was pleasantly tipsy. It had been a month since their first date, and, at Theo's request, she had taken the train to Chicago and a taxi to his office on LaSalle, where he met her in the lobby and took her to lunch. Theo had ordered a steak, Margie a wedge salad. And since Theo did not have to return to work, he suggested martinis. Now Margie felt she was floating just above the slick tile floor, grateful Theo seemed to know where he was going. They stopped in front of a glass case trimmed in walnut in the jewelry department.

"I saw something here the other day that made me think of you," Theo said. "I thought maybe you could try it on."

The clerk, a woman Margie's age in precise pink lipstick and a blue jacket with scalloped lapels, appeared and used her tiny gold key to unlock the case and slide open the door. With Theo's direction, she selected a slender watch from the row of pieces draped on the oyster-colored velvet display. "This one?"

"That's the one," he said. When Margie produced her wrist, the clerk laid the watch across it. It was gold, with a fine mesh strap and a face of mother of pearl and numbers almost too tiny to see.

After a moment, she handed it back to the clerk. "Thank you. It's very pretty."

"Would the lady like to wear it out? Or shall I wrap it up?" the clerk asked.

"Oh no," Margie said, realizing they weren't just playing dress-up. She turned to Theo. "I couldn't. It's too much."

He touched her elbow. "Of course you could. I want you to have it."

Margie glanced back at the mother-of-pearl face. Verna would say Margie should refuse the watch, that men don't give gifts out of kindness but instead because they think they will get something in return. And yet, feeling Theo's shoulder pressed up against hers, the nearness of him, Margie knew she wanted that thing too. Theo was a good man, and he was offering her something wonderful, not just in the watch but in everything that came with it. The question was whether Margie could let herself have it.

"It really does suit you," the clerk said. "Wear it for a day and see."

Margie gave her a decisive nod. "All right."

"That's my girl," Theo said, and as the clerk removed the tag and fastened the band, Margie basked in his words.

They walked back through the store and out the main doors to State Street, where it was starting to drizzle. Late that afternoon, she was supposed to return to Milwaukee. Theo kissed her cheek. "How about one more drink before your train?"

Margie nodded. "Somewhere quiet."

"How quiet?" Theo gave her a long look.

"Very."

The clouds opened then, and in the few minutes it took for Theo to hail a taxi, they got soaked. It was only six blocks to the apartment Theo rented on Madison for the evenings he worked too late to catch the last train back to Pottawatomi. In the polished lobby, a doorman sat on a stool with his arms crossed over his chest and his chin puddling as his head bobbed in sleep. Margie and Theo snickered as they tiptoed past him to the elevator, and Margie felt a thrill at the implied fiction, that her presence was illicit, that Theo was sneaking her in like a mistress.

In the elevator, Theo kissed her in a new, more urgent way, and Margie's breathing quickened as she let herself give in to it, give in to his hand pulling at the buttons on her raincoat. He broke away, his mouth still near hers, a raindrop from his sandy hair trailing down his nose. "Excuse me, miss. Do you happen to know what time it is?"

Margie giggled, delighted, and the warped-sounding bell rang for the ninth floor. But in moments of relief, even joy, her mind was quick to pierce them with the arithmetic of loss. *I am twenty-two*, Margie thought, out of nowhere, as she followed Theo from the elevator to his door. *I am twenty-two, and that makes Timothy five.* The bridge of Timothy's nose flashed across her mind. His tiny hand. Any day, that lawyer might call with news, something he could tell her about where Timothy was, whether he was all right.

No. She pushed the images away.

The studio was small and sparsely furnished, but clean. In the kitchen was a small electric stove with just two burners, and a half-size fridge like the kind the fathers of Sycamore Ridge kept in their garages to chill the beers they cracked open after mowing the lawn. There was a small brown loveseat in the corner and a twin bed by the only window. An orange popcorn-stitch bedspread hung over it, and its fringe graced the floor. The bare window looked out on an airshaft.

Theo must have been watching her take it all in. He laughed to cover the uneasiness in his voice. "I know it's not much. But it really is just for sleeping and the occasional pizza delivery. I promise, my actual house is much nicer."

It occurred to Margie that it was possible the house Theo had mentioned a few times was a figment or a dump. Maybe this studio was actually all he had, and maybe he was lying about his job too. Then again, he had those business cards that looked so official. The greatest shock of all might be meeting a man who was exactly who he said he was. Because Margie walked through each day masking the most important thing that had ever happened to her, she assumed that everyone carried a secret just as explosive.

He sank onto the loveseat and yanked his tie loose. Extending a hand to Margie, he pulled her down next to him and began kissing her again as he had in the elevator. Together they peeled her raincoat down her shoulders, and though the touch of his fingers at her neck drew her closer, Margie was now concentrating hard on corralling her mind away from all the things she did not want to think about in this moment. Timothy, of course, but also the touch of other hands, the touch she did not want on the basement floor of Mr. Grebe's workshop, the touch of Dr. Samuels's speculum, and the groping hands of the fraternity boy on the fire escape. There was no such thing as being alone in this moment with Theo. All of them were in the room with her too, touching her body as he touched it, and it didn't matter at all that the other men's intentions were perverse while his were pure. All the men were touching Margie in all the ways they wanted to touch her, and she was barely there at all.

But I'm with Theo now, she told herself in a stern voice inside her head. *Only Theo.*

She tried to stay with his lips at her neck. With the feel of his fingers pushing up her skirt to trace the edge of her pantalettes at the top of her thigh, as he brushed his thumb against her. He, Theo, here on the brown loveseat. He, the fraternity brother; he, the doctor; he, Mr. Grebe. It was suddenly loud in the room. There were so many men and so many thumbs. Margie felt herself falling back, back, back against the pillows, a choking sound coming out of her throat.

"Margie," Theo said, his voice urgent, and she opened her eyes to see him peering down at her, his forehead creased in worry. "Are you all right?"

"Oh," Margie said. She blinked at him, put her hand to her throat, and swallowed. "I am. I'm fine."

Theo pulled her skirt back down to her knees and helped her sit up. "What happened? It sounded like you couldn't breathe."

"I couldn't for a moment there." Margie felt her face flush.

His unbuttoned collar was splayed, his lips marked with her pink lipstick. "Have you . . . has that ever happened before? I was going to call it a fainting spell, but you didn't really faint."

"No, I didn't faint. It's hard to explain. I go into, well, it's sort of like a tunnel in my mind. In my memories. And when I am in there, it is more real than what is happening right in front of me." Margie realized Theo might interpret this as a slight, that she had wanted to escape. "I don't choose it, to go away. And I always come back out of the tunnel." She gave him a tired grin. A headache was starting to bloom from the martinis. "There's nothing I want more than to be here with you right now."

Theo flexed his brow. "I'm sorry if things have moved too fast. Sometimes I forget about the age difference—I can hardly believe you're only twenty-two. It's only because you're so easy to be with, and you have a wisdom about you I can't explain. But I never want you to feel pressured. There's no reason we can't take our time."

"But I don't want to wait," Margie said. She leaned in and began kissing Theo's neck. Girls spent most of their early dates with someone trying to determine whether he was a good person, worthy of trust, but Margie was already certain of those things with Theo. The challenge for Margie came not from unmasking Theo but unmasking herself, determining whether she could stay out of the tunnel long enough to accept the affection Theo was offering. She wanted to make it true that she could. She had to push through. "I want to be with you," she whispered.

"Are you sure?"

She nodded. Theo stood and pulled Margie to her feet, and they moved together to the bed. Theo began to kiss her once again, this time with perhaps a little more solemn devotion, and then, one button at a time, he began to take off her clothes, slowly, too slowly. To keep herself in the room, Margie pressed her fingernails hard into the heel of her hand.

Theo's shoulders were as freckled as the rest of him, and he had a surprisingly muscled chest and arms. More than anything else it was the feel of his skin against her skin, the sound of his breathing as they moved together, that kept Margie in the moment and stopped the other men from intruding. When he slipped to the bathroom and came back with a condom, Margie wasn't jealous, wondering if there were other girls, but only grateful that he was a Boy Scout, even in this, that she wouldn't have to worry.

A while later, Margie drifted into a happy half sleep, still conscious of the sheet soft against her feet and Theo's warm exhale on her shoulder. When he finally stirred and reached for the lamp on the bedside table, it was the first time she thought to wonder about the time.

"I think I've missed my train," Margie said.

Theo propped himself up on his elbow. "I'd say so."

"I was thinking—"

"Margie, there's something—"

They exchanged a smile. "You go first," Theo said.

"Well, I was just going to ask whether you're hungry. I'm *starving*."

Theo laughed. "Wouldn't it be nice if this apartment came with room service? I'm afraid the cupboards are bare."

"I'll be the judge of that," Margie said and pulled on a few articles of clothing so she could walk across the room to the kitchenette. She felt loose all over, full of relief, and incredibly thirsty. At the sink, she drank down a glass of water, then found a can of tuna and a box of stale crackers in the cupboard. She opened the refrigerator. "I don't suppose you have any eggs?"

"Afraid not," Theo said, and the grin on his face made her laugh.

"What?"

He smiled. "Nothing."

As she stuck her head back into the chilly cavity, rooting through the impressive array of condiments to find the mayonnaise, she said, "What were you going to ask a minute ago?"

"Just whether you would marry me."

The door slipped from her fingers and banged against the wall as she stood up and looked at him, holding the glass jar and a butter knife.

Theo was sitting on the edge of the bed now in his boxer shorts. "Don't say anything yet. I shouldn't say it out loud when we've only known each other such a short time. But I love you, Margie. And I can say firsthand that life is short. I'm not going to play a lot of games or bide my time and pretend I don't have the future on my mind. I would marry you tomorrow if you'd have me."

Margie steeled herself for the panic she thought would rush into her chest, but it didn't come. She set down the jar and the knife. She closed the refrigerator door and stood looking at the can of tuna. It hadn't even been two months since the day she and Theo met on the train. Any rational person would say this was not enough time, not enough evidence on which to make such a monumental life decision. And yet in that time Margie had experienced actual, relaxed happiness. Theo had quieted down the cacophony enough for her to hear her own voice, to understand what she wanted, to ask for it. Of course, she still wasn't being honest with him, never could. But what she wanted now, hearing his words, was to say yes.

Her family would think she was crazy. Verna would assume she was pregnant again—"Why the rush?" There were so many questions: Where would they live? What would she tell her friends? And the dark cloud that always hung nearby: How would she be able to keep Timothy a secret? What if she somehow succeeded in finding him? What then? But Margie pushed all the questions away. She didn't have to know all the answers today. They could have a long engagement, hold off on the wedding until she finished school next spring. There would be time on other days to fret over it all.

She sat down beside Theo on the bed, and his hand touched her shoulder.

"I'm sorry, Margie. As soon as the words were out, I knew I should have bitten my tongue. The last thing I want to do is scare you off."

She shook her head. "I love you too. And I'd love to marry you."

He smiled in surprise. "You would?"

She nodded. "On one condition."

"Of course. God, I feel bad—this was sort of impulsive. I don't even have a ring yet. So name it, anything."

"You take me down to the diner so I can get a hamburger."

26

Doreen

On Carla's birthday, Danny had the idea to borrow his boss's new two-door Impala ragtop and pick their mother up in style from her long shift at the hospital. Carla loved beautiful cars and, maybe as a consequence of having a son who worked on them all day, could name the style of every fender and fin and hubcap.

"Ma will love it," Danny said. "No one should have to take a Chicago city bus on their birthday."

Doreen was touched by Danny's thoughtfulness, which made her feel a little guilty for always being so dismissive of her brother. There was a big heart knocking around in there with his pea brain, she had to admit.

"Don't rush home," she said. "Take her on Lake Shore for a while and then drive around the neighborhood so her friends can see her. She will want to make them as jealous as possible."

Doreen needed the extra time to finish cooking Carla's birthday dinner—chicken cacciatore from scratch, thank you very much—and to get Summer ready in the dress Doreen had bought for the occasion. She had spent the past few weeks trying to get back into Carla's good graces after the four a.m. stomach flu disaster. She made sure the laundry was done and put away before Carla got home from work. She got up early to make the coffee. But Carla, who typically relished all three acts of an argument, from wailing crescendo to slammed door to silent treatment, had been strangely subdued. Besides her terse words at Summer's bedside, she hadn't asked where Doreen had been or who she had been with. She hadn't berated her or given her the silent treatment. More than anything, she seemed, simply, sad. This was not an emotion Doreen had ever seen on her mother, and it was alarming.

Summer, of course, was oblivious to all of it. It paid to be five. After she had spent a day in bed recovering, Doreen lying beside her tallying receipts and trying to keep her eyes open, Summer was back to her old self and delightful (exhausting) chatter from morning till night.

"Will Nonni get a balloon?" Summer asked as Doreen parted her hair with a wide-toothed comb and fastened it in her standard two pigtails the shape of softballs. She put a little water on the comb and used it to try to smooth the short, fuzzy hairs that sprang up around Summer's hairline like tufts of clouds. The water never really tamed them for long.

Summer herself had gotten a balloon, red with a silver ribbon, on her own birthday the previous spring, and she had treasured it and petted it as the helium dissipated and, day by day, it sank lower until finally it rested on the floor, a dying animal laying down its weary head at last. Wiser for the experience, Summer cautioned, "If we do, we should warn her about what happens. You know, how it doesn't last forever?"

Doreen put her hands on her daughter's shoulders in the mirror and kissed the top of her head. "You're right. We wouldn't want Nonni to be disappointed. I think this time, instead of a balloon, we're going to have a nice dinner, and then I have a present to give her."

She tried not to think about what she would have done if something really bad had happened to Summer while she was lying in Cal's bed play-acting what it would be like to be free. One quality of motherhood no one warned you about was the ambush: periodically waking up to the *fact* of it—how permanent it was, the sober reality of what it meant to be responsible for the safety and care of a growing human—and being shocked all over again by that reality. She loved Summer so much that it made her crazy, the love and obligation all mixed up together, tethering her for life. There was no way under it or around it, which was both wonderful and terrible. Luisa had hinted at feeling this way too, and remembering this made Doreen think of Margie. *What an ungrateful shit I am*, Doreen thought. She could touch her daughter, standing right in front of her. She could see, now that the stomach virus was gone, that Summer was all right. Margie would never have that with Timothy.

"Is it a necklace?" Summer asked and touched her heart-shaped charm.

Doreen shook her head. "Keep guessing."

"A new car?"

"I wish!"

Doreen hoped that this very minute Danny and Carla were sailing along the lakefront as the sun set behind the skyline, glinting orange off the glass and steel. Even if it was only for an evening, Carla deserved to get a taste of the good life.

Summer's eyes went round. "Is it a kitten?"

"No, baby. Are you sure we're still talking about things *Nonni* likes?"

Summer's new dress was white eyelet with ruffled cap sleeves and a wide ribbon belt. Doreen helped her tie it and buckle the stiff new Mary Janes that were still a size too large for her feet. She was in the kitchen pulling the baking dish from the oven when Carla and Danny came through the door. Carla's cheeks were pink and shining.

"So?" Summer cried, her boisterous voice sounding just like Carla's. "How was it?"

"A dream! I felt like a Hollywood starlet on her way to a premiere." She pulled her scarf off her hair and then picked up Summer to kiss her on the cheek. "Did you see the sunset? I love your new dress."

"Danny, let me borrow your camera," Doreen said. When he brought it to her, she made Carla sit at the head of the table so she could take her picture. She held up her glass of wine in a toast.

Summer insisted on serving her grandmother the chicken and salad, and Doreen helped her pour the wine. Doreen was nervous. It had been years since she had played, really played, the piano for her family, and longer than that since she had played a song of her own. Cal talked endlessly while they were in bed (kissing was the only thing that shut him up) about what it would be like when the Suspects went on tour, when the Suspects couldn't go outside without getting mobbed by fans, when the Suspects would play on *Ed Sullivan*. He thought he was going to get all the glory without doing any of the work. But Doreen *wanted* to do the work. She wanted to sit at the piano and solve the puzzle of the songs that distracted her all day long. And she didn't really even care all that much about glory. She just hoped to hear one of her songs—just one!—on the radio someday. What made her nervous was not the work itself but her ambition to do it—how much she *wanted* to see her name on one of those album covers. The wanting was the precarious and wild and dangerous thing.

"Should we have cake?" Doreen asked, glad for one more chance to delay.

"I think I'd like my present first." Carla looked at Doreen with a gentle smile, and Doreen had the strange sensation of hearing an echo: the ambush she had been thinking about, the no-under-it, no-around-it kind of love. Maybe Carla had that too.

"No!" Summer cried as if mortally wounded. "Cake first!"

"She has been waiting very patiently," Doreen said and laughed. Summer had only asked fifteen times in the last ten minutes when they would be finished with dinner and move on to dessert. "It will just take a minute."

"No candles!" Carla said. "I don't want to think about the number."

"All right." Doreen went into the kitchen and popped the string on the bakery box. With Summer bouncing at her side, she lifted the chocolate cake on its cardboard plate and set it on a platter.

"Summer, count out four forks," she said, and Summer raced to the drawer. In the dining room, Doreen set the cake and a stack of plates in front of Carla. Danny, who had loved to sing as a child but never did anymore, revealed his rich tenor as he began the birthday song, and Summer belted out the lyrics in her idea of a glamorous and grown-up voice.

Carla cut the cake and passed the slices around. "Go on," she said to Doreen, nodding at the piano. "I know you've been practicing."

Doreen pushed back her chair and walked to the piano bench. Her heart was pounding, but when she sat down and put her hands on the keys, she felt the familiar comfort of their smooth caps and it helped a little. "It's just a silly little song," she said to Carla. "Don't get your hopes up." She might have been saying it to herself too.

"Dorie, just play," Danny said.

Doreen closed her eyes and tried to channel the sound of the strings and the swishing Latin percussion on "Up on the Roof" by the Drifters. Carla's song was a little like that one, she hoped. Simple in a way that disguised the longing behind it.

Summer pulled on her sleeve. "Play, Mommy!"

So Doreen played.

When I was eight,
I baked my first cake
and I left out the eggs by mistake.
You could have said, "What a waste!"
Instead, you rescued me.

When I was sixteen
and ripped my prom dress sleeve
ten minutes before it was time to leave,
you could have said it was too late.
Instead, you rescued me.

You rescued me when I came to the end of what I knew.
You found a way to make it okay.
You rescued me.

Five years ago
I came home
with a bundle in my arms, all my courage flown.
You could have said I'd made my bed,
who could blame you if you had,
but just the way you always did,
you rescued me.

When she finished, the room stayed quiet for a few seconds, and Doreen was suddenly terrified to turn around. She heard Summer's small hands begin to clap, then Danny's, and just when her heart was about to plummet, Carla crossed the room and squeezed Doreen's shoulders. She kissed the top of her head, just the way Doreen had kissed the top of Summer's head earlier that evening, watching their reflection in the bathroom mirror. "Thank you," Carla whispered.

It was a silly song. The lyrics were trite and the chords were too simple—she could do better. But it just felt so *good* to make something out of nothing, and to try to tell Carla how she felt. She would never forget that night when Danny helped her up the front stairs, Summer wrapped in a blanket Sister Joan had stolen from the Starlite Motel. When they came into the kitchen, Carla was standing in the middle of the front room, the light of Vincenzo's reading lamp glowing orange behind her. Maybe she hadn't really believed that Doreen would agree to come home, maybe hadn't really believed the baby was real. Her hands went to her mouth. For a moment, she stood frozen there in her white nurse's uniform and stared at her daughter and granddaughter. To Doreen, it had felt like the spinning earth creaked to a stop and all the saints in heaven held their breath.

And then Carla had crossed the room and pulled them into her arms.

Now, Doreen scooped a drowsy Summer out of Vincenzo's armchair and tucked her into bed, and Danny brought the bottle of wine over to the table. With her eyes shining, Carla told them stories of their father when he was a young man, tales they had heard before but wanted to hear again because of how much she wanted to tell them. There was something restful about being with people who all knew the same stories.

But when Carla was in bed and Danny went down the street to meet his friend for a beer, Doreen slipped out too, back to the warm bed of a guy who didn't know *any* of her stories, and, if she had anything to say about it, never would.

27

Margie

It wasn't until patient Theo had asked three times—once when he met her for dinner in Milwaukee, once over the phone, and once in the silly notes he stuck in her purse when she wasn't looking—that Margie realized she needed to go home to Sycamore Ridge and tell her parents about him. She had been hoping to wait until the time was right, but the truth was, the time would never be right to have a conversation about her future happiness with Verna.

"Just in time," Verna said, closing the oven door with her hip. She set the baking dish on a hot pad and gave Margie a brisk peck on the cheek. "How was the train?"

Her dad, who had picked her up from the Sycamore Ridge station, followed her in through the kitchen door. "Fine. Not too full."

"Any coloreds bother you in the station?"

"No, Mother. And you shouldn't talk that way."

"Why not? They're tearing the city apart."

"Now, Verna," Frank said. "Let's not get riled up. All that has nothing to do with us."

"They're angry," Margie said. "Wouldn't you be angry if you had to pay double the rent to live in a dump just because it's in the Black Belt? This is supposed to be *America*. We should be ashamed."

Verna widened her eyes theatrically and clucked. "Well! What are those nuns teaching you? You look puffy. Are you eating too much salt?"

Margie sighed. "Not that I know of. Actually, I've lost five pounds."

"Set the table, please."

Tomorrow, Margie's brother and sisters would come over with their children for Sunday supper, but tonight it was just the three of them together at one end of the dining room table. Still, Margie tried to make it special. She took the kitchen shears into the backyard and cut three white roses from Verna's bushes, set them in a vase at the center of the table, and put out the wineglasses.

"Ah, lovely," Frank said when he took his place at the head of the table. "I think there's a bottle of wine in the liquor cabinet."

Margie found it and poured a bit in each of their glasses. In the kitchen, Verna was opening and closing the oven, pulling a serving spoon out of the drawer, and all the while coughing a light hacking cough Margie had never heard before.

"Has Mother been sick?" she asked Frank.

Her dad was still staring at the roses. After a moment, he said, "Oh, just a cold. It's going around the Optimist Club."

When Verna came in with the casserole, she paused in the doorway. "What's all this?"

"I just wanted to make it nice," Margie said.

"Well." Verna gestured to her wineglass with her elbow as she set the hot dish in the center of the table and laid a serving spoon on top of the crisp shoestring potato crust. "None for me."

"And I have some news."

Frank raised his eyebrows. Verna sat down in her apron, oven mitts still on her hands. "What is it?"

"Let me help you get the plates and the salad," Margie said, standing up. "I can tell you when we're all—"

"Just tell me," Verna said. "You know how I hate your surprises."

"It's not *bad* news. Why would you assume that?"

"With you I never know," Verna said. This was her signature comment and the closest she ever came to referencing Holy Family. Frank held up his own end of the bargain they seemed to have made long ago by saying, as always, nothing. By pretending he didn't know exactly what Verna was doing, he demonstrated that his loyalty would always be to her.

Margie tried to think of what to say. *I met a man* sounded ominous and would draw too much attention to Theo's age. *I'm getting married* sounded presumptuous—Theo had not yet asked Frank's permission. *I'm in love* was the worst possible thing she could say, sure to spark Verna's ire. Who was Margie to fall in love? La-de-dah.

"There's someone I want you to meet," she finally said. "His name is Theodore Barrett. Theo. He's from Pottawatomi. Works in the city and—"

"Works doing what?" Verna was quick on the draw.

"For the mayor, actually," Margie said and lifted her chin. "It's a very good job, in statistics. I think you'd really like him, Dad."

"I'm happy for you, Mars Bar, though I will say Pottawatomi is a surprise," Frank said. "So far from the city. How'd you meet him?"

"On the train, actually. It was funny—I spilled my juice on him by accident when I nodded off, and he was such a gentleman about it. It could have been such an awkward situation, but he . . ." As she told the story, she felt the buzz of nostalgia. Already, she and Theo had a story. So far in her life, all of Margie's stories had been the kind you couldn't tell anyone.

Verna watched her carefully. "So he's not a student?"

"No." Margie steeled herself. "He's a bit older than me."

"Than I."

"Than I." Margie clenched her toes hard inside her shoe. "A widower, actually."

"He was *married* before?"

"That's what widower means, Mother. His wife died last year. It was sudden and tragic, and he has been alone all this time. They had no children. He needs someone—he wants someone. And that someone is me, I guess." Margie smiled weakly.

"And what about you?" Frank asked. Very gently. "Do you *want* to be that someone?"

Before Margie could say yes, Verna cut in. "It sounds to me like you're getting ahead of yourself. He hasn't even spoken with your father."

Margie took a breath. "I would like you to meet him. We'll all go together to Hackney's. That was his idea, Mother. You can have the whitefish."

Verna sat back and, finally, took off her oven mitts. She really did like the whitefish at Hackney's, Margie knew, because it was grilled, not poached, and they put buttermilk in the mashed potatoes.

"Well, I for one can't wait to meet him," Frank said. He lifted his plate. "Now can we please eat?"

After dinner, Frank went in search of his pipe, and Verna and Margie cleared the table. Verna waited until they were standing side by side at the sink, Margie washing, Verna rinsing and drying, before she began the second round of her interrogation.

"How long have you been seeing him?"

"A few months," Margie lied. "At first we would just see each other on the train to Milwaukee and catch up like old friends every time. And then one day he finally asked me to dinner."

If Verna were a different kind of mother, Margie might have tried to explain what happened the night of the date, when the fixture fell and cut the woman's shoulder, and Theo kept so heroically calm amid the panic. But Verna would only react to the freak nature of the accident, be put off by the talk of blood. She would not understand how something so unpleasant could be the basis of their romance.

"How well does he know you?"

Margie measured her words with the precision of a chemist. "He knows what he needs to know. That I am just starting out. That my life is ahead of me."

"He won't be so charmed by you if he finds out, so you'd better be careful."

Margie tried to still the quaver in her voice. "Mother, why don't you want me to be happy?"

"Oh, happiness. I don't understand this focus on happiness. It can't be a goal in itself. You can't *choose* it. Happiness comes from living right."

Margie went into the dining room and brought the butter dish and the vase of roses into the kitchen and set them on the counter. Verna would want the table empty so she could polish it, another thing Margie knew to do without being asked. What she felt for Theo seemed so fragile just now, the grip on her certainty that she really did want to be with him. It would be so easy to let Verna's doubts and warnings worm their way into her mind until she told herself she didn't really mind if the whole thing fell apart. To want something, to go after it despite her fear and despite Verna's poison, was so much harder than just numbing out into indifference. And yet somehow Margie knew it was almost a matter of life and death.

"I want to marry him. I am going to marry him."

Verna nodded, unmoved. "Well, that's wonderful. You had better do it soon. Men change their minds."

"Actually, Theo isn't the kind of man who would expect me to quit school. We'll wait until next spring, after graduation. You know, you weren't this way with Catherine and Alice. When they got engaged, you were happy for them."

"It was different with them." Verna dried her hands on her apron. "They never gave us any trouble."

Even all these years into her life as Verna's daughter, Verna's cruelty could still take the breath out of Margie's lungs. She would never forgive Margie for bringing Timothy into the world, no matter how much Margie needed and deserved that forgiveness. Verna wanted more than lifelong penance. She wanted to see Margie suffer.

Verna hung her apron in the pantry and went into the den to ask Frank what he wanted for dessert. Margie stood looking at the roses for a long moment and then, with an angry swoop of her hand, yanked them from the vase and tore the petals from the stems. She left the mess on the counter and went up to bed.

In the end, Margie gave Theo the number to her father's office phone so they could arrange a time to meet and Theo could ask for Margie's hand in the customary way. On Friday, Margie took the train home for the weekend so she could accompany her parents the next day to the restaurant where Theo would be waiting to meet them. When it was time to leave the Ahern house, Frank was already sitting in the driver's seat with the engine running. Verna, who had taken an unusually long time to get ready, was still upstairs, presumably fussing with her hair, so when the phone in the kitchen rang, Margie picked it up.

"Ahern residence."

"Miss Ahern, this is George Michelson. We met in my office?"

With the phone to her ear, Margie stepped into the hallway, from which she could glance up the carpeted steps to the second floor and judge whether Verna was nearby. She stepped back into the kitchen, keeping her voice low. "Of course. I remember."

"Someone at your dormitory gave me this number. I hope it's all right that I've called."

"Yes, I was hoping I would hear from you."

Mr. Michelson cleared his throat. "Yes, well. I wish I had better news. I made a call to a colleague who works more frequently in this area, and I'm sorry to say that it is what I expected. There is no getting around that 1945 statute, I'm afraid. You may place a letter in the child's file, which will be opened to him when he turns eighteen, and at that time he could initiate contact with you if he wishes. But in the meantime, there is no way for you to obtain information."

With her wrist, Margie blotted a tear that had run to the end of her nose. "I see. Well, thank you for making the call. How much do I owe you for your time?"

"Oh, nothing, Miss Ahern. I'm just sorry I can't be of more help."

"Well, thank you," Margie said and hung up. She took one long breath in, her hand still resting on the phone. She knew she had been foolish to expect anything else.

Verna clicked into the kitchen on her heels, her head tipped into her palm as she adjusted an earring. "Oh lord, is your father already in the car? We should go. Who was that calling?"

"Wrong number," Margie said.

A half hour later they stood under the awning at the main entrance to Hackney's, and Frank offered Theo his hearty handshake as if to an old friend.

Margie gestured toward Verna. "Theo, this is my mother, Verna Ahern."

"It's a pleasure to meet you, Theo." Her voice cracked at the end. "Oh, excuse me," she said, and turned away from them with the hacking cough Margie had heard the other night, three short bursts. Then she rejoined them with a bright smile. "I'm so sorry! Nobody likes a summer cold. Theo, I understand you work for the city?"

Margie could see from the angle of her mother's shoulders that Verna was surprised by Theo's age and also by the fine quality of his jacket, a mercifully conventional herringbone, she noted. He was too old for Margie, but old-fashioned in a way Verna couldn't help but like. All this she could discern from the tiniest shift in her mother's posture. It was as if Margie were a prolific poet in a language so dead, no one had even heard of it before. Her translation skills had no value to anyone but herself, and even there she knew it was poisonous to her well-being to spend so much time thinking about what was in Verna's head. She wondered if she would ever escape it.

Theo slipped his hand into Margie's as they walked two by two into the waiting area of the restaurant. She gave him a reassuring smile—it was going well after the first thirty seconds, she thought—but Theo did not seem to be nervous. Now they just had to get through the meal without Verna insulting Theo, by accident or on purpose, and it would be behind her.

But fate introduced a new wrinkle. As they waited for the hostess to prepare their table, Margie felt a rush of air on the backs of her legs and turned to see two new people enter the restaurant. She felt a cold awareness in her throat before she understood the cause of it. The sun reflected off the glass in the door as it swung slowly closed on its damper; yellow fragments that shifted across the wall glinted off the man's hair, slick with pomade. Mr. Grebe.

"Well, Jan, will you look who it is," he said to his wife and extended a hand to Margie's father. "Frank, how are you?"

"It's good to see you, Harvey. It's been years."

Margie watched Mrs. Grebe and her mother exchange greetings, her father asking how business was, and then she felt her gaze being pulled against her will back to Mr. Grebe. He looked exactly the same, with his heavy gold watch and the cigarette case that made a bulge in the front pocket of his shirt. When Theo gave her a funny look, she realized her whole body had stiffened, that her tongue had gone dry.

"And little Margie," Mr. Grebe said. "All grown up now, I see."

"How are Richard and Susan?" Margie managed to ask.

"Well, let's see. Rich is captain of his Little League team now. They're 10–0 this summer. And Susie is off at Girl Scout camp."

At the edge of his smile was the one yellow tooth that stood out from the rest like a kernel of corn. She only knew it was there because, once, she had been pressed so close to his face on that cold basement floor. Her stomach turned.

"Congratulations are in order for us too," Frank said, proud and clueless. "We're here to celebrate Margie's engagement to Theodore Barrett."

"Little Margie engaged!" Mr. Grebe said.

Margie could feel that he was trying to catch her eye, but she wouldn't give in to it. She introduced Theo in a bland voice, and as they shook hands, the hostess appeared to take them to their table.

"Many happy returns, Margie," Mr. Grebe said.

She wanted to cover her ears but instead nodded, gave him a weak smile.

Theo leaned over to her as they passed through the bar. "Are you all right?"

She took a deep breath through her nose. "Oh fine. Just nerves."

They took their seats, and Frank ordered a bottle of champagne—Hackney's wasn't exactly the kind of place for that outside New Year's Eve, and the bottle the waitress brought them was slightly tacky with dust. Frank filled their glasses and lifted his to Theo. "We're very happy for you both, isn't that right, Verna?"

"It is," she said and smiled, and Margie could see that she actually meant it. Verna had now verified that Theo's "good job" was real and understood that he had enough money, maybe more than enough. He was not covered in some strange pox. He was articulate and mild-mannered, and her finely tuned radar could not detect any reason he would not be able to make a nice life for them. Margie allowed herself to bask in finally having pleased her mother, but of course that would be short-lived.

"Next you'll have to meet Margie's brothers and sisters. I think you'll fit right in," Frank said.

"Let's talk about the wedding," Verna said cheerfully. "What colors are you thinking?"

Margie took a gulp of champagne. "Oh, I'm sure Theo doesn't want to be bored with that. Anyway, we have lots of time."

"We do?" Theo asked.

"Well, sure. We won't need to book anything until this fall if we want next May."

Theo turned to her. "Surely you don't mean waiting until next spring."

"I thought that's what we—"

Verna broke in. "Of course she doesn't mean that. Returning to school now just doesn't make sense, Margie. What does a married woman need with college?"

Margie stared at Verna. They had only just talked about this in the kitchen a few days earlier, Margie announcing so confidently that Theo would never ask her to quit school, Verna saying nothing at all in reply. Margie had never felt the age difference with Theo so much as she did now.

She had been naïve, a fool. And she recognized this sinking feeling because it had happened to her before, when the priest told her parents she would have to leave in the middle of the semester to go to Holy Family. Here she was again, the comfort of school yanked away. The end of poetry seminars and afternoons in the library and the walk up the long curved drive to her peaceful little dorm room. No more late nights at her typewriter, no more abandoning her work to join a gossip session with the girls on her floor. It would be the end of the one thing that was all her own.

Theo's neck had grown slightly pink, but he glanced between Verna and Margie, understanding that he had waded into something tricky. "Margie, maybe we can discuss this in private. I'm sure we can work something out. Right now we should celebrate."

Verna folded her hands. "But what's to discuss?"

"Verna, leave it alone." Frank, who was last in and first out of every conflict that had ever bloomed near him, finally piped up. "It doesn't concern us."

Margie plastered on her most convincing smile and laid her napkin on the table. "Theo, you're right. I'm sure we can find an answer. I'd like to run to the ladies'. Will you order the chicken for me?"

But after she walked back through the dining room and bar, blurring her gaze so that she would not see the Grebes, she turned right instead of left and went out through the front door and into the air. Just moving felt so good she didn't want to stop, and she continued between two rows of cars to the back of Hackney's parking lot. Beyond was busy Pace Road, on a Saturday mostly full of mothers in station wagons doing the shopping, picking up dry cleaning, probably counting the minutes until it was time to get home and relieve the sitter. Margie finally slowed her pace, air returning to her lungs at last, and realized with a dark laugh that she had stopped at the back of Mr. Grebe's turquoise Eldorado Brougham, a little worn around the fins six years on, but the flashiest car in Sycamore Ridge. She knew it was his, HGHG1 on the license plate. What was better than his own initials once? How about twice.

All of this had started with him, hadn't it? He had altered the course of her life when he decided *for* her what would happen *to* her. Because of his decision, because she was then going to have a baby, her parents did the same: decided for her what would happen to her, and away she went to Holy Family. Away went the life she knew, away, away, away, the baby she never even got to touch. Even a lawyer couldn't undo their decisions. And now Theo, deciding. Everyone but Margie, deciding.

Her anger swung in her head like the tongue of a bell. *Clang*. Before she really knew what she was doing, her keys were in her hand—*clang*—the jagged edge of her dormitory key pressed against the iridescent paint—*clang*—her wrist tight as she dragged the key down the length of the car, curving it up and down, rubbing it back and forth. The back of her dress dragged along the car parked next to his, surely streaking it gray. The metal-on-metal screech was horrible, but she couldn't stop, barely heard the approaching footsteps.

"Margie, what in the hell are you doing?"

She turned to see Theo, the key still pressed between her fingers. The sun was trying to break through the haze, and she squinted against it.

Theo's eyes were wide, his mouth an O of shock. "What are you . . . I don't even know what to say." He looked back over his shoulder at the restaurant, the large windows of the dining room that faced out on the parking lot.

"Then don't say anything," Margie said.

"You have to get away from here before someone sees you." He grabbed her elbow and gave it a shake. "Goddamnit, Margie. Put the keys away!"

The crazed feeling had subsided enough for her to see he was right. She swallowed down a wave of nausea and slipped the keys back into her pocket.

"Come on. Let's walk over a few rows and back up another way."

Margie nodded and followed Theo back into the restaurant, back to the table where their meals were growing cold. "Oh, please eat," Margie said as she sat down.

"Yes, let's eat," Theo said brightly. "I think Margie is feeling better now."

Somehow they made it through the rest of the meal, though her hands shook a bit in her lap. Verna seemed satisfied she had stirred up some turmoil, and Frank was mostly clueless and enjoying his rare steak. When the bill was paid, Theo said he had promised to drive Margie to the train station. She retrieved her overnight bag from her father's car, and they all said their goodbyes. Just an hour ago, she remembered as she followed Theo to his car, she had thought if they could just get through the meal with her parents, everything would be fine.

Once they were in the front seat and Theo had started the engine, his amiable smile fell away. "All right, Margie. Are you going to tell me what just happened?"

She rested her hands on top of the overnight bag in her lap. "I don't know what to say."

"You don't know what to say."

Margie sighed.

"Do you know how expensive that car is, Margie? You wrecked it! It will cost a fortune to fix. I mean, the owner will probably call the police."

Verna's words—*men change their minds*—went through her head. Theo's opinion of her was sinking fast, and while she might be able to save it by confiding in him, how much truth could she tell? How could she explain what Mr. Grebe had done to her but not tell him about Timothy? And of course she could not tell him about Timothy. She felt paralyzed. How could her own small story have the power to destroy everything around her—her parents' reputation, Mr. Grebe's nice life, her own shot at happiness with Theo—and yet she herself was powerless over it?

Theo was still looking at her like she had transformed into an entirely different person. "I didn't know you felt so strongly about finishing school. Let's talk about it."

Margie shook her head.

Theo made an exasperated noise. "You're acting like a crazy teenager. Is this what you always do when you get angry? Find some property to damage?"

"I'm not angry," Margie said.

He laughed. "Yes, you are."

"I'm happy."

"No, you aren't. And if we are going to make this work, you're going to have to start telling me the truth. Don't you know you can trust me?"

She had never wanted to tell anyone the truth as badly as she wanted to tell it to Theo right now. But she couldn't do it.

They drove in silence, and Margie was puzzled when he passed the turn for the highway. Then she realized he wasn't going to drive her all the way downtown to Union Station but instead planned to drop her at the Sycamore Ridge commuter train. She would have to go to the Loop from there, then catch the Hiawatha that doubled back north to Milwaukee. The trip would take another hour at least.

When he pulled up to the curb at the station, he did not turn off the engine. "Let's take a little breather for a few days. I need to think. You need to think." He looked at his watch. "You should be able to catch the 4:32 to the 6:15 Amtrak."

"I don't need you to tell me the goddamn train times, Theo." She could have screamed, but the full force of it was trapped in her throat.

"But you're not angry."

I could melt this car with my rage, she wanted to say, but instead she got out and walked away.

28

We

We did not tell the truth to the men we married because we wanted to have a respectable husband, and a respectable man would never marry a girl like us.

We had more children, and each one was a joy and a torture, a reminder of every birthday and skinned knee and fever and recital and picnic we had missed. We smothered them; we kept them at arm's length. Even when those children were sleeping soundly at night, there was no peace.

We could never bring ourselves to have another baby. We made birth control a religion; we refused men's advances until they spread rumors that we were frigid, lesbians, freaks of nature. We got pregnant and had abortions. We got divorced. We lived alone and we were lonely. We lived alone and took comfort in the silence.

Though we asked the question in a thousand ways—in our prayers, in our dreams, through binge and denial of booze and food and pills and sex and money, in traveling to the other side of the world, in locking ourselves in rooms, in sacred things and common things, in trying and failing to cease to be, in succeeding—we never got the answer to whether that first baby was all right.

We got the answer. It helped; it didn't help.

We believed what we had been conditioned to believe: that though we had given birth, we were not mothers. Unwed girls don't have that right.

We woke up from that belief. We got angry at the world, and the limitless rage terrified and powered us. It was a riptide sucking us down; it was the life preserver that carried us to the distant shore.

29

Doreen

Doreen and Summer were an hour into a session of beauty parlor in the front room—Summer was the beautician, Doreen, the customer—at eight on Saturday morning, when the phone rang.

"Hold on, kiddo," Doreen said, lifting Summer's fingers from her hair. She could feel at least five barrettes clipped on the right side of her head, and the tail of a ribbon twisted around the three ponytails on the back of her head tickled her neck. "I'll be right back."

Doreen hustled to the phone in the kitchen. Carla had been called into the hospital early that morning, and Danny was still sleeping off last night's Old Style.

"Coniglio residence," Doreen said. The top of the receiver clicked against the arc of barrettes around her ear.

"Doreen?" Though the voice sounded a little like his, there was no way it could be Cal at this hour. Anyway, when he wanted to talk, he always called, let it ring once, and hung up so that Doreen knew to call him back. She had told Cal it was to avoid an awkward conversation with Danny, but she actually wanted to make sure he never interacted with Summer.

"Yeah?"

"It's Lew. From Sound Town Records?"

"Oh." It took her a beat to think what to say. More and more over the last few weeks, Doreen had been going straight to Cal's and skipping the pretense of a visit to the store. "Hey, Lew. What's up? Is everything okay?"

Summer, still in her nightgown, had followed Doreen into the kitchen on all fours and was mewling like a cat, brushing her cheek against her mother's calf. Doreen reached down to pat her head. *Good kitty*, she mouthed, to Summer's delight. They had already been up for two hours and eaten breakfast, washed the dishes, put together a puzzle, and played five rounds of Twenty Questions before the beauty parlor game began. At some point, Doreen had to get to the books for A+ Hardware and the Polish bakery. It was going to be a long day.

"I don't know if you knew, but Cal and his band were supposed to come into the studio to record again this morning. They didn't do much with the last demo they made, but I told them we could try again. As long as we made it really early so we could wrap up before I open the store at eleven."

"Let me guess," Doreen said, imagining Cal sprawled across his mattress in much the same manner as Danny was in the other room. "They didn't show?"

"You got it," Lew said.

"Well, if you're looking for him, I don't know where he is. I haven't seen him since last week."

"Oh no, it's not that," he said. "I'm calling to ask if you want to take their spot."

Summer was scratching Doreen's ankles now with her "claws," and Doreen stooped to bat the girl's hands away. "What do you mean?"

"Bring your notebooks over. Let's see what you've got, and maybe we can get something recorded for you. The engineer is scheduled to be here all morning, and I have to pay him either way."

"Are you serious?" Doreen said. For months she had been working steadily to nail down some songs she could imagine sharing. They still weren't perfect, but they were coming along.

"Yeah," Lew said, and she could hear the smile in his voice. He knew he had just made her day. "But you've got to get here as soon as you can."

"Meow?" said Summer, tipping her head up to look at Doreen. Carla's shift didn't end until four, and Danny would be dead to the world for hours to come.

"Shit. Wait. Lew, I . . ." Doreen closed her eyes and pressed her forehead to her fist. "I can't come."

"What do you mean? This is no time for false modesty, Doreen. Studio time is hard to get—take it."

She sighed. "It's not that. I have to tell you something, but the thing is . . . Cal doesn't know. And I need to be the one to tell him, so can you keep it under wraps for a little while longer?"

"Sure thing."

"Do you remember how I told you I had been away for a while? That I had to grow up pretty fast a few years ago?"

"Yeah?"

"Well, I had a daughter. She's five now. I'm home with her this morning, and I don't have anybody to watch her."

"Oh. Wow." God bless Lew. He only let the revelation of this enormous secret throw him for a second. "Well, bring her with you."

"Really?" Doreen tried to picture Summer in the same room where, back in August, Cal had leaned in and asked for her phone number. It felt wrong to let those two worlds collide.

"Sure. She'll love all the buttons on the mixing console."

When would she ever get a chance like this again? Free recording time? She knew she would be an idiot to pass it up. "All right. We'll be there as soon as we can."

"Meow," Summer said as Doreen hung up the phone. She pretended to lick her paws. Doreen took the canvas market bag off a hook by the front door and started shoveling crayons and paper inside, Summer's sticker book, a Barbie who was missing one of her blue high heels.

"Are you ready to go on an adventure?" Doreen asked. She dashed into her bedroom and without even looking in the mirror exchanged her nightgown for a pair of black cigarette pants and a green blouse. From Summer's dresser, she pulled a pink gingham shift.

"Meow," Summer said from the doorway.

"This is an adventure for humans." Doreen reached for Summer's wrist and tried to pull her to her feet.

"Meow-meow," Summer said, then whispered, "That means 'I'm not a human' in cat language."

Doreen inhaled slowly through her nose. "Hon, we're kind of in a rush. I really need you to help me out here. Let's get dressed."

Summer crawled off into the front room, wagging her behind as if it had a long, twitching tail attached to it. Doreen followed her. "Meow."

"*Summer.*" The clock on the mantel was approaching 8:30.

"Meow."

"Get up, Summer. I'm not kidding."

Summer began to whimper and mewl dramatically. Then she whispered another stage direction: "It's not nice to yell at cats. They get scared."

Doreen crammed her notebooks into the bag that held Summer's toys. She found Summer's sandals under the kitchen table and stood by the door. "You know, cats can't have candy. But girls can." Bribery had become her only play lately, and while she wasn't proud of it, there was no question that it got the job done.

"Meow?" Summer looked down her back at her mother. Doreen had her attention now. "Meow what kind of meow candy meow?"

Doreen closed her eyes and counted to five. Generating the bottomless patience motherhood required, day in and day out, sometimes felt like it took years off her life. "Any kind you want. But you have to get up right now and put on your dress and shoes. And you have to be a good girl all morning. Can you do it? I'll buy you candy every day this week."

"Every day? I mean, meow?"

"Every day," Doreen said. God, you had to admire how stubborn this kid was once she got something in her head. If they stayed home, Doreen knew Summer would keep the cat thing going for hours. She would ask for tuna for lunch and want Doreen to put it in a bowl so she could eat it on the floor.

"Meow, I need to think about it."

"Summer, please." Doreen pictured Lew sitting in the store, tapping his pencil on the counter. She felt like crying. "Please, just this once, help Mommy."

Summer heard the thick sound come into Doreen's voice and snapped to attention, looking alarmed. Pushing herself to her feet, she came to the door. "Okay, Mommy."

Outside, Doreen pulled her along the block by her wrist, wishing she had the money to pay for a taxi. Her heart pounded as she glanced at her watch yet again. The bus only came every twenty minutes this time of day. But they got lucky—it pulled up just as they were rounding the corner.

"Thank you for being such a good girl," she said, smiling at Summer once they took their seats. They faced the morning sun, and it painted them gold. Summer's eyes looked like pennies in the bright light. "I never would have made it without your help," Doreen lied through her teeth, as only a mother could.

Summer beamed. "I did a good job on your hair too. You should let me do it every day."

Doreen touched her head with her fingers and laughed. The barrettes were still clipped all around her ear, the strange pigtails sticking out the back of her head.

Lew was waiting inside the store to unlock the door for them when they arrived, and Doreen felt the buzz of fear that gripped her every time Summer met someone new. She dreaded the flash of surprise that almost always crossed the person's face, however well they thought they covered it up, when they took in Summer's hair and skin, and the penny dropped. But all that was on Lew's face was a warm smile. "Welcome, ladies," he said. He crouched down in front of Summer and put out his hand. "Hi there. I'm Lew."

"I'm Summer," she replied with a hand on her hip. "Pleased to meet you."

Doreen stifled a laugh. Just last week they had practiced the mechanics of the handshake, the importance of making eye contact and smiling. But Summer had added her own withering take on the greeting—it was Lew who should be pleased to meet her. *Charmed, I'm sure.*

Lew looked up at Doreen, delighted. "I don't know which one of you is going to be the bigger star here." He winked.

"It's me," Summer said.

"No doubt about that," said Doreen.

Lew led them down the stairs. Though Doreen had been here once before, the studio looked different with all the lights on, without the distraction of Cal's shoulders and cigarettes and the bottle of whiskey. Lew had moved the piano to the center of the room and set up the mics. Doreen felt a wave of nerves.

"Let's get you set up," Lew said. He introduced her to Ron, the engineer who would run the mixing console and make the demo tape. He was a big white guy built like a linebacker, with fingers like Polish sausages, and Doreen wondered how they could work all those little buttons on the board. Diana, his assistant, was a Black girl about Doreen's age, as delicate as her boss was whopping. She moved around the equipment in her smart silver mules, reaching to plug cords in, and gave Summer a friendly wave.

Once Summer was settled happily in the corner of the room with her toys, Doreen took her notebooks to the piano, and Lew pulled up a chair next to the bench.

"Why don't you play through some of what you've brought, and we can talk about what might be strongest? But there's no rush. Take your time getting warmed up—whatever you need."

Doreen gave him a faint smile. Imagining what this would be like was something different from the real thing. Even as she was all too aware of the three people waiting for her to begin, her brain felt full to bursting with the hardware store's third-quarter taxes, the groceries she had to pick up at the market on the way home, the growing hole in Summer's right elbow of her jacket. Carla had asked her to call the plumber, she just remembered. And she had been fifty cents short on the grocery order at the end of last week. The man had been nice about it, but she needed to get back there to repay.

Doreen took a breath. Her songs were in there somewhere too, amid that swirl of anxiety, and she tried to calm her mind enough to focus on just one of them. The first she played for Lew was called "Housekeeping," about a girl washing dishes and folding laundry and cooking dinner, but the whole time she's thinking about the boy she'll get to see that night when her chores are done.

"Interesting," Lew said charitably when she had finished. "I don't think I've ever heard a song with the word *potato* in it."

She had come up with the melody for the next one years ago, the kind of hook she would mysteriously find herself humming out of the blue. It had the stickiness she knew you needed, something with earworm potential. But she hadn't come up with the right lyrics for the song until the night Danny picked Carla up in his boss's car on her birthday. It was such a good surprise. In the song, Doreen made the car red and the girl young (no offense, Carla) and the boy picking her up was, of course, the object of her affection. This was the first time they were going to be alone together, driving through the night with the windows down. The chorus went: *Every time I feel him accelerate / I know in my heart I'll be home late . . .*

"I like this one," Lew said. "You sound a little like Dusty."

Doreen felt her cheeks color. "I guess I've been listening to her new record a lot."

Lew knocked her shoulder with a soft punch. "That was a compliment. I think we should record that one."

Doreen tucked the comment away like a shiny penny she would take out later to admire, when no one was watching. She accepted his praise because she knew the song worked. It had that element of fantasy that was just a little bit magical, where the song says what it wants and then *gets* it. So unlike real life, where you never get to the bridge that tells you resolution is coming in that last verse. Real life was more like the metronome, ticking endlessly.

"There's one more I think might be good enough," she now had the confidence to say, and she flipped to the song she had been saving, the one she took around her like a shawl when she was trying to fall asleep at night. Another boy and a girl, another summer night, but this time they were in the tall grass on Wooded Island, surrounded by dragonflies at dusk. And it was love, the real deal, and the kind they had to keep a secret. In the third verse, the boy gets on a Greyhound bus, and the girl knows she will never see him again. But she has something to remember him by. The song was called "Wooded Island." As she played, Doreen glanced over to where Summer lay on her stomach in the corner, drawing with a green crayon.

She played the last chords and then looked at Lew.

His eyes were wide. "Now that's a song."

"You think?" Doreen feigned humility, but she knew what he meant. This one was different from the others. There was a spark in the lyrics, maybe because they were true. When she played it, she wasn't thinking about the chords or what was coming next. There was just an open channel from her mind to her voice to her hands.

"Definitely," Lew said. "Ron, I think we're ready to get started."

They spent the next hour trying a few different versions of "Pick Me Up" and "Wooded Island": faster, slower, moodier, jauntier. They had a long conversation about percussion and backup vocals, how they might work on "Pick Me Up," though it was all speculation given that they didn't have a drummer or singers on hand. Still, digging into the work of building the songs, being taken seriously by real musicians, felt so damn good. They made some decisions and recorded. At some point, Summer had abandoned her drawing and joined Doreen on the piano bench. Lew put his finger to his lips to remind her that they had to be quiet to keep any other sounds from ending up on the recording. Though

Summer didn't typically take this kind of direction very well, she seemed entranced by the big instrument and the sound it made, the sound of her mother's voice, which she knew so well, but in this space, with these people looking on, sounded different and a little magical. She sat still as a rabbit beside Doreen, listening.

Lew helped her gather up the loose sheets of notes they'd made, and Doreen tucked them into her notebooks. "You know," he said, "Elektra is hiring songwriters by the dozen right now, if your stuff is strong. Do you ever think about going to New York?"

What she pictured was her songs on the radio in every city of the country—she never thought about where *she* might be. And anyway, leaving Chicago was out of the question. She had made a promise to Margie to watch over Timothy, and she intended to keep it. Instead she gave Lew a weak smile and shrugged. "Maybe someday."

Diana took her reel off the machine and put it back in the red cardboard Ampex box. Ron wrote Doreen's name and the titles of the songs on the front in black marker, then handed it to her. "Good job, honey," he said. "I wish you the best of luck."

Doreen turned to Lew. "So what do I do with this now?"

"You get it to Roger Sharp at WLS. See if he will play it."

Doreen laughed. He made it sound so easy. Summer was still at the piano, plunking on the keys, and Doreen sat back down on the bench next to her. She bumped her lightly with her shoulder. "You think they'll play my song on the radio?" she said.

"Yes, they will," Summer said. "Play that one about the island again, Mommy."

So, at the risk of wearing out her welcome, Doreen played "Wooded Island" one more time, and while she did, she allowed herself to remember Mosel and that brief, magical few weeks they'd had together. Even though Doreen hadn't really known him well, Summer provided some clues. The little girl was such a combination of her mother's take-no-shit attitude and her father's razor-sharp mind. Doreen had accused Mosel of trying to untangle the secrets of the universe while he was kissing her—his mind was always a little bit elsewhere, and now she wondered whether Summer already had numbers twirling through her mind like he did. She realized all at once how important it would be to tell Summer about Mosel's abilities. They would shape what she thought was possible for herself. But then, how would Doreen explain his absence? Someday soon, Summer would realize her family was different from the families of the other kids at school.

While the song's final chords still hung in the air, the door burst open suddenly and there was Cal. Doreen felt her mouth go dry.

"The red light's on," he said. "What's going on?"

Lew sighed. "Good morning."

Cal looked at Doreen. "What are *you* doing here?"

She started to answer, but Lew stepped between Cal and her. "You and the band were supposed to be here at seven."

Cal kneaded the back of his neck, and his signature lock of hair flopped forward, limp and greasy. "Come on. It was a late night, okay? I'm here now. Did the rest of the guys not show?"

Doreen slipped over to the corner of the room and began putting the toys back in the market bag. Summer kept uncharacteristically close to her hip, almost as if she knew that her mom had erased her by omission for all these months. Doreen felt sick with regret.

"Cal, I'm sorry, but it's too late now. Ron has to be over to Chess by one."

Ron shrugged as he zipped his jacket. "Sorry, man." He eyed the door, and so did Diana as she wrapped her scarf around her neck, both of them eager to avoid the coming storm. But Cal was in the way, oblivious to everything but the betrayal.

"Wait—so you called *her*?"

Lew adjusted his glasses, and in that nervous gesture was every punch he had taken when they were kids and Cal took their good-natured wrestling too far. "Doreen is talented. Don't you know that? You should. We cut a great demo this morning, didn't we, Doreen?"

Doreen swallowed and, realizing at once that Cal must have assumed Summer was Diana's daughter, plastered a smile on her face. Maybe they could all leave and she wouldn't have to get into it with him. "Don't be mad, Cal. It was just for fun. Lew didn't want the time to go to waste. I'll find a way to pay you back for it."

"No, you won't," Lew said. "That's on the house."

Cal exploded. "Are you kidding me? Why do I feel like the two of you are going behind my back?"

Lew groaned and threw up his hands. "Yeah, I'm moving in on your bird right here in front of Diana and Ron and Doreen's little girl."

Doreen closed her eyes.

"Her what?" Cal stared at her, shock darkening to something it took her a moment to name, given Cal's many soliloquys on the dangers of conventionality—disapproval.

"I was going to tell you," Doreen said. "I swear. It just never felt like the right time." She unpeeled Summer from her torso. "Cal, this is my daughter, Summer."

Summer took a deep breath and stepped forward. Just as she and Doreen had practiced, she put out her hand. "Pleased to meet you," she said.

But Cal didn't shake her hand. He just stared at Doreen. "I don't know what's worse: that you have a kid—a brown one!—or that you have a kid and *lied* about it."

"What in the hell is wrong with you, man?" Lew muttered.

Summer, anguished by the swift rejection, buried her face in Doreen's middle and began to cry. Doreen wrapped her arms around her. Maybe because she was the only other woman in the room, Diana's eyes found Doreen's and a channel of commiseration opened between them that straightened Doreen up.

"We're leaving," she said. She lifted Summer onto her hip, took the notebooks from the piano and clutched the boxed demo tape to her chest.

"I'll walk you out, honey," said Ron, who had clearly had enough teenage drama for one day, and used his bulk to cut a path to the door at last.

"I'm so sorry, Doreen," Lew said. "Cal, you are an asshole."

Cal looked at everyone, genuinely bewildered. "How am *I* the asshole here?" he shouted.

Doreen's anger snapped like a rubber band. "Don't say *asshole* in front of my kid, you asshole."

Cal pointed at Lew. "He said it first!"

"But he's not an asshole."

Ron held the door, and Doreen began to climb the stairs, still carrying Summer.

"Doreen, wait," Cal yelled up after them.

"Don't follow us," Doreen said.

Then Summer lifted her head and hollered down the stairwell, "I don't know what a asshole is, but they sure have bad manners."

On the bus home, Summer was quiet and watchful of Doreen as she tried to work out, within the limits of her five years of life experience, what she had just witnessed. Doreen felt like hell, but she was relieved too, and in addition to the guilt, she felt a strange sense of vindication. Her instinct that Cal couldn't handle this part of her life, the most important part, had been correct. He had revealed himself and hurt Summer, and she would never forgive him for that—would also never forgive herself for letting it happen—but in the tussle, she had saved what was important and walked away from what was not.

"Summer, I promise you will never have to see that man again. I promise our life is going to be bigger than this."

Summer pursed her lips. "His breath stinked."

Doreen laughed. "It did."

She would go to the ends of the earth for this kid. For Cal, she wouldn't bother walking to the corner store. There was a peace in affirming those facts. Still, though she hadn't loved Cal, damn if she didn't want to love somebody, someday, and it depressed her to think about how unlikely that was to happen. Her life was locked on a set of rails, the future nearly certain to disappoint her recklessly large hopes.

Nearly, Doreen reminded herself. After all, the demo was in her bag.

30

Margie

"Margie!" Shawna called from the telephone table that sat outside the sitting room near the stairs. Margie left her desk and stuck her head into the hall.

"Phone for you."

"Who is it?" Margie said.

Shawna, the receiver pressed against her short-sleeved sweater, bugged out her eyes. "Who do you think?"

Margie swallowed. After three days of silence, in which she had prepared what she would say down to the word—*I understand. Don't feel bad. It was crazy to think this could work after just a month. You deserve every happiness.*—she realized she wasn't ready to have this conversation. "I'm not here."

Shawna tipped her head and mouthed, *Are you sure?* Margie nodded. She hadn't told the girls in the dorm about the engagement, and she wasn't yet wearing a ring because Theo's grandmother's diamond was still at the jeweler being placed in a new setting. It wouldn't take many awkward conversations in order to sweep all this away.

"Hello, uh, sir?" The other girls still didn't quite know what to make of Theo's age. "I'm sorry, I thought she was here, but you just missed her.

She's gone to the library. Yes. Yes, I know, that's Margie for you. I'll give her the message. Okay, bye." She hung up the receiver.

"What did he say?"

She shrugged. "That he wants to talk to you. Did something bad happen, Margie? Did you two have a fight? You look terrible."

"Gee, thanks."

"Oh, you know what I mean." Shawna had come to Mount Mary all the way from Ironwood, on the border with the Upper Peninsula of Michigan, to learn about accounting and have a big city adventure before she went back home to help her father run his grocery store. She had the coiled energy of a person on borrowed time, and Margie had never seen her with a book in three years of college. "Me and Linda are going to see *Frankie and Johnny* again. You should come."

"Oh . . ."

"Don't stay in your room feeling sad—come on."

"Thanks, that's nice," Margie said, and meant it. The other girls really tried to make her feel included, and sometimes she even said yes. Today she wouldn't dream of subjecting them to her dark mood. "But I think I actually will go over to the library for a while."

"You and that Sylvia Plath." Shawna smiled and shook her head. "You know, you can't go steady with *her*. She's a girl, and she's dead."

Margie laughed. "Yeah, I'm aware."

"You're sure I can't convince you?"

"Thanks, but no. Have fun. Say hi to Elvis for me."

When the girls had gone, Margie packed some books and her twin composition notebooks, one with notes from the poetry seminar and one full of letters to Timothy, and walked down the long curved drive and out to the street to catch the bus. The funny thing about living in the dorm at Mount Mary was that it wasn't so different from staying in the rooms at Holy Family. Girls came from all over for a short time, all of them waiting for a big *something* to happen to them—getting pinned or engaged, getting an internship or grad school fellowship or a job. Waiting for the due date to approach, when they'd slip down the dark tunnel to where their life would finally begin. The difference with Margie was that her big something had come and gone, maybe twice now.

She wondered what had become of Yvonne, the girl with the big glasses, and Laurel, that one who seemed to be wasting away from her endless morning sickness. Or Ingrid, the girl who was so young none of them liked to think about how she had ended up at the home—though Margie herself had an idea. What had happened to all of them? Did they comply willingly with the doctors and nurses? Were they simply grateful to everyone who had helped them get out from under their problem and back to school to pretend everything was fine? She thought of all the babies that had come out of Holy Family over the years. There had to be hundreds.

It always made her ache a bit to think of Doreen because she missed her so much, but there was consolation in knowing for certain that Doreen was all right. Not that her life would be easy, not by a long shot with a baby and no husband and not much money. But at least she had gotten to choose what happened to her. That was what separated the girls who got better from the ones who stayed angry forever: whether one's life was her own or just the product of a bunch of decisions other people had made for her without asking. Margie's anger was steady, limitless, depthless, a darkness that stayed clamped to her feet like a shadow. Theo had been the first person in her life to name it out loud. Even Margie herself couldn't do that.

And then the question etched in her mind: Where was Timothy? How would she ever go on with her life not knowing if he was all right? Just that morning she had written him another letter she would never send: *Dear Timothy, When something ends, you must accept it gracefully. No matter how much you flail on the inside, you must stay on the surface as still as a pond. It helps if you can tell yourself you never wanted the thing at all.*

At the library, Margie took her time selecting a table and arranging her books in a stack, turning through her notes from *Ariel*, finding just the right pen. The final grade for her poetry seminar would come from a presentation to the class on Plath ten days from now, but Margie knew that if she had to give the talk today, she would do well. She was ready. Working with the poems like a kind of code-breaker, lifting an allusion to the light to unspool the story it contained, writing and speaking in the analytical voice the literary critics used—all of it came naturally to her. She felt like a man when she wrote this way. She felt like Adam naming the animals.

It helped. She walked the stacks, pretending she couldn't find a book she needed even though she knew precisely where it was, just to burn through a little more time. Finally she packed up and headed back to the bus, the sun low at the end of the afternoon. It would be one of those June evenings that seemed to last as long as the day itself, orange, then peach, then pink, then purple, then finally pale blue again before the darkness came. A thing to savor if you weren't just trying to get through to tomorrow and the next day and the next, when you might feel better.

When she was about halfway up the curved drive, she saw Theo's gray Fairlane parked at the top of the hill and Theo himself leaning against it with his arms crossed. He wore a yellow short-sleeved, button-down shirt and olive-colored slacks and a straw fedora—just a fashion disaster. She had to laugh, even as terrible as she felt. The brim was tipped low but not so low that he didn't see her walking toward him. She was no more ready than she had been earlier to have this conversation, but there was no way to dodge it now. She would have to face it.

Margie clutched the straps of her book bag with both hands and forced her feet to keep walking.

"Hi," he said.

"Hi."

"You're a hard woman to get ahold of."

"I've been studying for this presentation."

He nodded. "Margie . . ."

He was too nice to do it well. He would drag it out and sputter and backtrack. She wanted to make the cut herself, quick and deep. She stood beside him and leaned against the car. "It's okay, Theo. It was nice of you to come, but we don't have to make it harder than it has to be. I really do understand."

"What do you understand?"

"Maybe it was never going to work with the age difference and everything else. You thought I was a different person than I am. We are probably saving ourselves a lot of trouble later on."

Theo laughed. "Margie, I'm not here to break things off with you."

She turned to him. "You're not?"

"I've been trying to get you on the phone so I could apologize."

Margie's mind was trying to work the angles, but she couldn't come up with any reason he should be here now, saying this to her. "What do you have to apologize for?"

He pushed his hands into his pockets and sighed. "For assuming that what happened in the parking lot was about me. For forgetting that you had a life before I came along that is maybe none of my business."

For a moment, she thought about what would happen if she just told him the truth. She felt like a wolf cub just dying to eat out of a hiker's hand, but at the last minute losing heart and darting back into the woods. "You don't owe me an apology."

"I think—and I'm not trying to press; I mean what I said about it not being my business—but I think that car belonged to the man we met when we were waiting for our table. Is that right?"

Margie's eyes flashed to his.

Theo nodded and put up a hand. "You don't need to say anything. I saw the change that came over you when he walked up, but I didn't think about it again until later on."

Margie stared straight ahead again. She thought about that day in Father Keene's office, when he talked about how much her parents' reputations could suffer if word about Margie got out, how just their association with her could harm them. The idea was that she would keep the secret forever, just change the truth through sheer force of will. What would Verna think of her if she cracked under the pressure now, after all this time? "I wish I could tell you," Margie said, which in itself was a dangerous admission: there was something to tell. "I've never met anyone I wanted to tell before, until you. But I can't."

Theo nodded and didn't say anything for a moment. "I believe you. Both that you want to and that you can't."

"Thank you," Margie whispered.

"I just wish I had known what you were going to do to that car."

Margie cringed. "Believe me, it wasn't something I planned."

Theo turned to her again and touched her elbow. "I would have slipped my steak knife in my pocket. I could have helped you with it."

When this pledge of solidarity registered, her breath caught. Her face crumpled, and before she could stop it she began to weep.

"Oh, Margie," Theo said, and pulled her into his arms. He held her for a long time. After a few minutes, she could open her eyes enough to see the trees that towered over the quad, the sparrows bouncing among them. Finally he said, "What time do you have to be back?"

"No time."

"Come with me for the night."

Margie had never been to Theo's house in Pottawatomi, ninety minutes' drive from Milwaukee, ninety minutes' drive from the Loop, an hour from her parents. It was at a comfortable remove from any place you might be, which made her like it before she even laid eyes on it. Then she laid eyes on it.

The Barrett home was a three-story painted lady, blue with buttercream trim, sitting up on a small hill on a corner lot. Just from the car window she could see it had a big front porch and a fence with a garland of climbing hydrangea, a backyard with three apple trees and a vegetable patch.

Margie looked at Theo with her eyebrows raised. She had half expected there was no house at all.

He grinned, pleased to have taken her by surprise. "It looks best in the morning, I think. With a cup of coffee on the porch. You'll see."

They entered through the front gate and went up the brick path, past the brass mailbox with the hinged lid and BARRETT engraved on the front. Inside was a tiled entryway with coats and market bags hanging on hooks, the living room to the right; to the left, the dining room with built-in corner hutches jammed with mismatched china. Beyond that, an old-fashioned country kitchen with a big sink and weathered butcher-block counters, a door that led to the backyard and a length of clothesline. The floors creaked, and the simple white curtains ballooned in the open windows. And Margie knew that, in the winter, the radiators would hiss through the night. It was like a house from a story.

Theo leaned against the counter. "My father spent years walking by this house when he and my mother were still teenagers, just sweethearts then, and telling her he would buy it someday. But neither of them had any money. After school, he got a job as an errand boy for the Pottawatomi Typewriter Company, then a janitor, then worked in product testing. He saved every spare dime in strongboxes in the basement of his parents' house because he didn't trust banks. But the whole family thought he was crazy. No one, including my mother, I think, believed that he would ever be able to buy it. This was the kind of house the company executives had, not a working man.

"But then the market crashed, and the family who owned this place lost it in foreclosure. My father walked by on his way to work every day, watching it fall further into disrepair. Finally, after ten years of saving and that well-timed economic collapse, he had enough money to buy it. He married my mother the next day, and I was born a year later in the bedroom upstairs."

"It's like a fairy tale."

Theo laughed. "Well, it's a pain in the neck to take care of, to be honest. The porch sags at a troubling angle, the pipes leak, the wiring is wonky. I'm the town handyman's best customer. But there's Olga too, my housekeeper. It's a lot of house to keep up."

"Seems worth it to me," Margie said.

"What *do* you think of it?"

She thought about how Lorna had lived here too for all the years she and Theo were married, but, oddly perhaps, Margie didn't find that upsetting. Lorna was a part of Theo's history, just like the typewriter company and the strongboxes and the old-fashioned birth at home, more nineteenth than twentieth century. Lorna's death, too, and Theo's year of living here alone. That his life seemed to be an open book made Margie all the more conscious of everything she was keeping from him.

"I think it's a wonderful house."

"Could you see yourself living here?"

She grinned. "Oh yes."

"And . . . wouldn't you like to start that life in a month or two instead of a year?"

Margie tried to keep her voice level. "It's only a year. Why does it matter so much to you?"

He sighed. "A year in which anything could happen. You could meet someone else, change your mind. Twelve months is a long time, believe me."

Margie could see that he was thinking about Lorna, diagnosed in March and dead by Christmas.

He wrinkled his brow in confusion. "You know you will never need to work, don't you? You will never need to worry about money?"

It was so tempting to give in to his sense of urgency, because she *wanted* to be his wife, to live in this house; she wanted that right alongside the other things she wanted. "I'm trying to get you to see that it's not about that. It's just . . . I haven't had very many things in my life that were mine. I have two older sisters—I played with a lot of hand-me-down toys." She smiled to crush back the wave of sorrow that came with the memory of Timothy, hers so briefly, taken away. "A lot of things have . . . fallen through. And it seems now you want me to quit school, just because you are impatient."

He gave her a pleading look. "Impatient to make you my wife. Impatient because I love you."

Margie wouldn't look at him or else she would crumble. "My mother wants me to quit school because it's not practical for me to continue.

But what I feel about it is not about practical things. School is *mine.* I don't know how to explain it to you any other way besides that. It's mine alone. And I can't let anyone take it from me. I don't want to have that to blame you for."

Theo held up his hands in defeat. Margie had been so intent on expressing herself that she hadn't thought to wonder whether he would accept her explanation. But he didn't accept it or reject it. He slid closer to her along the edge of the counter, leaned in to kiss her neck. "Let's go to bed."

The warmth of his touch was a welcome distraction from her racing mind, and she let herself kiss him. But the urgent voice broke through again. "Theo, we haven't decided. We have to decide what to do."

"No." Theo put his hands on her shoulders. "*You* have to decide. If you're asking whether I will wait another eleven months to marry you, the answer is of course I will. I'm not trying to keep you in suspense or something. But it's not really about when. It's about whether you will let yourself do it. Whether you will let yourself have something good, whether you will let yourself trust me. I can't decide that for you, Margie."

31

Doreen

The parent-teacher organization of Our Lady of Pompeii, where Summer and Timothy would attend kindergarten in the fall, organized an open house, inviting the children to spend two hours after lunch exploring what it felt like to sit in a real school desk, make a craft with scissors and paste, and walk in a quiet line down the hallway to the cafeteria to eat the same cookies served at the church's funeral receptions and wait for their mothers to pick them up. Doreen had offered to collect both kids when it ended and keep them busy for the remainder of the afternoon so Luisa could keep an appointment downtown.

She saw the pair of them before they saw her. Timothy, whose fair skin was unusually red and blotchy, held Summer's hand as she led him down the steps. He was moaning in that stoic way kids did as they continued to move through a task while crying. Doreen tipped her head to the side. "What happened?"

"He fell down outside the cafeteria," Summer explained when they reached the sidewalk.

"I didn't fall," Timothy said. "They pushed me."

"Who pushed you?" Doreen crouched in front of him and brushed his cheek with her thumb.

"Some big boys." Timothy was trying mightily not to let his voice quaver.

Summer patted his back. "I think they just didn't see you. There were so many people coming through at once."

"Could I give you a hug?" Doreen asked him. He nodded. Still kneeling, she scooped him into her arms. Because she was accustomed to embracing Summer's solid frame, Timothy's light, almost fragile shoulders were a surprise, as if he were a bird instead of a boy. When she relaxed her grip to let him go, he clung to her neck with his little wings and rested his cheek on her shoulder. "It's okay," Doreen said, her voice catching in her throat. Summer continued to pat his back tenderly.

While she held him, Doreen recalled marching across the snow in front of Holy Family as she called goodbye to Margie. She had only turned back once, to wave and say something smug about Sister Simon, before picking up her pace to get out of the glow cast by the light above the front door. Now, with Timothy in her arms, she amended the memory to make herself turn back again and look more closely at her friend. Her protector, her savior. There was Margie in her pink quilted bathrobe, face and hands still swollen from the intravenous fluids she had received while under anesthesia, one arm raised to wave back as Doreen rushed to leave that terrible place behind. To leave Margie behind. In the beginning, Doreen had written Margie off as a doormat and a drip, but that night Margie summoned a fortitude that still seemed impossible. Doreen thought she would never get over her guilt, nor her gratitude. Margie deserved so much more than being abandoned to the emptiness of her old life. She deserved to know the truth, but Doreen had not been brave enough to tell her.

She kissed Timothy's temple. Not wanting to be outdone, Summer did the same, kissing the top of his head as if she were his older sister instead of his contemporary, and Doreen smiled at her approvingly. Had Timothy been just one year older, he might have squirmed away or wiped the offending action off his hair with a *yuck*. But for now he was still just little enough to allow himself the pleasure of being soothed by two girls who adored him.

"Let's go to the drugstore," Doreen said. "We can try the new milkshake flavor."

Summer squealed. "Milkshakes!"

"Does that sound good to you, Nicholas?" Doreen smoothed his hair.

He took the shuddering breath that follows a big cry and nodded as Doreen led their party across the street.

"Don't you want to know the new flavor? It's liver and onions."

Summer stopped, midstride, and locked her elbows in horror. "Mom, *eww*!"

"What? I think that sounds delicious. And very high in iron," Doreen said.

"She's not telling the truth," Timothy said solemnly to Summer. "They would *never* make a milkshake like that."

"How do you know?" Doreen asked. "Maybe some people really like that flavor. I think I would choose it over any other kind of milkshake in the world. Especially if they could add some sardine sauce—and maybe some whole sardines for sprinkles."

Timothy's dour face broke into a grin. "No, you wouldn't. A sardine milkshake is the worst thing I've ever heard of in my whole life."

"In your whole life? Well, goodness. I suppose we could ask for chocolate. They might have a little left."

"Mo-*om*," Summer groaned, driven crazy and loving every bit of it. "We are getting chocolate."

"Not me," Timothy said with the quiet courage of his convictions. "I'm getting strawberry."

Summer began relating a complicated theory she had about why tornadoes never came to Chicago, and Timothy rubbed his elbow, still soothing the wound from his fall. Doreen let them walk ahead of her a few steps so that she could slip Danny's camera out of her purse and snap a couple pictures of them: First, twirling. Then giggling, holding hands and walking backward with their faces turned toward Doreen. Then

Summer's face in profile, turned toward Timothy, her hand whirling in the air to show the tornado's speed. Timothy listened patiently as he watched the sidewalk ahead of them, thinking maybe about the frightening capabilities of weather or the strawberry milkshake that would soon be cold in his hands or something else entirely in the secret world of his mind.

After the milkshakes, they stopped at the playground, and Summer and Timothy, enlivened by sugar, ran full speed for the swings. Summer reached them first and threw her stomach onto the band of rubber as if she were belly-flopping into a pool. While she squealed with delight, Timothy reached his swing, turned around, and carefully fitted his bottom to its curve. Slowly, he tiptoed backward on the mound of woodchips that kept the mud at bay, and only when he was carefully aligned did he lift his toes and let himself sail in a perfect arc.

"Nicholas," Summer cried. "This is our spaceship. We're driving to the moon."

He looked solemn. "People can't go to the moon, Summer."

Just then, another kid appeared. She was younger, wearing pink rain boots, with skin darker than Summer's, and she took the third swing. Doreen turned to see a woman following the girl into the park. She wore a red cotton top with a Peter Pan collar, and her hair was styled in a smooth bob. Doreen felt a wave of recognition, followed instantly by dread. Maybe Diana wouldn't remember her.

Doreen gave a friendly wave. "I guess the swings are the place to be today."

Diana's smile was warm, outlined by deep red lipstick that made her eyes bright. "Fine by me. We were bouncing off the walls at home."

"I wish I had their energy." Doreen kept her eyes on the kids.

"Hey, don't I know you?" Diana said, recognition breaking on her face. "From Lew's studio, right?"

"Yeah," Doreen said, forcing a smile. "We met the other day."

"I'm Diana. Remind me of your name."

"Doreen." She cringed as she thought about the scene Diana had witnessed the last time they had been together. "That was . . . maybe not my best day."

Diana waved the comment away. "All I remember is a couple great songs." She gave Doreen a reassuring grin and gestured to the kids. "You have a son too?"

Doreen exhaled. "Oh no—the girl is mine. Summer. And Nicholas is our friend."

"They play cute together. My daughter's Sharon. She just turned four."

"She's gorgeous. Looks just like you. I'd like a pair of those boots in my size." Doreen fiddled with the strap of her purse. "The kids will start kindergarten at Pompeii this fall. We come here any day it's not raining." She knew she was babbling, but she couldn't shake her self-consciousness. Diana had seen her at her most vulnerable—first, when she played her music, and then when Cal had shown up and thrown his tantrum. Doreen wanted to melt like snow and disappear down the storm drain.

Instead, she had to stand there and wait for the awkwardness to pass. Diana was too experienced in the studio to ask what was happening with the demo. That was likely a touchy subject with most musicians, when so many of their efforts went nowhere. Doreen watched Sharon and Summer swinging side by side. Sharon's hair was braided in neat rows, and the braids were decorated at the ends with pink beads that made a pleasant clicking sound as she moved through the air.

"I love how you style Sharon's hair," Doreen said.

"Oh." Diana looked surprised. "Thanks."

"I wish I could do something like that for Summer. You can probably tell I don't really know what I'm doing when it comes to her hair."

"Well . . ." Diana said, stretching out the word. Together they gazed at Summer's style, or lack thereof: today her frizzy curls were held back with a headband. Doreen liked to tell Summer her hair was like a thick, beautiful vine in a garden, or a rich crown, but her natural texture was inconsistent, running from dense to curly, and Summer often wasn't patient enough to let Doreen comb it. Even if she had been, Doreen had to be honest with herself: there was more to caring for Summer's hair than she understood, and she hadn't tried very hard to learn what to do.

Doreen gave Diana an embarrassed smile. "It's okay. You can tell me the truth."

"It's not your fault," Diana said. "Her hair texture is different from yours. How would you know what to do?" Then, carefully, "But it could look a lot nicer. It's going to start to matter a lot more to her as she gets older."

Doreen winced. "I know." She remembered how many hours she had spent on her own hair in her teenage years, the clouds of hairspray that had probably done permanent lung damage, the sleepless nights in rollers, after which she woke in the dark to unwind her curls and spray them again so they fell just so around her shoulders.

"I could help you," Diana said.

Doreen turned to look at her. "Seriously?"

"Sure." She didn't sound sure. Having already seen the mess behind the curtain of Doreen's life, Diana was likely wondering whether it was a mistake to get involved. But her obvious compassion was winning out. "We just moved into the neighborhood, on Laflin."

"Oh, we're on Ada. I grew up here—we live with my mother." Doreen hadn't meant the comment to be anything other than informative, but given the tensions over who was moving in and who was moving out of the neighborhood, she hoped Diana wouldn't take her reply the wrong way. "Welcome," she said. She wished she had said that first.

"Tomorrow's Saturday," Diana said. If Doreen had offended her, she wasn't showing it. "Why don't you come over in the morning? My husband will be at work, and the paper said it's going to rain. I could show you a few things, and the girls can play together."

"It's such a generous offer. I really don't want to put you out."

Diana twisted her mouth into a crooked smile. "Well, I'll level with you. *Somebody's* got to help you. Summer's hair's so dry it's going to start breaking, if it hasn't already. You need to learn how to take care of it to protect it, and so that you can teach her how to do it for herself. Much as we hate to think about this, our girls won't be little forever."

There were at least three alarming pieces of information in Diana's words. Doreen nodded at her, embarrassed and grateful. "I'd really appreciate it. I don't have a clue what I'm doing."

"No offense," Diana said, "but that's pretty clear."

"What do you take in your coffee?"

"Just a little milk," Doreen said. "Thank you."

"Sure." Diana prepared their mugs and sliced a small coffee cake into bite-sized squares. She was as easy-going as Doreen was nervous. In her tidy galley kitchen, the scouring pad and sponge were tucked in a cup beside the stainless steel sink; on the refrigerator door was Sharon's drawing of a rainbow-colored ice cream cone. Doreen realized that despite sharing the ultimate intimacy with Mosel, she had never been inside a Black person's home before.

Diana and her husband, Paul, lived in a newer apartment complex, one of many built within the past few years after the highway split the neighborhood and forced so many Italian families out to the suburbs. Or that's what they said, anyway, that they were *forced* out by the highway. Doreen knew some of it had more to do with people who looked like Diana—who looked like Summer—moving in.

"Have you worked with Ron a long time?"

Diana laughed. "Only since I was a teenager. My father was a sound engineer too, for Chess and Delmark. Ron learned from him and then taught it all to me, since my father was gone by then."

"Oh," Doreen said. "I'm sorry. My father died when I was in high school."

Diana looked at her with a simple, open expression. "Then you know."

She carried the tray to the coffee table. The front room was furnished with a pale-pink sofa and two gray chairs draped in a chintz fabric, brass table lamps with delicate white shades. Not trendy, but classic and tasteful in the steady way that Diana seemed to be steady. Down the short hallway was the ceramic-tiled bathroom and two bedrooms. Sharon and Summer were playing school in Sharon's bedroom, and Summer, to Doreen's shock, had offered to let Sharon be the teacher. ("She doesn't know how to do it right," Summer had confided to Doreen in a whisper, "but it's okay.")

They settled at either end of the sofa and sipped from their cups. "Your apartment is lovely," Doreen said.

"Thanks. It has taken some time for us to get settled in. There are so many decisions to make, and my husband does not like to spend money." Diana grinned and took a square of cake. "So I've had to get creative."

"Well, you've done a fantastic job."

"And Summer's father?" Diana asked. "What's he like?"

It was funny: no one had ever asked Doreen this question in casual conversation before. Every person in her life, from Carla and Danny and Luisa on down to Summer's teacher and the man who owned the corner market and had known Doreen all her life, steered the conversation far from this topic and the shame they assumed it provoked in Doreen. They knew one thing about Mosel, the thing they had gleaned from Summer's complexion, and that one thing made them conclude it would be rude to acknowledge his existence.

"He's very smart," Doreen said, puffing up with pride, as if the halo of Mosel's accomplishments somehow extended to her. "He would be done with college by now, I think. Maybe on to graduate school. That was his plan, anyway."

Diana nodded, quickly understanding what that *would be* indicated. "Well, that doesn't surprise me. Summer seems like a very bright girl." One woman could always put another at ease by complimenting her child. It provided a merciful pivot for just about any awkward conversation. But now that Diana had opened the door, Doreen found she didn't want to change the subject. She wanted the chance to talk about Mosel.

"He and I were together for just a little while, and then he went off to college. I only found out that Summer was coming after he was gone, and it didn't seem right to make him change his plans. He won a mathematics scholarship. I'm not just saying this because he was my guy—I mean, I had it bad for him, of course, so what do I know—but I think he really was brilliant or something. The university seemed to be making an awfully big deal about him, and I couldn't mess that up." Though she felt bold enough to tell this part, for the rest of her life she would probably never divulge to anyone what came next: that for a time she had considered giving Summer up.

Diana was quiet for a moment, looking at her hands. "Well. That is something to be proud of." She set her cup and saucer on the coffee table just a little too roughly. "Should we talk about Summer's hair now?"

And though the best course would have been to stuff it and move on, Doreen couldn't help herself. (It was no mystery where Summer had gotten her mouth.) "You don't believe me?"

"What?"

"About Summer's father. You don't believe that he got the scholarship."

Diana drew back. "Of course I do."

"Then what is it? Why did you just get so quiet?"

With her hand up and a new wariness in her voice, she said, "Look, we hardly know each other. And I don't make a habit of sticking my nose in other people's business."

Doreen grinned. "Aw, go ahead. Stick your nose in. Everybody else I know is too scared to ask about my business because they think they're going to say the wrong thing. They think I must be walking around feeling ashamed every second of the day. Especially because . . ."

Diana's eyes shot up to hers, and there was both sympathy and anger there. "I can imagine."

"So tell me what you were thinking."

"I . . ." She pressed her lips into a line, considering. "I was thinking that if I were in your shoes—which I'm not, but if I were—I'd feel that it isn't right to keep a man's child from him, no matter who he is." She stirred her coffee. "Don't you think he deserves to know he has a daughter?"

"Even if it's going to ruin his life?"

"But you don't know that would happen. If he is as smart as you say, he knows what's important in life. Besides, how could that little girl ruin anyone's life? She is a ray of sunshine."

"She is. It's just . . . he has worked so hard to get where he is. I can't take that away."

"But who are you to make that decision for him? He is a grown man and a father."

Diana's blunt words startled Doreen, but she tried to consider them instead of snapping back to say she'd changed her mind about Diana sticking her nose in. Though Doreen thought of Mosel often, it was mostly to reminisce about the only real romance of her life, not to think of him as Summer's father. She kept this secret from him just like she kept the secret of Timothy from Margie. Just like she had kept the secret of Summer from Cal. She did it because she thought she knew what was best for the people she cared about, and for herself. But, maybe for the first time, she wondered whether they would appreciate being cared about in that particular way.

"You're not on an easy road. I'm sure your people were not too happy about the whole thing."

Doreen raised her eyebrows, remembering Carla taking to her bed, threatening Danny with swift death. "It has been . . . interesting."

Just then, the girls came barreling into the room, Summer yammering in her aggrieved voice and Sharon managing admirably to keep up.

"Mommy, we switched places, and now I'm the teacher, but Sharon won't do the pledge like I told her. She doesn't even know to put her hand on her heart."

Poor Sharon stood behind the girl she hoped to impress, with her palm pressed to her blouse. "Yes, I do!"

"Summer!" Doreen scolded her. "Sharon is younger than you. It's your job to *teach* the younger kids, not make them feel bad."

"You know what?" Sharon said in what had to be a perfect imitation of Diana hitting her breaking point. "No more school! I don't like this game."

I'm sorry, Doreen mouthed to Diana over Summer's head.

But Diana just clapped her hands. "Girls, we've got a new game to play. Beauty parlor!"

By the end of the morning, Summer's hair had been washed, conditioned, and combed through with Posner's Bergamot until her curls tightened beautifully and every bit of frizz was gone. Diana told Doreen where to buy the product, what kind of comb to use, and what she should stop doing forever: no more harsh shampoo, no more brushing.

"This girl may be part white, but her hair is all Black," Diana said.

She parted Summer's hair into sections and wound them into four thick braids tied off on the ends with blue barrettes in the shape of butterflies. Instantly, Doreen knew Carla would hate this look that wasn't even *trying* to be white, but Doreen was elated. Summer looked polished and well cared for. Just what Doreen had longed to be able to do.

She stood behind her daughter as Summer gazed at herself in the mirror. "You look like a princess."

Summer turned her head one way, then the other, ran her forefinger along her hairline and touched the end of one braid. She gave Doreen a dubious glance in the mirror. "A princess? Try again, Mommy. I look like a queen."

32

Margie

On the morning of her poetry seminar, Margie rose early so she would have the communal bathroom at the end of the hall to herself to take a long shower, dry her hair, and put on her makeup, leaning over the sink in her cotton bathrobe, without having to talk to anyone. All the while, she thought about Sylvia Plath, picking up where she had left off at midnight practicing what she would say. If anything, Margie had overprepared. She had so much material to pack into her fifteen minutes in front of the class, she would probably never get through it all. But she had to prove to Verna, to Theo—to herself—that her classes weren't just a waste of time.

The lecture room was quieter than usual, all the girls sorting nervously through their index cards and whispering to themselves. Index cards would have been a good idea, Margie realized with a sinking feeling. She had been planning to rely on pages of notes written longhand.

"So many nervous faces this morning," Professor Butler said when she called them to order. "Take a deep breath, girls. You will do beautifully."

This broke the tension some, but Margie was still glad she didn't have to go first. She sat through Millicent Carl's talk on Wallace Stevens, Julia Reese on Edgar Allan Poe, Bernadette Coyle on Marianne Moore, growing more anxious with each presentation because her classmates finished a few minutes early, with time to spare for questions.

"Margaret Ahern," Professor Butler said, and Margie pulled her notebook from her bag and walked stiffly to the front. A sea of eyes stared at her, and she tried not to look directly at them but instead at the wood grain of the door at the back of the room, behind their heads.

Margie cleared her throat. "My topic today is Sylvia Plath. I want to show you the difference between two of her poems that have made the biggest impact on me. The first is called 'The Eye-mote,' and the second, a poem from the volume published after her death, 'The Moon and the Yew Tree.' While they are different stylistically—I think the older one is more formal and constrained—it has always been interesting to me that they are both about looking out, across a field, from a window, and how the speaker isn't always right about what she thinks she sees."

As Margie spoke, she began to relax and realized she wouldn't need her notes anyhow until it came time to read a portion of the poem. "In a way, I think you can really see Plath's state of mind changing, to a kind of hopelessness, between the poems. Let me show you what I mean."

Margie opened the notebook and folded back the cover, flipped a couple pages to find the poem. She felt her lungs constrict. A long moment passed in which she stood, frozen, unable to look up from the page.

"Margaret," Professor Butler said gently. "Are you all right?"

She stared at the words *Dear Timothy*. "It's . . . I've made a mistake. This is a notebook of . . . my own writing. I mixed it up with the class notes. I left those in my room."

Professor Butler twisted up her mouth. "Oh dear."

The eyes continued to stare at her, now with pity, and every second that ticked by only made it worse.

Professor Butler had the kind of gentle manner that in past decades would have doomed her to teaching grade school, despite her scholarly accomplishments. "Margaret, forgive me for treating this as a teachable moment, but I would say to the class that this sort of thing is why I chose to make the final exam a presentation instead of a written test." She turned to the others. "In poetry, as in life, we can only expect the unexpected, and our success depends on the ability to pivot, to recover when our plans go awry. You don't have your notes on Plath handy, Margaret, so what could you do instead? How can you pivot and recover your remaining minutes to engage the listener and teach her something new?"

"I . . . well . . ."

Professor Butler nodded to the notebook of letters to Timothy, the open page now tacky with perspiration from Margie's hands. "You said it's your own writing, didn't you? Why don't you read us something?"

Initially, Margie recoiled at this impossible prospect, but then Professor Butler whispered, "Remember, you can pivot."

Margie stared at the words on the page and thought about the longing they held, the cumulative hours they represented, of calling and calling into the darkness with no expectation that she would ever be heard, of striving to be a conscientious custodian of her secret. She was so tired of it.

A couple girls shifted in their seats as the moment dragged on. Margie flipped through the pages and landed on a fragment from six months back. "This is . . . Well, I won't try to explain it." She swallowed again. "I'll just read it.

> *"Do you remember what happened on the last day we were together? I swear this was real: You were still mine, and I buckled us into a rocket that left the earth. I can still feel the rumble of the engines beneath my feet, your scalp soft against my hand. You couldn't see, but I could see for you: the rising, the world diminishing below until it was just the two of us in orbit, the two of us and the black sky and the stars. But then there was too much sky, and the worst part came. When I tried to lift you to the window, you disappeared in my arms."*

Margie closed the notebook and looked up. Without realizing it, she had expected the other girls to reflect back her own feelings, of terror, of acute vulnerability, as if the brief excerpt could reveal everything she had gone through at Holy Family and every day since, the endless and invisible and shameful war she waged, now on display. Instead, her classmates stared blankly at her. Millicent's forehead was creased like an elephant's. Anita's mouth hung open in an O of confusion.

Blinking her eyes for a moment, Professor Butler seemed to be grasping for what to say. Before she could get a word out, a laugh exploded from Margie's chest, sharp and unwieldy in the quiet room. She clapped a hand over her mouth to try to contain the sound, but her shoulders were shaking with laughter, her eyes beginning to well with the pure absurdity of the situation.

"Thank you, Margaret," Professor Butler said. "That was very . . . unexpected."

Margie nodded, still unable to get a word out, and went back to her seat, laughing at her bad luck with the notebooks, at her deep pain simply lost in translation to a room full of people who had no idea what in the hell she was talking about, at the sheer strangeness of her life. Margie wiped away her tears with the backs of her hands and noticed as her chest continued to shudder with peals of laughter that it felt open in a new way. She would certainly receive a bad grade on the assignment. It had been a disaster. But even though they now thought she was nuts, Margie had read her carefully guarded words to a roomful of people, waiting for the sky to fall, and nothing had happened. A surprising and beautiful nothing.

Instead of heading straight back to her room to get started on a make-up assignment Professor Butler told her she could complete to rescue her grade, Margie stopped first at the main desk outside the administrator's offices to fill out a registration form for the fall term. Somehow, the fiasco with her presentation only made her more sure that she should continue through to the end. It was a revelation: she didn't have to be a perfect person to deserve a chance to keep trying. The form was in triplicate, and she searched for the four courses she had left to take to graduate. Two of them, Early American Novels and Advanced Rhetoric, were offered in the fall.

The receptionist was new, a woman Margie had never seen before, and she smiled as Margie filled in her name on the top of the form.

"Oh, you're Margaret Ahern?"

Margie stopped writing and nodded.

"Someone has called for you a couple times this morning." The receptionist handed Margie a pink message marked urgent. The return number was for her parents' house in Sycamore Ridge.

"Thank you," Margie said, flustered. She folded the incomplete registration form in half and took it with her to the phone booth at the end of the hall. She had no change in her purse. She would have to call collect.

"Ahern residence. I'll accept the charges."

It took Margie a second to recognize her sister's voice. "Alice?"

"Margie, thank God. We've been trying to reach you."

Though Margie didn't have particularly strong feelings about either of her sisters—essentially, they were strangers to her—Alice, the older one, had always been kind to Margie. "I'm sorry, I was in class. What's wrong?"

She sighed. "You should come home right away. Mother is sick."

"What kind of sick?" She curled the black cord around her finger, that momentary openness in her chest now closing like the shutter on a camera.

"Margie, I'm sorry to have to tell you over the phone, but it's cancer. In her lungs. She has known for months but hasn't said a word to any of us. I really can't believe it. But there's no hiding it now. You should come as soon as you can."

33

Doreen

"Mommy, why does that man have that long coat on? It's so hot today."

Doreen cupped her hand over the finger Summer was using to point at the bum standing under the awning of the pharmacy to get out of the sun. She lowered her daughter's hand. "Hon, you shouldn't point at people."

"Why not?"

They walked on to the end of the block, pausing to wait for the light to change. "Because it's considered rude to point."

Summer turned her face up to Doreen and squinted against the sun. "But how else am I supposed to show you what I'm talking about?"

"I know." Doreen tried to keep her face solemn. "Manners are . . . kind of complicated. But we have to learn them."

"But why?"

Doreen shrugged as they crossed the street. "Because we don't want to make people feel bad, even by accident." She figured they were about a third of the way into the mile-long walk to the Des Plaines station, where they would take the West Side subway to the Loop and the Social Security office in the federal building. The journey was a continuation of her penance to Carla to make up for the late night out when Summer had been sick. A few days ago, Carla had received a scary-looking certified letter that said the Social Security Administration needed proof she still resided at the same address, or Vincenzo's checks would stop coming. Why in the world they thought she would have moved, when she had lived on Ada Street since 1941, was a mystery for the annals of bureaucratic history. But Doreen recognized at once an opportunity to get back into her mother's good graces. "You don't need to take off work just to go down there and stand in line all afternoon," she had said. "Summer and I can do it."

"Anyway," Summer said now, the conversation still going, "you never answered my question."

Doreen plucked her blouse away from her damp lower back. Once they got east of Morgan Street, it seemed like there wasn't a single tree on the planet, and this had been the hottest June she could remember. "What's that?"

Summer sighed with the weariness of having to explain things to a simpleton. "About the man in the coat. Isn't he hot wearing that?"

"Well, I think he doesn't have a home, so he brings all his stuff with him wherever he goes. He probably wears all the clothes he has because it's easier than carrying them in a bag."

"But where is his bed?"

"He doesn't have a bed."

"But where does he sleep?"

"I don't know. Probably in the park somewhere."

Summer looked stricken. "But you can't sleep in the park. The squirrels will bite you at night."

Doreen put her hand on Summer's shoulder. "Well, I don't know about the squirrels, but you're right that no one should have to sleep outside. It's sad."

"It's *terrible*," Summer said.

"I agree."

They walked another block as Summer contemplated this new information, and Doreen enjoyed a brief moment of silence as they passed the new University of Illinois Chicago campus, with its hulking concrete buildings with tiny windows that looked more like prisons than classrooms. She wondered whether this was what Ohio State's campus looked like too, or whether it was one of those older colleges that looked like colleges were supposed to: white buildings with columns, stately stone dorms with stained-glass windows.

"This is taking *so long*," Summer whined.

"I know. We're almost there," Doreen lied.

Summer brightened. "But at least we're not germs."

"What?"

"Don't you know? Germs are so much smaller than us. Nonni told me that there are a million germs in just one drop of water!"

"Well, I guess you're never alone if you're a germ."

"That's why I'm glad we're not germs, because if a germ had to walk from our house to the train, it would take *way* longer."

Doreen laughed. "That's true. And they don't even have legs."

"Mommy, rent is money, right?"

"What?" Doreen tried to keep the annoyance out of her voice. She lifted her hair off the back of her neck and wished for even the slightest breeze, or to be able to follow the train of this conversation. "Well, yeah. You pay money to rent an apartment or a house, to the person who owns it."

"Like the Quinns pay rent to Nonni?"

"That's right."

"Well, we have money from your job and Nonni's job and Uncle Danny's job. Why can't we give it to that man so he can get a bed?"

They were crossing the bridge over the Kennedy now, trucks whizzing below and the rails vibrating when each one passed. Doreen waited until they were on the other side before crouching down to look her daughter in the eye. "You are good, through and through. Do you know that? You have such a big heart."

"So we can give him the money?"

Doreen closed her eyes and smiled. "No, I'm sorry."

"But why not?"

She sighed. "Hon, it's complicated to explain, but the world just doesn't work that way."

"But why not?"

She wanted to be proud that Summer seemed to be a person disturbed by the world's injustices, but she was mainly just hot and tired and irritated. "Summer, we're going to take a little break from talking now. The sun is making my ears hurt."

This summer was already putting the city through the wringer and it was only June. Three weeks before, the police had shot a Puerto Rican boy about four miles away in Humboldt Park, and the PRs rioted for days. You got the feeling it wouldn't take much for a whole lot of other people to join in, they had put up with so much abuse for so long. The whole city had the feel of a beaten dog about to break its chain to fight back. Doreen worried what the cops would do if things got worse. Every Italian hated Daley's guts for running the Eisenhower expressway right through their neighborhood, and by the transitive property of enemies, that meant they hated his police department too. Those guys put more stock in the Klan than the Constitution, and they took it as a personal insult when any Black man spoke up for himself. There were so many neighborhoods where Doreen would never take Summer. The stares they got when they were walking together on Taylor Street were bad enough, but at least there, most everyone knew her.

On the train, Summer asked about how the tracks worked, why the windows didn't open, why the brakes made a screeching sound, and was not satisfied with any of the answers to her questions. When they finally reached the office, with its waiting area corralled into an orderly line by faded velvet ropes draped from bronze pedestals, Doreen was so relieved to see the bank of chairs about six feet away from where she would be standing, she thought she might cry. She pulled a small notebook and pen from her purse and handed them to Summer.

"I have an important job for you. I need you to draw me ten pictures of cats. Ten *really detailed* pictures. Three of them should have stripes, and you can decide what the others are like. Do you think you can do it?"

Summer nodded solemnly and took the notebook to the chairs. Doreen felt the momentary relief that came when she got a break long enough to think a thought from beginning to end. But then the avalanche of tasks began tumbling in her brain: They needed milk. The uniform exchange at Pompeii was on Saturday, and if she wasn't in the front of the line, the only jumpers left would be the ratty ones, or too small or too large. Carla would kill her if they had to order a new one, and anyway they were almost out of time for it to arrive ahead of September. Either way, it would need to be hemmed. And then, what she really wanted to think about: her demo, in the top drawer of her nightstand at home. How in the world she was supposed to get it into the hands of that man at WLS?

There were three people ahead of her, two women and then a tall man in a tan belted jacket. Doreen glanced over to check on Summer. She knelt in front of the chair, using its seat as a little table. Doreen winced, thinking how dirty the floor probably was, but at least Summer was occupied.

The line shifted forward. The man ahead of her turned his head to assess the length of the line behind him and looked at the clock. She felt his gaze pass over her, and though she didn't meet it, she could tell he was good-looking, with dark skin and a nonchalant posture. He turned back around.

A moment later, he looked at her again, and she couldn't avoid acknowledging him. She met his eyes and grinned politely, nodded. But something there jolted her.

"I'm sorry, miss, but . . . don't I know you from somewhere?"

The eyes were Mosel's, but the rest of him was not: too tall, too broad-shouldered, his chin a different shape. "I . . . I don't know."

His eyes widened, and he lightly slapped his left palm with the folded papers he held in his right hand. "You're that girl my brother met at the Regal."

It was coming back to her now: Mosel and his brother sitting in the row next to Doreen and Wanda. The brother talking about the architecture. Mosel staring shyly at his hands. Doreen felt the shiver that comes when you think back on a night that changed your fate. Mosel wore an olive jacket, an orange pocket square. She had thought about it ten thousand times. But why should his brother remember her all these years later?

"Wow, what are the chances we'd both end up in this line?" she said, keeping her voice cool. "I can't believe you remember me."

"I remember your friend," he said, a smile spreading on his lips.

She couldn't help but laugh. "Wanda."

"Oh, Wanda. What's she up to these days?"

Doreen shook her head. "You know, I really couldn't say. We sort of lost touch." The last time Doreen had seen Wanda, she was pushing baby Summer down the street in in her stroller. Wanda had promised to come by for coffee so they could catch up—she said she couldn't wait to hold the baby—but then she never called. It was like she thought Doreen had a disease she was afraid of catching.

The line was not moving. Doreen glanced at the chairs. Summer had lost interest in her drawings and was now examining the leaflets in a wooden rack on the wall. The peril of the situation was creeping from Doreen's tight lungs to her brain: if he saw Summer, she would have to be ready to explain quick. But what would she say?

Mosel's brother slid the papers back in his jacket pocket. "You're right—it has been a while. We were young back then, weren't we? Before we had to grow up and get jobs. Before we had to stand in the line at Social Security."

"Yeah," Doreen said. "We didn't know what we had."

"Your name's Doreen, right? I remember that too. *Doreen*. Mosel could not stop talking about you that summer. He kept your picture on his dresser. I think that's why I recognized you."

It was like hearing your echo across a cavern. The one you loved, loving you back.

"I'm Raymond," he said. "I'm sure you don't remember."

"I didn't. I'm sorry." She shook his hand.

He shrugged. "Well, why would you? Now, that Wanda." He winked. "I bet *she* remembers my name."

The clerk called the woman ahead of them in line, and they stepped forward, but not fast enough. Summer called to her from the chair.

"Mommy, look at my cats." Then she was at Doreen's side, talking a mile a minute. "You can't tell since I don't have my crayons, but this one's orange with a white stripe. He's a boy. And this one is his sister. She is all white with a pink nose."

"I really like them," Doreen said softly. She ran her fingers over the soft skin on the back of Summer's neck, hugged her close to her hip.

She glanced up to see Raymond's face. First it was amused in a distant way, taking in the big personality of a child who had nothing to do with him. Then something slid into place, and his eyes sharpened. He looked at Summer more carefully, then at Doreen.

"So you got married."

She was going to have to decide what to do here. And fast. "Actually, no. I never have been married."

"Oh, I see," he said. "I'm sorry. I didn't mean to be rude." He looked at Summer again. It didn't help that she was Mosel's double, not just in her features but her mannerisms too—the way her long fingers moved over her drawings, the wonder in her voice. Raymond looked at Doreen again, and she knew there was no way to sidestep it. "Doreen," he said, "is there anything Mosel needs to know?"

She didn't deny it fast enough because she didn't *want* to deny it. She only looked at him with pleading eyes.

Summer was so bright. She had already discerned that something important was happening. Her eyes bounced from Doreen to Raymond.

"It's probably not a conversation we should have here."

Raymond put his hand to his mouth. "I can't believe it." His face cycled from shock to anger to tenderness, and then he crouched down in front of Summer. "Hi," he said, offering his hand. "I'm Mr. Palmer."

Summer pumped it up and down. "I'm Summer. Pleased to meet you."

"Summer. What a pretty name. I like your drawings. Do you like cats?"

"They are my favorite animal." The clerk called the woman in front of Raymond, and they shuffled forward.

"What do you know? Me too. Do you have one?"

Summer shot Doreen a look. "Mommy says we can't because they're too much work."

"Ah, well. Your mother may be right about that. Someday, when the time is right, though, Summer, I think you'll have one."

"Me too."

Raymond stood up, his eyebrows high. "All you have to do is take one look at her eyes."

Doreen nodded. "Yeah, I know. She's lucky that way."

"Doreen, he has a right to know."

She thought of what Diana had said: *He is a grown man and a father.* Doreen had treated Mosel like an idea instead of a person. A memory she could treasure but always control. She was terrified that if she saw him again in real life, if he knew about Summer, he might lose respect for her, or that she might learn that she never really meant that much to him. It was safer to keep him at a distance. "I know."

"I don't want to interfere," he said, "but I can't keep a secret like this from my brother." He asked Summer if he could borrow her notebook and pencil. Inside the back cover, he wrote an address and phone number. "Mosel lives in New York City now."

The clerk called Raymond forward.

"He does?" Suddenly Doreen was desperate to ask the thousand questions that cycled through her mind at night: Was he married? Did college go okay? Was he happy?

"He's in graduate school. Doreen, are you still at the same address?"

"Sir, next please," the clerk called. "Don't hold up the line."

Doreen nodded.

"You've got to call him."

"I will."

"If he doesn't hear from you . . ."

"I'll call him. I *promise.*"

He looked at Summer one more time and turned to the counter. All Doreen could think was that this was another one of those days that changes your fate, except this time Summer's fate was involved too. She was tugging on Doreen's sleeve now, ready to begin her interrogation. "Mommy," she said, whispering because she had gleaned enough from the interaction to understand that no one should hear this question, "who was that man?"

34

Margie

Theo drove south on I-41, fast but not too fast, occasionally glancing at Margie. "You doing all right?"

Margie shrugged, her eyes puffy from crying, her mouth dry. She tried to remember if she had packed her toothbrush when she rushed back to the dorm to gather her things after calling Theo. His secretary had put Margie through, and he left work right away, driving all the way to Milwaukee to collect her, then doubling back south to deliver her to the hospital in Sycamore Ridge.

"I forgot to tell you, there's some sandwiches and a thermos of coffee in back. I wasn't sure whether you'd had the chance to eat. Though I don't suppose you're very hungry."

Margie gave him a weak smile. "No, but thank you. That was so thoughtful." She wouldn't have minded the coffee right now, especially if it were scalding. It was eighty degrees out at five o'clock in the evening, and she thought something bitter and hot would be just the opposite of comfort. It would be wrong to expect comfort now, when she was crying not for Verna but for herself.

Margie ran her fingertip over the seam in the black vinyl seat and tipped her head against the window. She thought it couldn't be true, what Alice had said, that Verna was so near the end. Margie had just seen her mother two weeks ago and she was undiminished: beautifully styled and more than a little cruel, as usual. Margie remembered that hacking cough, her "summer cold." It didn't seem possible that she could go from being her usual self to gone in a matter of days, and with so much unfinished business. She felt panicked. What if Verna stayed angry with her right through to the end? What if Margie could never get her forgiveness?

At the hospital, Margie went into the room alone. Verna's breathing was shallow, her face ghost-gray. She wore a blue terrycloth nightgown Frank had brought her from home and a scarf that covered the hair she had not been able to get fixed that week at the beauty parlor. Margie had not once in her entire life seen Verna without her hair set. That was when Margie knew for sure the end was just days away.

On the bedside was a full glass of water and the tube from the oxygen tank that Verna was supposed to keep in her nose. Her favorite rosary hung on the headboard.

"Mother," Margie said softly, both afraid to wake her and afraid not to.

Verna's eyes fluttered and she opened them, her face creased with tension.

"Are you in pain?" Margie asked.

Verna shook her head slightly. "It's just . . ." She wheezed. ". . . bright in here."

"It's okay," Margie said. "You can close your eyes if you want to. I'm just going to sit with you. Would you like me to read the paper?"

"You're going to have to check on your father when I'm gone. He's helpless."

"Oh, Mother. I will. But let's not talk about that part now."

"Don't be stupid. Now is the time to talk about it. Right now. There isn't much time, Margie."

Margie took a breath. "He's not going to be alone for a day." She said this sincerely, emotion rising in her chest. Bumbling Frank was going to be lost without Verna, even though she mostly abused him. "It's the blessing of a large family, isn't it? You have three daughters and a daughter-in-law to look in on him. We'll take turns, fill the freezer in the basement with meals. Let us worry about it now. You've taken such good care of him all these years."

If these promises calmed Verna's anxiety, she didn't show it. "Don't let Alice bully you when it comes time to divide things up. There is . . . an emerald ring in the bottom drawer of my jewelry box that you should have. It belonged to my mother."

Margie blinked in surprise. "All right. Thank you, Mother."

"She had fat fingers . . . like you. If Alice takes it, she will have to waste money on getting it sized."

"Oh. Of course." Margie absorbed the familiar sinking feeling of anticipating Verna's favor and swiftly being relieved of that hope.

They sat in silence for a while, and Verna closed her eyes. Margie looked at her mother's spotted hands. Now was the time to bring it up. Now or never. "I have something to say."

One of the machines began to beep, and a nurse slipped in, pressed a button and left again.

"Where are my Chesterfields?"

"You know you can't smoke them with the oxygen tank here."

"Then take me to . . . another room."

"Mother, I will. But first—I, well, this is difficult."

Verna must have sensed something coming, because she straightened her back on the pillow, refolded her hands expectantly.

"I want you to know how sorry I am for everything I put you and Dad through, with the baby." As she spoke, she felt the odd sensation of her muscles coiling, her body rejecting her own words. She nearly bucked out of her chair when the word *sorry* passed her lips, it felt so wrong. What about Mr. Grebe and the doctor and Sister Simon? Had they ever apologized to anyone for what they had done? What about her own parents, who had shipped her off to that place, who had worried more about their own reputations than what would happen to Margie there?

Her apology was really a plea to Verna: *Acknowledge what happened, at last. Don't die without saying it out loud.*

"Will you ever forgive me?" Margie asked.

Verna made a smacking sound with her lips and gestured to the water glass on the bedside table. Margie reached toward it, so transparently eager to please, as always, and brought the straw to her mother's lips. Verna sipped for a long time and swallowed, painfully, and closed her eyes. She made a strange sound in her throat and then went so quiet Margie thought she had fallen asleep. After a long moment, she said, "It's not up to me. Read your catechism. It's God who forgives."

Margie held her arms across her stomach and pitched forward with a whimper. "Don't you have *anything* to say to me?"

Verna turned away with her eyes closed. How little it would have cost her now to acknowledge Margie's pain. Even Sister Simon, who had been nothing but cruel to Margie throughout her stay at Holy Family, had softened toward her when she returned to the home that final night after Timothy's birth. Margie had done what they all said was the right thing, the only thing, to do, and Sister Simon had acknowledged Margie's concession by gently offering to help her put on her nightgown. Verna, on the other hand, had set her teeth against tenderness, right to the very end.

Eventually, with nothing more to say, Margie left the room. All through the night, in and out of the waiting room and the cafeteria and the bathroom, waiting to hear the news, wanting both to be in the room when it happened and to be as far away as possible, Margie clutched at that dark and terrible feeling. Alice dropped Theo off at the bungalow to change clothes, so Margie was alone in the waiting room, staring at a *Life* magazine, when the nurse came in to deliver the news. Her father had been in the room with her when she went.

The nurse took Margie back to the room. Verna's body lay still, her palms resting on her breastbone. The smell of rubbing alcohol filled the space.

Frank looked up. "I'm sorry, honey."

Margie's breath distended her lungs. She felt she couldn't exhale. "Did she say anything?"

"The nurse?"

"No! Mother. Did she say anything at the end?"

He shook his head. "You know how hard it was for her to talk today."

But Verna had just been talking to her. "Are you sure?" Margie's voice was high and tight, and then it became a shriek. "Are you sure?"

Frank looked alarmed. He shifted in the vinyl chair, and it squeaked. "Honey, I'm sure. I know how hard this must be."

She paced at the end of the bed. An image of herself slapping her dad with all the strength in her shoulder flashed through her mind. "*Do* you know?"

"*Margie.*" Frank looked as tired as she had ever seen him. He glanced at the door, worried they might be disturbing people in the hallway. "Please."

A primal scream spewed from Margie's lips. "She made me go to that place. The place where they took him away."

"What? Took who away?"

"And I will never know if he is okay. I will die without knowing."

Frank's face moved from confusion to anguish.

"And she never, for one minute, she never had a drop of regret."

"Oh, Margie." Frank put his head in his hands, his shoulders shaking. He drew a breath and wiped his eyes with the back of his hand. "She wasn't the only one who made that decision. She isn't the only one who owes you an apology."

Some faraway part of herself was frightened by her complete lack of empathy for her father's pain, the fact that she was yelling at him across her mother's corpse. But that part was not in charge right now. She paced at the foot of the bed. "Didn't you ever want to know how I got pregnant? Didn't you ever *wonder* how that could happen to a girl like me? I hardly had any friends, much less a date."

Frank held up his palms in the helpless gesture she'd seen him make ten thousand times in her life. "I did. Of course I did. But I thought it would be better if we could just . . . move on. Get back to normal."

He had really believed that if they came up with a credible cover story for her absence and, upon her return, dedicated themselves to collective amnesia about her bleeding onto every chair she sat on for weeks, about her crying in the night from the pain of binding her breasts, the fever from mastitis, that they could make it go away. He had assumed that forgetting was within Margie's power, because he was a man. No one had ever taken something from him that he hadn't agreed to give.

Margie pressed her face into her hands, hard, then threw them down at her sides. "I am so . . ." The word for it was rising to the surface like a shark. "I am so . . . *angry*!"

Frank nodded, his face sorrowful.

"You didn't help me, Dad. You didn't stand up for me. No one did."

"And I regret it. Margie, you have no idea how much I regret it."

Margie looked at Verna, inert on the pillow. "She didn't, though."

He was quiet for a long moment. In thirty-three years of marriage, he had never contradicted his wife, never won an argument with her. "She was sorry in her way, though she never could have said it. She didn't want to hurt you. That was never her intention."

In the hallway, a nurse knocked on the glass window to tell them it was time for them to take Verna's body away. Margie wiped her eyes.

"Well, she did. That's just the truth," Margie said, and the power of saying it out loud, finally, was not needing to say it again. It was all over now. She went to the chair where Frank sat hunched, his forehead propped on his hand. He hadn't slept in thirty-six hours, and soon he would go home to an empty house. Margie draped her arm across his shoulders. She kissed the bald spot on the top of his head.

35

Doreen

The beige telephone sat on a small end table next to the sofa. Beside it, Summer's notebook of cat drawings was open to the back page, where Mosel's phone number was written in smeared pencil. All Doreen had to do was pick up the receiver and dial.

Except she needed more coffee first. Even as she moved without haste in the kitchen—pouring from the percolator, adding milk, stirring with a spoon and rinsing it—she knew she didn't have much time to complete this task she had promised Raymond she would do. It was rare to have the apartment to herself, even for an hour or two, and especially on a Saturday. With Carla and Danny off at the Maxwell Street Market, and Summer playing at Timothy's house under Luisa's supervision (for a change!), Doreen knew it was now or never. By lunchtime, they would all be home.

Back on the sofa, Doreen pulled the end table in front of her and put her mug on a coaster beside the phone. *Pick it up, Doreen.*

And say what?

For five years, I have been lying to you.

Or, *I have to confess a secret that's going to change your life. Unless you don't want it to, and then, I guess, you could just pretend I never called.*

Or, *The good news is, you have a daughter. The bad news is that you missed every important moment of her life so far. And there is no way to get them back.*

Or, *I wanted the best for you, Mosel. I wanted to make sure nothing would stop you, and it looks like I succeeded. But it was wrong of me to keep her from you. Your own daughter. Wait until you see how incredible she is. Brilliant, like you. I almost lost her too, so I know a little of what you are probably feeling right now. Can you ever forgive me?*

But what if she couldn't bring herself to say the words? What if he didn't pick up, or he picked up and became furious and hung up on her?

Doreen stood up again, with her hands on her hips, and stared at the phone for another minute. Then she went to Vincenzo's desk and took out a sheet of paper and a pen. A letter would be better. She could say everything she needed to say, and she couldn't chicken out. Then Mosel could decide what to do next. Maybe she would never hear from him again, and then she would know that he wanted to go on with his life and didn't want anything to change. He wouldn't get hurt, and Summer would never have to know.

She took a deep breath and wrote *Dear Mosel*, then explained the situation as clearly as possible. She didn't say anything about Raymond being the catalyst for her finally telling the truth. The idea that she had only come clean when she feared she would be outed made her sick to her stomach. She would simply tell him the truth and offer him the chance to meet his child. Whatever would happen after that was too much for Doreen to even begin to imagine. *I'm sure you have moved on with your life*, she wrote, *and I don't want to disrupt it. But I wouldn't be telling the whole truth if I didn't say that I loved you then, and still do. I hope you can forgive me. If you can't, I understand, but I hope you won't take that out on her.*

As she signed her name, she realized she should include a picture of Summer. She glanced around the living room. There was a posed shot from Christmas on top of Vincenzo's desk, but Summer had already changed so much since then, and Carla would kill her if she took something out of a frame. Then Doreen remembered the pictures she had taken with Danny's camera the day she took Summer and Timothy to the park.

She fished them out of the kitchen drawer and couldn't help but smile flipping through them. In one, the kids looked like two blurs, and she remembered that Summer had been schooling Timothy in the ways of tornadoes. One showed Timothy's face clearly but not Summer's. But in the next one, Summer's face was clear and her personality was on full display: hands raised as she explained the science, her eyes bright and full of excitement. This was the one.

As she picked up the kitchen scissors to cut the photo in half, she paused. There was one more part of Summer's story that she wouldn't try to tell Mosel yet because she could barely admit it to herself: Even if she cut Timothy out of the photo, he and Summer would always be linked by one person. Margie. Margie, who had brought Timothy into the world; Margie, who had kept Doreen and Summer together. Just like Mosel, she deserved to know the truth.

Maybe it was momentum, maybe writing the letter had opened the floodgates. Maybe it was Doreen's awareness of the clock ticking toward lunchtime. Whatever it was, she didn't stop to mull over the possibilities. Doreen picked up the phone, dialed the operator, and asked for the numbers and addresses for all the Aherns in Sycamore Ridge.

The first Ahern was a man with no children. The second Ahern said his household wasn't the right one either, but he knew the one she wanted—"Margaret's my brother's kid. You want John Francis Ahern." And so it only took five minutes and three tries to find Margie's number, despite having told herself that it would be impossible to find Margie out there in the great big world. Only five minutes and three tries and five long years.

"Margie's not here yet," said the woman who answered. Maybe her sister? "She's still over at the church, but they will all be back here at the house in the afternoon. May I take a message?"

"No, thank you," said Doreen, who did not pause to consider what the woman's words might mean. "I will see her there."

For as many years as Doreen had spent deriding the suburbs from the vantage point of crummy but gutsy Taylor Street—her entire life—she had never actually been to one. The funny thing about Chicago was that people didn't tend to explore. They were loyal as hell to the block they were from but not especially curious about anyplace else.

So when the UP-NW train pulled into the sparkling clean Sycamore Ridge station and she emerged to find an art deco movie house, a bank with a big white clock, a public library with a wreath on its front door, Doreen was surprised. She wasn't sure what she had expected to find here, but this place was *nice*. Vincenzo would have scoffed, though, at the tidy yards and well-kept storefronts. In his mind, people who wanted that safe life had given up on adventure. Not a lot of bars where you could play late-night piano in Sycamore Ridge. But there was something else too, something that felt menacing about the pleasantness and order. As "safe" as this town seemed, Doreen knew it was only safe for white people. She could never bring Summer here.

After so many years of inaction, it felt good just to be in *motion*. Doreen had hung up the phone, put the photos in her purse, and called Luisa to ask her to keep Summer for the afternoon. Then she wrote a quick note for Carla and Danny and put a stamp on Mosel's letter. On the corner of Taylor and Racine, she put it in the mailbox and lucked out finding a taxi to take her to the train station. Now she showed the address to the man behind the window in the station. He showed her Margie's house on the map, just six blocks away.

As she walked, Doreen's nerve started to dissolve. *Just keep going*, she told herself. *No turning back now.*

The redbrick bungalow was on a corner lot surrounded by a chain-link fence, with rose bushes blooming in the backyard and a tidy lawn that somebody obviously spent a lot of time taking care of. In the context of some of the other houses she had passed along the way, Doreen could see they weren't well-to-do, but every window in the house sparkled. And it was crowded, she realized. Several cars were parked in the street out front, a few more in the driveway. On the sloping front porch, three women wearing black dresses stood talking in a circle, smoking. A teenager poked his head out of the door to ask them something. He, too, was wearing black.

Doreen, still on the sidewalk, paused and put her hand on top of the fence. She had a sinking feeling, remembering what the woman on the phone had said: "She's still over at the church, but they will all be back in the afternoon." If everyone was gathering here, the funeral had to be for one of Margie's parents.

Shit, what timing. Doreen thought she should leave and come back when things settled down. But could she trust herself to do it?

"Oh my God—*Doreen*?"

Now there really was no turning back because there was Margie, standing by the back door, stuffing a trash bag bulging with dirty paper plates into the can and staring across the rose bushes at Doreen. A tiny puff of air escaped Doreen's lips. Margie. Her hair was shorter and well styled, but her face was the same. The image of her last night at Holy Family flashed through Doreen's mind, waving to Margie across the snow. Doreen nodded. "It's me."

"I can't believe it." Margie fitted the lid on the can and crossed the yard, passing through the gate to join Doreen on the sidewalk. "I can't believe this is real."

"I know. It's been a few years."

Margie shook her head. "How did you even hear about my mother?"

Doreen thought about whether to lie. "Actually, if you can believe it, I hadn't heard. I had . . . a kind of whim to try to find you today, and it was easier than I expected it to be. So I thought I would just hop on the train and come out here. I had no idea it was her funeral today. I'm so sorry."

Doreen's heart was pounding, and her voice was uncharacteristically shaky. So many times, she had imagined what she would do—what she *should* do—if she ever found herself face-to-face with Margie again. Now the moment had arrived, but her courage was failing her.

Margie stared at her in confusion, trying to work out the purpose of Doreen's errand. "I thought I would never see you again. I mean, it's great to see you—I'm just surprised."

"The timing stinks. I'm really sorry."

Margie shrugged. "It's okay." Her eyes widened. "Gosh, how is your baby? She's not a baby anymore, I guess."

"I had a girl."

"I know. Sister Joan told me. I saw her one last time, right before my parents came to take me home. She wouldn't tell me anything else about how it went for you except that you and the baby were all right."

Doreen felt her throat tightening. "We were." Now wasn't the time to tell the story of the Starlite Motel. Every year, Sister Joan sent a card for Summer's birthday. She lived in San Francisco now, having left Holy Family to join an order of renegade nuns who passed out birth control in grocery store parking lots. "We made it through. Her name is Summer."

An almost indecipherable flash of pain crossed Margie's face. "Oh, that's beautiful. A perfect name. Do you have a picture?"

Doreen put her hand on her purse, where the photos were tucked in the pocket next to her sunglasses. "I wish I would have thought to bring one." What would hurt Margie worse—showing her the photo or not showing her? "She's five now."

Margie gave Doreen an amused look. "Yeah, I know."

"Margie . . . you know that I wouldn't have her if it wasn't for you, don't you?" The words fell so far short of what Doreen felt.

Margie's forehead creased. "Oh, that's not true. You fought for her. You wouldn't have given up the way I did."

For Doreen, telling the truth to Mosel, to Margie, meant surrendering control over what they knew about the past, but also what they knew about Doreen herself—her limitations, her failures, the part of her that was small and selfish and fearful. But she couldn't let this go on any longer.

"Oh, Margie," Doreen said. "I don't know if . . . this is the right place." She glanced behind Margie to see the women on the porch still smoking with their elbows propped on their hands. A radio sprang to life in the garage, the sound of the Cubs game. "But there's something I have to tell you."

Margie's shoulders tightened. "What. What do you know?"

"I—"

She grabbed Doreen's forearm. "Did something happen to him? Is that why you came? But . . . how would *you* know about it when they won't tell me anything?" She took a step back, her palm pressed to her stomach. "Oh, please, Doreen. If it's something awful, I don't think I can—"

Doreen reached for her arm. "Margie, he is perfect. He is happy and healthy and the sweetest little boy."

Margie's face was a twisted mess of pain and confusion. "But how . . ."

Doreen tried to say it as fast as she could. "The first thing to know is that he was adopted by a very nice couple who wanted him so much. They take such good care of him. He doesn't go without a thing."

"You've *seen* him?"

Doreen nodded. "They live in my neighborhood."

"But . . . how long have you known about this?"

Doreen paused. It wasn't a real confession if she didn't tell the whole truth. "Too long. Since the beginning." Doreen explained how she had stumbled upon the Messinas in the waiting room at the hospital and watched the nurse hand the baby over to them. "I have no excuse except that I was scared. And I didn't know if it would be worse for you to know or not to know. Then, when I realized I should have told you, it was too late. I was already gone." Doreen's voice broke. "I'm so sorry, Margie. I should have tried harder to find you."

"Five years," Margie whispered.

Doreen couldn't tell if she was angry or hurt or in shock. "I know. I can't imagine what it has been like for you. I wouldn't blame you if you clawed my eyes out right now."

Fury and relief clashed on Margie's face, and suddenly her entire demeanor changed. "I want to see him."

"What?"

"I want to see him. Today. Right now."

Doreen had imagined many possible outcomes, but somehow—stupidly, she now saw—not this one. "Margie. It's the day of your mother's funeral. You can't just leave."

"I don't care."

"Margie . . ."

"I'm not going to do anything crazy. I don't have to talk to him—I can see him from across the road. But I have to see him." Margie's face was pale, her eyes absolutely wild. "Doreen, you have to understand how long I have waited."

Doreen looked at her for what felt like an eternity. Then she glanced at her watch and tried to calculate what time it would be when they got back to Taylor Street. She could pretend it would be tough to find him, but the truth was he and her own daughter were probably playing with the neighborhood kids in the empty parking lot beside the church or in Vernon Park. She could find him.

"Doreen. Please."

"I don't have a car."

"No problem. Theo went with my brother to buy more beer, but they took Bud's car. I have Theo's keys. We can take the Fairlane." Margie started walking toward a gray car parked at the curb on the side street.

"Who's Theo? Don't you at least want to get your purse?"

Margie shook her head and opened the car door. "No. I want to go."

36

Margie

Speeding southeast on the Jane Addams in Theo's Fairlane, Margie felt all the cells in her body tipping forward like pins pulled to a magnet. A remote part of her, which she hoped to attend to later, was overjoyed to see her friend. How Margie had missed Doreen! She had so many questions about Chicago and Summer and the boyfriend and motherhood. The other girls from Holy Family—did Doreen know what had happened to them? But at the moment, nothing could overcome her driving urge to reach Timothy.

"How often do you see him?"

Doreen seemed to hesitate, then exhaled. "Almost every day."

Margie looked at her, blinking, and turned back to the road. The rhythmic whish of the tires on the asphalt matched her heartbeat.

"He and Summer play together. They live just a few streets way," Doreen said, as if that would somehow soften the revelation that she had known where Margie's baby was for more than two thousand days.

"You see him every day," Margie whispered. She felt Doreen's eyes on her. She felt her own jaw hardening until it was difficult to speak. "And you never tried to find me?"

"I know."

Margie swallowed. "I thought . . . all this time, I always thought about you. I . . . *missed* you. I thought you were my friend."

"I am, Margie. More than that. I owe you everything. If it wasn't for you, I wouldn't have Summer."

"But that's all the more reason— Can't you see? You *knew*. You knew that day, and you kept it from me. Do you have any idea what the past five years have been like? It never goes away. I have worried and worried. I thought he could be dead, and I would never know."

Doreen nodded but didn't try to interrupt.

Margie's voice shook. "What you did—it's just as bad as the people at the hospital taking him away. They thought they knew what was best for me. You thought you knew what was best. You decided *for* me. But who gave you the right?"

"No one," Doreen said. "You're right. I think I thought I was protecting you, or maybe . . . I think, that day in the hospital lobby, I think I knew that telling you was the right thing to do, but I couldn't get the words out. I chickened out. And then I just never made it right. Believe me, if I could change it, I would. I would do anything to go back."

"Well," Margie said, and her voice was softer now, maybe because she had said what she needed to say, "we can't go back, can we?"

They rode in silence for a few minutes. Then Doreen began to fiddle with the clasp of her handbag, *slide click*, *slide click*. "I know this doesn't fix anything, but when I left, in my head I promised you that I would watch over him. And I've done it, all this time. It isn't enough, I know. But I kept my promise."

Margie turned to her in surprise. "You did?"

Doreen shrugged. "I mean, it's no big deal. But yeah. Since he was a baby, I have just tried to keep him real nearby so I could be sure he had everything he needed. That he was happy, you know? That they were taking good care of him. I always tried to think about the things I would want to know about Summer. He's a bit of a picky eater, but that's not their fault, I don't think. They give him nice haircuts, and he always had new shoes. Brand-new toys too. None of this yard sale stuff like I buy for Summer."

Margie stared at her. Their speed had dropped to about forty-five miles per hour, and the steering wheel felt hot in her hand.

"Hon," Doreen said, pointing out the windshield at a curve of orange cones lining the shoulder ahead. "You should probably watch where you're going."

"What?" Margie said, then, "Oh, yeah." She swallowed, still thinking about his haircut. Was his hair fine or thick? What color was the curve of his ear? "What do they call him?"

"Nicholas. I don't ever hear them use Nicky. He's always Nicholas. A big name for a little guy."

Margie almost felt embarrassed to bring it up, but she couldn't help herself. "Do you remember what I named him?" It had been such a long time, but she thought she would never get the music of it out of her ears.

"Of course," Doreen said. "He has always been Timothy to me."

They had to circle the neighborhood for a while because Doreen said the kids weren't in the park where she expected to find them, closest to Timothy's house. "They're probably playing over by the church," she said. "We'll find them."

"I know." That wasn't just a statement of reassurance. Margie didn't know what Doreen had planned for the rest of the day, but she had no intention of leaving until they found Timothy, even if she had to knock on every door in the neighborhood.

They drove through the alleys from Carpenter to May that ran between two-flats and three-flats with chain-link fences around their yards, where Doreen said they sometimes played capture the flag, then went back to Taylor Street and passed a fruit market, a hardware store. A long line of people stood at the Italian lemonade place. Then Doreen pointed to the parking lot beside a large yellow-brick Catholic church. "There they are."

Margie slowed the car along the curb. They got out and stood in front of it on the sidewalk. There was a group of boys and one girl in a flowered sundress standing near a bench inside the fence that encircled the park. The oldest ones looked to be ten or twelve, and the rest were younger. The girl wore a straw sunhat, though the sun was low in the sky now.

"Is that Summer?" Margie asked.

"Yeah."

One of the older boys held a beagle puppy by his leash. The kids made a circle, and the boy unhooked the leash from the puppy's collar to let him run around. One kid threw a ball, and the puppy went running after it, returning it to his encouraging hands. Margie scanned the faces of the boys as they shouted the puppy's name and whistled for him, patting their knees to call him. Summer knelt down too. Margie felt she should be able to recognize Timothy among them. It was a test of all those hours she had spent dreaming about him over the years. Now that she was finally seeing him in the real world instead of in her mind, would she know him?

"You all right?" Doreen asked softly.

Margie nodded, taking small breaths because her lungs wouldn't open all the way. There was one little boy in a light blue polo shirt who crouched down right in front of the puppy. He had a smaller voice than the rest of the boys, who shouted and jumped around, trying to get its attention, trying to get it to leap and chase, so Margie couldn't hear what he was saying. But, like the puppy, she couldn't take her eyes off the boy's arms, stretched low on the ground reassuringly, nor his cheeks, kissed pink by a day spent outside in the sun. In the midst of the chaos of the other kids, the puppy chose to come to him, and he pulled it gently into his arms.

"Is that him?" Margie asked, her throat tight. "The one holding the dog?"

Doreen nodded, watching her warily, probably worried Margie would start hollering his name or dash across the park to snatch him up and make a run for it. But Margie felt no such impulse. Here was Timothy alive, breathing, laughing, his fingertips stroking the puppy's ears. The ease in his face, the tenderness with the dog, showed her that he hadn't been hurt. That he mattered to the people he spent his days with. It was the only thing she had needed all this time—to know for certain that he was all right. There was Timothy, and then there was the sky and the concrete racing up to meet her hip, her elbow, her temple.

Time, bending in its strange way, passed, and then she had the vague awareness of being helped into the front seat of the car and watching Doreen get behind the wheel. A little while after that, there was a stairwell and a bright kitchen, women's voices, the voice of a girl saying, "Shhh." And, finally, the softest pillow she had ever known. Margie sank into a velvet ocean of sleep.

It was like being back at Holy Family, caught up in one of those dreams where she didn't know if she was asleep or awake. Margie felt the lumps of the old mattress beneath the small of her back, but it wasn't an unpleasant feeling. She liked sleeping where Doreen had slept. It made her feel connected to Doreen and Summer and Timothy. A space opened beneath her, and she felt her body moving down through a dark tunnel. She could see nothing, but she wasn't afraid, only curious to see where it would lead. The tunnel shifted in direction, and Margie had the sense that she was moving up again, rising through space, weightless. Up she went, up, up, up, and light began to come up around her field of vision, just enough that she could make out her silhouette and then the fabric of her dress. In the womblike darkness, Margie stopped moving through space and rolled off the mattress onto a soft rug. Somehow, she knew not to stand but to crawl, like a baby learning the world, toward candles and the scent of woodsmoke, cinnamon. She came to a stop when her nose brushed a velvet curtain.

Or was it something else? Now Margie was being lifted by two enormous hands, which she understood at once to be both the most powerful and the gentlest force in the universe. The velvet was not a curtain but the folds of a skirt, and she was being pulled onto an expansive lap, nestled against a fleshy belly. "Rest," came a feminine voice from above her, and it sounded like the sweep of a bird's wing, a rush of wind, lapping tongues of fire, and as Margie fell asleep, pulled into the soft flesh, cradled and soothed and consoled and loved, she realized she knew who this was.

37

Margie

Margie rested.

38

Margie

In the morning, fortified by Danny's atomic coffee, Carla's Eggs in Purgatory, and Summer's candy-apple-red manicure—miraculous, startling Summer, not a baby at all but a full-on *person*, who did not stop talking about how ancient Egyptians made mummies of their cats, how unicorns were both not real and also extremely powerful in ways that should give us all pause, how Tommy Johns was the best pitcher in the history of forever and she couldn't wait for baseball season to start, all of those things, interchangeably, and if you lost the thread, well, that was on you—Margie drove to Pottawatomi.

Theo, it turned out, had waited in Sycamore Ridge all night for Margie to return, eventually sleeping, in fact, in her childhood twin bed, in his underclothes, because he had not thought to bring pajamas. So it turned out that Margie was waiting for him, instead of the other way around, when her sister Alice dropped him off, his tie hanging loose around his neck as he walked into the kitchen.

"I'm sorry if I worried you," Margie said. Despite its being February, Theo's freckles looked more prominent than ever, and Margie felt an undeniable fondness for him. She recalled the Plath poem about the girl with the splinter in her eye that forever changed how she saw the horses in the distance. Theo was the same Theo he had been since the beginning, but somehow, knowing that Timothy was all right made her see Theo differently now. Or maybe she was finally able to see him for the first time.

He pulled out a chair and sat down across from her at the table, looking tired and maybe a little amused.

"You stole my car."

"I know. I'm sorry."

"Your friend Doreen called the house about midnight and said she had just realized she should probably tell everyone where you were," he said. "So it was okay. After that I wasn't worried anymore. Maybe curious."

Margie nodded. "I wouldn't blame you for that."

"You know, Margie," Theo said, "I have the feeling, based on what probably seems to you like my vast life experience, that you might be about to tell me something. And, before you do, there's something I want to say."

Margie watched him. A few weeks ago, she might have tried to anticipate what Theo was going to say, to calibrate her response so that she could do what was within her power to protect her heart. And his. And hers, from his. But now she just sat still, her hands folded on the table, and waited.

"Margie," Theo said.

"Hm?"

"I love you."

Margie laughed. "Okay."

"I'm not sure you know what I mean by that."

"I'm not sure I do either," she admitted.

"I mean," Theo said, "that there is nothing, really nothing at all that I can conceive of, that would change the way I feel about you."

Margie wanted so badly to look away, but she made herself stay inside the warmth of his gaze.

"Well?" Theo said, and more than anything else at that moment, his tone was defiant. It said *try me.*

Margie blinked. A tear fell from the far corner of her left eye and settled at the edge of her mouth before she brushed it away.

"I have a son," she said. "He was adopted by a couple in Chicago just after he was born, and yesterday I got to see him for the first time since we were separated."

Theo leaned forward. "Oh, Margie. You must be reeling."

"He didn't see me. I only saw him from across the road. I don't know what he knows about me."

Theo nodded once and waited a moment. "And what else do you want me to know?"

"I think," Margie said, "I want you to know it all."

And for the first time in her life, Margie told her own story from beginning to end. In a measured, unhurried voice, she told Theo about Mr. Grebe and his workshop in the basement, the diaper pin that held her straining uniform skirt, her parents going to Father Keene for help. How they decided *for* her what would happen *to* her.

How they took Timothy away.

Theo listened to everything as if there was nowhere he would rather be. Maybe there wasn't. He passed her his monogrammed handkerchief and placed his hand gently over hers. When she came to the end, to Timothy and the puppy and her rest in the bed of her friend, he stood up and pulled Lorna's blue teapot down from the hutch. He was quiet as he fixed the tea, found the cups and saucers, cream and sugar because he remembered that Margie took both.

As she watched him, it was Verna's voice she heard in her mind, of course, warning her that Theo's opinion of her must be sinking fast, that he was eyeing the exits and wondering what it would take to disentangle himself from her. How he would be feeling relieved they hadn't married yet.

Theo brought the tea things over, poured her a cup and slid the saucer across the table. She remembered back to their date at Dante's, how Theo had waited for her to order her food and what a surprise that had been. He wasn't going to direct Margie now either. She was going to have to say what she wanted.

"I wouldn't want to interrupt his life. That's so clear to me now that I've seen him and seen that he's a real boy and not just the baby in my memory." She took a sip of her tea. "And I am grateful to his parents. They have taken such good care of him, and they all deserve their privacy. But a few years ago, someone from the home told me that I could write him a letter and they would place it in his file so that, when he turns eighteen, he could find me if he wants to. I want to do that."

"Okay," Theo said. "Then I think you should."

Margie thought of the stack of letters in the bottom drawer of her vanity upstairs, hundreds of them, that she had written across these years, and the frantic incantations they contained. Though they had been addressed to Timothy, they weren't really for him, Timothy the person. They were for Margie herself. They were messages to the future she tried to imagine, where she might be whole and well and free, or on her way to those things and relieved of the question, *Is he all right?* that thrummed in her body like a heartbeat. She saw now that the letters had worked—in writing them, Margie had called herself into that future. What she had gone through would continue to shape her, and the hurt would always be there. But she was here. She had found a way through it.

Today, for Timothy's file, she would write something new and simple. *I wanted you so much, and that will never change. It's okay if you wait a long time to decide. I will be here.*

"The thing is," Margie said, "and this is probably silly, but I don't think I can just put it in the mailbox and believe it will get to the right place. After all this time not knowing about him, I need to at least know about the letter. I need to put it in someone's hand."

"I can understand that."

"The drive is a few hours. Will you come with me?"

Theo smiled. "I'll pack us a lunch."

39

Doreen

The bus station was on Harrison and Des Plaines, a cheap cab ride away, but Danny again insisted on borrowing Benny's Oldsmobile—which was more than ten years old now and succumbing to the rust that eventually devoured all cars in Chicago—to deliver Doreen and Summer and their luggage with plenty of time to spare. Doreen had tried not to overpack, but as Danny loaded the trunk, the back end sank a couple inches closer to the pavement.

"Christ Jesus, Doreen," Danny said. "How in the hell are you going to carry all this down the street when you get there?"

Doreen faked a confident shrug. "I've got a plan. We'll find somebody to help us. They have cabs there, you know."

"Yeah," Danny said, rolling his eyes. "I think I've heard something about those."

In fact, Doreen really did not have much of a plan. She had been flying by the seat of her pants since the day she sent Mosel the letter about Summer. The thing about telling the truth was that it made you feel so much better, but it blew up your life. She had expected Mosel to mull over the letter's contents for a few weeks, then maybe write back himself—after all, she happened to know that he was an accomplished letter writer—but just three days after she dropped it in the mailbox on the way to Margie's house, he had called her around lunchtime.

"Coniglio residence."

"Doreen, this is Mosel Palmer." He was speaking in the tone of a teacher preparing to chew out an unruly student.

With a slow, somewhat shaky hand, she had slipped off her earring. "Well, hello."

"I just read your letter."

"I figured." Summer was in the bathroom swimming her Barbies through a bubble bath in the sink. She heard Summer's voice making one Barbie tell another, "You have a great figure for your age."

"Doreen, I can't believe it."

"I know." She pictured him sitting at a round table at the edge of his kitchen, the cord of his phone stretched long, the way hers was now. "I'm sorry that I told you that way. I'm sorry I didn't just call."

"I don't even know what to say. Five *years*."

"I know. You have every right to be angry, of course."

"I don't need you to tell me that."

"Okay, I'm sorry."

"I mean, I don't know if I'm angry. Of course I am. But I think I'm in shock too." The line was quiet for a moment. "Amazed? Can I be amazed?" Mosel's voice was beginning to soften, and Doreen's eyes filled.

"She's pretty amazing, all right. She looks just like you. I mean, we're not going to need Joe Friday to get to the bottom of who her father is—put it that way."

"*Father.* Damn. Doreen, you have to let me see Summer."

"Of course you can see her." She sniffed, wiped her eyes.

"I mean soon. I'll come to Chicago."

And that was when she decided, the words making themselves true as she said them aloud. "Well, part of why I wanted to get back in touch is that we're moving to New York." Now that she no longer had to keep an eye on Timothy for Margie, now that Margie knew he was all right and Doreen knew that Margie would be all right, she had been thinking about what Lew had told her about the jobs at Elektra. She had her demo and enough money from her bookkeeping work saved to get them through a couple months. There wouldn't be any guarantees, but if she didn't try, she would never forgive herself.

"You are? Well, that's even better."

"Yeah, I think it is. I have a line on a job. You and Summer can get to know each other. I mean, if that's okay. I just realized you're probably married by now. I'm sorry you're going to have to explain all this to everybody, to your wife."

He paused, and she couldn't be sure, but she thought she heard the crackling sound of his lips drawing back into a smile. "I'm not married, Doreen."

"Well, that makes two of us," she said. She cringed now, remembering how she had written that she loved him that summer and always would. God, how she hated showing her hand. Another reason telling the truth was such a pain in the ass.

"I am really mad at you," he said. "And I'm going to stay mad, probably for a long time."

"Okay. I deserve that."

"But I'm really . . ." His voice grew thick. "I'm really glad you told me, Doreen. God, I'm so grateful to know. Not to miss any more of her. I can't wait to meet her. Does she know about me?"

"Not yet, but she will."

It took a few weeks to make her plans: letting her customers know, talking to Lew, who gave her the name of the guy he knew at Elektra and some people to call about sublets in the Village. Summer could start kindergarten at the public elementary school in the neighborhood, where she wouldn't be the only kid who wasn't white. They could see the Statue of Liberty.

The Coniglios piled into the Oldsmobile, and Danny turned on the radio. Just as she had on the trip to Holy Family six years ago, Carla sat in the front seat crying and carrying on.

"What kind of person takes a grandchild away from its grandmother? To somewhere even more dangerous than this hellhole?"

"Ma, give me a break," Doreen said, grinning. She couldn't stop grinning. "You love Chicago."

"I love Chicago because my family is here."

"Why is Nonni talking like that?" Summer whispered.

"Goodbyes are hard for her," Doreen explained. She happened to know, however, that Carla was secretly thrilled to see Doreen go after the job. It was only after Doreen had made her plans, after Carla had hosted a goodbye party with Timothy and Luisa and Art and the girls from the diner, Diana and her husband and little Sharon, that her mother began her superficial campaign to stop them. Her voice said, "Don't leave me!" But the money she had pressed into Doreen's hand, cobbled together from selling the last of Vincenzo's suits and her double shifts, said otherwise.

"Right Now and Not Later" by the Shangri-las came on. It felt like a sign.

Carla looked over her shoulder at Doreen. "Promise me you'll go straight to that record company with your songs, and you won't leave until they give you the job."

"I think that's how to get them to call the police." Doreen laughed. Her actual plan was to get a waitressing job, at least for the time being. It was probably wishful thinking, but she still had a good feeling about "Wooded Island." Someday Lew would carry that single in his store. Someday Mosel would hear that song on the radio. Would they be together when he heard it?

"Uncle Danny," Summer said, "have you ever been to New York?"

"Can't say that I have, kiddo," Danny said over his shoulder as he backed the car into a parking space. "But then, I never had a reason to go there before. Now I do."

"Mommy said we can get a kitten!" Summer squealed for the eleventh time that morning.

"That's great news, kid," Danny said. He took the suitcases out of the trunk. Summer looped her arms through a backpack as big as her. Doreen would take the rest, one handle in each hand and her biggest purse slung over her shoulder.

"It's going to sleep right on my pillow."

Doreen looked at the luggage and took a deep breath. "Let's go before Nonni starts crying again," she said to Summer.

They each hugged Danny. "You keep my niece away from those East Coast boys."

"Danny, she's five!"

"I'm just saying. We can't have any Yankee fans marrying into this family."

When Doreen hugged Carla, she held on for a long time. "I love you, Ma."

"I love you too."

"You'll come to visit."

"New York," she said, rolling her eyes. "I can't go to New York."

"Sure you can."

Carla kissed Summer about a thousand times. Then she crouched down to look her in the eyes. "You can always come home, do you hear?" Summer nodded. "If you try it and you don't like it, you can just come home. But I think you're going to like it." Summer nodded again, almost certainly thinking that New York was the only place in the world she wanted to be because that was where her cat was. She didn't yet know that was where her father was too. The long bus ride would give Doreen and Summer plenty of time to talk.

They walked away backward, Doreen unable to wave because of the suitcases, Summer waving until her arm was about to fly off, and then they turned a corner and couldn't see Carla and Danny anymore. Doreen stopped to take her new camera out of her purse. She wanted to take a picture of the sign above the bus's windshield that said NEW YORK CITY. She thought it would make a nice addition to the letter she planned to send to Margie when they got settled in. Doreen had promised she would keep in touch, and she always kept her promises.

Author's Note

Between 1945 and 1973, when *Roe v. Wade* upheld the right to abortion as a matter of medical privacy, 1.5 million pregnant girls and women in the United States were sent away to maternity homes run by organizations like the Salvation Army, Louise Wise Services, Florence Crittenton, and local Catholic dioceses where they passed the long months of their pregnancies and in some cases were coerced into surrendering their babies for adoption. By the 1960s, more than two hundred of these homes were operating in forty-four states.

In trying to understand what is now called the "Baby Scoop Era," contemporary historians have examined birth records, adoption statistics, and other quantitative data. They have also turned to a powerful tool: oral histories. It may not seem radical to ask the people most impacted by maternity homes to speak in their own words about what it was like, but for many years, no one did. In *The Girls Who Went Away,* Ann Fessler gathers recorded and transcribed interviews with women who experienced the homes firsthand. Published in 2006, the book was the first chance most of us ever had to learn how those women were treated and how *they* felt about what happened to them.

Prior to that, the official story went something like this: Girls who came to the maternity homes were careless and promiscuous and were only disappointed to get pregnant because it ruined their good time.

They were eager to surrender that baby and be free of the inconvenience it caused. Fortunately, a maternity home was there to provide compassionate care until the birth, at which point the baby could be placed with a married couple and avoid the stigma of growing up "illegitimate." The birth mothers, now appropriately chastened, returned to their lives, put it all behind them, and forgot. It was a win-win scenario: maternity homes "saved" the babies and gave the birth mothers a chance for a fresh start.

People with societal power, like church and community leaders, told this version of the story—which was a story not just about teenage pregnancy but also about the value and role of women, the meaning of motherhood, and the primacy of maintaining a "nice" middle-class lifestyle—in many ways. Through school textbooks (what was in them and what was not), from the pulpit (who was good and who was bad), in the subsequent laws they created (who had rights and who did not), and in popular culture (the stories we heard and the stories we did not), the messaging was extremely consistent and all-encompassing.

The Girls Who Went Away takes an axe to that official narrative. The most important thing we learn from the women interviewed is that the decision to surrender their babies was far from easy and, in many cases, no "decision" at all. Often the birth mother was rushed through signing papers while still under anesthesia. If she resisted, nurses or social workers would remind her that her family would have to pay the maternity home back for the cost of her prenatal care, room and board—even the baby's christening gown. If *that* didn't work, birth mothers were regularly threatened with commitment to a mental institution.

Alongside these extreme cases, several women described willingly complying with the process at the time but later experiencing deep shock and regret. They describe a sense of having been conditioned throughout their time in the home to believe things about themselves, their value and their competence, that made surrender possible.

Because I have been lucky never to experience it, I struggled at first to understand this particular loss of agency—it sounded like these women were describing actual brainwashing, and that seemed far-fetched. But then I came across the research of psychiatrist Robert Jay Lifton, which transformed my understanding of the context in the maternity homes. Lifton is best known for testifying at the 1976 bank robbery trial of Patty Hearst about his theory of "coercive persuasion," which attempted to explain how Hearst's treatment at the hands of her kidnappers, the Symbionese Liberation Army, conditioned her to willingly participate in an armed robbery. Lifton's theories apply to the practices of any cult or coercive ideology—and they accurately describe the conditions of midcentury maternity homes.

Here are just a few characteristics of these environments: leaders strip followers of their individuality, giving them new names and prohibiting communication with the outside world; they articulate a "higher purpose" to justify followers' suffering; they demand purity and require confession; and they use repetitive language that becomes a script for dismissing followers' doubt ("your child will be called a bastard on the playground," "this doesn't happen to nice girls," "no man wants to marry a single mother"). Eventually, this conditioning deprives a follower (or captive, we might say) of her own interpretation of her experience. She stops fighting the overwhelming current and allows herself to be swept away.

The women's own accounts should be enough to persuade us that in many cases they were coerced into giving their babies up. We shouldn't need a robust body of research explaining the psychological process behind it. But, for the skeptical, we have that too.

Many women realized only later, when they were out of what Lifton would call the "totalistic" environment of the home—when the spell was broken—that their legal rights had been violated and they could have kept their babies. Whether these young women could have provided for their children, whether those babies were better off with a married couple of means, is a question that came up then (and comes up now) in conversations about adoption, but it elides the more important point: Who but the pregnant woman herself should choose what happens to her child?

The biggest lie of the official narrative about these closed adoptions was that the birth mothers would forget and move on. They never forgot.

Many of them were haunted by grief for the rest of their lives. This haunting haunted *me*. I could not stop thinking about what had happened to these women. How were the wounds of 1.5 million women—wounds which, when denied, did not disappear but traveled through their bodies and across time—shaping our society, even now?

Because the official narrative did not acknowledge their experience, many women lived in shame and never spoke about it. Not permitted to view what happened to them as a loss, they were supposed to be grateful that someone had solved their problem. Silence reigned. Their priests and parents and siblings and classmates embraced collective amnesia; the men they went on to marry often remained in the dark. Predictably, some women began to doubt their own memories. They wondered whether they had just made the whole thing up.

Fessler reports that many of the women she interviewed described surrendering a child as "the event that defined their identity and therefore influenced every decision they made thereafter, including their education, career, decision to marry and have other children, how they parented, and relationships with their partner, parents, and friends." As life continued on, they experienced all the symptoms associated with unacknowledged and complex grief: depression, anxiety, shame, difficulty with intimacy and attachment, and physical manifestations of their pain, such as severe headaches, serious unexplained illnesses, and substance abuse. One woman reported developing a problem with speech. She literally lost her voice.

And the false narrative wasn't just harmful to the women themselves. The young birth fathers, who were in many cases encouraged by adults in the community to deny paternity or forge on with plans for college or the military, were robbed of the valuable and fortifying life experience of taking responsibility for their choices. Or becoming fathers, if that's what the young couple might have chosen. And because the myths about women's motives were accepted as truth in the culture, it was common for children who were adopted to be told or to believe the traumatic lie that their birth mothers didn't want them.

This novel imagines the experience of birth mothers who were white and middle class because that is the population the maternity homes recruited. As historian Rickie Solinger explains in *Wake Up Little Susie: Single Pregnancy and Race Before Roe v. Wade*, there are a few reasons for this. Structural racism that made segregation the norm, and that placed a higher value on white babies, created homes that either explicitly or implicitly barred nonwhite girls and women. Cultural, historical, and economic factors also played a role. While white families prioritized maintaining their economic and social standing above all else (which is what created the demand for a place to send unwed pregnant girls), Black families were more likely to accept the pregnancy and reorient themselves to provide for the care of both mother and child. According to a 1963 study, nine in ten single pregnant Black women chose to keep their babies. Though they did not necessarily experience the grief of separation from their child, we know their lives were far from easy. We need to hear their stories too.

I also deliberately chose not to turn the lens on the children who were adopted. That, too, is a story for another writer to tell.

Describing the truth about what happened in the Baby Scoop Era is not a condemnation of adoption, which can of course be an affirming and love-filled experience for everyone involved. Adoption is not the trauma here—instead it was the loss of agency, the fact that the "choice" these women supposedly made was no choice at all, and that losing control over your body and your life causes objective harm that cannot be erased by a lie. Taken together, the oral histories of these birth mothers tell a powerful *collective* story of multiple generations of women. To try to acknowledge and honor the power of that collective, I created the brief chapters told from the point of view of "We."

While their stories draw on details of the experiences of real women, Margie and Doreen are fictional characters. Doreen's impulsive decision to leave the home before her baby was born was rare. And because of the rules about anonymity, it was unusual for women who met in the home to see each other again. It did happen, though. One woman described passing another on their college campus, their eyes meeting and widening in recognition, but neither of them spoke. It was like seeing a ghost. It was like *being* a ghost.

Did this happen to your aunt or grandmother? Did it happen to you? If you are one of the 1.5 million women, I wonder if you keep finding your way back to the "book of myths in which [your name does] not appear," as Adrienne Rich writes in the poem that serves as the epigraph to this novel. I hope in some way that Margie's and Doreen's stories might help you write it there yourself.

Acknowledgments

To better understand the experiences of young women who spent time in American maternity homes, I relied on *The Girls Who Went Away* by Ann Fessler; *Wake Up, Little Susie* by Rickie Solinger; the work of historian Kim Heikkila on birth mothers who surrendered babies at the Salvation Army's Booth Memorial Hospital in St. Paul, Minnesota; Sheeka Strickland's essay "The Forgotten Home"; and the work of Robert Jay Lifton on the psychology of Totalism. Also helpful were *Secret Daughter: A Mixed-Race Daughter and the Mother Who Gave Her Away* by June Cross; *Unveiled: The Hidden Lives of Nuns* by Cheryl L. Reed; *Always Magic in the Air: The Bomp and Brilliance of the Brill Building Era* by Ken Emerson; and *Songwriters on Songwriting* by Paul Zollo.

Thank you to dear friends and fellow writers Eleanor Brown, Erin Blakemore, Ellen F. Brown, Claire Zulkey, Molly Backes, Wendy McClure, Kate Harding, Lori Nelson Spielman, Julie Mosow, Kelly Harms, Susan Gregg Gilmore, and Meghan Murphy-Gill; to my O'Connor and McNees families; to my husband, Robert McNees; and especially to writer and artist Willa McNees.

I am grateful for the dedication and good humor of my agent, Kate McKean, to Andrea Guevara, and to Jessica Case, Claiborne Hancock, April Roberts, Maria Fernandez, Amanda Hudson, Lisa Gilliam, Rita Madrigal, and everyone at Pegasus who worked to put this book in readers' hands. And special thanks to Mary Therese Gunter and Megan McNees-Smith.

Stephen O'Connor helped me select the cars. Mary O'Connor talked me through important details of the era. Ethan Holben provided information on the music business and recording process. Bob provided and explained the number theory problem Mosel might have solved to win his college scholarship. I am so thankful for their help, and any errors of fact—or taste—are mine alone. For better or worse, I chose the songs.